PENGUIN BOOKS

1268

JUAN IN CHINA

ERIC LINKLATER

Eric Linklater

JUAN IN CHINA

PENGUIN BOOKS

Penguin Books Ltd, Harmondsworth, Middlesex
AUSTRALIA: Penguin Books Pty Ltd, 762 Whitehorse Road,
Mitcham, Victoria

—

First published by Jonathan Cape 1937
Published in Penguin Books 1958

Made and printed in Great Britain
by Hunt, Barnard & Co, Ltd,
Aylesbury

'*Fierce loves and faithless wars*' – I am not sure
  If this be the right reading – '*tis no matter;*
The fact's about the same, I am secure;
  I sing them both, and am about to batter
A town which did a famous siege endure,
  And was beleaguer'd both by land and water. . . .

It is an awful topic – but 'tis not
  My cue for any time to be terrific:
For checker'd as is seen our human lot
  With good, and bad, and worse, alike prolific
Of melancholy sentiment, to quote
  Too much of one sort would be soporific; –
Without, or with, offence to friends or foes,
  I will not *sketch your world exactly as it goes.*

BYRON

NOTE

THE earlier adventures of Juan Motley – a lineal descendant of Byron's Don Juan – were recorded in *Juan in America*.

Towards the end of his sojourn in America, Juan met a young lady from China to whom he was much attracted. Circumstances, however, prevented him from pursuing the acquaintance.

Some weeks later, when misfortune had temporarily reduced his spirit, he was rescued from defeatism – he had almost decided to enter his grandfather's bank – by a newspaper paragraph that fortunately gave him news of Kuo Kuo and her intentions.

She was going to join a Nudist Colony, governed by the well-known Dr Salvator, at Arroyo Beach on the coast of California. Juan immediately discovered that his plan of settling-down was premature, and determined to follow Kuo Kuo.

His meeting with her, at Arroyo Beach, is described in the introductory chapter.

END-PIECE

NAKED and ashamed, Juan had been a member of Dr Salvator's Nudist Colony for five unhappy days. He had lived healthily in the sun, he had been urged to play solar games, to dance eurhythmically, and attend lectures on the Ethics of the Neo-Pagan Zeitgeist; and he had escaped these revolting activities only by insisting that what he most urgently needed was solitary meditation. His recent mis-adventures had somewhat diminished the natural fortitude of his spirit, and the proximity of so much obviously corruptible flesh was begin-ning to create in him an almost vegetarian disfavour. Nostalgic thoughts came to his mind of tweed suits, white waistcoats, and fine frocks for ladies; and he listened angrily to Mr Lippincott, the oldest nudist, who sat beside him in a deck-chair.

'In the midst of an effete and decadent civilization,' Mr Lippincott was saying, 'we nudists stand for an heroic effort to recapture the grand old virtues and the vital body-urge of primitive man.'

'I deny your assumption,' said Juan rudely. 'From China to Spain the world is seething in war and rebellion, hissing with industrial strife, bubbling over with military philosophies and martial economies. How can you say that our civilization is effete when its most obvious symptoms are the warts and pimples and boils of an indecently robust adolescence?'

'That is a very interesting point of view,' said Mr Lippincott. 'But the unnatural standards of modern life and the hectic gaiety of our great cities . . . Pardon me while I go fetch that ball.'

He rose from his chair and amiably pursued a large red-and-white air-ball that rolled flightily down the beach to a whispering blue sea. He was a shrivelled little man with rimless eye-glasses and a gallina-ceous rump. Forty yards away, slender, expectant, and golden-brown, stood three ripely nubile girls who had lately, with graceful move-ments, been tossing the ball from one to another. In a rude arc of the neighbouring cliffs was another group of nudists, some twenty-five or thirty, many of them middle-aged and scarcely at ease as they squatted on the sand. They were listening to a deep-chested woman who, in a hoarse contralto, stood in their midst, and recited a poem by Gertrude Stein. Her words reached faintly to the sea's antiphon that rustled the sand:

'If she bowed. To her brother. Which was. A fact. That is.

If she bowed. Which. If she bowed. Which she did. She bowed to her brother.

Which she did. She bowed to her brother. Or rather. Which she did. She bowed to her brother. Or rather which she did she bowed to her brother.'

Scattered along the beach, ambulatory or in supine contemplation of the sun, were the other members of the colony. Few could claim aesthetic justification for their nakedness, but those who had less cause for pride in it were more conscious of their merit in its display. Juan, bare as the others except for a hat – the sun shone hotly – deflected his gaze from the three young women who were waiting for their ball, and looked instead at two elderly thigh-shrunken gentlemen whose conversation, as they walked to and fro, was earnestly of lumbago and the healing power of light. After five days in the colony he was still subject to occasional embarrassment.

He was, moreover, worried by the non-appearance of Kuo Kuo. He had come to Arroyo Beach in the expectation of finding her already in residence, but despite the difficulty of recognizing anybody except the most intimate of friends, he had soon made sure that she was not there. Now he wondered uneasily whether she had changed her mind and had no intention of coming. If that were so, he was wasting his time in this unnecessary New Congo, and had shocked his modesty for nothing. He had no faith in the benefit of gregarious nakedness, and there was no pleasure to be got from looking at it. To contemplate it was either aesthetically distressing or socially disconcerting. He wished he had been less headstrong in his movements, and had learnt what Kuo Kuo's plans really were before trying to anticipate them.

Mr Lippincott returned to his chair. 'As I was about to say,' he continued, 'the current trend towards elementals is an index of man's capacity for survival. There is, in our racial preconsciousness, a system closely akin to the traffic lights in our great cities. We call that system Instinct or Intuition, and when it shows the red light we know it's time to turn around and ride back to Nature. . . .'

Again Mr Lippincott was interrupted. With a sudden exclamation

Juan sat up and stared at two figures walking towards them along the level beach. One was Dr Salvator, decently clothed in the lion-skin he used for the receiving of visitors; the other, slim as a reed, was a girl in a pale green Chinese dress, a narrow dress as straight and nearly as simple as the green skin of a reed. She came nearer with small quiet movements, like tall grass shaken by the wind, and her hair was bright as black lacquer in the sun. Juan was immediately torn by the most painfully conflicting emotions. He was delighted to see her, and appalled at the prospect of being seen. He was very excited, and exceedingly abashed. He acutely despised the disorder of his mind, and was ill-naturedly jealous of Mr Lippincott's equanimity. 'An Oriental, I presume,' said Mr Lippincott. 'There's room for many guests in Nature's mansion.' Juan was tempted to flee, and prevented by fear of seeming still more ridiculous. Before he could resolve his emotions Dr Salvator had turned towards them, waved a muscular arm in their direction, and confronted them with a countenance as leonine as his costume.

'Mr Lippincott and Mr Motley,' he exclaimed. 'Let me present, Miss Kuo Kuo; Mr Lippincott, Mr Motley. Miss Kuo Kuo is a visitor from China.'

Juan raised his hat. 'How do you do,' he said. 'I don't know if you remember me. . . .'

Suddenly as the serenity of a goldfish-bowl is ruffled by a cat's paw, the ivory smoothness of her face was ruffled by laughter. Neither recognition, nor surprise at the circumstances of recognition, had changed the placidity of her eyes or the soft firmness of her lips, but laughter in a moment took and dispossessed them of calm. She laughed aloud, and louder than anyone could have expected. It was very musical and pleasant laughter. At another time and in another place it might have been compared to the ringing of many little bells among a greenery of bamboos; or to the filling of the summer air with the music of pigeon-wing pipes, as the Chinese so agreeably practise. But it was more unexpected than the former, and louder than the latter. It was incongruously loud and hearty, coming as it did from a person of so delicate a shape and such exquisite features. Dr Salvator was manifestly indignant. Mr Lippincott took off his eye-glasses, felt for a handkerchief with which to polish them, and failed to find one. And all the surrounding nudists, rising like penguins at a zoo

9

when the keeper comes with fish, rose and came slowly, slow and bewildered, towards the noise of the little bells in the spinney of bamboos, to the shrilling of the pigeon-wing pipes.

Furiously angry, Juan put on his hat and walked stiffly away. He squared his shoulders. His demeanour was extraordinarily dignified, but his straw hat seemed either redundant or inadequate. He felt, in his dignified retreat, its redundancy – or inadequacy – and threw it away. Kuo Kuo was still laughing.

'To hell and disaster with nudism!' Juan exclaimed. 'That's the finish of it for me. I'll take off my clothes to swim and to sleep and to die and make love, but God forsake me if ever again I undress on principle.'

With force and ingenuity he continued to curse himself for his folly and Dr Salvator for his charlatanism till he came to the colony's headquarters. There, from a Filipino servant, he demanded his suit-cases, and rapidly dressed. After the indignity of five days of nudism, the humiliation of being laughed at was unbearable. He was going to leave the colony at once.

He filled the tank of his shabby second-hand motor-car with Dr Salvator's petrol, and drove to the imposing iron gates that protected the nudists from the world without. While he was waiting for them to be opened he heard Salvator's voice booming and thundering behind him, and turning he saw the Doctor and Kuo Kuo, with servants pursuing them who carried a steamer trunk, a cabin-trunk, three suit-cases, a dressing-case, and a couple of hat-boxes. Perceiving the civilized profusion of Kuo Kuo's wardrobe, and correctly guessing that she had already been expelled from the colony, Juan was immediately conscious of a warm and grateful sympathy with her. – Being decently dressed, he was again capable of generous emotion. – He got out of his car and waited.

'Why, Mr Motley, you're not leaving us, are you?' said the Doctor.

'I am,' said Juan.

'Now I realize you've been grossly insulted, and believe me I deplore it. But this is the first time our colony has been profaned by foolish laughter, and I give you my word that never again will you suffer a like embarrassment.'

'I certainly shall not.'

'The human body – '

'Is greatly indebted to human tailors, shirtmakers, breeches-makers, bootmakers, couturiers, milliners, and haberdashers. If nudism prevails, then all will be ruined; and their faculty of invention – so much more ingenious than Nature's, which can't give us any larger variety than a chest and a breast – will be entirely lost. And why should Nature be flattered for doing slovenly, slipshod, ill-cut work that no tailor would be seen dead with? Look at Mrs Wibloe, Miss Urt, and Mr Lippincott: do you think any decent tailor would sell you a suit as badly cut, poorly finished, and shoddily lined as they are? You can have Nature if you want her, but give me tailors. For their sake I'm going to remain orthodox, unnatural, and well-dressed; so if you'll tell your servants to put Miss Kuo's luggage in my car . . .'

'I have rather a lot, I'm afraid.'

'The more the better,' said Juan.

'You are throwing away your chance to lead a simple healthy life in communion with the primal forces of earth,' shouted Dr Salvator; and clutched his lion-skin.

'That is my exact intention,' Juan answered, and noisily started his engine. 'Where shall I take you?' he asked.

'I don't know,' said Kuo Kuo. 'What a pity I laughed. Now I shall have all the trouble of making new plans.'

The admirable road stretched smooth and almost white before them. It was made of cement and stained by the excreted oil of many motorcars. There was nothing natural about it. It was a magnificent road, and it ran for hundreds of miles through country in which Nature was everywhere in obvious and proper servitude to humanity. Villas and oil-wells spoke of her subjection. Spanish architecture and gas stations proved it. Straight-eights, high-tension cables, and hot-dog stands triumphantly proclaimed the sovranty of Man. To hell with Nature, thought Juan, and was happier than he had been for a week.

'I'm going to San Francisco,' he said. 'To the biggest, newest, noisiest, most abominably over-heated, and absurdly luxurious hotel I can find.'

'It sounds horrible.'

'It sounds delightful. After five days of nudism one has a craving for the superfluities of civilization.'

'Why did you go to Arroyo Beach?'

'I thought you were going.'

'And if I had gone there first, and you had come later and seen me undressed, you might have been the one to laugh.'

'I'm sure I wouldn't.'

'There is a great difference between men and women,' said Kuo Kuo.

'Life has its compensations,' answered Juan. 'Why not come to San Francisco with me?'

'Wouldn't that be rather improper, as we are almost strangers?'

'How nice of you to take it like that.'

'Oh, I don't, if that isn't what you meant. In any case I am certainly not going with you, to San Francisco or anywhere else.'

'But we aren't really strangers. We're acquaintances, and I'm very fond of acquaintances. I've always been willing to give two old friends for one new acquaintance. It takes so long to get used to an old friend.'

'But if acquaintances live more lightly, it is because they have no burdens to carry, of friendship and consideration.'

'I dislike burdens,' said Juan, 'and at my back I often hear Time's wingèd chariot changing gear.'

'That is nonsense. In China we are never afraid of Time. The days are our servants, not our masters.'

'So in China the business of courtship is a fairly long one?'

'Very long indeed,' said Kuo Kuo.

'And are Chinese marriages always happy?'

'No, not always. It depends on who is married, of course. My father had seven wives – my mother was the fifth – and they were all rather frightened of him. They used to run and hide when he came in. But most of them were quite happy, I think.'

'And would you be happy with a husband who had seven wives?'

'Why not, if they were all friendly and agreeable?'

'You must come to San Francisco,' said Juan.

'But I am really a serious person, and I cannot go idly to places, for no purpose or reason.'

'Then why were you going to Arroyo Beach?'

'Because I thought there would be very silly people there, and I could learn things from them that can't be learnt from wise people.'

'I often behave foolishly myself.'

'But are you as foolish as your actions?'

'Most decidedly not.'

'Then what could I learn from you?'

'If I were a jazz singer, a torch singer, a radio minstrel, a whispering baritone or a crooner, I might tell you. But the words have been battered and tattered and flattened and flayed till everyone else is ashamed to use them.'

'I think I shall not come to San Francisco,' said Kuo Kuo.

Juan stopped the car. 'I think you ought to.'

Kuo Kuo twisted round, lifted her knees on to the seat, and gravely faced him. Her eyebrows were outward-curving, black and thin, as proud and delicate as a peewit's crest. Her lips were like the rose-flaws in a pied magnolia, her chin was narrow and round. 'I am Chinese,' she said, 'and in China to-day there is so much misery that to look for pleasure would make me a traitor to my country.'

Juan was unwilling to accommodate his mind to such heroic seriousness. He was fairly ignorant about China. The name created for him little more than a blurred image of enormous yellow plains, a gigantic and crenellated brown wall, pagodas, umbrella'd armies, sampans in the deep gorges of the Yangtze, and Li Po fishing for the moon. 'I think you're taking too solemn a view,' he said. 'If we were all as preoccupied as that with our national problems . . .'

'We might solve our national problems.'

'Now you're being totally unreasonable,' said Juan. 'You're talking like the guest of honour at a Rotarian breakfast who's graduated from selling bonds to selling Utopias. I believe — well, I've never thought about it till now, but I'm quite sure I believe — that the world is spasmodically getting better, but that nine out of ten amateur reformers only succeed in leaving banana-skins on the pavement. The less we interfere with a biological process the better.'

'That is a very Chinese thing to say. For four thousand years we have done nothing but mind our own business, and now China is being destroyed by bandits and Communists and opium and the Japanese and our own inefficiency.'

'But I don't see what you can do . . .'

'When the proper time comes, I can fight.'

Juan looked sceptically at her hands and narrow wrists.

'You do not need much strength to fire a machine-gun,' she said. 'When I came to America, which is the modern country of the world, I thought I would meet some philosopher who knew as much about modern times as Confucius knew about his. But the most honest man

I have met was a soldier. So I asked him to teach me about machine-guns; and he did.'

Juan by chance had stopped the car about fifty yards from a wayside petrol pump. Beside the pump was a stall displaying cigarettes, chewing-gum, crackers, fruit, and soft drinks. The pump was a golden yellow, and the framework of the stall was bright red. They looked very smart, and compared with the grey thought of machine-guns they were comforting to the mind and agreeable to the eye. Juan got out and bought two cardboard-sealed bottles of milk.

'You'll need to build yourself up if you're going to handle a machine-gun,' he said. 'Have you ever fired one?'

'Not actually, but I know all about them.'

'And what's going to be your target? Bandits, Communists, opium-eaters, or Japanese?'

'The Japanese, of course. They are much the worst. We have always had plenty of bandits and criminals in China, and we do not really mind them. But the Japanese are trying to destroy China, and make us a subject people.'

'You're really serious about fighting?'

'Of course I am!'

A man's impulse to succour beauty in distress is neither pure nor revoltingly hypocritical. It is altruism sweetened by self-interest; but it is also a noble and hazardous enlargement of self-interest. Juan's sentiments had hitherto been simple and vivid. Kuo Kuo delighted and excited him, and he wanted to extend and enlarge the pleasure of being with her. Her attractions were magnified by her nationality. She was Chinese and unfamiliar; in the unknown there may be bliss unknown. Her beauty was strange and new, her character unexplored; and all men are sailors. But now altruism – a young man's altruism – began to plait itself into his simple motive, and in a very short time he felt astonishingly confident about several things, all of which, half an hour earlier, had been total strangers to him. He felt sure he could help Kuo Kuo in her trouble about China; indeed in any of her troubles. He felt sure it would be the pleasantest thing in the world to help her. He was sure she was right in judging China's condition to be desperate, and in arraigning the Japanese as her worst enemies. He began to feel strongly about China himself. He thought again of Li Po, and of Confucius, and of cherry-blossom – no, that was Japanese –

and of Willow Pattern plates, and several hundred million patient farmers. Why the devil should Japan go in to ruin their peace? Japan, he was sure, had never produced anything as lovely as Kuo Kuo, with her ivory skin, her narrow green dress, and the gold buttons on its collar. He was more than half-ready to fight for China himself.

'Look here,' he said, 'if you come to San Francisco with me, I'll go to China with you. And I'll bring my own machine-gun.'

'Do you think that would be a good bargain for you?'

'I am neither a huckster nor a lightning calculator,' said Juan. 'Neither am I afraid of yielding to impulse. Nor have I ever found any difficulty in knowing what I want. At present I have twin desires. The other is to see China. I am a simple person easily pleased with the best of everything, and I have been told that Chinese scenery is superb. As for the rest, I have two eyes, but single vision. I refuse to be contradicted.'

I

WITH portentous joint-stock banks for its battlements, and granite-walled huge offices for its watchtowers, Shanghai stood like a robber-keep at the entrance to China. Behind its tremendous walls were the incessantly toiling, tirelessly spawning provinces from which it took toll to build and maintain its magnificence. Out of rice-fields and poppy-fields and the little labour of many millions of men had risen those great buildings; and from the sweat of innumerable simple peasants that luxury had been distilled. Merchants had founded it, and merchants ruled it. As daring and fanatical for wealth as ever soldiers for honour and priests for their God, they had crossed the world, and sat themselves down in a hostile land, and stayed there despite hostility, and in a few generations raised to a wondering sky this imperial city, where before had been only some wattled huts and a stinking swamp.

It was achievement of the largest kind. Running-board to running-board, hundreds of motor-cars stood on the Bund, and other hundreds in the bannered streets were as restless as the weaver's shuttle. They had been bought with money made in a land where a wheelbarrow was wealth, and where the commonest kind of highway was still a foot-path through the fields.

In the Whangpoo, the river that washed the city's wharves like a defensive moat, were ocean-going liners from France and Britain, America and Germany and Japan. Their cargoes had been brought to them in junks that naked coolies hauled through the fierce waters of the Yangtze, or in sampans laboriously poled through interminable muddy creeks. They were pirate ships, and Shanghai was a pirates' roost.

But the keep, the pirates' roost, was not without benevolence. The robber merchants, for their own purpose, had established law in their settlement, and contrived for those who lived there a very reasonable degree of security. It therefore presented yet another contrast to the unspoilt hinterland, whose charms included banditry, extortion, armed assault, and such reverence for the Confucian principles as to leave invested capital without any adequate protection. The result was that worldly and wealthy Chinese, in ever-increasing numbers, had discovered the amenities of the roost, and come to the conclusion that the pirates' law was better than their own lack of it. Many who had been thrifty enough to save a little money or so clever as to swindle their fellow-villagers, and others who merely had ambitions about saving or swindling, made their homes in the foreign settlement, whose population presently numbered more than a million, the vast majority being Chinese. Two million more came to live on the periphery of the settlement, where they enjoyed the over-flow of its beneficence, such as decent roads, tramcars, cinemas, the service of a fire brigade, an opportunity to make money, and a chance to spend it before it had been stolen from them.

The robbers' keep was therefore regarded as a Centre of Civilization; the conquering merchants built more temples to Progress and Industry, which, though scarcely as beautiful as Lincoln Cathedral or the Taj Mahal or a Greek Artemis, were more immediately useful; and all the patriotic Chinese politicians, who called the foreigners running dogs and said they must be driven into the sea, and the Chinese generals who fought or evaded each other for their country's good, put their money into foreign banks and acquired town residences under the foreigners' protection. Shanghai might have developed peacefully on these lines – collecting the wealth of China, returning some small change to the natives, and providing an asylum for retired Chinese statesmen – had it not been for the unruly ambition of the Japanese.

The Little Dwarfs of the East Ocean, as the Chinese called them, were a pleasing example of a psychologist's hypothesis. For centuries they had been bullied, swindled, and humiliated by the Chinese, the Russians, and anybody else who had the opportunity. Then they had become civilized, and discovering in civilization the very weapons they needed, had adopted along with it a modern code of ethics, imperialism, and revengeful efficiency. In their rapid progress, how-ever, they had scarcely had time to reconcile some contradictions in their national character.

They were, on the one side, as clean and tidy and orderly, as fond of flowers and bright colours, as the Dutch; the other side they were apt to be hysterical, fanatical, and curiously addicted to suicide. They boasted of their reverence for their ancestors, and often behaved like arrivistes who had never owned a grandfather. They were in many ways as clever and energetic as the devil; and they were so foolish as to want, not merely China's trade, but much of its unwieldy land and undisciplined people. Because of their militant avarice the streets of Shanghai – that most benevolent of pirate polities – became a bloody and untidy battlefield.

It was raining when the yellow-funnelled *Empress of Hawaii* came into the Whangpoo River. Over the wide clumsy perspective of grey buildings, and the staccato chimneys on the other bank, the sky hung dismally low, and the air was cold. Juan and Kuo Kuo stood on the boat deck and silently regarded the cheerless view.

Four months had passed since their going from Arroyo Beach, and for twelve weeks they had been living together so contentedly that their relations had become almost domestic. Kuo Kuo, for instance, no longer troubled to conceal the blemishes in her character. She was unpunctual, illogical, and opinionative. She spat orange-pips on the floor, kept toilet requisites, peanuts, and sweetmeats under her pillow, and often, when Juan was talking well and judicially about some matter that had newly drawn his attention, she would interrupt him with a cool 'I'm reading, dear'. But in spite of these and other flaws in her behaviour he loved her inordinately. He loved her so completely that often he felt – with the injustice and forgetfulness of love – that he had never loved before. Three months of happy fidelity had convinced him that man was properly monogamous, and he an exemplar of blissful virtue.

That Kuo Kuo should be so blindly and totally enamoured as this was clearly impossible; for she kept thinking about the part she was to play in the affairs of China. But she was in love, sometimes passionately, sometimes tolerantly, often with gaiety, and occasionally with petulance; for Juan, as was natural after they had dressed together for several weeks, had lost something of his spontaneous admiration for her frocks and complexion, and paid her fewer compliments about them. But they were mutually in love, and now, as they stood looking at Shanghai and Shanghai came nearer, her hand was in Juan's coat-pocket, held closely by his, and they had no thought of parting.

The river was busy with the passing of ships and lighters and high-sterned country-craft. Tugboats sped swiftly under plumes of furious smoke, ferries crossed, and narrow destroyers were anchored in mid-stream. It was, though hardly a peaceful scene, a scene that made no suggestion of war. But suddenly a procession of boats – a tug and two lighters – enormously erupted. A funnel of grey and yellow fumes shot upwards from them, expanded, and spread into cumulus. In the very moment of expansion it was split by a lurid flame, and the city shook to the roar of the explosion. Out of the smoke descended a shower of dismembered arms and legs and other human fragments.

Staggered by the shock and dazed by the infernal roar, Juan and Kuo Kuo held tightly to each other. 'The war has started,' she said. Her voice was awed and thrilling. 'China will win,' she added.

A pair of blue cotton trousers, stripped in the upper air from the lower half of a bisected coolie, sailed absurdly by and collapsed on the rain-pocked water. Boatmen and rickshaw-pullers screamed and fled; laden coolies on the wharves dropped their burdens and ran. But already the disciplined movements of rescue-work were opposing the wild activity of panic. The destroyers were lowering boats, a motor-launch raced to the storm-centre, and bearded Sikh police-men strove stubbornly to create order out of the sudden chaos on the streets. With a frenzy of klaxons and the blatant hullabaloo of bells, fire-engines hurry-scurried along the Bund.

'They wouldn't call the Fire Brigade to put out a war,' said Juan.

'Well, it sounded like a war, and a lot of people were blown to pieces.'

But some of the passengers had already got more accurate news of the disaster, and presently Juan heard that the lighters had been loaded with gunpowder, and the explosion was probably caused by sparks from the tugboat's funnel, or a casual cigarette-end, or an act of God. For once the Japanese were innocent. Juan was thankful that hostilities had not yet begun, for he felt strongly the desirability of becoming acquainted with the lie of the land before entering into battle. He was largely ignorant of military service, but he knew that personal recon-naissance was highly commended by professional soldiers, and he fancied that the first thing to reconnoitre was a line of retreat. If war were imminent – and apparently it was – he was pledged to fight, but by no means to die for China. 'One must keep one's head,' he thought.

Of the many friends whom Kuo Kuo had expected to meet her, only one appeared. He was a plump little man in a felt hat and a long black gown. His name was Min Cho-fu. 'Excuse me,' he said to Juan, 'I speak only a little English.' He spoke less than that, however. But talking to Kuo Kuo he was extremely voluble. He explained that all the others who had intended to meet her had probably been delayed by the confusion that followed the explosion; or perhaps they would arrive later, as some of them were not very punctual. But they would all meet that evening, he said, for they were to dine at the Mei-sum restaurant in Szechuen Road, where there was the best Cantonese food to be got in Shanghai, and there they could discuss the situation.

It was very grave. For several days past there had been serious rioting in Chapei, an industrial suburb of Shanghai, and the Japanese admiral had delivered an ultimatum in which he demanded the instant suppression of anti-Japanese sentiment and the immediate establishment of a sincere and lasting friendship; and to assist in these matters he had landed five hundred marines. Japanese residents in Shanghai were insistently demanding their government's intervention, and Japanese reservists in plain clothes, armed and numerous, were already patrolling certain streets. The Chinese, on the other hand, were busily erecting barricades of sandbags and barbed wire, and were momentarily expecting reinforcements. Their own organization, the Conquering Youth of China, said Mr Min Cho-fu, was ready for action and waiting only for Kuo's leadership. War was imminent, bloody and serious war.

But Juan, for whom Kuo Kuo translated these tidings, found it difficult to regard the prospect seriously. During their civilized conveyance to an hotel, in a very good taxi-cab that avoided other cabs in the most civilized fashion, he could see nothing but the evidence of an apparently secure and civilized existence. There were handsome shops and bright electric lights, traffic-policemen and smooth office-buildings, and Englishmen in bowler hats. True, there were many thousands of blue-clad Chinamen in the streets, and a hurrying stream of rickshaws; but in spite of their foreign appearance he could discover nothing fierce or combative in their demeanour. It was ridiculous to suppose that war could invade such peacefully busy thoroughfares.

Their hotel was almost Americanly tall. There were Chinese residents in the lounge, and Chinese servants; but the lift rose swiftly and smoothly, their room was furnished with the clean elaborate impersonality of an hotel in London or New York. 'It's nonsense to talk about war,' said Juan.

But Kuo Kuo was busily unpacking. From a pile of underclothes she took two automatic pistols, one of which she gave to Juan. 'When wisdom rules, the world will be common to all,' she said. 'Till then we must protect what is rightfully ours. The youth of China will lead the whole country into action.'

'But it's absurd for you yourself to think about fighting! There's a Chinese army, isn't there? Well, why not leave it to them? I'm not going to let you run into danger for the sake of nonsensical, quixotic, sentimentally blood-and-thunderish romantic notions about patriotism . . .'

'I'm going to have a bath,' said Kuo Kuo, and deafened herself against his sudden anger with the noise of rushing water. But Juan continued to talk, to expostulate, and denounce her folly. He walked impatiently to and fro, talking loudly in the heated air. He sat on the edge of the bath and continued to talk. But in the middle of a sentence he stopped, and was silent.

In spite of his disbelief in the likelihood of war his nerves had reacted to the atmosphere of danger, and in a very natural and illogical fashion he now felt responsible for Kuo's safety. Love had never before contented him so well or troubled him so deeply. Her narrow beauty delighted his eyes and his arms; but beauty was only partly the cause. There was poetry and prose in her; the poetry of a people who had for many generations cultivated the poet's vision and loved the poet's tongue; the prose of an old nation that accepted the dirt and discomfort of life, and could laugh loudly and live strongly till its death. She had beauty, and strength of character, and many small faults that did not matter in the least. Because they loved so well they could be casual in their love without hurt to it. Such happy love was like a mountain stream, bubbling and shallow at one moment, then passionate and deep, but always in the same course. To think of losing her was misery and darkness.

But Kuo lay calmly in her bath, and said, in the unexpected silence, 'I suppose Japan has been too straitened to acquire riches and good manners. Mencius said, "To be very poor and yet law-abiding is possible only to the cultured". And Confucius said, "Cultured people

22

must inevitably become poor; but when the mean in spirit are poor, they are lawless".'

'I wish you'd forget about Confucius and Mencius,' exclaimed Juan. 'If it weren't for them you might have had time to learn something useful in the last four thousand years; and China wouldn't be in the mess it's in to-day.'

'Give me a towel,' said Kuo. 'And if you're going to put on a clean shirt you'd better hurry, because in China we dine early.'

Juan was still unpacified when they reached the Mei-sum restaurant. They climbed a narrow and rather dirty wooden stair, and came into a warm smell and a clattering noise of talk and eating and the shifting of dishes. The restaurant consisted of eight or ten small private rooms. They passed a black and narrow kitchen, and arrived at a room where Kuo Kuo was warmly greeted by seven men and a short, slim, pretty girl. When Juan was introduced they bowed in turn, shook hands with themselves, and began a lively conversation with Kuo. For some minutes Juan was forgotten. He examined the furnishing of the room, and saw bare matchboard walls, rather shabbily painted; three large spittoons that had not recently been emptied; heavy chairs and a round table; and a battered sideboard of a curiously Victorian pattern. Presently Mr Min came round and again introduced him to the slim pretty girl, who was his sister. 'She speaks good English,' he said.

Unfortunately Miss Min was so shy that she could use no more of her English than a whispered yes or no. It was a relief to Juan when they sat down, and dinner was ordered. But his relief was short-lived, for looking at the table equipment he found before him an array of tiny bowls, a little plate, a small porcelain ladle, and two ivory chopsticks. Tea was served. Then a waiter put a dish of little birds in the middle of the table, at which Juan stared helplessly. Everyone else, reaching forward with strangely prehensile chopsticks, pincered a bird and eagerly began to eat. Juan was still trying to find the proper grip with which to hold his skewers, when Miss Min obligingly offered him, on her own chopsticks, a blackbird, lark, or such small fowl. He was very grateful, and hurried to empty his mouth of splinters of bone in order to tell her so. Before the little birds were finished another dish was brought in, of small hard mushrooms and a long green vegetable. The mushrooms, by some remarkable device of the cook's, had become slippery and slightly elastic. Some of them evaded Juan's chopsticks with a coy squirming motion, and others leapt lightly about the table. Even the soft green tendrils slid snakelike from his grasp. But Miss Min again took pity on him, and filled his plate, from which, abandoning his chopsticks, he ate with the porcelain ladle and a surreptitious finger.

A large fish, very ugly to look at and dressed with a sweet-sour sauce, was brought in and rapidly pulled to pieces. Then came a couple of chickens, chopped into gobbets, and after them a great bowl of vegetable soup. A dish of pork succeeded that, followed by bean-curd and a fat duck. Intermittently they drank hot wine, poured from a tea-pot into little cups. It seemed that the polite and friendly thing to do was to salute one of the party with a cry of 'Kanpei!' – which was Chinese for No Heel-taps, or Bottoms Up – and swallow the wine at a gulp. Conscious of his deficiency with chopsticks, Juan determined to show his proficiency with wine. 'Kanpei!' he exclaimed to Miss Min. 'Kanpei!' she whispered in reply. He drank Kanpeis with everyone whose eye he caught. He drank one with Kuo Kuo, who sat farthest from him.

'I wish you'd tell me what you're all talking about,' he said to her.

'We're discussing terms for uniting the Conquering Youth of China with the Student Volunteers and the Death-Defying Corps of the National Salvation Association.'

'I hope the Japanese don't get to hear about that,' said Juan.

'They have many spies in Shanghai,' said Mr Min.

Juan turned to Miss Min. 'Are you interested in politics?' he asked.

'No,' she whispered.

'Then what do you do on a wet afternoon?'

Softly she breathed, 'I go to the pictures.'

More dishes were brought to the table, which was now so crowded that it was impossible to distinguish them or remember the sequence of courses. None of the earlier dishes had been removed, and a great confusion lay there of broken meats, abandoned fish, and little birds limed in dark gravy. Juan drank Kanpeis with a man who wore horn-rimmed spectacles, and with another who grew a soft thin beard. The wine was not strong.

'Who is your favourite film star?' Juan asked Miss Min.

She hung her head and murmured shyly, 'I don't know.'

After a long time, when the table was unbelievably congested, the dinner came to an end. Apparently some conclusion had also been reached in the discussion about the union of the Student Volunteers, the Conquering Youth, and the Death-Defying Corps of the National Salvation Association; for after a violent coda the conversation suddenly expired, and everybody got up and prepared to go. They all spoke politely to Juan – but in Chinese – and he felt as remote from the party as the Severn from the Yellow River.

He was last, and alone, as they left the derelict room. Passing an open door some two or three yards along the passage, he saw, at a half-disclosed table, a Japanese who had been aboard the *Empress of Hawaii*, and with him a figure so familiar, and so wholly unexpected, that for a second Juan stood motionless in the hypnotism of utter astonishment. It was a bulky and tough-seeming man with a face carved out of brightly coloured rock – blue where he shaved and elsewhere brick-red – and the last occasion on which Juan had seen him was when, with Red-eye Rod Gehenna and Wonny the Weeper, he had come with equal unexpectedness to Egret Island. It was Rocco, Red-eye's bodyguard, who had punched him with merciless force and precision, at Red-eye's orders, because his daughter Lalage said she had been integrated. Where was Lalage now, and who shared with the palms and the azure sea the solitude of that lovely island? And what was Rocco doing in Shanghai?

Juan went into the room, and the Japanese immediately rose with an exclamation of pleasure and a smile that revealed several gold-capped teeth. He had joined the *Empress of Hawaii* at Yokohama, and as they were both of a friendly disposition, he and Juan had rapidly become acquainted. His name was Hikohoki.

'Mr Motley!' he said, 'I am rejoiced to see you again. You will join us and have some refreshment? Let me introduce my friend Colonel Rocco.'

Recognition showed in Rocco's bright little eyes. 'Well, for Christ's sake!' he exclaimed.

'We've already met,' said Juan.

'I'll say we have.'

'Your promotion's been rapid, hasn't it?'

'Maybe it has.'

'So you are old friends?' said Hikohoki. 'That will aggravate your

25

pleasure considerably, and we must celebrate your happy reunion. Sit down, Mr Motley, and we shall drink some Chinese wine.'

'I'd like to, but some people are waiting for me outside.'

Hikohoki, hissing politely, expressed his regret.

'But perhaps we shall meet again,' said Juan.

'I am rejoiced to think so.'

'Good-bye, Rocco.'

Rocco made a surly gesture of farewell, and Hikohoki bowed from the waist. Very much puzzled by Rocco's presence in Shanghai, and his acquisition of a military title, Juan left them and hurried down the narrow stairs. Outside he heard a confusion of human noise, as though a great crowd were passing. The pavement was filled with the untidy fringes of a procession. The main body had passed, with banners and torches. There was a good deal of thin shouting.

'That was a demonstration, I suppose,' thought Juan, and looked for Kuo and her friends.

But they had disappeared. They had either been swept into and away by the crowd, or come out in time to escape it. There was no sign of them. In the wake of the procession the street was almost empty. Its innumerable coloured banners, painted with Chinese cryptograms, depended on vacant pavements. They were red and black, red with black ideographs, and black with gold. They were red and gold, and red and white. Red was a brave colour in a crowd but sinister in the shuttered half-darkness of an empty street. And Juan had forgotten the way back to his hotel.

He turned left, by chance, and walked for some distance under the gently moving banners. The unmeaning characters fascinated him, and the more he looked at them the stronger became his conviction that their purpose was rather to delight the eye than inform the mind. Instruction or communication was a secondary affair, significant form came first. The Chinese were artists, and so long as their writing was aesthetically satisfying, what matter though its meaning were dubious or none at all. 'Kanpei, China!' he exclaimed, and was startled by the sound of his voice in the quiet street. It occurred to him that Chinese wine might be less innocuous than he had supposed. And what, he thought again, what was Rocco doing in Shanghai?

He continued a little farther, and presently, on either side of the street, he was surprised to see Roman characters easy to decipher.

The Daisy, he read; Happyland, Forget-me-not, and Tumble Inn. These, he decided, were some of the several hundred resorts where Shanghailanders – those famous night-hawks – took their nocturnal pleasure. Their occupants would therefore speak English, and so could direct him to his hotel. He chose the modest entrance of The Daisy, and, passing a somnolent Chinaman, opened a frosted glass door and looked inside. Opposite him, in a silent row, were seven youngish women with blank expressions, and one older, with copper-coloured hair and a robust figure. She rose briskly as Juan looked in.

'Zdrástvitye!' she greeted him. 'Come inside. Come and have a good time.'

'Thank you,' said Juan. 'Merci bien,' he added, deciding with an assurance clarified by Chinese wine that French was the more appropriate language for such an occasion.

'Je serais ravi,' he continued . . .

'Ce serait tout le contraire,' Madame courteously interposed.

'. . . de faire la connaissance de toutes vos jeunes filles – bon soir, mes chères – mais il y a une faite intransigeante qui m'empêche. Je cherche mon hôtel.'

'Mais pourquoi?' said Madame. 'Vous l'avez trouvée.'

'Pas du tout,' said Juan firmly. 'Je veux dire, j'ai perdu ma route, et si vous aurez la bonté de me montrer la vie . . .'

'Bien sûr! Par ici, m'sieur!'

'Non. Non pas la vie. Je veux dire la rue. Ou la route. La route à mon hôtel.'

'You don't speak any English?'

'Of course I do,' said Juan indignantly.

'Then sit down and let us have a drink. Boy!' she called. 'Piva! It is good beer, only the best. Put on the gramophone, Sonia. The gentleman wants to dance.'

'No, I don't,' said Juan. 'I want to go back to my hotel.'

'You like blonde or brunette? There is Stasha, she has a good figure. She dances well, too. Stasha, come and dance with the gentleman.'

A fair-haired young woman, apparently the youngest there, came and stood so close to Juan that her corsage brushed his cheek. Madame took his hat and gloves. 'Help him lift off his coat,' she said.

Still protesting, Juan was pulled to his feet, his overcoat was removed, and Stasha, tightly holding him, bunted him into the middle of the narrow floor. A desolate wild music came from the gramophone. It was the gipsy song *Black Eyes*. Stasha, her mouth at his right ear, began to sing it in a hard and vibrant tone. In a futile effort to escape this irritation, Juan danced with great energy.

The song finished with a scratch, the needle scraped, and the noise stopped. Juan turned and saw all the young women sitting at the table with bottles of beer in front of them. A Chinese waiter gave him the bill.

'Now look here,' he said. 'I really am going. I must go. And if you'll tell me the way . . .'

'Drink your beer,' said Madame. 'It's early yet. We'll have a good time.'

'Za váshe zdaróvye!' cried the young women, and drank heartily.

'Good luck,' said Juan. 'But I simply can't stay.'

'Maybe you like a brunette better? Try Olga next time,' said Madame.

Before Juan could answer, the door was smoothly opened, and to his great relief Mr Hikohoki came in.

'Aha!' he said. 'So we have met again already. You like girls? So do I. They have always been my principal hobby.'

'I only came in to ask the way to my hotel,' said Juan. 'I'm in a great hurry to get back.'

Mr Hikohoki made a hissing sound that indicated sympathy. 'I understand,' he said. 'This is not a very good place. But there is a better one not far away. Really high-class. I will take you there.'

This suggestion was instantly and angrily opposed. The young women grew shrilly indignant, and Madame – her mind in a tumult that revealed itself in the agitation of her hands, her bosom, her eyes, and her speech – assailed Mr Hikohoki with indescribable fury; who answered her with equal vehemence. They argued in a mixture of Russian, Japanese, and English, and Hikohoki, though the poorer linguist, had so much the better of the debate that in a few minutes Madame was reduced to impotent muttering.

'Let us go now,' said Mr Hikohoki.

'He must pay for the beer,' said Madame.

'Of course!' said Mr Hikohoki.

Juan paid the bill, and wished the ladies good night. They did not answer.

'And now,' said Mr Hikohoki, 'we shall go to a more fashionable place, where there is very good tone and many high-class girls.'

'I'm sorry,' said Juan, 'but I'm going straight to my hotel.'

Having protested and pleaded and word-painted in vain, Mr Hikohoki shrugged his shoulders and said, 'As you will. There are times when I also do not care for even the most refined pleasure. You are staying at the New Celestial Hotel, are you not?'

'Yes.'

'That is where I am, so we can go together. It is a good hotel, but do not buy any jade from the shop they recommend. It is too expensive. Also silk. There is very good jade, very good silk, in Shanghai, but if you want the best and also the cheapest you must buy at some places I shall tell you. I shall arrange special low price for you, which I always do for my friends.'

'That's very kind of you.'

'It is nothing. I am rejoiced to be helpful.'

'How did you persuade that woman to let me out of her night-club?'

Mr Hikohoki made his amiable hissing noise. 'It was quite easy. I told her she would be discharged for rudeness to a customer. We have a motto, in such places, that the customer is always right.'

'But . . .'

'I am a director of The Daisy. I am also a director of The Happy Valley, to which I would have taken you. It is a most interesting avocation, to be a director of night-clubs.'

'And profitable?'

'Sometimes it is happily remunerative, but we have suffered from the depression, of course. And now, when we of the business community desire only the loyal co-operation and esteem of China and the rest of the world, we are encountered with waves of hatred and suspicion. They are difficult times, but I am not without hope for the future.'

Dark banners and the golden ideographs hung over tenantless streets. From the innumerable town behind them came faintly, because they were far off and untranslatable, the sounds of anger and excitement. In front of them rose the tall and solid strength of European buildings, and yellow in the misty darkness shone the lights of ships in the river. Mr Hikohoki spoke of Japan's unbounded sympathy for China.

'What,' said Juan, 'is Rocco doing here?'

'Colonel Rocco? He is Military Adviser to a Chinese general called Wu Tu-fu.'

'Good God!'

They crossed a bridge. In the Soochow Creek lay a countless fleet of sampans, side by side, odorous and over-populated and twinkling with the glow of their little fires. 'The Orient,' said Mr Hikohoki, 'has been lashed and washed by the stormy waves of civilization, but undoubtedly the present crisis is merely lurking under the verge of a golden age. Japan is forging ahead with full sail on the sea of world politics, and both emotionally and rationally we perceive that our destiny is to establish order out of chaos in the whirligig of the Far East. May I inquire whether you are interested in Life Insurance?'

'Not in the least,' said Juan.

'You are making a great mistake. If you are staying in Shanghai there will certainly be danger to your life and limbs, and it is your duty to think of the plight of your near and dear ones should their bread-winner become demised.'

'I don't think I've ever done much breadwinning.'

'That is only a figure of speech. It includes the other comestibles and necessaries of life. Now I am agent for the Nippon Provident and Mutual Welfare Insurance Company, Incorporated, and as your friend I shall see that you will get the most highly favourable terms. We can also insure your personal effects against fire and burglary at excessively low rates.'

'What are your rates for happiness?' said Juan gloomily.

They had come to the elaborate bronze doors of the New Celestial Hotel, and Juan was suddenly afraid that Kuo might not be there. Love's cowardice attacked him, and he thought the roaring procession might have confused her; or she had deserted him, being more deeply in love with China. Abruptly he said good night to Mr Hikohoki, avoided him, and caught an ascending lift.

Kuo Kuo was in their room. She also had been afraid. She ran to him, and threw her arms round his neck, and clung to him.

'You're making a fool of me,' said Juan. 'I was frightened you wouldn't be here, and my bowels felt like a cold sponge.'

'Where have you been? I thought you were lost, and I remembered I had treated you badly – I didn't speak to you at dinner, I wasn't nice to you – and I was miserable. Juan, do you love me?'

'I love nothing else.'

'But where have you been?'

Juan picked her up, carried her to a deep chair, sat down, and settled her on his knee. 'I took the wrong turning,' he said, 'and you've got to thank Hikohoki – you remember him on the *Hawaii*? – for bringing me back to you. He found me at a critical moment, when hope was waning, and led me home.'

'Did you talk to him?'

'We discussed international politics. He told me that Japan was China's truest friend, and tried to sell me life insurance.'

Kuo Kuo sat up. 'He is a spy,' she said. 'He is in the Secret Police.'

'Honeyheart,' said Juan, 'milk of Paradise, blissful, heartsease, my soul's adrenalin; you're talking nonsense. He told me the best place to buy silk underwear.'

'That is his cover. He is either engaged in espionage or counter-espionage. That means he may think that you are a spy.'

'My darling . . .'

'Don't call me darling in that tone of voice.'

'Well, you're talking poppycock, balderdash, and double-bottomed hooey. Hikohoki's a tout, and nothing more.'

'I know more about affairs in China than you do.'

'And I know more about everything else.'

'Then why haven't you learnt to be sensible?'

'Campaspe by her beauty,' said Juan, 'so enslaved the philosopher Aristotle that she could, when she so desired, drive him round the town like a beast of burden. And who was Campaspe? A Peloponnesian trollop, a fly-by-night under the Acropolis, a two-dollar pushover in Piraeus. Shall I compare her to you? A short-in-the-heel garlic-eating Greek? Compare her with white jade and the first day of spring, which are the only things to be remotely compared with you? The mere thought of it shames me. Nor shall I put myself on a par with Aristotle. But if he was a fool for Campaspe, haven't I a lien on lunacy under the new moon of China?'

Kuo sighed. 'You do talk a lot.'

'We men of action are incurably loquacious,' said Juan complacently.

But when he turned out the light and opened the window he felt less assured; for the silver shafts that tunnelled the darkness over Shanghai were not the rays of a Chinese moon but searchlights from a Japanese cruiser.

2

FRIGHTENED people from the outer parts of Shanghai were beginning to invade the Foreign Settlement. They came in motor-cars, on foot, in rickshaws, and pushing wheelbarrows. The more prosperous brought such of their possessions as they thought were valuable or immediately useful; the poor took with them everything they could carry. The rich could afford to be sensible, to abandon the greater part of their property; but to the poor it seemed that every trifle they owned was part of their lives, and they had burdened themselves with all the penny furniture of their tiny rooms. The less poor, the not-wholly poor, sat four or five together in rickshaws, huddled on each other's knees, children in the crook of an arm or the corner of a lap, with that gift for occupying a minimum of space which is a pitiful faculty of all the poor. Their possessions were tied in dark bundles, and often there was a girl who carried a bird in a yellow cage. The rickshaw coolies, sweating in front of such heavy loads, moved slowly with bent shoulders. They scowled and grimaced as they strove to keep their places in the fleeing column, but their expression had no more meaning than the solemnity of an old horse in a mill.

The colour of the fugitive throng was dark. They wore tunics and trousers of sombre blue, or long black gowns. The red banners above them were the brighter by contrast. In many places the scarlet papers, printed with greetings, with which they had welcomed the New Year, were still stuck to walls and windows. And no matter what ill luck the future brought them, their children and survivors would welcome the coming years with the same arrogant colour of their hearts' blood. War and disaster were a transient thing, but the life of China was eternal, and their eternal misery would always be lighted with bursts of laughter like red banners in a dismal street.

In the Foreign Settlement the Europeans were very angry, and worried about their investments. They were mobilizing their Defence Force. With stern impartiality they were making ready to defend their property against the aggressor, and against fugitives from the aggressor. Brokers spent sleepless nights, but English matrons refused to cancel their bridge-parties, and the Shanghai Scottish, stepping out of their vocational trousers and wrapping their loins in the heart-taking filibeg, said that war was a damnable thing, but a welcome change from going to an office every day of their lives.

Yet work, on the whole, was done with the same intensity and almost in the same volume as though nothing threatened the profitable continuity of life. Merchants and accountants bought, sold, and calculated; caterers drove their cooks to redoubled toil and trebled their prices as the swarm of fugitives demanded sustenance; and the coolies on the wharves beside the incoming ships staggered beneath their enormous burdens and chanted the interminable song of labour. 'Ley-la, hui-la, hui-la, hang-la,' they sang without ceasing and were dwarfed by their loads. Labour for bread could not halt though all the world were at war, and labour for profit would not cease before the shell-holes that showed the end of profit.

Traffic, it is true, was more and more impeded by the barricades that were being erected. Ramparts were made of sandbags, and fascines of barbed wire disposed across the frontier streets. Chinese soldiers in grey uniform untidily occupied strategic positions, Japanese gunmen moved warily into Chapei, and machine-gun classes were conducted on patches of waste ground. But while these preparations for war were being openly made, the greater part of Shanghai was busily pursuing its normal interests. The situation was as incongruous as if a garden suburb had presented its playing-fields and church hall to a batch of homicidal lunatics.

For two days Juan had observed, with increasing bewilderment, the setting of the stage for tragedy. He found it difficult to understand the necessity for war. It was true that some Chinese had killed a Japanese monk. It was also true that some Japanese had set fire to a Chinese towel factory. But was it worth going to war about the loss of a Buddhist acolyte and some face-cloths? The Chinese, of course, said that the Japanese were secretly installing a garrison of plain-clothes gunmen in Chapei; and the Japanese said that the Chinese were surreptitiously massing an army on the outskirts of Chapei. But could not the truth of these charges be ascertained? Chapei was not a hidden city in impenetrable hills or the deserts of Sinkiang. It was a dismal industrial suburb of Shanghai, continuous with Shanghai, as open to investigation as Salford from Manchester, and not unlike Salford in appearance. So far as Juan could discover, the only valid reasons for war were the Chinese refusal to answer the Japanese admiral's ultimatum – the ultimatum that had demanded love and admiration for Japan and all its works – and Kuo's decision that China could only be saved by charging with its embattled youth on the invader's guns and bayonets. She had not so far discovered a proper site for the charge; but Juan had gathered that he was expected to participate in it.

In the late afternoon Juan was sitting in the overheated lounge of the New Celestial Hotel, pondering these questions, when one of the tallest and the fattest men he had ever seen came in and looked inquiringly through the room. He was red-faced, with an amiable mouth, close-cropped grey hair, blue eyes, and a fine, high-bridged, fleshy nose that supported gold-rimmed spectacles. He stood proudly behind his enormous paunch. It was no mere pudding-basin of a paunch, no petty tumescence or adventitious hummock of fat; it was a rolling down, a Border hill that marched from his broad chest to a broader top, and from there declined steeply, but not without dignity, to the spacious anchorage of an heroic pelvis. It was a truly noble paunch. It was far more than the simple consequence of a hearty appetite. It was a monument to his spirit, and a testimonial to the strength of his back. It was a paunch that made one think not of greed but of grandeur, not of gluttony but of the profusion of earth and the magnanimity of humankind.

Puffing like a hot harvest-wind over corn, the fat man sat down. But the chair he selected had a fault in it; worm-holes or a dislocation or a greenstick fracture. It collapsed beneath him, and he sat heavily on the floor.

'God in a Flaming Bush!' he exclaimed, with annoyance indeed, but hardly with surprise. His voice was curiously mild. He looked up at Juan, who came to help him, and said: 'That's the forty-third I've broken since I started to count the paltry things.'

A number of people rose and regarded him with curiosity as he sat among the wreckage. 'Pigmies!' he exclaimed, but without rancour, and broke a leg of the demolished chair across his knee. 'Stuff for a doll's house,' he remarked.

'Have something to drink,' Juan suggested.

White-gowned waiters came to remove the wreckage. 'Take away the rookery and bring two whiskies and soda,' said the fat man; and sat more carefully on a sofa.

He drank his peg as the desert drinks summer rain. 'Are you going to stay and see the war?' he asked.

'Yes,' said Juan. 'Are you?'

'And be a target for recruits?' said the fat man. 'Not on your life. Any wall-eyed conscript, with his sights rusted at nine hundred, could hit me somewhere. If he allowed a yard for windage on the wrong side, he'd score an outer on my ribs. Machine-gunners would use a swinging traverse against me. I'm too fat to miss and too broad to defend. I'd fill a battalion's frontage, and need divisional artillery to cover my retreat.'

'So you don't approve of war?'

'Did I ever say that? Would you refuse to eat a fried egg because you don't want to lay one?'

'I don't see the connexion,' said Juan.

'There are more ways of looking at war than over the parapet of a front-line trench,' said the fat man. 'That was how I looked at the last one, and the view was horrible. But others made money out of it, and I'm going to make money out of this one.'

'Good luck,' said Juan, and drank his whisky and soda. For some time they talked inconsequently of Shanghai, the weather, and the catering of various shipping companies. The fat man spoke with a certain rotundity of phrase and richness of allusion that accorded nicely with his figure, and Juan was delighted to have made his acquaintance.

'Have you been long in Shanghai?' he asked.

'Fourteen years, and this is my last week. I'm going home to a Christian country, to die where I was born, in Gloucestershire.'

'That's my calf-country.'

'Gloucestershire? What part of it?'

Juan told him, and the fat man, glowing with a new geniality, smacked him on the leg and exclaimed, 'There's no land like it, and we're the pick of England there. You'll dine with me tonight?'

'I don't know if I can . . .'

'Nonsense. We'll dine and talk till midnight, canvassing every hedge and village in the county.'

Juan, however, was more anxious to talk of matters in Shanghai, and presently he asked, 'Have you ever heard of an American here called Rocco? He's apparently known as Colonel Rocco.'

The fat man looked wary. 'Yes, I know him. A friend of yours?'

'No. But I saw something of him in America.'

'A gunman, wasn't he?'

'Yes.'

'I thought as much. He was a soldier at one time, a sergeant with the American army in France, and a bruiser, a prize-ring man, before that. Then he rose in the world and became a gangster, and now he's ploughing fresh fields in China.'

'I met him the other night. He was with a Japanese called Hiko-hoki . . .'

The fat man was suddenly enraged. 'Hikohoki?' he exclaimed. 'God's uncle in Hell!'

'What's the matter?'

'Half my pension's gone, that's all. I've lost my annuity, I've slept in on Maundy Thursday. This war would have been breakfast and dinner and a good roof for my old age; but the roof's going to leak now.'

Juan said he was sorry to hear that, but still did not understand.

Over the benignity of the fat man's face there passed quick darkness of anger, furious grimaces, like rain-squalls over a broad wood. He muttered and grumbled and swore disjointedly. Fragments of imprecation bubbled softly from his lips; his gentle voice pronounced the disarticulated syllables of curious anathemas. Juan waited for an explanation.

Presently the fat man said: 'I'll tell you the whole story. You know something of Rocco, you come from Gloucestershire, and you look like a man of imagination. You may help me in the tangle I'm in. Now to begin with, there's a General in Nanking called Wu Tu-fu, with the title of General Commanding the Victorious Division of Ever-Invincible Tanks; and so far he hasn't any tanks to command. But I have. I've four of them, that I bought for twenty thousand Mex, plus six thousand to Hikohoki, who smuggled them in, the jaundicey two-headed tapeworm. At the other end there's Rocco, who's bodyguard, and calls himself Military Adviser, to Wu Tu-fu. And Rocco, acting for him, is buying my tanks for a hundred and eight thousand, less twelve thousand commission. But if that rat's tooth, Hikohoki, has been talking to Rocco, Rocco's going to cut the price and double his squeeze. For I told him the tanks had cost me eighty thousand; and Hikohoki knows better.'

'But Hikohoki's a Japanese,' said Juan, 'and if the tanks are being sold to a Chinese general . . .'

'It's surprising how commerce broadens the mind. As a matter of fact they were made in Japan, and I don't think they're worth much anyhow. But they were going to be a pension for my old age.'

The fat man sighed prodigiously. 'My name's Flanders,' he said.

'And mine's Motley.'

'Have a drink.'

'Have it with me,' said Juan, and called a waiter. 'Has it ever occurred to you that Hikohoki might be a spy?'

Flanders shook his head. 'There's not enough money in spying.'

'He tried to sell me life insurance. There's no fortune in that.'

Flanders scratched his grey head and eased the fork of his trousers. Then he looked slyly at Juan. 'You've given me an idea,' he said. 'Rocco's frightened of the Japanese. He thinks in terms of the Yellow Peril, and believes they spend all their time in plotting and assassination. If we tell him Hikohoki's a spy, or in the Secret Police, and there's a plot against his life, he'll stink with fear.'

'And how will that help?'

'He'll pay on the nail. He's coming here this evening, with the money in his pocket. Tell him there's a deadly, soft-footed, knife-in-a-corner conspiracy against him, and he'll pay without counting, and get back to Nanking like a terrier going down a drain.'

It seemed to Juan that Flanders's confidence was excessive, but he agreed to wait and corroborate the suggested fiction with such details as might occur to him. He had no reason to feel friendly towards Rocco, and the idea of a little tail-twisting was pleasant enough. They had another drink and waited thoughtfully till Rocco should appear.

His entrance was impressive. He came into the lounge, quick and heavy-shouldered, like a boxer conscious of spectators, and stopped for a moment to look this way and that with the searching gaze of a ham actor in melodrama. Then he caught sight of Flanders and advanced with determination in his gait, and saluted him – an American gesture – with a kind of truculent bonhomie. He had not noticed Juan, but when he saw him he scowled and thrust forward his head, again with rather theatrical vehemence, and his lips twisted to an unfriendly shape as though his mouth were filled with bitterness. 'Getting around pretty fast, aren't you?' he said.

'Sit down and have a drink,' said Flanders.

Rocco took off his coat. It was a handsome garment with a red check in it. He wore an olive-green tweed suit, cut in the extreme of New York sporting fashion, with a yellow waistcoat, and a large diamond ring on his little finger. He sat down and made himself comfortable. 'What's the dirt?' he asked.

'Very cold weather,' said Flanders. 'I trust you're keeping your health in this unfriendly climate?'

'I'm getting along pretty good.'

'Excellent. You know Motley, I think?'

'So what?'

'Nothing, nothing at all. I thought you'd be pleased to see an old friend; that's all. But perhaps you prefer business to amicable chit-chat. Well, have you brought the money, Rocco?'

'Yeah. If you want to talk turkey, I'm with you, Major Flanders. But not before a stranger, see?'

'Oh, come. Motley's no stranger. He's a mutual friend.'

'Well, now I know.'

'Have you seen anything more of Hikohoki?' said Juan.

'And what if I have?'

'You ought to be careful. He's one of the most dangerous men in Shanghai.'

'You're crazy. I've seen plenty of these Japs, and I don't like 'em. But Hikohoki's on the level.'

Juan looked at Flanders. 'He's stubborn,' he said.

'Tell him what you know.'

'Hikohoki's in the Secret Police,' said Juan.

'That's a lie!'

Flanders shrugged his enormous shoulders. 'Well, if you won't take a warning, I can't help you,' he said. 'We'd better talk finance.'

'I told you already: not before a third party.'

'He knows everything,' said Flanders. 'He's a Government man. Counter-espionage. It was he who told me about Hikohoki.'

38

Juan concealed his surprise at this unexpected announcement, which was more than he had bargained for. But he had a talent for acquiescence . . . There are people whose temper expresses itself naturally in *No*, that graceless and obstructionary plug of a word; and there are others whose eager nature must always find release in the runnel of a fluent *Yes*. – Negative and affirmative created He them. – And because *No* will timeously stop a leak, they that use it see nothing but virtue in it, forgetting that what will prevent wine from running out, must also withhold men from drinking. But *Yes*, that wasteful syllable, that running tap of a word, will carry those who utter it, as if on a pleasant stream, through rich and various country. It is a bridge that leaps over stagnation, a sky-sail to catch wind in the doldrums. It is a passport to adventure, birdlime for experience, a knife for the great oyster of the world and the pearls or the poison that hide within. *Yes* is the lover's word, for peril and for bliss, and *No* the miser's and the word the barren womb has said. The trumpet sounding for the charge cries *Yes*; and the key in the rusty lock squeaks *No*. They are an opening or a shutting; creation or criticism; life – or in all probability a very much longer life. Juan said *Yes* by nature, and had in consequence enjoyed many delightful experiences and several disastrous ones. Now, having rapidly adjusted himself to the situation, he decided to accept the role that Flanders offered him. He found sufficient reason for this decision in his liking for the fat Major, and his lack of liking for Rocco. He assumed an expression – or so he judged – of inscrutable omniscience, and with his finger-tips tapped on the table-top a sinister little rhythm.

Rocco corrugated his narrow forehead and stared suspiciously at Juan, at Flanders, and again at Juan. 'You're trying to double-cross me,' he said.

'What did Hikohoki tell you?' asked Juan.

'He told me plenty.'

'Well, well,' said Flanders, 'we'll have no more gossip-mongering. How about the muniments of war? Have you the money for them, Rocco?'

'Yes and no, if you see what I mean.'

'No, but I smell it,' said Flanders. 'There's an odour of double-dealing, a little stink of tergiversation, in that out-of-step conjunction. You're trying to go back on your bargain, eh?'

'Now be your age, Major. There's no use running around with your pants on fire. You've got certain goods, and I'm prepared to buy them; but only if the price is reasonable. And I've been hearing things, see? I've heard what you paid for the goods, and it wasn't the same as what you told me by a long way. There was so big a difference between those figures they'd need a suspension bridge to join them. So I'm just knocking thirty grand off my previous offer.'

'And that's the tale that Hikohoki told you? What squeeze do you pay him? What's his cumshaw? And when does he spring the trap on you?'

'There's isn't no good talking like that, Major. It won't get you nowhere, and when I'm trying to figure out a fair price . . .'

There was a lady who wished to speak to him on the telephone, said an ivory-yellow waiter to Juan. He left the disputants – Flanders leaning sideways towards Rocco, like a red moon gibbous on the edge of a cloud; Rocco watching with a boxer's eyes – and in the telephone-booth heard Kuo Kuo's voice. She was going to Nanking, she said. She was going at once, and she would not be back for two or three days. She was speaking from Min Cho-fu's house. No, Juan could not see her before she went, and she would not tell him why she must go with such precipitation to the capital. Her mission was important, of course. Perhaps there was going to be a change in their plans. They had decided to postpone the attack. The Conquering Youth of China would not, for the present at any rate, be asked to sacrifice themselves upon the guns. But the alternative plan was too important to discuss. Juan protested, said he would come with her. Kuo Kuo would not listen. They argued, and their voices met in sharp little waves, like conflicting tides. Then Kuo rang off, and Juan, suddenly unhappy and with anger for a core to his unhappiness, went back to the lounge and stood for a moment to look at the idlers who drank and did not know the bitterness of love. He wanted revenge, irrelevant but quick revenge, for the bruise the telephone had dealt him. He returned to Flanders and Rocco, and found them still arguing. But Rocco was clearly worried.

'How long are you staying in Shanghai?' said Juan.

'Till to-morrow evening.'

'You'd better get out before then. I can't guarantee your safety after midnight.'

'I should worry!' said Rocco. 'I've never asked for protection yet.'

'You'll probably ask for it too late. I've just been talking to one of my men, who has shadowed Hikohoki for the last three days. You're being led into a trap, Rocco.'

Rocco began to look uncomfortable, for Juan's manner was cold and convincing.

'Well, did you ever!' he retorted in an uneasy voice. 'So they're leading me into a trap, huh? And it's just my dumb luck that I've never walked into a trap before, is it? Say, what do you think this is?'

He opened his olive-green coat and showed, in a holster under one arm, the butt of a revolver. 'And nobody ever saw the big blow on my hip?' he asked scornfully. 'I've been in plenty traps, and come out again with the cheese in my pocket.'

'You know your own ability, I suppose,' said Juan, 'but I know the Japanese Secret Police, and I know this: that if you want to get out of Shanghai alive, and take your tanks with you, you haven't much time to lose.'

Suddenly Rocco appeared to weaken. 'I'd catch a ride to Nanking right away, if Major Flanders would only be reasonable,' he said.

'Reason be hanged!' bellowed Flanders – but soft and melodiously bellowed, his voice muted by the fat that encircled his neck and padded the sounding-board of his cheeks – 'Reason be hanged, for you listen to that yellow nark of Nippon, and stick your neck in the running-knot of his lies, and call that reason! Reason's a fair price, and pay on the nail!'

The argument recommenced, but now Rocco's bargaining was a mere formality. There was no feeling in it. His offer rose by ten thousand as though money had no meaning for him. He was anxious to be off, and Flanders, pressing his advantage home, forced up the bids. Juan took no further part in the negotiations except to say casually: 'They meant to take your body to a house in Chapei, and set it on fire.'

Rocco went up another five thousand, and Juan thought gloomily of Kuo Kuo. Love was a fire that must be given fuel, or it burnt the hearth. When Kuo Kuo was beside him, love was a dancing flame; but when she was away, a devouring coal. To be in love was to be like a country that pushes its conquests over sea, and wins for its pleasure a city with silver battlements, a sweet-smelling island, and a snow-capped hill; and thereafter is always afraid for the safety of its possessions.

Flanders and Rocco, it seemed, had come to an agreement. They exchanged papers, and Flanders counted a thick bundle of notes. They went out together, and spoke in turn through the telephone. They came back to the lounge and had another drink.

Rocco said to Juan, 'I guess the Japs won't start anything to-night, will they?'

'You're perfectly safe till midnight.'

'Well, I'm kind of sorry about that,' said Rocco with false regret. 'If I got my hands on that bastard Hikohoki I'd pull his guts out.'

He put on his red-checked overcoat.

'Why,' asked Juan, 'did you leave America?'

'The depression,' said Rocco. 'There wasn't no more money in bootlegging. Red-eye muscled-in on the kidnapping racket, but that didn't look good to me. I've always been sort of fond of kids, and it just burned me up to hear 'em crying for their ma. So I beat it out here.'

He waved an airy salute, and swaggered off.

'I never suspected him of sentiment,' said Juan.

'He carries his frailties well,' said Flanders tolerantly. 'Now you'll dine with me to-night, for you've done me a noble service. You've saved my bacon, Motley. I've an old-age pension in my pocket – ninety thousand I got from him, and that's more than seven thousand pounds in Christian money – and if friendship's any use to you, mine is yours till the worms and the sexton make room for this fat body of mine. And God help the sexton, for it's a quarry he'll have to dig to hold me. They'll look at my grave and think of foundations for a cathedral, or a dry dock for battleships, and when the turf covers it there'll be a new playground for children, a public park, and room for a bandstand over my head. If I were to die abroad I'd make a new province for England, and younger sons would build a town upon me. But thanks to you I'm going home, Motley. I sail on Monday, with money in my pocket and a gentleman's life in Gloucestershire waiting for me like a child's picture of Heaven.'

'I'm going home myself before long,' said Juan.

'Then come with me, and we'll live like lords together with the Severn to spit in and the Forest of Dean to light our fires.'

'No,' said Juan. 'I can't go yet. I must stay in Shanghai for the present. I'm interested in China, and I've certain responsibilities.'

'A woman?'

'Yes.'

'God's made millions of them,' said Flanders.

'And sometimes all but one are irrelevant.'

'All but half a dozen,' said Flanders. 'Time and time again have I said it. Leave me with five or six of them, or perhaps only three or four, and you can do what you like with the remnant splinters of Adam's rib. I'm an old soldier, and a man of sentiment myself. But by God's bounty I've money in my pocket, and it's time for dinner. Come and dine, and the larger you dine the more she'll love you.'

'She's gone to Nanking,' said Juan resentfully; and then, with a more cheerful expression – for though in love he was not much given to love-sickness and did not nurse its symptoms – 'Where shall we dine?'

'At the Club,' said Flanders, and they went out into a drizzling darkness and walked along the Bund. The black pavements were almost deserted except for armed guards who stood before the pillared banks and the heavy-fronted offices; but on the road was a thin stream of burdened refugees, and twice they saw, going northwards, a group of fifteen or twenty men, running fast and silently. In the Whangpoo a British cruiser was cheerfully illuminated.

3

'THE longest bar in the world,' said Flanders affectionately, as they crossed the imposing entrance hall of the Shanghai Club, and went into a crowded furlong of a room whose appointments had the unlikely look of ecclesiastical furniture. The bar was indeed enormously long, but to estimate its length more accurately was quite impossible, for its perspective vanished in a haze of tobacco smoke, and no one could essay the journey from one end to the other whose heart was less stout and wily than Odysseus' when he set sail for Ithaca.

But as though to forestall the criticism that such immeasurable facilities for drinking could only denote the most brutal self-indulgence, the reredos was decorated with what appeared to be a succession of altars. There were ten or a dozen of them, with architrave and pilasters of bright mahogany – the colour for the feasting of martyrs – and upon the *sedes corporis et sanguinis Bacchi* a various and elegant arrangement of spirits, wine, and liqueurs. The devotional atmosphere was increased by the multitude of Chinese bartenders who, in white raiment, worked with the single mind and the quiet enthusiasm of pious acolytes. The worshippers comported themselves with decency, and on Saturday mornings, at the most popular service, they were present in such numbers as to crowd four or five deep against the whole length of the bar.

'Drinking in Shanghai,' said Juan, accepting another glass of sherry, 'appears to have acquired something of a ritual.'

'That's just what an American told me the other day,' said a man with a moist eye and a drooping lip with whom Flanders and Juan had fallen into conversation. – His name was Harris, and he was a journalist. – 'He said, "You've got the finest bar in the world, and you don't take advantage of it. You come here, and drink enough hard liquor to kill a cowboy, and go out looking sober as a judge. You're too darned civilized. You've lost the reality of drinking, and kept nothing but the ritual".'

'I like America,' said Juan.

'And I like China,' said Harris. 'I like the Chinese.'

'I'm willing to believe almost anything you tell me about them.'

'They've had a raw deal,' said Harris. 'They've been getting a raw deal for two hundred years. They're the wisest people on earth, and yet anyone can make suckers of them.'

'If there are fish in a river, there'll be a fisherman on the bank,' said Flanders complacently.

'Did you ever hear about Sun Yat-sen's glass coffin? Well, when he died the Russians offered to present one for him, the same as Lenin's. The Chinese thought a lot of Sun Yat-sen, and they liked the idea of keeping him so that they could always see him. So they had him embalmed, and waited for the coffin. It was a handsome affair, all plate-glass, and the old man looked fine in it. You could see him as plain as a gold-fish. But presently he began to dimple, for the coffin wasn't airtight, and he hadn't been very well embalmed. So they took him out, and puttied up the holes, and put him back again. But it wasn't any good. He just got worse and worse. And that's typical of a lot of things that happen in China.'

'Tell him more,' said Flanders. 'Disillusion him and change his mind. He wants to stay and see the war.'

'He won't have long to wait,' said Harris. 'It's going to start to-night.'

There was a manifold and quick response to this announcement, for Harris had a loud voice, and all who heard him at once began to ask how and where hostilities would begin. The bar, though not crowded, was well filled, and more than a dozen men were in uniform, for the Volunteers had been mobilized some hours previously. In half a minute Harris was the centre of an excited group, and Flanders and Juan were hemmed in with him against a segment of the bar on which drinks stood closer than primroses under an April hedge.

'The Japs are going to shell Woosung at half past ten,' said Harris. 'But that's confidential, so don't tell anyone I told you.'

'And what about Chapei?' someone asked.

'I don't quite know, but there'll be something happening there too. The Marines in the Kong Da Mill are all ready to move.'

A little silence followed, so that it seemed as though a human attacking force, infantry advancing with bayonets, appeared more serious and terrible to those who listened than the mechanical assault of guns.

'Poor bloody China,' said a voice.

'Serves 'em right,' said another. 'They've been asking for it.'

'It's going to be 1926 all over again.'

'But the Japanese will respect the Settlement.'

'Don't be too sure. They may this time, but they won't the next.'

Harris's audience, having heard all his news, disintegrated and formed smaller groups in which the imminence of war was discussed from many points of view. Beneath a surface layer of excitement the disputants revealed their profound anxiety. War was coming, and no one could foresee its limits or foretell its end. They were living on a threatened frontier, not as men prepared for war, but encumbered with wives and children, houses and furniture, offices and warehouses, all the apparatus and the means of livelihood. A city living at peace, among the infinite complications of civilized peace, was about to experience the brutal simplification of a battlefield.

Juan, Flanders, and Harris dined together, solidly and well. Juan, who had been silent for most of the time, was now approaching,

45

by way of fatalism and Clos Vougeot, a happier frame of mind. His first sensation, having heard of the immediacy of battle, was pure dismay at the prospect of being separated by it from Kuo Kuo. Then he had been glad to think that she, in Nanking, was out of danger. But on the heels of that relief had come the fear that in Nanking, or rashly returning thence, she might encounter worse danger, without his knowledge and far from his presence. Nor could he prevent, despite anxiety, a tingle of impatience, an eagerness for the war to start – now that it was so near – and growing curiosity to see what a battle was like. But this combat and confusion of hopes and fears had exhausted both, and into their place had come a philosophical acceptance of his inability to do anything for Kuo Kuo's safety; with that a bottle-fed intuition that all was well with her; and underlying both a very pleasant sensation of physical well-being. He listened with amiable attention to Flanders and Harris, who were debating the difference between Chinese face and English honour.

'The Chinese only fight when they've got to,' said Harris. 'They fight to save face, and for no other reason. And face is more serious than honour, because it's more real. Honour's something in a particular code of behaviour, but face to a Chinaman is what colour is to paint. It's also the right to sign a dud cheque and make your banker accept it. The Chinese are realists, and they don't give a damn about being honourable in private. But they'll go to a lot of trouble not to lose face.'

'You're getting old, Harris. That's why you despise honour, and belittle it. We lose sight of it in middle life, as we lose sight of our knees. For honour's a quality of youth. Young men have the taste of it in their mouths, like sweet apples, and the smell of it in their nostrils like a sea breeze. I was honourable myself once – no, by God, some three or four times – but that's long ago now. Life wears it out, and you lose the knack of it.'

'That's why I say that face is more serious and more real, because it's always important.'

'The Chinese,' said Juan irrelevantly, 'believe that the heart is on the right side of the body and the liver on the left.'

'I've liver all round me,' said Flanders. 'I'm as full of liver as a Strasbourg goose.'

'I don't want to be unfair to the Chinese,' said Juan, 'but if, after

46

four thousand years of civilization, they still think their hearts are on the right, isn't that rather a criticism of the Chinese mind?'

'I've been driving a car for ten years,' said Harris, 'and I still don't know where the battery is. But I'm a very good driver.'

'And do you think,' asked Flanders, 'that you can't make love without studying a plan of your sweetheart's arteries and internal viaducts? Must you think of her like a railway map of London, so that every time you take hold of her you can say you've a hand on Notting Hill and another on Regent's Park, and here's where I change for the Elephant and Castle?'

'It's just as well to know the difference between Kensington High Street and Stratford Low Level,' said Juan.

'The surface only,' said Flanders. 'The surface is enough for a gentleman. Leave the rest to midwives and mechanics. Behaviour's the thing, and too much knowledge is a ball and chain on a leg that was meant to walk. If man were designed to burrow he'd be built like a mole, but he was made with a long leg to go upon the top of the earth. Respect the surface of things. If everyone had a proper respect for surface, honouring a greater surface before a less, I'd be a duke at the least, and as rich as an Indian prince, for I've more of it than most.'

Harris returned stubbornly to the original argument. 'Suppose I agree with you,' he said, 'and say that Chinese face is the surface of honour, and so, as you must admit, its most important part?'

'There's a kind of argument,' said Flanders in a temper, 'that comes like a lump of a wave out of the Dead Sea of wordiness to cover meaning as if it were a half-tide rock. I tell you the difference between honour and face is the difference between a good regiment and the General Staff. Regimental honour and a bull-sergeant can turn a coward into a decent soldier, and a good soldier into a hero. But who ever died for the honour of the General Staff? Face is their flag, and we marching officers, all but a few of us, were butchered to save it. But I was thinner in those days. I could run like a hare.'

'What's that?' asked Juan, sitting forward and turning his face to the north.

Harris looked at his watch. 'They've started,' he said.

'Boy!' called Flanders. 'Bring more brandy.'

Muffled by the intervening air, they heard the distant gunfire like a heavy pulse in their ears. It resembled no other noise. It was a dull

47

violence that struck their nerves. Two wine-glasses, touching and vibrating, sent out a high thin note. The air shuddered and a window rattled.

'I'm going over to Chapei to see what happens there,' said Harris.

'Can I come with you?'

'You bet. Are you coming too, Flanders?'

Holding a balloon-shaped glass in the cup of his hands, Flanders warmed his brandy. 'I'm a rich man,' he said, 'and rich men take care of themselves. Do you think a Japanese bullet is a better end than peace and plenty in Gloucestershire? Go to your war if you like, but I'm going home, and my limbs are going with me.'

4

HARRIS had a car waiting for him, and he and Juan drove northwards and crossed the Soochow Creek. Juan asked when he would write his description of the fighting, if there was any.

'I've got most of it written already. It's a damned shame, isn't it?'

'You mean the war?'

'The bloody war. Did you ever come across a Chinese poem that says, "When I was away from home in winter and spring I used to long for letters. But now, when I'm coming back to my village, I daren't ask anyone for news." That's what war means; you're frightened to ask about people. Hell! I've drunk too much.'

The Chinese chauffeur stopped and said he could go no farther. Harris and Juan got out. In front of them the street was closed by a rampart of sandbags and barbed wire. In the white illumination of the headlights the dark wall, the fascines of wire, and the waiting soldiers had a theatrical look. Except for the soldiers the street was deserted. The lamps had been put out, and there was no light in the houses. The bombardment at Woosung had stopped, and the air was quiet.

'You'd better become a newspaper correspondent,' said Harris, and took from a bulging pocket-book a number of visiting-cards. 'I always keep the cards that people send in,' he said. 'You never know when they're going to be useful. Here's half a dozen – Kettledrum of the *Express*, Dearborn of the *San Francisco Examiner*, Gibbon of the *Times* – you can take your choice.'

They passed the barricade, and turned into another deserted thoroughfare. The night was dark, and Juan looked uneasily into the obscurity of the streets, for already he felt rather lost.

'We're in Chapei now, are we?' he asked.

'On the outskirts of it,' said Harris. 'Listen!'

They stood for a moment, and heard, still small but coming nearer, the noise of motor-engines and their muffled reverberation against the walls of a distant street. Into that steely purring and plangent echo came the sound of a shot, another shot, and then a brisk fusillade.

'This way,' said Harris, and began to run, with awkward arms and whistling breath. Stumbling in the darkness they ran the length of a desolate street, turned a corner, and were halted by half a dozen Chinese soldiers who came suddenly from a pitch-black lane. Harris spoke to them, breathlessly, and after a short argument they returned to the shadows of their ambush. Juan and Harris ran on.

Presently Harris stopped, gasping for breath, in the doorway of a little shop. 'Here they are,' he said.

A motor-cycle and sidecar, with a machine-gun mounted in the sidecar, came slowly down the street. Behind it were two lorries, crowded with Japanese troops, and following them, marching swiftly on the pavements, were more soldiers carrying flares. The bayonets and the round helmets of the men in the foremost lorry were il-lumined brightly by the vehicle behind. The headlights of the lorries and the motor-cycle splashed the road and the houses with a livid radiance, and the flares of the marching men were reflected from darkened windows.

A Japanese officer spoke sharply to Harris; but learning who he was, changed his tone, became courteous, and laughed a little as he explained what his men were doing. While he was talking a shot was fired into the second lorry, and before its echoes died there was a burst of fire from either side of the street. The Japanese at once began to shoot into blind windows, and storming parties invaded the houses, smashing down doors with their rifles. Far ahead, like jerky shadows on the edge of the light, three or four crouching figures ran from one pavement to the other. The machine-gunner in the sidecar opened fire against them, the walls of the street repeated the savage stammering of his gun, and the driver, accelerating his engine, took him swiftly in pursuit of the disappearing snipers. Another motor-cycle, swinging recklessly past the lorries, followed in support.

The officer who had previously spoken to Harris came out from one of the invaded houses, and said, 'We found a most notorious person in an upper room.'

'Is he dead?' asked Harris.

'Not yet,' said the Japanese, showing his square teeth in a smile.

The column moved on, sweeping away the darkness with headlights and flares, and leaving gross darkness behind.

'Where shall we go now?' said Juan.

'This way, I think. We'll get into Dikwell Road. I heard there was likely to be a good deal of fighting there.'

Juan was not sure whether this was a really cogent argument for proceeding to Dikwell Road, but he did not like to interfere with Harris's plans. During the engagement between the Japanese column and the snipers he had felt an almost overpowering temptation to join the latter and assault with all his strength the round-helmeted invaders. Patriotism has foster-children as well as its native sons, and having lived so long with Kuo Kuo, Juan had inevitably been infected by her national sentiment. Ignorant as he was about China, except for what she had told him, he had had no knowledge to protect him against enthusiasm, and now, when bullets were flying and the dark air carried the contagion of anger, he discovered, what hitherto he had but faintly suspected, that an alien passion had got into his blood and he was become a hot defender and a partisan of China. Kuo Kuo had read poetry to him, and in his mind there was the image of a land whose poets were countrymen and scholars, whose countrymen were craftsmen and poets. It was a land of laughter and grief, where the mountains and drinking-cups were of jade, and the cruelty of love found a lenitive in songs of an exquisite felicity. Wars had troubled it, but war had not darkened its lanterns, nor frightened the pheasants from the clumps of willow, nor the old roguery from the hearts of its people. True, cities had invaded it from the West, and cities obscured the realities of poetry: the mulberries and the pine-trees, the wine and the wedge of geese and the girl behind a vermilion screen. But poetry, when Kuo Kuo read it, was a light that drove back the shadow of civilization as the flares that the soldiers carried thrust off the darkness of the streets; and when Kuo Kuo spoke of her country's enemies, they were the Little Dwarfs of the Eastern Sea.

Juan had been well coached, and his anger, though partly a natural response to the surrounding atmosphere of anger, was largely a tribute to Kuo Kuo's eloquence and ardour. But when the Japanese soldiers had gone and the firing had stopped, he remembered that several bullets had come unpleasantly close, and he doubted the wisdom of deliberately going into still more dangerous places. It was Harris's job, however, to watch the progress of the battle, and wherever Harris went Juan must go too; for without Harris he could not find his way home.

'How did you feel when those bullets hit the window behind us?' he asked.

'Scared to death,' said Harris. 'Come on. They've started firing again.'

Once more they ran through the darkness. Juan tripped over a steel helmet that a Japanese marine had lost, and nearly fell.

'I remember being damned frightened in Chicago,' he panted, 'when I got mixed up in a gangsters' battle.'

'You needn't come if you don't want to,' gasped Harris.

'That's all right. Do you mind if I take a crack at a Japanese if I get the chance? I've a pistol in my pocket.'

'Better not. Don't let anyone see you if you do.'

'I've just remembered it. The pistol, I mean. A friend gave it to me.'

'Never carry one myself. Too dangerous. Might go off.'

Still running, Juan fumbled in his hip-pocket and pulled out the automatic pistol that Kuo Kuo had given him. He felt for the magazine.

'It isn't loaded,' he said.

'That's fine. Wait a minute, I've got a stitch.'

Harris stopped, and bowed in agony, with Juan solicitous beside him. Suddenly, with a vicious crack, a bullet struck the wall above them and flew off with the trembling whine of a ricochet. They leapt into the shelter of a deep doorway.

'That's cured my stitch,' said Harris with a gasp.

Juan looked out, and another bullet hit the lintel directly over his head.

'He must think we're Japanese,' he said.

'He must have the eyes of a cat,' said Harris.

A voice behind them remarked, 'That appears to be characteristic of these animositous snipers. They have made themselves highly inconvenient, and I have been compelled to wait here for more than half an hour because of their inopportune attention.'

Juan recognized the voice immediately, but Harris, badly startled, exclaimed, 'Who the hell's here?' and directed a small flashlight at the smiling features of Mr Hikohoki.

'Good evening, Mr Motley. And Mr Harris, is it not? I know you quite well by sight.'

'Hikohoki's an old friend of mine,' said Juan, and thought with interest of his share in the negotiations between Flanders and Rocco.

'I am rejoiced that you should so describe me,' said Hikohoki.

'This isn't a very healthy part of the town to be in,' said Harris.

'I had business here. We business men are the slaves of our vocation.'

'What sort of business?' asked Juan.

'Now indeed you are claiming the privilege of old friendship,' said Hikohoki with a smile. 'But that is O.K. with me. I had a client in this neighbourhood who was backward in the payment of an instalment on his insurance policy, so I came to collect it before civic discipline should be wholly disorganized. He was a Chinaman, and a most undesirable client. It is very difficult to make the Chinese pay money. They are bitten by the fangs of materialism.'

'You took a risk in coming here,' said Harris.

Hikohoki shrugged his shoulders. 'And you, Mr Motley, you have come to seek evidence of the deplorable misunderstanding between China and my country? I ask you, as impartial observer, are the Chinese, as they were requested, doing their utmost to eradicate hatred?'

'I don't know,' said Juan. 'I was talking to your friend Rocco this afternoon.'

'Is he also your friend?'

'No, he isn't.'

'I am rejoiced. The Colonel is prone to avarice of the English or American type. He endeavoured to sell me information about the Chinese military dispositions. But I told him that was not necessary, for Heaven will ultimately disclose what man tries to hide.'

'What's all this about Rocco?' asked Harris.

'He's a common acquaintance,' said Juan. 'Do you know him too?'

'I know everybody.'

The street filled with mechanic noise and an advance guard of light, in which a drizzling rain shone like quivering needles of silver. More Japanese troops were advancing. This time, preceding the soldiers in their lorries, there came an armoured car, its turret painted with a red sun on a white field; but in the artificial light the red sun looked black.

'Thank heaven, we are preserved,' cried Hikohoki dramatically; and waving his umbrella to attract attention, he called to his passing countrymen. An officer came to investigate, with whom Hikohoki had a short and apparently satisfactory talk. Harris explained his own and Juan's presence, and the officer, using Hikohoki as an interpreter, suggested they should fall in at the rear of the column.

The solitary sniper had fled, and the column encountered no opposition. Harris and Juan marched in silence, but Hikohoki, who had put up his umbrella, was in high spirits and exchanged facetious remarks with the soldiers in the rearward lorry.

Juan was greatly puzzled by Hikohoki's presence in Chapei, and by his readiness to admit, though he claimed a virtuous part in them, the nefarious trend of his dealings with Rocco. It was possible, of course, that Hikohoki had told the truth and really come to collect an overdue instalment on some insurance policy; and it was also possible that he had seen Juan in conversation with Flanders and Rocco, and had decided to defend his own character by attacking the Colonel's. But Kuo had been positive that he was a spy, and though Juan had no great faith in feminine intuition, he now began to wonder whether Hikohoki's strange activities and curious knowledge might not be explained by some such hypothesis.

As though he suspected the nature of Juan's thoughts Hikohoki turned and with great affability inquired, 'When are you coming to further discuss with me the matter of your life insurance, Mr Motley? For that, I think, was the subject of our last felicitous conversation.'

'We might have a talk to-morrow morning. I'm still at the New Celestial.'

'That is most agreeable to me. About eleven, perhaps?'

Before Juan could reply, the column was halted by several shots fired from an upper window. In the darkness above the headlights they could see the thin orange flash of the sniper's rifle. His shots were apparently a signal, for they were followed by machine-gun fire from a side-street, and also from straight ahead. In a moment the lorries were deserted, and the Japanese were lying flat on the road or pressing themselves into thin shapes against the walls of the houses. Then the crew of the armoured car opened fire. There was a villainous bang, and the scream of a shell. Half-a-dozen rounds were fired, and the machine-gun in front was silenced. Slowly the armoured car advanced.

Ahead of it rose a red glare and smoky tongues of flame, small at first and low to the ground, but quickly spreading and growing in brightness. Two or three houses had been set on fire.

Japanese riflemen engaged the machine-gun in the side-street, and the noise of their firing, doubled and redoubled by the echoing houses, was presently increased by the clamour of advancing motor-cycles and the thunder of reinforcing lorries. Encircled by this iron hullaballoo, Harris put his mouth to Juan's ear – they were lying on the pavement with their heads raised like inquiring seals – and shouted, 'I think we've seen enough here. Let's try and get round to the other side.'

'Wait a minute,' shouted Juan.

Seven or eight Japanese soldiers were coming out of a house with a pair of prisoners. The captured snipers were in dark clothes. An officer, a revolver in his hand, walked up to them and after a word or two shot one of them at point-blank range. Juan, evading Harris's restraining hand, scrambled to his feet. The officer pointed his revolver at the second sniper, but before he could fire Juan threw his own empty pistol – a hard throw, a lightning return from cover-point – straight at his face. It took the Japanese between the eyes, and he went down like a coconut at a fair.

'You bloody fool!' Harris exclaimed, and seizing Juan by the arm, pulled him into the darkness. 'This way,' he said, and for the third time that night they took to their heels and ran.

'They'd have killed you if they'd caught you,' he gasped.

'It was rather a pretty throw-in,' panted Juan. 'The sniper got away, didn't he?'

'We're not out of the wood ourselves yet.'

'You oughtn't to drink so much, if this is the kind of work you have to do.'

'I'll never touch another drop.'

They came into a street where the air, washed by the rain, tasted sweet and clean after the acrid stench from which they had escaped.

'Have you any idea where we are?' Juan asked.

'If we keep on this way, we'll come into Range Road, I think. My God, you were a fool to throw your gun at that fellow.'

'I lost my temper.'

'And nearly lost your life as well. I can't run any farther.'

'We ought to be safe here.'

The street was empty, but the stammering din of battle continued, and it seemed as if only a single row of houses separated them from the crowding of angry soldiers. Harris, walking with drooping head and shambling steps, was breathing painfully; but his spirit was undaunted.

'We'll try and get round to the railway,' he said. 'The Chinese are properly dug in there.'

They turned a corner and came into a street that was not wholly deserted, nor entirely dark. Here and there were little groups of people, obviously nervous, patently on the point of running, but yet sufficiently enthralled by their nearness to danger to wait and see if it should come closer.

The characteristic of the street was a small and dreary respectability that struggled against decay. The houses were of dark red brick on a foundation of small shops. Here, behind their shutters, lived a patch-tailor and a shabby modiste. There was a sweet shop, a fruit shop, a cabinet-maker's shop. There were two dingy little restaurants. And the houses over the shops were inhabited by elderly clerks and superior artisans, by unlicensed dentists, and widows and their lodgers.

The rattle of machine-gun fire came nearer, and there was a movement of panic among the scattered groups on the pavement. Then, with a screech and a wild explosion, a shell burst on a roof and sent a whistling flight of tiles and splinters into the street. Half a mile away the gunner of an armoured car, with blood trickling into his eyes, tilted his gun too high and fired again and yet again. The second shell burst in a restaurant, and made ragged cantlets of all its poor furniture; the third, taking a chimney-pot on its way, crashed through the milliner's back wall and exploded among silk blouses and smart knickers for typists. It slaughtered a high-busted corset-model, and blew another, that wore a ten-dollar blue party frock, end-over-tip through the front window. The people in the street, sobbing for their losses or crying aloud their fear, ran wildly in the wrong direction. Ten miles away, at Woosung, the naval guns began a new bombardment, and filled the air with their dull violence.

At this inopportune moment an old-fashioned bus came into the street, and stopped abruptly when another shell, screaming for plunder, burst in an upper room and uncovered a fountain of broken slates and shattered rafters. The driver leapt from his seat and bolted for cover. From the back of the bus, shrieking with fright and scrambling to escape, tumbled a dozen young women, bare-headed, with coats and wraps that flew open to show their many-coloured evening dresses. They ran to the other side of the street and crowded into a narrow doorway, beating on the door and crying for entrance.

'They're Russian girls from one of the night-clubs,' Harris explained. 'A lot of them live here. My God, where are they going now?'

Some new panic had assailed them, for suddenly they took flight, away from where Juan and Harris were standing, and like a levee of pigeons in a wood fled noisily into shadow.

Harris hurried after them, but Juan, having followed him for some forty yards, stopped when he came to the bus. Its interior was brightly lighted, and to his surprise he saw two girls in it. He went to the door, which was at the back, and got in. The girls were arguing with some heat.

The bus was of that old-fashioned kind which has, in the middle of the gangway between the seats, two brass uprights to support the roof. The girls, standing shoulder to shoulder, were on either side of one of these uprights, and though their language was incomprehensible, their animated gestures appeared to indicate that they were debating the subject of precedence. Each of them demanded the right to go out first, and each, apparently, was restraining the other from exercising that asserted right. They were very pretty girls, and in appearance remarkably alike.

'I apologize for interrupting you,' said Juan, 'but do you realize that you're in a rather dangerous position here?'

'That is what I have been saying to my sister for the last five minutes,' said the girl on the right. 'Now, Masha, will you not be reasonable when you hear this gentleman declaring the same thing that I have been telling you so often?'

'But it is my turn to get out first,' said Masha. 'It is you who are being unreasonable, Varya.'

'This is no time to split hairs,' said Varya impatiently. 'We are in danger, and I ask you to yield to me.'

'My danger is equal to yours,' replied Masha, 'and if you will yield we shall get out as quickly as if I were to yield.'

'It was I who got up first, and you who impeded me.'

'Because it was certainly my turn to go first, and that you cannot deny.'

'You have a petty mind, Masha. You are egotistic, a bitch in the manger, and you cannot see farther than your nose.'

'And you are overbearing, and stubborn as a donkey, and I hate you!'

Varya replied in Russian, and Masha, speaking the same language, discovered a remarkable volubility. Their gestures became wider and more threatening, but still they retained their original positions on either side of the brass upright, against which, in moments of exalted temper, they appeared to lean their united weight, as if trying to thrust it out of their way.

A spent bullet interrupted their argument. It broke a window and struck with an unpleasant sound the steel framework of a seat.

'Now will you let me go, or do you wish to murder us both with your stupid pride?' cried Varya.

'But why should I give in to you? It is always I who must give in. I wish you would learn about fair play, Varya.'

Juan had listened with interest and some perplexity to this acrimonious debate, but circumstances now persuaded him that it had lasted long enough. Two or three of the houses struck by shells had caught fire, and were blazing fiercely. The heat was considerable, and both he and the girls were profusely sweating. In addition to this discomfort, he thought he could see, at the far end of the street, some new signs of military activity.

'I suggest,' he said, speaking with great calmness in order to pacify the young women, 'that you solve your difficulties by coming out together. Simultaneously, I mean. Concurrently, or *pari passu* and hand in hand.'

'But this brass pole is in our way,' said Varya sullenly.

'Surely you can come on either side of it?'

They stared at him in honest bewilderment. Then Masha began to giggle self-consciously; but Varya said coldly, 'I thought, of course, that you had recognized us.'

'I'm afraid not,' said Juan.

'Give him our card, Masha.'

'It was I who gave a card to the last man we met. It is now your turn, Varya.'

'Do not be silly, Masha. You are wasting time.'

'I do not have any cards left,' said Masha.

Varya, frowning, fumbled in a handbag, and having found a card gave it to Juan. He took it and read:

THE SISTERS KARAMAZOV
THE ONLY GENUINE RUSSO–SIAMESE TWINS

'I should never have guessed it,' said Juan, looking at them with the greatest admiration.

'In other ways we are naturally quite normal,' said Varya.

One of the burning houses suddenly collapsed, and with a wide-throated roar the flames shot upwards. The heat in the bus grew unbearable. At the same time there was the sound of brisk shooting at the farther end of the street.

Juan made a sensible decision, and sidling past the Sisters Karamazov, he got into the driver's seat. 'It's time to go,' he said. 'Where would you like to be taken?'

Backing and turning, he headed away from the fire and the advancing soldiers, and drove the lumbering bus into the coolness and comparative peace of a street as yet immune from all the ills of battle except its noise.

'Where shall we go?' he repeated.

Varya and Masha, though in agreement as to their most suitable refuge, gave him contrary instructions as to reaching it, and Juan continued to drive, so far as he could judge, in the direction of peace and security. Then Varya took command, and directed him by way of several obscure streets and narrow corners into a broader thoroughfare that Juan recognized as North Szechuen Road.

'It is rather a long way to go,' said Varya.

'It is not far if you go by the nearest roads,' said Masha.

'But even the nearest roads are not very short.'

'They are much shorter than the way we are going.'

'It was you who told the driver where to go when we were in Manila, and every time we used to get lost. Please admit that, Masha.'

'That happened once, and only once; and this, in any case, is not
Manila.'

'It is a much larger town, and so more easy to mislay yourself in it.
You will please turn right at the next corner,' she added to Juan.

'That is not the way to Avenue Joffre,' said Masha.

'No, it is the way to Avenue Foch.'

'But good Heavens, Varya, how can you get to Rue des Andouilles
from Avenue Foch?'

'It is the only way you can get to it, Masha.'

Juan drove through the spacious streets of the Settlement with all
the speed of which the ancient bus was capable. It was a noisy progress.
Every window was loose in its frame, the seats were loose, the bonnet
clattered as though a score of little boys were rattling sticks along park
railings, and the engine so roared and complained that all its pistons
and cylinders appeared to be as much at variance as the Sisters Karamazov. But the sum and total of these noises, the dissonant addition
of stridor and roar, of snorting, thumping, and horrisonous rattle,
was a friendly and reassuring total. It was the sound of machinery
grown old and decrepit in the employment of man. It was a flattering
and respectable sound, as of an aged servant whom neither asthma nor
crutches nor chalky joints could tear from his demi-century of service.
And though it was almost as deafening as the din of battle in Chapei,
it nowise resembled that murderous tintamarre. Juan held the shuddering wheel with an approving hand, and turned a corner with inadvertent acceleration.

How delightful, he thought, to have been in a battle and escaped from
it! And not merely to have escaped without increment, with nothing to
show for it except a whole skin, but to have eluded death with a motor-
bus and Siamese twins for a prize! Fortune had indeed been open-
handed. She was a Lady Bountiful who might have graced Trimal-
chio's table, a prodigal who spilled the munificence of her cornucopia
with a princely hand. Was there another, in all his generation, who in
one short night had seen war's anger and driven the dark streets of
Shanghai with geminate and lovely Russians? Had they been separate
they would have been exciting enough, and each in her own person

sufficiently charming; but being joined, and as it were one person –
though speaking with a divided tongue – their charm was doubled
and became unique. It was true that they wrangled a great deal, but
they bore the brunt of that themselves, and to a third person they
might be as equable as the angles at the base of an isosceles triangle.

In obedience to Varya's direction – Masha without success opposed
it – Juan turned left out of the Avenue Foch, and presently came into a
street whose most noticeable features were quietness and discretion.
He stopped beside a modest house with green jalousies, and briskly
opened the driver's door.

But jumping out with some precipitancy, in order to assist the
descent of Varya and Masha from the rear of the bus, he caught his
foot in a loose floor-board, and pitched head-first on to the road. He
felt a moment's indignation with his own carelessness, a shattering
blow, and lost consciousness.

5

JUAN returned to life in mingled circumstances of luxury and discomfort. He was lying, partly undressed, on a broad bed in a room
whose ornate furnishing included a horizontal wall-mirror on a level
with the accommodating couch. His head lay on a damp pillow, that
grew steadily moister from the large wet bandage which covered his
brow; and his bare feet were in painful apposition with an im-
moderately hot water-bottle.

He opened his eyes and perceived that the Sisters Karamazov,
seated by the bedside on a small Empire sofa, were eagerly watching
for signs of his recovery.

'It was I,' said Varya proudly, 'who put the cold-water compress
on your forehead.'

'And I,' said Masha, 'laid the hot water-bottle at your feet.'

'Do you mind taking them away?' asked Juan.

They rose, and Masha, who was the left-hand twin, reached in
front of her sister for the wet bandage; but Varya impatiently slapped
down her hands and endeavoured to remove the hot bottle.

'It is burning his feet,' she said. 'I knew it would.'

'It is better to have burnt feet than to get pneumonia, and possibly rickets, through lying with your head in a puddle,' retorted Masha.

Summoning his returning strength, Juan rolled over on the bed to escape from the sodden compress and the burning bottle. In his head there was the unpleasant sensation of a battering-ram that struck, at regular intervals, a splintered but resisting door, and his brow was embossed with a large swelling on which, diluted by water, there was a rivulet of blood. He lowered his feet to the ground, and got up, but dizzily and without confidence. He stood for a moment or two, and returned to bed. The Sisters Karamazov gave him a dry pillow and covered him with a heavy quilt.

'Do you always quarrel?' he asked.

'We?' exclaimed Varya. 'During the whole of our life we have never exchanged an angry word. We are devoted to one another. Aren't we, Masha?'

'We live only for each other,' said Masha. 'Varya is often selfish and inconsiderate, but none the less I have the most cordial feelings for her.'

'How can you say that I am selfish when I am always thinking of you and trying to save you from committing follies? It is I who bear the heavy end of the stick. It was I who took the heavy end of this gentleman when we brought him upstairs.'

'I'm extremely sorry to have given you so much trouble,' said Juan drowsily; and dreaming, while still half-awake, that the pain in his head was the booming of Japanese guns, he was carried upon the rhythm of that dream and fell sound asleep.

'On spatet,' whispered Varya.

Masha, with affectionate interest, leaned over him to see if this were really so, and murmured, also in Russian, 'Perhaps we should stay with him, in case he needs anything.'

'Nonsense,' hissed Varya. 'It is very late, and we must go to bed.'

Reluctantly Masha was led away, and the Sisters Karamazov went out with the broken pace of stretcher-bearers, or of children in a three-legged race, for the ligament that joined them, hip to hip, made it almost impossible to walk in step.

Juan slept for eight hours and woke to a feeling of drowsy comfort. His head no longer ached, and his body was full of the exquisite stirring of strength renewed, as of a meadow waking out of winter, to which his mind, released from battle and concussion, was pleasantly complementary. He could hear, from far away, the dull explosion of shells or bombs; but the sound had lost its novelty. The war, he supposed, was continuing. A column of pale sunshine divided the heavy curtains that covered the window, and was reflected as a luminous gap in the long mirror. In this diminishment of darkness he could see the outline of unfamiliar furniture, and presently curiosity persuaded him to get up.

He drew back the curtains, and the room filled with the bright glare of a fine winter noon. It was a curious apartment, deficient in much of the usual equipment of a bedroom, but in other ways very usefully appointed. The nature of the house was obvious. It would, in the ordinary way, be described as disorderly. But such a description was ungrateful and inaccurate, for everything was as orderly as it could be, and its accounts were strictly audited. Its function, indeed, was the raising of love's status from the primitive level of a romantic obsession to the civilized plane of a marketable commodity. Juan, thoughtful but not really embarrassed, washed his face and hands, and wiped the dry blood from his forehead.

No sooner had he made his toilet than the door opened and the Sisters Karamazov came in, the one carrying a cup, the other a glass of tea. They wished him good morning in the friendliest fashion, and then, putting down the glass and the cup of tea, marched with unusual agreement to the window and closed the curtains again. Varya switched on the electric light, and Masha said, 'That is much nicer, isn't it?'

'It makes it even more difficult to decide which of you is the lovelier,' said Juan courteously.

The twins were enchanted by this politeness, but immediately, in the Karamazov manner, began to dispute it, each protesting that her sister was by far the prettier, and prettily maintaining that urbane chiasmus. Then they remembered the tea they had brought, and Masha said she had thought he would rather have it made in the English fashion, but Varya was sure he would prefer the Russian style. So Juan took the cup in one hand and the glass in the other, and having assured them that English habit and Russian custom were equally agreeable to him and immeasurably improved by conjunction, drank them both.

Varya and Masha watched him with solicitude. Masha's expression

62

was the more affectionate, but Varya's the more considerate of his comfort. It was Varya who remembered to thank him for having rescued them from the perils of the previous night.

'It was so noble of you,' she said. 'You are kind to others and fearless for yourself.'

'And you drove the bus very cleverly and fast.'

'That is a minor thing,' said Varya.

'If he had not been able to drive, he could not have rescued us,' said Masha with justice.

'But the nobility of his mind – why, Masha, we do not yet know what the gaspaden is called.'

Juan, having told them, hoped they would allow him the usage of their Christian names. And how, they asked, could they refuse this small courtesy to one who had so recently saved their lives? 'I am Masha,' said Masha.

Their costume was the morning's négligé, but only in the technical sense could it be described as such. Masha, whose hair was the mild gold of an old spade-guinea, wore a blue silk peignoir as soft and pale as hyacinths in a wood; and Varya, whose hair was bright as a new penny, had a green silk robe de chambre as agreeable to the eye as young beech leaves. Their maquillage had been chosen with taste and skilfully applied, and their red leather slippers added two inches to their height.

'Are there many other people in the house?' asked Juan.

'There is no one except Anna Ivanovna, the old servant,' said Varya.

'They were frightened, and they ran away,' Masha explained.

According to Anna Ivanovna, they said, Madame la patronne and the young ladies of the establishment had been seriously perturbed by the arrival, on the previous afternoon, of a party of Japanese, two in uniform and one in plain clothes. What they had come for, Anna Ivanovna did not know; but clearly their purpose was not that of the majority of visitors. After they had gone the young ladies ran hither and thither, in great fear and derangement, making large untidy parcels of their more valued possessions, and though Madame at first had endeavoured to calm their panic, she had presently been infected by it and eventually was the worst of them all, crying, 'Make haste, make haste!' and leaving the house with nothing but a hairbrush and a tumbler containing an infusion of senna-pods. But what the Japanese had said to intimidate them and start such a wild stampede Anna Ivanovna could not tell, though she thought it might have something to do with General Sun Sat-lo, who was in love with a girl called Nina Fyodorovna, and during the week before he had visited her on three successive nights. All that one could say for certain, however, was that the only occupants of a once populous residence were Juan, the Sisters Karamazov, and Anna Ivanovna.

The twins told their story with great animation and little contradiction, and no sooner was it finished than Anna came in with an enormous tray on which were six glasses and a dozen small dishes of caviare, smoked salmon, gherkins, sausage, and so forth. Masha could not restrain her pleasure at this felicitous entrance, and greeted Anna with boisterous delight. Varya, with more self-control, merely glanced at the refection and hoped that Juan had a good appetite. But in making ready to eat, her alacrity was equal to Masha's, and with remarkable agility she and her sister hop-shuffled on to the broad bed, gyrated on Varya as a centre, and squatted on their retracted legs to face the tray that Anna set upon the gold-threaded counterpane. Juan, at their invitation, assumed a semi-recumbent attitude on the opposite side of the tray, and Anna, having made another journey downstairs, brought a bottle of vodka and three bottles of champagne. She filled the smaller glasses with vodka, and Juan and the Sisters Karamazov drank each to the others' health with willing kindness.

'Anything in the nature of a picnic,' said Juan reflectively, 'has always, until now, filled me with displeasure. The common attempt – common in England, that is – to avoid the tedium of a conventional meal by eating it cold in the company of ants, gnats, and wasps, and with the addition of sand and nettles, inevitably reminds one of the fatuity of trying to cure a chilblain by sleeping on an iceberg, which is known as homeopathy. But though feasting *al fresco* has all the discomfort of farce, I am now ready to admit that skilly *al letto* – but this is a banquet – might have merits unknown in a stalled ox and the dining-room mahogany.'

Seeing that Varya and Masha were somewhat puzzled by his allusive and unnecessary periphrasis, he obligingly added, 'Your arrangements are superb and the sausage is swell.'

'Have some more vodka,' said Masha. 'It will not do you any harm.'

'In moderation it would not,' said Juan. 'But what are the attractions of moderation, in beauty or anything else? You have put me in a mind for excess and extravagance, and all my thoughts are committing bigamy.'

He rose from the bed and kissed them in turn, Masha offering her lips and very heartily responding, but Varya turning a prim though not unfriendly cheek. Anna Ivanovna grunted and left them.

The atmosphere at once became warmer and more intimate. A new easiness informed their demeanour, as though in the minds of Masha and Varya some half-conscious doubt had been resolved, and Juan was no longer a stranger who might criticize and must be entertained, but a friend to be enjoyed. Such virtue is there in a kiss, that rather gives than takes, that throws away all the advantages of aloofness and detachment – the right to question and condemn – and by surrendering the judicial privilege of one who stands apart, wins in exchange the fellowship of the oldest conspiracy of humankind. Not only is it to sensation as a T'ang horse to the eyes or Menuhin's violin rustling the tufts of the auditory nerve; but in significance it is like a judge who puts off his ermine to share the thirty-shilling waterproof of the prisoner in the dock. With this kiss – so must a man say – I may not wed thee, but to thine arms I yield my strength, and to the numerous beauties of thine aromatic and depilated person I surrender my wits. Judgement is mine, and individuality; but both I forfeit in respect of thine eyes, which are lambent, of the well-contrived volutes of thy hair, the anfractuosities and pneumatic pleasances of thine expedient anatomy. I renounce what is secondary in evolution, which is of the intellect and masculine, in favour of all that is primary, which is emotional, physiological, and feminine. I am, in brief, no longer thy senior and tutor, but for a little space, a specious and happy interregnum, thy postulant and suitor.

Having thus had the courtesy and good sense to define his position, Juan was rewarded with confidence and amiability. Their curious room enclosed them, and their temporary isolation was made agreeable by their mutual interest. They could hear, muted by walls and the distance, the intermittent sounds of battle. But nobody referred to the war.

Juan asked the twins to tell him their history, and they responded with willing but often perplexing volubility. They had been born, they said, in the city of Kazan, in the year 1912, their father having been a leather merchant in respectable circumstances. Their mother had died within a few days of their birth, and during the first three years of their life they had been cared for by the nuns of the Bogoroditski Convent, to the great relief of their father, who, a man of conventional ideas, had been greatly shocked by so unexpected a sequel to what he had always regarded as a perfectly normal activity. Had he been allowed his own inclination, the sisters would have remained in the convent, where the nuns indeed were quite willing to keep them.

Their father, however, had a brother, who was a subordinate teacher of mathematics in the university. He, whom the sisters called Uncle Georgy, was a sentimental bachelor who felt as proud of his exceptional nieces as their father was ashamed of them. Their birth had been one of two notable adventures in a life whose monotony had otherways been variegated only by ascribing, in an odd-numbered year, the quadrature of the parabola to Pythagoras, and to Archimedes when the calendar was even. His previous adventure had been a visit to London. This took place in 1895, immediately after assuring his students that beyond question it was Pythagoras who first quadrated a parabola, and his motive in undertaking so long a journey had been a passionate desire to see Lord Salisbury, for whose Conservative principles he had a great admiration.

He was so fortunate as to see him on two occasions, and also to witness, in the Agricultural Hall at Islington, an admirable performance by Lord George Sanger and his company. By Uncle Georgy this excellent circus was taken to be part of the enlightened policy of the Conservative Party, and after several weeks of sight-seeing he returned to Kazan with unbounded respect for the way things were going in England. He became an ardent Anglophile, and having already acquired some colloquial knowledge of the language, set himself to become thoroughly acquainted with it, a project in which he succeeded with the help of Hall Caine, Mrs Humphrey Ward, Miss Marie Corelli, and other novelists of the time whose works he assiduously studied.

'So it was Uncle Georgy who taught you English?' said Juan.

'He began when we were three, after we came home from the Bogoroditski Convent,' said Varya. 'But he lost all his books in the Revolution, of course, when we had to go away from Kazan.'

It was Uncle Georgy who had persuaded their father to remove them from the Convent. He adored his geminate nieces, and in childhood, indeed, their doubled prettiness must have been curiously attractive. Their father, that conventional man, had refused to flee when the Red Terror came to Kazan, and had died, it was said, in defence of a side-saddle he had just made for a Countess Orlov. But Uncle Georgy, moving with the same decision as he had shown in 1895, effected with no more trouble than might be expected the escape of the children, himself, and three valuable ikons that he sold at a very fair price in Vladivostok. Their journey, of course, had been long and tedious and often dangerous. They had lived for three months, on a lonely siding, in a coach that had gone off the rails and been abandoned. This was a valuable period in their lives, for having nothing else to do they learnt a great deal of English. Uncle Georgy looked after them with tireless love, and when they came to Vladivostok he found them a room where they lived very comfortably for some time on the proceeds of their ikons. Then again they were forced to flee, and found refuge in Harbin, where, eighteen months ago, Uncle Georgy had died peacefully in his sleep. Varya and Masha burst into tears when they told of finding him in the morning, with a little smile on his bloodless lips and a Tauchnitz edition of *Robert Elsmere* on the pillow beside him; and Juan, after considering whether it would be kinder to acquiesce in their grief or try to dispel it, decided on the latter course and persuaded them to have a little more champagne.

Uncle Georgy had saved their lives and taught them English. They would always remember him with gratitude and great affection. But he had also, and less successfully, tried to instruct them in singing; and as his ear was defective he had launched them on the mathematical undercurrent of music, beginning, as if he had been Pythagoras himself, by teaching them the numerical proportions of the intervals in the diatonic scale. And this unfortunate introduction had had a disastrous effect on their voices.

'Nobody seems to like our singing,' said Varya sadly. 'We have good strong voices, but people say we do not sing in tune.'

'You must let me hear you some time,' said Juan kindly. 'No, not now. Tell me what happened after your uncle died.'

'Varya had an admirer,' said Masha.

'No, Masha! You are not to talk about that.'

'Oh, come,' said Juan. 'A love affair, especially an unhappy love

67

affair, is the best stuff in the world for conversation. It may happen to anyone – and so everyone is interested. Do tell me about your admirer.'

'He was a scientist,' said Masha.

'Be quiet!' cried Varya.

'I was once in love with an ichthyologist,' said Juan encouragingly. 'But she always had damp clothes and I used to catch cold.'

'Boganov was a physiologist,' said Masha, 'and he used to take our blood pressure.'

Varya began softly to cry, and Juan, removing the tray from the bed – they had finished their meal, and there was nothing left on the plates but crumbs and heteromorphous moist fragments – sat down beside her and with an embracing arm, a caressing hand, did what he could to comfort her.

'Now,' he said to Masha, 'tell me the whole story.'

'Boganov was very good looking,' said Masha, 'and when he first began to pay attention to Varya she was awfully well-pleased and I was terribly jealous. But then one day he came and tied something on her wrist that he called a sphygmo——, I do not remember the word.'

'A sphygmomanometer,' suggested Juan. 'It tells you how hard your pulse is beating.'

'Of course it does. That is what he put it there for. He made love to her, and looked at the sphygmo – what you said – to see how much it was measuring. Then he put it on my wrist, and made love to Varya again, to see if I also got as excited as she did.'

'He did love me, all the same,' sobbed Varya.

'Certainly he did. But he was a scientist, and so had many other things to think about. He wanted Varya to have a baby, because he thought it would be interesting if I got sick as well as she did, and also wanted to make little garments. He said that someone had done experiments with rats to show that the maternal instinct could be aroused by sympathy and imitation.'

'So we told him to go and make love to rats,' said Varya, recovering some of her self-composure.

'But all the same,' said Masha, 'he was very useful, because he introduced us to a man who had a café cabaret.'

The man who had a café cabaret was a Mr Alzerian, of no recognizable nationality. He had seen potential value in the Sisters Karamazov, and persuading them to sign a three-years contract had found a teacher who instructed them in tap-dancing, and another who taught them some popular songs. Mr Alzerian, as it happened, was tone-deaf, and admired their singing wholeheartedly. Having thus equipped them as popular entertainers, he presented them at his café cabaret, where their appearance created a sensation and their duets a riot; for Uncle Georgy's Pythagorean education, instructing them to find the right key by calculation – and they never did sums alike – had resulted in their always singing in different keys. Mr Alzerian, however, was undismayed, and staking everything on his belief that Masha and Varya were destined for fame, he had had them taught several new steps and some more songs, and then, after exploiting Harbin, had taken them on tour to Mukden, Dairen, Tientsin, and as far as Manila.

But Mr Alzerian was an artist, and when he found that even their most emotional songs could move an audience only to laughter – and this he learnt in Manila beyond hope of forgetting it – he was persuaded to transfer his contract, at a fair profit, to an entrepreneur less sensitive to ridicule. And their new manager had brought them to Shanghai.

'He is a very nice man,' said Masha. 'He is going to take us to London and Paris some day, and he says we shall make a great deal of money. But meanwhile we have been appearing at the Continental Night Club, where we do not earn very much.'

'But he is more clever than Mr Alzerian,' said Varya. 'He will know how to arrange things. He is a Japanese, and they are all clever.'

'What is his name?' asked Juan.

'Mr Hikohoki,' said Varya.

6

OF Varya's tears, both those called out by the story of Uncle Georgy and those more saltily evoked from memories of the scientific Boganov, there were now no traces but a few faint flaws in her maquillage, like raindrops dried on a bright window. She wore, indeed, an expression of some complacency, leaning against Juan's shoulder with the air of a young queen negligent in the corner of her familiar throne.

But Masha, detecting a hint of permanence in the snugness of her attitude, regarded it with restless misgiving, for she was well aware of the ease with which a habit is formed; and Juan, conscious both of Varya's contentment and Masha's restlessness, decided he had done his duty by the former and now owed a little courtesy to the latter. He therefore transferred himself from the right to the left-hand side of the twins, where Masha welcomed him with enthusiasm, so that his status, which had previously been that of a throne, now more closely approximated to that of a prince consort.

He had been surprised, but not overwhelmed with surprise, to hear of Hikohoki's connexion with his new friends. He had been surprised, not with the emotion of Dr Livingstone when Stanley greeted him at Ujiji, but of the guest at a house-party who meets the same people with whom, in other mansions, he has spent the two previous week-ends. The surprise of encountering Hikohoki, or new evidence of his many activities, was fast becoming a familiar surprise, like the unexplained but anticipated plenishment of a Christmas stocking, or the daily pint in the widow's cruse. Juan partially released himself from Masha's amorous hold, and inquired, 'Does he own this house? Hikohoki, I mean?'

'No,' said Varya. 'I don't think so. But he found employment here for two girls that we know.'

'We used to know them in Harbin,' Masha explained, 'and since coming to Shanghai we have visited them. That is why, when we found there was a battle in Range Road, we thought we could take refuge here.'

'In Harbin,' said Varya, 'they were quite respectable. They were dancing-partners at a night-club.'

'They are still respectable,' said Masha indignantly. 'They behave themselves very nicely.'

'It is not a nice thing to earn your living in a house like this.'

'But they were getting too old to be dancing-partners. They were growing fat, and they had no money, so they had to do something. You are too self-righteous, Varya.'

'And you are not very dignified, to be hugging someone like that, when I am here to see you.'

'Then why don't you go to sleep, and then you would see nothing?'

'Because I do not feel sleepy, thank you.'

'When Boganov came to see you I always used to sleep, except when he brought his sphygmo machine.'

'And how often did you open your eyes while you were sleeping?'

'Well, I had to look and see if he was still there before I could wake up, didn't I?'

Varya, in a voice and manner that emphasized the difference between her and her sister's understanding of polite behaviour, inquired of Juan, 'Have you ever been married, Mr Motley?'

'No,' said Juan. 'No, I've never been married.'

'It must be very agreeable, if one has found the perfect partner. I, for my part, should like to be married in a cathedral.'

'I don't care where I get married,' said Masha. 'But I should like a nice house to live in afterwards.'

'In England,' said Varya, 'there are many cathedrals, are there not?'

'Yes, all over the place,' Juan answered. 'They used to build a lot of them.'

'We were in a house in Manila,' said Masha, 'where they had a cocktail cabinet, a radio-gramophone, and a frigidaire. I should like to have things like that when I get married.'

'Come and tell me about the English cathedrals, Mr Motley.'

'Oh, go to sleep, Varya!' cried Masha impatiently. 'He was hugging you for a long time before he came to hug me. It is my turn now.'

Varya stretched an inviting hand in front of her sister, but Masha, thrusting it away, imprisoned Juan in a firm embrace. It occurred to him that it might be advisable to prevent an open quarrel between the twins, for though he supposed they were quite firmly attached, he knew neither the precise nature nor extent of the attachment, and he became suddenly alarmed by the possibility of their being hurt, if the dispute became violent. Releasing himself as gently as possible from Masha's embrace, he rose to open the remaining bottle of champagne.

'There are times,' he said, 'when I prefer talking to anything else on earth, and when you consider how rapidly the art of conversation is dying – principally because most of our recent inventions, like aeroplanes and modern music and the radio, are so noisy that all one can do in their presence is to utter loud exclamations – I think you'll admit that it's our duty to talk as much as ever we can, in case we sink, in a social way, to the level of small dogs, who only dribble and sniff each other, and give a paw. Didn't that pop nicely? – I wonder how the war's getting on? – Have some champagne, Varya. Here's your glass, Masha.'

Juan drank his own glass at a gulp, and sighed with relief. The situation was no longer quite so threatening, but both Masha and Varya wore very sulky expressions, and though momentarily quelled by his volubility, they were certainly not yet captured by his arguments. Without giving them time, therefore, to snap even once at the bone of their own contention, he continued his impromptu monologue in defence of conversation.

'Take, for instance, the business of making love,' he said. 'No one who has studied the history of social relations can deny that the art of love-making is decadent, and its decadence is directly due to the fact that modern lovers are generally inarticulate. When girls were all tied-up like a registered parcel or a stowed topsail, their suitors would talk for hours and hours, because they couldn't do anything else; but nowadays, when there's no obstacle but an elastic belt and a couple of suspenders, the whole thing's over by eleven o'clock, mainly because the poor young men are tongue-tied, and can't do anything else. And do you think that's progress? Of course it isn't. It's no more progress than flying to Paris so that you can get back to Tooting in time for dinner. In my opinion – and God knows I'm not proud, but whenever I think of other people's opinions I'm increasingly pleased with my own – in my opinion, if a man's in love with a girl he ought to learn, not only how to talk to her, but how to talk about her. About her eyebrows, and the shape of her nose, and the precise inflexion of her lips, and the little undulations, like moonlight on a slow river, on her companionable bottom when she goes out to powder her nose. He needn't be afraid of having no one to talk to, because she'll listen to that sort of conversation till the milkman comes. And why shouldn't she? You find great oafs of men, and pinheaded splinters of men, and tedious tiresome old men, who go to infinite trouble to acquire the technicalities of golf, so that they can talk about club-faces and loft, and what they do with their hips and elbows and wrists; and they'll have scores of equally gravel-blind and dismal companions to listen to them. Well then; do you mean to suggest that the face of a beautiful woman isn't more interesting than the face of a Number Two iron? Is anyone so totally bereft of reason as to think that the hips of some scrawny old medal-winner, or the disgusting forearms of a hulking baffy-addict, are more engaging than the corresponding parts of a girl so lovely that daffodils look dowdy beside her? But where's the golfer who could describe her movement, the beauty of her stillness, the little lofting of her lip, with the minute particularity he would use in discussing his favourite chip-shot? There isn't one. And isn't that an insult to women, and a sign of the degeneracy of men as well as of conversation? I give it you as an absolute fact – and St John is with me in this – that you can't make love properly, because you don't realize what love is, until you have put your feelings into words. St John's support of this apparently rash statement may be found in the sentence: *"In the beginning was the word."* Words are the beginning of everything. Primitive man could hardly tell the difference between such various and fundamental matters as hunger, love, death, and a rainy day, till someone had invented names for them. All he realized was that the inherent discomforts of life sometimes made themselves evident in one part of his body, sometimes in another, and sometimes all over. And that's by no means an adequate appreciation either of love or a shower of rain, though it's what we're returning to unless our golfers take a pull at themselves and learn a few more words than "birdie" and "windcheater" and "God blast that bloody foursome in front of us!" I'm a feminist – I say it with as little apology as a Quaker would use in declaring himself a pacifist – and it grieves me to think that women, in spite of their so-called emancipation, are probably worse off to-day than they were in Elizabethan times, when their lovers prefaced every caress with a sonnet. They weren't always good sonnets, but at least they were an indication that the young man had studied the appearance of his young woman and tried to analyse the emotions she roused in him; which was flattering to her. Anyone, moreover, who has taken the trouble to compose fourteen pentameters on half a dozen rhymes is going to stick around the fair recipient of his verses a good deal more closely than the casual donor of a couple of cocktails; and that's the difference between a proper love affair and half an hour's untidiness on the sofa. Of course you may object that an Elizabethan sonnet wouldn't cut much ice to-day, because the figures of speech are out of date – summer's honey breath, for example, largely consists of carbon monoxide, and directional wireless is much more useful than a star to every wandering bark – but we must cut our metaphors according to our cloth, and I daresay a really ingenious wooer could make quite a good impression by comparing his lover's brow to a radiator, her legs to cylinders, and her bosom to a graph of commodity prices in America before and after the slump, with a pretty reference to the rosy hue of 1929. At any rate the principle is clear, and what we need to-day is a more ample vocabulary, a greater fluency of speech, and such an exact understanding of things as can only be acquired by talking about them in a precise, accurate, and spacious manner, and going to as much trouble to give the proper words to the component parts of emotion and the innumerable articulations of thought as golfers do in describing their unnatural attitude on a tee. Let us once again conscribe verbosity in the service of love, and remember that when Ben Jonson said, *"There goes more to matrimony than four bare legs in bed,"* he spoke a granary of wisdom in a single grain; and what he meant was that every young husband should study a first-rate dictionary so as to acquire a plenitude of good words with which to adorn his pillow-conversation, and above all to equip himself for capacious, vivacious, but not necessarily veracious discussion of that which will be of perennial interest to the wife of his bosom, which is to say her own person and personality.'

Juan, who had been walking to and fro while he gave utterance to this very reasonable thesis, stopped to pour out another glass of champagne, and looking more closely at the Sisters Karamazov he perceived that all danger of their quarrelling had long since disappeared. They sat quietly, not so much bewildered – though bewildered they had been – as slightly stunned, like country cousins, whose only previous experience of music has been *The Gondoliers*, towards the end of a Bayreuth performance of *Götterdämmerung*.

'That was very interesting,' whispered Varya.

Masha, stirring slightly, asked. 'Do you never make love until you have talked as long as that?'

'We cannot always live up to our ideals,' said Juan. 'And how much less eventful life would be if we did,' he added, finishing the champagne.

The consciousness of benevolence invaded his mind. He had defeated, by eloquence, the menace of a disagreeable scene, and his little triumph, notably abetted by the benignity of wine, inspired in him that magnanimity which, now natural only to slight intoxication and the fleeting of an occasional happiness, is the vestigial heritage of an age of gold. His urgent desire, in this delectable mood, was that everyone should be as happy as himself, and advancing on the twins he kissed them with the amiability of a bachelor uncle and the heartiness of a storm-delayed sailor. 'Now sing to me,' he said.

Masha sighed with pleasure and the extremity of her relief. 'I thought,' she said, 'that you were tired of kissing me.'

'All that I said,' declared Juan, 'was an expression of my passionate conservatism. I am prepared to laud for ever the oldest delight on earth.'

'You are not interested in our blood-pressure?' asked Varya suspiciously. Boganov, in his own way, had sometimes been given to excessive wordiness.

'Only in its effect on your complexion,' said Juan, and kissed her again.

'I have just as big a blood-pressure as Varya,' said Masha jealously.

'I'm sure you have,' said Juan hurriedly. 'And now what are you going to sing? Do you know *Black Eyes*?'

'Of course we do!'

The twins arranged themselves, more conveniently for song, on the edge of the bed; muttered a word or two of warning to each other; expanded their chests; and burst into a fine presentation of discords:

> '*Kak ty chornaya,*
> *Kak ty strashnaya . . .*'

They sang with fervour and feeling, and their voices rubbed against each other like a wet finger on glass.

Juan listened in astonishment greater than that with which the twins had heard his oration in defence of eloquence. At its best their singing was like the inadvertent double-stopping of an illiterate fiddler; at its worst it resembled the noise of a tram-car running on lines that had been laid for a train. Each had a voice that was, in itself, powerful and melodious, but in apposition they were like an isosceles triangle whose superior angle was a horrid gap that nothing would close. Uncle Georgy had told them that music was a matter of sums; and both were constitutionally incapable of such an elementary addition as sevenpence-ha'penny and elevenpence-three-farthings. Their singing was a farce that their humanity disguised as tragedy.

'That was a most unusual performance,' said Juan, and tilting the last champagne bottle over his glass, found to his dismay that it was empty.

The twins got up, and hurrying towards him, Masha came first and sat on his knee. Varya was left standing.

'Go and look for Anna Ivanovna,' said Varya. 'She will give you another bottle.'

Juan lifted Masha to reluctant feet. 'That's a very good idea,' he said. 'In such a company as this, which is triangular and therefore incapable of linear solution, wine is our only consolation. It was Meredith I think – but correct me if I am wrong, for I am totally uneducated – who expounded the theory that Bacchus is morally superior to Venus, inasmuch as Bacchus in his bounty is generous and inclusive, while Venus is jealous and shuts the door against intruders. Where, by the way, is the door?'

Varya pointed the way to it, and Juan, descending an easy flight of stairs, came to a narrow hall in which, on a hatstand, he recognized his coat. He opened the front door, and looked out at blackness slightly relieved by the reflection of an unseen light and faintly striated with rain. It seemed a long time since he had been out of doors. The war had stopped – but the truce was temporary – and the night was quiet. He breathed the mild darkness, and as though it had dispelled a proscriptive atmosphere, peculiar to the house, he suddenly remembered Kuo Kuo and her mission to Nanking. He thought of her with a little pang, as though his conscience had slightly twisted an ankle in a downhill run through the heather. It was not his dalliance with Varya and Masha that occasioned the pang, but his realization that for the better part of a day he had never thought of or recalled the existence of Kuo Kuo. Such forgetfulness was infidelity indeed, and Juan, stiffening his moral fibres with a harsh rebuke, resolved to leave at once this Lethean household.

Or almost at once. For it would be churlish to go without saying good-bye to Varya and Masha, and before he had given them some more champagne. He re-entered the house, and finding Anna Ivanovna, who was sleeping on a little iron bedstead in the kitchen, he indicated by signs that he was thirsty, and specified his desire by putting a finger in his mouth and withdrawing it with a loud plop! Anna, rising creakily from the bed, took the twenty-dollar note he offered her and used it to hide a yawn. She gave him a bottle of champagne and some inexplicable advice in Russian.

Juan went upstairs again, and found the twins singing loudly. They ignored his entrance, but when the song came to an end, Varya explained: 'That was a song called *Stenka Razin*. Our home is at Kazan, which is on the Volga, and Stenka Razin was a great hero who sailed on the Volga and fought against people. It is a very well-known song, and we shall sing it again.'

They sang it again. It sounded like a gramophone being played with two needles, like the jarring of split trumpets:

> '*Kak vskochíl tut grózen*
> *Stenka Razin.*
> *Podhvatíl Persídskuyu tsarevnu,*
> *V volny brosil krasruyu . . .*'

But the Sisters Karamazov were enjoying themselves. They found no fault in their own voices, but were assured by mathematical calculation that they sang correctly. They took the champagne that Juan gave them, and began a very melancholy song. They finished that, and sang *Kólokol*, *Ya nye barin nye tartarin*, and *Vecherni zvon*.

Juan listened with increasing amazement and no little pleasure, for to relish the unusual, the grotesque, and the heteroclite, was one of his more notable faculties; and despite their voices the twins were enchanting to look at. But half-way through yet another one, called *Ya tsiganka maladaya*, he decided it was time to go. He stood up and prepared to say good-bye.

Masha and Varya, however, were drowned in melody, drunk with delight in the loud noise they were making, drugged with nostalgic thoughts of Holy Russia. They paid no attention to him, nor looked his way when softly he opened the door.

He decided to walk back to his hotel, and turning by chance in the proper direction he soon came to the Avenue Foch, from where he found his way without much difficulty; though now and again he detected in his progress a slight tendency to circularity, which he defeated by a resolute series of tangential movements. He was also impeded by a recurrent desire to stop and talk to anyone he met, but this amiability, that in other circumstances might have made his noctambulation interminable, was fortunately parried by the linguistic poverty of Chinese wayfarers and Sikh policemen. Persuaded at last that further entertainment was unfeasible, he went to bed.

7

WHILE Juan had been engaged with the Sisters Karamazov, the Japanese had occupied themselves with the bombing of Chapei. From early morning their seaplanes had flown over that dull but useful suburb, dropping bombs on plain and unpretentious streets, on squalid lanes, on a multitude of industrious small premises where human beings had scratched from circumstance a narrow livelihood with the bright-eyed patience of hens in a backyard. At first the aeroplanes had flown at a great altitude, cautiously releasing their explosives from the heights of the sky. The weather was mild and clear, and wherever a bomb burst there rose a shape of reddish dust, like a vaporous dark cauliflower, that slowly spread and lost the deceptive firmness of its outline, and presently subsiding became nothing but dust with a fragment of wall or a broken gable in the middle of it. The seaplanes carried four bombs apiece, and when they had dropped their destructive cargo they returned to the river for another load.

As the day grew they became bolder, and flew nearer to the houses. Their shadows raced along the streets, and the noise of their engines, echoing on broken masonry, was like the vibration of a fevered nerve. Sometimes a pilot would come so low that the upflung shape of dust, from an exploded bomb, obscured his machine in a rufous haze. Here and there, on the house-tops, were Chinese machine-gunners who fired hopefully at the invading planes, but the noise of their guns was little more than the stammering of impotent wrath. It is not easy to hit an aeroplane, and the Chinese, who were in any case indifferent marksmen, were using ammunition of inferior quality. Much of it had been imported from Japan.

The principal target of the bombers was the north station of the Shanghai-Nanking railway, on the outskirts of Chapei. Like so many stations it had been built in a poor and dismal neighbourhood, as if to say that railway passengers should enter a city only by the back door. It was surrounded by black shunting-yards, by cinder-dumps, and dirty streets, and crouching rows of little smoky houses. When bombs burst there, they filled the air with fountains of coal-dust. The Chinese had chosen this sombre neighbourhood as the core of their resistance. Troops from the 19th Route Army had already arrived there, and taken up a strong position. These were Cantonese soldiers, well-equipped and drilled, whose morale and reputation were both excellent. An armoured train had come from Nanking, which materially stiffened the defence till it was withdrawn after having been hit by a bomb.

In the early afternoon an aeroplane registered a direct hit on the station, and the buildings were almost wholly destroyed in the subsequent fire. But in the midst of this infernal scene, among dust and falling debris, scorching flames and the shattering impact of the bombs, the men of the 19th Route Army held their position and would not yield.

A few yards away, on the northern boundary of the International Settlement, the mobilized companies of the Shanghai Volunteers performed the arduous and complicated duties of policemen, an interested third party, and touch-judges. Their most important function was to prevent the war from overflowing into the Settlement, and their most difficult job was to deal with the hordes of panic-stricken Chinese, who at one moment would try to force their way across the frontier with the whirring unanimity of locusts, and the next were endeavouring to hurl themselves back with the suicidal impetus of lemmings. The Volunteers, moreover, were frequently under fire from both sides, and in spite of this recurrent provocation were not allowed to retaliate. They accepted their position with that curious humour which shows itself in the belittling of danger and adversaries. They were Shanghailanders, and therefore hard-boiled. They knew their reputation and were proud of it. They were ready at any time to drink heavily with their friends and fellow-countrymen, or to kick the Oriental bottoms of the rest of the world. They were, especially in their cups, merry gentlemen; and having put off their financial and social anxieties with their civilian clothes, it took a lot to dismay them.

Within these efficiently but somewhat contemptuously guarded frontiers, there was a great deal of worry and confusion. Chinese students were parading the streets in noisy demonstration against the iniquities of Japan and the Laodicean policy of Nanking. The Chinese Chamber of Commerce and the Chinese Bankers' Association declared a general strike, and innumerable engagements to play golf, football, bridge, or motor-car courtship – for it was a Saturday – were broken without apology. Chinese restaurants did some useful profiteering at the expense of refugees; and occasionally an alarm was caused by the discovery of a sniper, firing at nothing in particular, on the roof of a house far from the field of battle.

These events all took place in bright sunshine. At eight o'clock, when darkness had fallen, a truce was called; and most of the cinemas and night-clubs opened as usual.

Juan, sleeping late into Sunday morning, was wakened by Kuo Kuo, who came into their room looking tired but excited. She had just returned from Nanking. A white-gowned room-boy followed her with a small dressing-case, which was all the luggage she had. As soon as he had gone she turned to Juan, and told him he must get up at once.

'Sweetheart,' he said sleepily, 'how absurd you are. Approach the situation from another angle, and come to bed.'

'There's no time for nonsense,' she answered, with agitation in her voice. 'I've been very worried about you, all the time I was away, because you're in great danger here.'

'It's my native air,' said Juan, yawning. 'I went to see the war the other night. It's going to be a good one, I think. How did you get on in Nanking?'

Kuo took off her coat, looked into a mirror, and between worry and displeasure smudged her face with powder. Then she sat on the bed beside Juan, and putting her narrow hands on his chest, leaned over him, looking into his eyes.

'Juan,' she said, 'you must be serious.'

'What's the matter?'

'Hikohoki *is* a spy!'

Juan twisted away from her restraining hands, and shouted with laughter. 'My pumpkin!' he cried, 'of course he's a spy! And the moon's a thief, and clouds are costermongers. My father sells skipping-ropes under the Admiralty Arch, and my sister does sums for blind accountants in a houseboat on Plinlimmon. What else could he be than a spy? He's a pimp and a gun-runner, he sells insurance and post-cards and homeless girls, he's an entrepreneur, he's got a finger in every pie and the ace of trumps up his tell-me-if-you've-heard-it-before. You bet he's a spy. He sold the secrets of Aulus Splautius that day we overcame the Nervii. He's the two-timer who put skids under Guy Fawkes. He did the dirty on Enver, he traded an old horse to Marco Polo for spring lamb, and Prince Eugene wouldn't move a step till Hikohoki told him what Metternich had said to Bill Bailey. God knows when I've loved another man so much as that poly-dextrous buttercup!'

'I don't know what you're talking about,' said Kuo, with a tremor in her voice.

'Proteus,' said Juan, getting out of bed and putting an arm round Kuo to comfort her. 'Or Hikohoki. Tell me what you've heard about him.'

Suddenly Kuo, turning her face to his shoulder, began bitterly to cry. Her thin shoulders moved convulsively, and through his pyjama Juan could feel her warm breath, the moisture of her tears. He was filled with remorse. He had hurt her feelings with laughter that was like a slap on the face. He had laughed at her when her anxiety had been all for him, when she was tired and worn-out with travelling and Heaven knew what nonsensical making-up of plots and plans. He was a brute and a blackguard. He begged her to be easy, to stop crying, to forgive him, to be happy, to tell him what he could do to please her, and he would do it on the instant. He swore he would never laugh at her again. He was serious as she was about this wretched war, and everything connected with it. He would enlist to-morrow in the Conquering Youth or the Death-Defying Corps of whatever-they-called-themselves if only that would content her. He loved her, she was sun, moon, and stars to him, and a thorn in his heart when she was sad. He would even be serious about Hikohoki for her sake.

'He really is dangerous,' she sobbed, but more quietly now, weeping in comparative comfort.

'Yes, I know. Lots of things are dangerous, but it doesn't do to worry about them.'

'You say that because you're so brave.'

'No, I'm hanged if I am. When I got mixed up in the war the other night I ran like a scalded cat.'

'You were fighting?'

'Well, hardly fighting. You remember that pistol you gave me?'

Unfortunately I forgot to load it, but I chucked it at a Japanese fellow who was just going to shoot a prisoner, and knocked him for six. Then I set a course for home and did the hundred in ten and a fifth.'

'Juan, I do love you. Don't laugh at me again.'

'Honeyheart,' said Juan. 'Look here, your feet are cold. Let me take off your shoes and stockings, and then put on a dressing-gown and make yourself comfortable, and we'll have breakfast. You must be hungry. How did you get back from Nanking?'

'We flew. There were no trains running, but some military aeroplanes were sent here, and they let Min Cho-fu and me come with them. It was very cold. Then we had to walk for two miles, till we found rickshaws.'

Juan ordered breakfast, and Kuo Kuo, returning to the mirror, said wistfully, 'I look perfectly hideous.'

'You're lovelier than a five-pound note in time of trouble. By the way, I'd a letter from my mother the day before yesterday. She sent another cheque. The family's doing well at present. England's herself again, she says. Roaring business in the bucket-shops, and all the banks building marble palaces for a happy people's surplus wealth. How are you feeling now?'

Kuo ate with a good appetite, and her spirits returned. Her visit to Nanking had been more successful than she had dared to hope. It was going to have results of the very greatest importance. Everybody in Nanking was full of indignation, patriotism, and excitement. Japan had gone too far, and forced into them at last a realization of national injury, wakened with intolerable wounds their slumbering pride. The hour was ripe for a campaign that would unite all China, and a plan of campaign, which was also the canons of action and a new creed, was in their hands.

Kuo paused expectantly, but Juan, buttering a piece of toast, missed his cue.

'That's splendid,' he said. 'And what exactly did you find out about Hikohoki?'

Kuo, whose voice had been quickening to a curbed excitement, grew sober at once and she spoke with the utmost gravity. 'We must leave this hotel, Juan. Hikohoki has been watching you ever since we came here, and Min Cho-fu was positive that we were being followed when we went to Nanking. I know you think that spying is something to laugh at, but you're wrong, and Hikohoki is truly a most dangerous person. He tried to murder Colonel Rocco when he was here a few days ago, and only failed because the Colonel is a very good shot – he carries two revolvers – and got out of the trap that Hikohoki had laid for him.'

'Who told you that?' asked Juan weakly.

'Colonel Rocco himself. He is an American. He was a very distinguished soldier in France, and now he is Military Adviser to Wu Tu-fu. We were talking a good deal to him in Nanking. He had been in Shanghai to obtain new tanks for the Tank Corps, and Hikohoki first of all tried to bribe him, and then, because of course Colonel Rocco refused to sell the tanks to Japan, Hikohoki arranged to kill him. The Colonel was attacked, by at least twenty people, he says, in a very lonely place. But he drew his revolver and killed seven or eight of them, and escaped, though he was seriously wounded. He had a large piece of sticking-plaster on his forehead when I saw him, and his left arm in a sling.'

By prodigious self-control Juan kept a front of serious attention. He himself had invented Hikohoki's trap, and now Rocco had shot his way out of it, and Hikohoki was become a master-criminal. His mind bubbled like a pot on the boil, but he dared not laugh again, for Kuo could no more stand it than ripe crops could suffer hail. She was as full of her touchy love for China as an ear of wheat in August, and laughter was like hailstones to beat it out. But Rocco's revolvers and the plaster on his forehead! Making a final effort, Juan put the thought away from him. He had turned a little pale with the severity of his inward struggle, and there was sweat on his forehead. He walked to the window and pulled it open.

'So you see,' said Kuo, 'I was right after all.'

'Yes, dear,' said Juan humbly.

'And you must go into hiding at once.'

'What!'

'Or you'll be the next one that Hikohoki tries to murder.'

'But he didn't . . . Well, anyway there's all the difference in the world. I'm of no importance. There'd be no point in murdering me.'

'Hikohoki knows you are my lover, and he will think you know all about the plan.'

'What plan? And why should that make him want to murder me?'

83

'Well, he might kidnap you, and force you to tell him about it.'

'And how could I tell him about it, when I don't even know what it is?'

'That's because you wouldn't listen. I was going to explain the whole thing, but you interrupted me and asked about something else.'

'Sweetheart,' said Juan desperately, 'I love you very much and always shall, but for heaven's sake tell me what you're talking about.'

'The plan that Min Cho-fu and I brought back from Nanking, of course. The plan that's going to unite all China, and teach us how to defeat the Japanese, and live noble, useful, and peaceful lives.'

'That's fairly ambitious, isn't it?'

'We are ambitious,' said Kuo proudly, 'and our ambition is both good and wise.'

'Who's the author of this plan?'

'An old man called Lo Yu, who lives on a mountain. Oh, it's a wonderful story, and you must listen to it with faith and understanding. You know it is the custom for many Chinese, when they are growing old and have seen plenty of life, to retire to some lonely place, and spend their time in meditation? That is what Lo Yu has done. He used to be a bandit, and then a famous general, but he fell into disgrace because he sold all the rifles belonging to his army to another general. So he became a hermit, and for many years he lived alone, studying the sages, and seeking the truth. He is now well known for his piety and wisdom, and thousands of people go to him for help and advice. It was a friend of Min Cho-fu who went to him and asked: "What can we do to save China?" Lo Yu answered: "The world has fallen into decay, and right principles have disappeared. Wicked discourse and oppressive deeds are rife".'

'That's all very well,' said Juan, 'but it isn't really constructive criticism, is it?'

'You don't understand. He was quoting Mencius, who described in those words the condition of China in Confucius's time. So Min Cho-fu's friend waited, and presently Lo Yu said: "I am frightened by what I have seen, and therefore I have considered the work of reformation." Then he explained that the work must be undertaken by the youth of China, for only youth has both strength and faith, and the understanding which it lacks would be supplied by Lo Yu. At one time, he said, he had thought of revealing his plan to the Young Men's Buddhist Association, but he consulted the Book of Changes, and the stick that fell out was unfavourable. So he was waiting till events should declare who were the proper people to be his executives. Min Cho-fu's friend therefore suggested the Conquering Youth and the National Salvation Association, and when Lo Yu again consulted the Book of Changes the answer was affirmative. He said therefore he would wait till a propitious time, and then give the plan to suitable representatives of those societies. That is why Min Cho-fu and I postponed our idea of an immediate attack upon the Japanese, and went to Nanking, where we met Lo Yu and got the plan. We thought a plan would be better. Of course there were many other people with whom we wanted to talk about the state of affairs in Shanghai, but meeting Lo Yu was the really important thing. He's a very little and very old man with a thin grey beard.'

'And what is his plan?'

'It is written on a scroll, and he put it into a section of bamboo and sealed it with wax. Min Cho-fu has it, and we are going to read it as soon as we can have a meeting of our two committees.'

'So you don't know yet what the plan is?'

'Not the details of it. But it must be good because Lo Yu has all the characteristics of a Superior Person. He has sought what he needs in himself, and he has cultivated himself so as to confer peace and prosperity on the whole people.'

'A quotation from Confucius?' asked Juan.

'Yes.'

'Is it true that Confucius wouldn't shoot a sitting bird?'

'Quite true.'

'I'm really fond of China,' said Juan. 'It's very like the Church of England. It has all the proper ideas, and it doesn't go about worrying people to put them into practice. It's a gentleman's country, or was before it was spoilt. But don't you see that your interesting story makes it quite unnecessary for me to go away and hide? Because all I know about the plan is what you know about it yourself, which is precisely nothing, and that is all I could tell Hikohoki if he were silly enough to kidnap me.'

'Yes, but he doesn't know that.'

'Then he's a very poor spy.'

'He nearly murdered Colonel Rocco.'

Juan walked up and down the room in irritating perplexity. The joke was losing its freshness. It had been amusing enough to create a sinister figure in Hikohoki's likeness, so as to frighten Rocco and help Flanders to get his money, and delightful indeed to hear how Rocco had decorated his creation. It was, however, by no means funny to be compelled to leave this very comfortable hotel and lurk in some obscure retreat for fear of a creature of his own invention. But Kuo Kuo was not only as sensitive as a fiddle-string but as obstinate as a limpet. He dare not laugh at her fears, and if he tried to dispel them by telling her the whole story of Flanders and the tanks she would either refuse to believe him or find in it new confirmation of her reading of Hikohoki's character. He shrank, in any case, from the labour of so long an explanation. The easiest way, after all, might be to agree to her ridiculous proposal and live quietly for a day or two.

'You don't want me to go anywhere that's horribly uncomfortable, do you?' he asked gloomily.

'No, it won't really be uncomfortable, though you can't expect it to be as nice as this hotel. But you'll be safe, and that's what really matters. I'm going to take you to a Buddhist monastery in the Chinese City. It was Min who suggested it, because he knows the abbot. He was to go there this morning and make arrangements for you.'

Juan looked at her in dismay, but before he could speak Kuo had put her arms round his neck and was murmuring, in swift words that fell warmly on his cheek, how glad she was, how greatly relieved because he would be safe, and how much she loved him. Her arms imprisoned him, and against his will he smelt with pleasure the sweetness of her hair. It was unjust, he thought, to call love blind. Rather was it cock-eyed, for having importuned love in order to obtain your will, you were compelled perpetually to go contrary to your will, and to find pleasure perversely in doing what displeased you. He kissed the ivory-smooth side of her neck. 'Take me to the monastery,' he said philosophically. 'It would have been more broadminded to offer me a nunnery, but perhaps you know best.'

8

JUAN stood in the Hall of the Five Hundred Lohan with a feeling of uncomfortable singularity. Most of the brassy statues, of gods, godlings, saints, or seraphim – he knew nothing of the Buddhist theocracy – had a family likeness of chubby cheeks, heavy eyelids, and placid impersonality. He alone was strikingly different, his cheeks being lean, his eyes wide-open; while so far from feeling calm, he was uncommonly ill at ease. It was, of course, ridiculous to be disconcerted by statues, but there were so many of them, they sat on their tall pedestals with such ponderous immobility, and in the huge gloomy hall they shone with a sinister yellow light. There was rank after rank of them, not in the simplicity of a battalion on parade, but rather in the pattern of a maze, so that one might walk for a long time among them till their numbers were doubled and redoubled in a frantic multiplication of similar features.

It was, thought Juan, about five hours since Kuo Kuo had left him at the monastery; but looking at his watch he saw that it was only an hour and a quarter. They had taken rickshaws at the hotel, and running south through the Settlement, and through part of the French Concession, had come to the edge of the Chinese City, which lay hidden like a stone in a plum, solid and self-contained and unexpected within its modern envelope. Leaving the rickshaws, they had walked down a narrow street and a narrower lane, one side of which was the monastery wall. An arched doorway opened on to a long stone corridor, from which at right angles passages led to courtyards and temples, and stone stairways to upper apartments. In the corridor were many small groups of people, some quietly sitting with bundles beside them, others excitedly arguing, who from their appearance were probably refugees. From one of the several temples came the sound of chanting, and Juan caught sight of grey-robed monks, bare-headed, who walked in endless circular procession, intoning their monotonous hymn. One of them, leaving the leisurely gyration, came into the neighbouring courtyard, raucously cleared his throat, and profusely spat. He looked incuriously at Juan and Kuo Kuo, and having exchanged a word or two with a loafing spectator, returned to his vertiginous ritual.

Presently Kuo found a monk, unoccupied and amiable, who consented to inform the abbot of their arrival. He returned in a little while to say that the abbot was busily engaged, but the foreign visitor was expected, and welcome to their hospitality. He would find a room on one of the upper floors.

The monk, silent-footed while Juan trod the stone floors with resounding steps, led them by corridor after corridor, past scenes of diverse activity – past a warm kitchen, a room for silent meditation, a room where monks were entertaining their several friends to tea – to a small cell naked of all furniture but a pallet on the floor. This, he said, the foreigner could regard as his own.

'How long do you want me to stay here?' asked Juan, considering the apartment without much pleasure.

'Only till we have made sure that you are no longer in danger,' said Kuo. 'Hikohoki will lose your trail – he will never be able to find you here – and then perhaps he will go away, or become busy with other matters.'

Kuo had left him a few minutes later. She was anxious to see Min Cho-fu, at whose house she was going to stay.

'Give my love to his sister,' said Juan. 'If it hadn't been for her I'd have got nothing to eat at that dinner-party in the Mei-sum restaurant.'

He was, he thought, sitting lonely on his pallet, unlikely to get much to eat here, and the kitchen they had passed did not look very clean. But his stomach was healthy, and could deal with any but the most virulent of infections. Man, he reminded himself, was not only infinitely adaptable, but almost as capable of new growth as a coral reef. Perhaps, in this environment of prayer and contemplation, he might permanently enrich himself with new depths of thought and perceptions of reality. He pulled up his trousers and thoughtfully scratched his right leg. He had already acquired a Buddhist flea.

Then he set out to explore the monastery, and was a little troubled as to whether he should salute in some fashion, or politely ignore, the monks whom he passed walking casually in the corridor. They, for their part, showed no curiosity in him, except five or six in dirty saffron robes, wildish-looking men, slit-eyed, with wrinkled faces hairier than the others', whom he took to be visitors from Tibet. But the local monks, grey-gowned, their shaven heads scarred with ritual burning, paid no attention to him except, when tentatively he bowed, to return his bow with a little flickering smile.

The Hall of the Five Hundred Lohan, when he came to it, was deserted except for the gods and a small shuffling figure who slowly inspected their ranks and with seemingly haphazard choice lit a joss-stick in front of one in every thirty or so. He finished his devotions, and Juan was alone with the supernal army.

For some time he considered the brassy jowl and somnolent eyes of a plump godling who hugged his knees and looked blandly over Juan's head. Then, turning quickly with the feeling that he was being watched, he confronted a long score of cousin-gods – fat-chested, broad of shoulder – whose yellow eyes, though now above the level of his, so smugly reflected some superior kind of amazement that he felt they must, while his back was turned to them, have been quizzing his strange clothes and the reach-me-down tailoring of his suit. He felt like some new-found anthropoid before a committee of the stoutest, most scholarly, and socially elevated Fellows of the Zoological Society; like a poor candidate, up for his viva, tongue-tied before the awful knowledge of five hundred stall-fed co-examiners; like a burglar, with the jewels in his pocket, compelled to walk between endless rows of heavyweight policemen.

Making an effort – but with a quick glance over his shoulder – he walked a little way, and turned, and turned again, and found himself lost in the maze. In front of him, alone between two ranks of gods, was a glaucous deity whose face was twisted in wild and diabolical laughter. Not the benign amusement of the others, but laughter that tore the very fabric of life. A god more evident than the others – despite his lineaments of the devil – for only a god could see such comedy in the world and have the courage to laugh at it. His mouth, at one end, curled upwards like the horn of a young moon, and hung at the other like a hound's ear. In his eyes there was more merriment than a man may show, as a man is more capable of mirth than a monkey. He was a god, but clothed in sackcloth and rags, heaven's outcast, perhaps, because he had mocked the foundations of heaven in the same breath with his derision of the structure of the world. Or a god, it might be, who was God's jester, fed with ambrosial crumbs and lees of nectar, to cock a long snook at providence, to butter the stairways of paradise, and applaud the lunacies of mankind.

Hurriedly retreating from this dreadful apotheosis of humour, Juan explored, with growing agitation, yet another avenue of gleaming idols. Here was one whose eyebrows, like frozen water-spouts, grew to the ground, and there another with a bald head like an umbrella. One with the heavy eyelids of a camel, one who rode upon a tiger, one who flirted a fan. There was more variety among them than he had at first thought, but all except a few were united by the family likeness of remote amusement and well-fed peace; they were gods in clover, and their eupeptic superiority was more unnerving than all the torture and bloody wounds of the Christian hagiarchy.

Then in a place of honour, gleaming like a giant buttercup and three times as big as the other statues, he saw a Chinese Gargantua, rolling in fat and creased with laughter. Not the laughter of the god with the twisted mouth, that tore the universe like lightning, nor the tolerant amusement of the majority, but the rollicking mirth of a divine toper. This was Mi-lei-fo, the likeness of God in his second coming, the Messiah. He would not come with a sword, for there had been swords enough in China. He would not judge the quick and the dead, for the Chinese were too sensible to want justice. But he would bring wine and fatness, and in his reign the cloud-patterned sky would fill like a blue pavilion in a breeze, puffing and pouting over gales of laughter, for China would be at peace and the villains who had troubled the comedy of life had been sent to their own place. Christ, with memories of the Cross and a sanctifying hand, was no saviour for the Middle Kingdom, but Gargantua was its coming god, with chitterlings instead of holiness, wine barrels, and loud jesting.

They have, thought Juan, considering Mi-lei with amazement, no sense of sin. He was, to be sure, but lightly encumbered with any such thing himself, though in Detroit the prospect of having to commit murder had troubled him, and somewhere else – but he had forgotten where or when – he had been worried by something he had done, which at the time seemed morally indefensible, though what it was he could not now remember. He had, he thought, a fairly reasonable kind of conscience, and suddenly to perceive that China had none, was very shocking. There were four hundred million Chinese, all of them by Christian standards miserable sinners, and none of them realized it. They could not even have suspected it, or their conception of a Messiah would have been entirely different. People with a troubled conscience foresee the toils of Purgatory; the judicial questioning of Rhadamanthus; the infallible shepherd who will permit no goat among his virtuous wethers. But the Chinese, in their gross and un-pardonable innocence, anticipated translation to a Utopia designed by Rabelais for the illimitable satisfaction of all gluttonous delight!

It was abominable, he thought, his mind filling from the twin taps of fear and Britannic righteousness. It was alarming in the ex-treme; for innocence is capable of the most appalling misconduct. – Only the conscious delinquent can really be trusted to behave himself. – No wonder he had been frightened by the smooth-faced godlings, for they were the idols of a people whom error had not abashed, and who without fear looked forward to the commission of endless mis-demeanours in the future. Here he was, powerless and alone, in a very dirty and uncomfortable monastery, surrounded by the sinister deities of a people whose language he could not understand, and who at any moment might behave like tigers because their hearts were like lambs! Kuo had no business to leave him in such a place, and he was certainly not going to stay there.

The figure of Mi-lei was fortunately near the entrance to the maze, and Juan, to his large relief, found himself a moment later under the enormous trinity of Buddhas that half-filled the outer hall. He was still in the shadow when he heard the slippered scraping of approaching footsteps, and having been brought to a state of unusual nervousness by the alien gods and his discovery of China's irresponsibility, he retired with haste into the shelter of the nearest statue. The heavy door was pushed open on groaning hinges, and in came the six Tibetan monks whom Juan had previously seen. Their heads nodded this way and that, their hands were hidden by their sleeves, their feet slurred softly on the stone floor. Juan, having committed himself to retreat, found no courage to do anything but hide. It was, he told himself, absurd to be afraid. But was it, he asked? It was also absurd that a poor suburb of Shanghai should be a battlefield; that after four thousand years of civilization the Chinese should have no sense of sin; that he should have been deposited in a Buddhist temple: but it was, they had not, and here he stood. 'If nothing happened that wasn't reasonable, very little would happen,' he muttered; and peered round Buddha's gilded skirt.

The Tibetans stood for a moment in a close shoulder-touching group, that presently opened like a fan. Foot-slow and shambling, their hands in their sleeves, they approached the statues in extended formation. Juan could not hide for long behind Buddha's skirts, for some would come on one side of him, some on the other. He made a swift decision. A sortie was his only hope. He stepped out of the shadow, and with squared shoulders and a bold demeanour marched quickly towards the door. To cover his embarrassment with the pretence of being quite at ease, he took out his handkerchief with a flourish and fiercely blew his nose. '*Vvhimm!*' he bugled to the one side, '*Vvhooomm!*' to the other. The Tibetans were manifestly surprised, though whether by his sudden appearance or this warlike neighing, he did not stop to consider, but pushing open the half-closed door continued his audacious retreat at a rather greater speed, and came without hindrance to his cell on the upper floor.

In a few minutes' time his mind grew calmer and more reasonable, but he was still very angry with the Chinese for their wicked un-consciousness of sin. He had been prepared to think well of China. He had, indeed, been captured by all those aspects of China which Kuo Kuo in her conversation had exhibited and made much of. But this was the first time he had been alone in China, and the encircling pressure of so much that was alien and incomprehensible had squeezed his opinion to a less favourable shape. A certain degree of innocence was all very well, and agreeable to the jaded eye. It was like the prim-itive gaiety of a modern picture on a dull wall of the National Gallery. But such enormity of innocence, as he had deduced from the undis-criminating benevolence of their Rabelaisian Messiah, was a different thing altogether.

No one, it was clear, who had not a nature of great hardihood, could be expected to sympathize with this robustious irresponsibility; and Juan, perceiving in himself such an incompatibility, discovered its origin in the sensibility of his intelligence, a frailty that he had never before suspected. But now, having unexpectedly come upon it, he began to think with pleasure of the delicacy of his emotions and under-standing, and for half an hour considered this amiable weakness with melancholy enjoyment. He was, however, interrupted by visitors. At the door of his cell stood the six Tibetans.

But now they were too obviously friendly to cause him any alarm. Their wind-graven faces – with smoke in the lines that the wind had scored – were broken by cheerful smiles, and they came in talking and amiably nodding. Their language sounded like awkward hinges and the loose board in an old flight of stairs.

'I can't ask you to sit down,' said Juan, 'because there isn't anything to sit on.'

One of the monks, whose face was as wrinkled as a peach-stone, said something in a voice less tuneful than a raven's, at which the others laughed creakily; and Juan, feeling it was only polite to reply, however incomprehensibly, answered, 'I suppose we have no mutual friends whom we can discuss? There are few things so effective in the promotion of friendship as the exchange of scandal or innuendo.'

The oldest monk looked closely at the tweed suit he was wearing, and cackled harshly. The others, examining some toilet articles – a razor, shaving-soap, tooth-paste, and so forth – that he had laid on top of a dressing-case, were also laughing. They may, thought Juan, have no need for inventive gossip, since they find the ordinary apparatus of living so very funny. The youngest monk was holding his shaving-soap under the nose of a pock-marked colleague, and both were hoarsely chuckling. Another, while examining the tooth-paste, squeezed a long stalactite from the tube; and all the Tibetans laughed very heartily indeed.

'Ha, ha, ha!' exclaimed Juan. 'Ho-ho-ho-ho! Ha, ha! Hee, hee, hee! Ho-ho!'

The monks, silent now, regarded him with troubled eyes.

'That will teach you how disconcerting it is,' he said. 'I'm getting rather tired of humour, do you see? First from the gods, and now from you, and I don't see what you've got to be amused at anyway.'

The youngest monk, by means of signs and grimaces, wanted to know if he could keep the shaving-soap.

'Take it,' said Juan; and gave the tooth-paste to another.

Presently they left him, but for some time he could hear their unlubricated laughter echoing in the stone corridor.

For the first time in his life he felt home-sick. He had been alone before, often enough, in Australia and America; but never had he been solitary in a land where everything was so totally alien and whose habit of mind was framed in another dimension. He wished he had never come to this confounded monastery. He wished he was in England again, where the jokes were all mild and harmless. Flanders, he remembered, would be sailing to-morrow. He would be home in a few weeks, walking under trees tipped brightly with new green, under white orchard-bloom, on roads soft with the dust of March. Why had Flanders made him think of Gloucestershire, when he must stay in China till this damned war was over? But he certainly wasn't going to stay in this dismal monastery.

He took his hat and the small dressing-case, and went down to the main corridor. It was now so crowded with refugees that he could hardly force a way through them, and when he came to the outer door it was locked.

9

Juan spent a melancholy night, for there were bugs in his room, that bit him cruelly and left a nauseous sweet stink when he killed them. He had supped sparingly off a bowl of gruel that a monk had brought him, and a little smoky lamp had helped him against the bugs. But these were all his comforts, and when morning came he lay long, still dozing restlessly.

When at last he woke it was with a feeling of apprehension, but rising at once and going down to the main door, he found to his relief that it was open. He was at once in a great hurry to leave, for his dislike of the monastery was reinforced by the coming of another day. He had neither tooth-paste nor shaving-soap, and in other ways the monastery was ill-equipped for the conventions of the morning. He returned for his dressing-case, and with no more than a glance into the hall, where monks were again circulating to the endless drone of their infinitely reiterated hymn, he left their sour-smelling precincts, the untranslatable laughter of their gods, and went out with a feeling of joyous deliverance into the cool sunshine of the streets.

He was surprised, a few minutes later, to find himself in a very narrow, populous, gaily-coloured, and busy thoroughfare, where open shops, displaying for sale such various commodities as earthenware pots and jade necklaces, paper money for the dead and patterned silks for the living, confronted each other over a pavement crowded with sombre-suited Chinamen of animated appearance. Scarlet bannerets, with golden characters, hung thick on either side, and the chattering of innumerable voices made in the bright air a shrill murmuration. Here was a row of little shops whose open fronts were full of carved ivory, jade necklaces, and silver ornaments. There were cream-coloured statuettes, charming trifles, Buddhas and green bracelets. There was a display of crude and gaudy pictures, the art of China brutalized by European or Japanese example. But cheek by jowl with the oleographs – peach-blossom cheek by vulgar jowl – long scrolls depended on which, in exquisite line and faint colours, trees were drawn and dim mountains, finger-thin pines and brown rocks, a pale girl with narrow eyes, a butterfly ship on a flowering sea. Beside them, talking to a lean old man, pouchy of eye – the yellow pouches and his yellow chin all curved alike – stood a bland Chinese, black-gowned, hands hidden, his buttoned cap the shape of Brunel-leschi's dome, whose large round face split suddenly to laughter. Like tadpoles in a pond, the crowd softly jostled. There were faces like Buddha's, a coolie whose blank expression was merely the circum-ference of an open mouth, a girl with willow-leaf eyes and pointed chin, a man with a black silk wisp of beard, a wrinkled and clamorous beggar. A little way past the jeweller's shop a lane appeared, where joiners worked, splitting bamboos and hammering coffins.

This was a part of Shanghai that Juan had never seen before, nor would have seen now had he not once again mistaken his direction. The monastery was just inside the boundary of the Chinese city, but instead of turning to the circumference of the city he was going towards its centre. He was, however, not ill-pleased by his mistake, and turning down the lane where the coffin-makers were busy he came presently to a black alley noisy with smithies and the hammering of brass. Then, past a corner where great earthenware cauldrons for excrement were piled in high pyramids, by a little street full of the smell of cooking and the display of strange foods, of messes grotesque in appearance and of unthinkable origin, he came to the bird market. In a thousand wicker cages were quails and love-birds, doves and Java sparrows and tiny birds, sprinkled with crimson as though by a shower of blood, that sat on their perch as tightly as peas in a pod. Between the cages, that stood one on top of the other, transparent walls on either side, the crowd, sombre-hued among this chattering brightness, surged and thrust its opposing ways, or gathered like leaves in a windy corner, or flowed like a tide in a narrow channel.

Caught by such a stream, Juan was carried into a small open square, in part of which were stalls loaded with fish of a horrible and gaudy aspect, while nearby sat plump men intent upon their eating of these and yet more improbable confections. Suddenly, to this crowded square, came the sounds of war. A couple of miles away the Japanese had re-opened their offensive against the North Station, and their seaplanes were again bombing Chapei. At once the crowd rose, with sharp cries and a huge fluttering noise, like pigeons on the piazza of St Mark, and turned northwards, raising to the sky their startled eyes and open mouths half-full of cuttle-fish, bêche-de-mer, and salted cabbage. Here and there was a little movement of panic, but they soon were quietened, and presently the square was busy again with its own affairs and bargaining, and no one paid much attention to the explosion of the bombs and the rattle of machine-gun fire, though everyone spoke more loudly to overcome the noise, and with greater animation because of the proximity of battle.

Juan, being reminded of the war, immediately wanted to know what was happening and who was winning. He decided to return, without further delay, to the New Celestial Hotel, and grew somewhat annoyed when he discovered that this was not going to be easy. The Chinese city was a maze of intersecting alleys, and try as he might he could not walk in any one direction for more than a hundred yards. He returned to the bird market and passed a shop that he recognized, where funeral ornaments were sold. Ten minutes later he was back in the bird market, and stopped to look at a silver pheasant and find his bearings. Having chosen his direction he arrived, after struggling through a very dense crowd, at a kind of sluggish and dark green lagoon in the centre of which was an ornamental building like the house on a Willow Pattern plate. Here it seemed to Juan that he was making real progress for he had not seen the Willow Pattern house before. But presently he returned to the bird market.

He made another attempt, and came to the shop that sold flaring oleographs; or was it a different shop with the same sort of pictures? There were thousands of shops, all side by side, and hundreds of lanes, all crossing and re-crossing. He was sweating a little now, and very urgently intent on finding his way out of the labyrinth. But it took him a long time, and he revisited the Willow Pattern house and the bird market more than once before coming to a broader street whose character, though hardly European, was not so aggressively Chinese as the crowded lanes behind him.

After walking some little distance he got a rickshaw, and though the coolie could not understand a word that was said to him, he ran very vigorously and came by good fortune to the Bund, from where Juan directed him with imperative waving of the arms to the New Celestial.

He engaged a room, and had his luggage, that was still in the hotel, sent up to it. He was told, somewhat to his surprise, that Kuo Kuo had telephoned, about half an hour before, to inquire if he had returned. But she had left no message. He asked the reception clerk to ring up Mr Min Cho-fu, but after several minutes the clerk said he could get no answer. It seemed to Juan that bathing and shaving could be postponed no longer, and when that was done it was lunch-time. He was hungry, and ate heartily, though his meal was punctuated by the sound of rifle-fire; for the war was coming nearer.

He decided to go to the Club and see if he could find Harris, from whom he might get authentic news. But before leaving the hotel he asked, on a sudden impulse, whether Hikohoki was still there.

'No, sir,' said the clerk at the reception-desk. 'Mr Hikohoki checked out this morning. He was paying his bill just before I took your telephone message. He also inquired for you, and wished to know if you had left a forwarding address. That was not very long before you came in.'

If I hadn't got lost in that confounded labyrinth, thought Juan, I might have been saved a lot of trouble. I'll have to go and look for Kuo now, after I've seen Harris. There'll be a row, I expect, but I'm hanged if I'm going back to that monastery. I'd like to have seen Hikohoki, too. I missed him two days ago, because I spent the day with Varya and Masha instead of coming back here. He might have reacted to a little conversation about tanks, though I don't suppose he'd have given much away.

Harris was not in the club. He had had an early lunch, and gone out immediately after it. But in a corner of the reading-room, where in deep chairs a score of members most prosperously slumbered, Juan saw a large and familiar figure. He also slept. His spectacles had fallen down his nose, and his hands were crossed on his great paunch. The air about him was rich with such a perfume as overhangs a malt-house in the sun, while from his lips, that blew softly in and out, came a sound of bees among clover, so that he appeared to sleep in some high summer of his own.

Juan hesitated for a moment, and then took him by the shoulder and shook him awake.

'Flanders,' he said urgently. 'Flanders! Aren't you sailing to-day?'

Flanders looked blearily over his spectacles. He licked his dry lips and smacked his mouth. 'Like an old horse-cloth that the mice have been in,' he muttered. 'Come and have a drink.'

'When does your ship sail?'

Huge and ponderously, Flanders rose from the chair. 'You remember Rocco?' he growled. 'That shape of recrement?'

He led Juan to the bar. 'It was bred by a hatch of thimble-riggers out of a stale hyaena.'

'What's the matter?'

Flanders leaned on the bar and looked through the window at the grey river. The sun had gone, and a slant rain was falling.

'My ship's ashore,' he said, 'on a lee shore with her back broken, and Gloucestershire's at the other end of the world.'

A barman brought coffee and brandy.

'Pay for it,' said Flanders. 'I took you to dinner when I was rich, but anyone with two half-crowns can play host to me now. I'd drink with the hawker of fourpennyworth of leather laces, for he's more stock-in-trade than I have. He can hang himself when he wants to.'

'You haven't lost the money you got from Rocco, have you?'

'Lost it? No, but the dye's run, the silver's come off it, the prize canary's nothing but a stultifying sparrow!'

Flanders pulled a bundle of notes from his pocket and held them under Juan's nose.

'Look at that!' he softly roared. 'Paper and bad ink! The pulp of a sour crab-tree. Go and hang them in a jakes, for they're worth nothing more.'

Juan took the notes and examined them. They were well printed and differed little from others he had seen.

'Whoever made them did a very good job,' he said.

'And there's my pension! I could paper the wall of a shed with it, or wrap stinking fish for an errand-boy's Saturday night, or give it to my landlady's tabefied daughter to curl her hair. But it won't carry me to England and buy the muniments of my last years.'

Juan looked thoughtfully at Flanders and the counterfeit money. 'Rocco's in Nanking, I suppose?'

'He's out of reach,' said Flanders. 'These fools in uniform hold the railway, and Nanking itself may be at war to-morrow. But to tell the truth I wouldn't care to go there even if all were at peace, for he's got his cut-throat friends, and if it came to arguing, with them at his back, there'd be bullets in the syllogism or a cold premiss in the shape of a knife.'

'But can't you sue him for fraud and charge him with felony? He's cheated you out of your price, which is fraud, and used counterfeit money, which is felony. There must be some law in China.'

Flanders, with a rumbling cough, looked cautiously over his shoulder. There was no one else in the bar.

'The law's a man-trap,' he said. 'I want justice, which is ninety thousand dollars, but God give me hives if ever I ask for law. It's dangerous, Motley, and narrow as a snake's tongue. The law chooses its occasions, and has more shapes than a piece of putty. By daylight it's a policeman in blue uniform, but if you walk under the rose it's a man-trap in the grass. And that's the trouble now, for in the matter of selling those tanks I was a kind of trespasser. The law would say I'd no right to sell them, so any dog may bite me that can, till justice puts a stick in my hand.'

'It's difficult to know what to do,' said Juan. 'What are your plans? Are you going to stay in Shanghai?'

Flanders, in the depth of his disappointment, was half disposed to admit defeat. He said: 'I've been here for fourteen years. I can suffer a few more, and the problem of old age will solve itself.'

'Look here,' said Juan, 'can we go somewhere more comfortable than this, and fairly private? I've had one or two rather curious experiences during the last few days, and I heard a story about Rocco that will amuse you. There's just a possibility, moreover, that I can get in touch with him.'

'Touch him with a gaff, then. Bring him ashore and we'll cut him open.'

They went to a smallish room on an upper floor. 'The war seems to be spreading,' said Juan.

'Like mange on a mongrel dog,' said Flanders. 'But there's profit in it, there's forage for those who don't mind a little flavour of carrion.'

He filled his chair – a large brown leather chair with padded arms – so tightly that it looked too small for him, and this inadequacy gave to his whole body an appearance of discomfiture that matched the rueful expression on his face. His hands lay flatly on his thighs, his spectacles hung so crookedly that the upper rim of the right lens bisected his eye, and his white hair was ruffled. He broke the silence that followed his last remark with a prodigious sigh.

He had been in Shanghai for fourteen years, and he wanted to go home. But how could he do that when he had been robbed of the money that was to make him independent? He had always been improvident as well as unlucky, and even his most flagrant dishonesties had never shown such profit as he expected. He found it hard to live cheaply, for his appetites were urgent and large, his taste extravagant. Nor could he save, for he was prodigal by nature, and though he frequently took thought of the morrow, he was generally optimistic about it. He rarely thought of it as a rainy day. At times he had lived well, and often insecurely, but never with that cold prudence which passes for wisdom and writes its epitaph in a handsome will. Nor could he regret the wasteful richness of his life, but only his ill-fortune. A little luck would have made all the difference in the world. But he had always been unlucky. Or nearly always.

'Did you ever wake up beside a dead policeman?' he asked.

'No,' said Juan.

'It's a bad start for a day.'

'I'm sure it is.'

Flanders sighed again. 'I've had my difficulties, Motley, but they've never spoiled my appetite. The old tunes are as danceable as ever, and if there's a day I remember more than all others with gratitude, it's the day when a German shell saved my life by killing a staff officer – a military fashion-plate with a voice for tea-parties and scent on his handkerchief – who'd put me under arrest for cowardice and desertion in face of the enemy. I'd have been shot for it, and lost twenty years of my life. But though I was called it was he who was chosen, for the shell blew him to rags and tatters – there was very little blood in the man – and did me no harm at all. But what were you going to tell me? You've heard something of Rocco, that leech from a dirty horse-pond. What else is put down to Sergeant Blow-fly, who filled my fortune with his maggots?'

'It's rather a long story, if I'm going to make everything clear,' said Juan.

Flanders rubbed his thick nose between thumb and forefinger and listened patiently while Juan briefly explained his relations with Kuo Kuo and described succinctly her political views and ambitions. He showed more interest when Hikohoki came into the story, and insisted that Juan should tell everything he had seen or heard of the Japanese. Juan had not intended to say anything about the Sisters Karamazov, but Flanders so pressed him that he was persuaded to expand his narrative with a short account of them and their connexion with Hikohoki. Nor, having once heard of them, would Flanders let them go, but made Juan describe them in detail, their appearance, their manners, and their history, after which he began so discursive a debate on the advantages and disadvantages of their curious condition that the main point of the story was in danger of being forgotten. But Juan brought him back to it, and related the impudent use to which Rocco had put their fictitious tale of Hikohoki the Secret Agent.

Flanders listened with wrathful astonishment, and decorated his indignation with such copious invective that once again the purpose of the narrative disappeared from view.

Juan at last remembered it. 'Kuo Kuo heard that bit of fancy-work from Rocco himself,' he said, 'and as she's met him once she may meet him again, or she may know something about his movements. That's my idea, at any rate. I don't know exactly what connexion she has in Nanking, or what strings she can pull; and I haven't the smallest notion whether the work she's doing is really important or totally irrelevant. That doesn't worry me. But she certainly knows a lot of people, and she's got a line on Rocco. So, if she's willing to help us, we may get hold of him. Anyway, that's the only approach I can think of.'

'And the very top of deduction, the master-key itself!' exclaimed Flanders with enthusiasm. 'Fly and minnow and prawn have their seasons, but woman's the inerrable bait from February to hot August. Send out your lovely Sinologue. Cast her into the pool, let her dance and twinkle in the depths, allure the fish – a kelt, by God, a slimy kelt! – and prick him with her beauty, sink in his jaw the barb of her seduction, and so bring him to the bank and my long gaff. The Sinologue for Rocco, Motley. You've hit upon the very plan!'

'That's not my intention at all,' said Juan coldly. 'I certainly shan't allow Kuo Kuo to run into any danger, and even more certainly she's not going to let Rocco touch her, or make love to him by so much as a word or a glance.'

'She can do it virtuously,' said Flanders. 'Let her show like a light-house on a dark coast or a green tree in the desert, and he'll come the closer. Let her shoot with her eyes and turn like a Parthian where we shall be waiting. She can do all from a distance, coldly and without fear.'

'What I suggested was that she should get information for us. I never meant her to do anything more than that.'

'But it comes to them by nature! They draw us by their beauty as a valley draws down a stream. And if the stream turns a mill in its course, beauty has increment, and all are satisfied.'

'At present Kuo's turning her own mill, and I don't think she can be diverted to another.'

'Let me talk to her,' said Flanders impatiently. 'Put words in their proper order, and they'll bend resistance as though it were a twig. Good words are like beavers to build a dam, and like dynamite to open a new channel. Let me talk to her, let me tell her the virtuous use she can make of her eyes, and Rocco's her captive to-morrow.'

'What about a drink?' said Juan.

'Two drinks, and then to the lovely Sinologue!'

They had spent the whole afternoon in talking, and they found the bar, which had been deserted when last they saw it, populous again with evening drinkers. They were surrounded by fragments of conversation, casual notes and errant phrases, as though all present were members of an orchestra, tuning their instruments for a per-formance that would never take place.

A pompous fierce little man said loudly: 'Give me a battalion of my old regiment, sir, and I'd go through China like a hot knife through butter!'

'Four spades to the Ace, and five Hearts to the Knave, Queen, King,' said a quieter and more earnest voice.

'I went down to Windy Corner this morning. They're in the front row of the stalls there.'

'Kicked the bottom out of every market in the world . . .'

'She came to Shanghai in October . . .'

'I wouldn't give fifty dollars for it now . . .'

'And boy, she was a lulu!'

'A bloody great piece of iron, and knocked him arse over tip . . .'

'I doubled, of course, and took five tricks.'

'No discipline! What can they do without discipline?'

'She told me she played the races, so I took her to see Hai Alai . . .'

'No, I wouldn't say they were really efficient . . .'

'But what can you do when all the banks are closed?'

'And could she take it? She said it was in her blood.'

'You might compare the Japs with our armies in the Crimea . . .'

'Hallo, hallo!' said a more familiar voice, and turning, Juan saw Harris with a glass of whisky and soda that shook perceptibly in his hand. His eyes were red, he was badly shaved, and looked as though he had had no sleep since the war started. 'The last I saw of you was in Range Road on the opening night,' he said.

'A good lot has happened since then.'

'Well, have a drink.'

'No, it's my turn. How's the war getting on?'

'It's killing me, and thousands more. I haven't been in bed for a year. What are you doing here, Flanders? I thought you were going home.'

'An astrologer told me the times were out of joint, and warned me against thieves.'

'He ought to copyright that. Here, when's my drink coming? I saw two blasted children dead in the gutter an hour ago.'

For five minutes Harris spoke disjointedly and expressively of the war. Their trio became a sestet, then an octet, and presently Juan found himself in very friendly conversation with one of the newcomers. This was a hale man of some fifty-five years with a mellow voice, a bald head, supercilious eyebrows, a clipped moustache, and a top row of artificial teeth. His name was Fannay-Brown.

'Look here,' he said, having discovered that Juan had but recently arrived in Shanghai, 'd'you ride? Well, you must come paper-chasing with us next Sunday. We're going to arrange an armistice with the Japanese. Their admiral's a very decent fellow, very decent indeed. Harris, old boy, have you met the admiral?'

'The baby killer?' said Harris.

'Oh, that's a bit harsh, isn't it? I'd tea on the flagship this afternoon, and found him a very agreeable little fellow. Full of humour, in his own sort of style. Well, Motley, you're going to come paper-chasing on Sunday. I've a pony that needs exercise, and you'll find it rather good fun, I think.'

'That's very kind of you indeed,' said Juan.

'Not a bit of it. Only too glad you like the idea. And what do you think of Shanghai?'

Juan said he had found everything very interesting so far, especially the coolness with which the English accepted the existence of war at their gates.

'That's part of the Shanghai mind, of course. You've heard of our celebrated Shanghai mind? It's really an affliction, but on the whole we're rather proud of it. It means that we're equally resistant to good ideas and bad luck. No, that's not quite the proper definition. My wife has put it better. She says we've got high blood-pressure and low thoughts.'

'That's hard hitting.'

'Oh, my wife's a very witty woman. Sometimes a very cutting wit, and she doesn't really like Shanghai. She finds it rather provincial after London and Paris. She lived in Vienna, too, for a while. Look here, you'd better come and have dinner some day. Come and meet her, before we go out on Sunday. She'll be delighted to see anyone who's just out from home, and knows what's going on in Town.'

'I'm afraid I haven't been in England for some time. I've been living in America.'

'Well, that's better and better. We've scores of American friends, and we're both very keen about American humour. Their magazines are so much cleverer than ours, don't you think? The *New Yorker*, and that sort of thing. My wife always says they make our periodicals look like the parish magazine. Now, what day can you come?'

Mr Fannay-Brown was really very friendly, and Juan, who enjoyed meeting people and found entertainment everywhere, was amiable in return and said Thursday would suit him admirably. Mr Fannay-Brown thereupon scribbled a direction on his card, accepted a short drink, smiled with a bright flash of his artificial teeth, and waved a cordial good-bye.

'Has he sold you a pony yet?' asked Harris.

'Or persuaded you to go shopping with his wife?' said Flanders.

'He's offered to mount me for some kind of a hunt next Sunday. I thought it very friendly of him.'

'You'll come back with the pony in your pocket.'

'I rather liked him,' said Juan.

'A man must live,' said Flanders, 'and there's no vice in him. His wife sells pictures and pottery, and he's a horse-coper, for they've learnt that marriage is only made durable by the cement of kindred interests. He takes customers home to sherry-parties, and she persuades them to buy his ponies. They do very well, I believe. A happy couple, as things go.'

Half an hour later Juan said: 'I think we'd better have dinner here. It's eight o'clock, and the Chinese dine early. It might be awkward if we went to Min Cho-fu's and expected a meal.'

'Turtle soup, a chump chop, and some Camembert for me,' said Flanders. 'That's all I want. A snack and a bottle of Burgundy. This damned country's played the mischief with my stomach. I can't eat as I used to.'

They dined together, and were rather silent over their meal; Harris because he was almost too tired to sit in his chair, Juan and Flanders because each was composing and rehearsing a persuasive appeal to Kuo Kuo.

In silence they lighted cigars, and without remark sipped their meniscus of brandy. Harris, who had fallen into a doze, woke suddenly as he began to slide under the table, and with a great effort got to his feet. 'Bed!' he sighed. 'I must go to bed. A night's sleep, or I'll die in my boots.'

'A cab,' said Flanders. 'We'll take Harris home, and then to the dazzling Sinologue.'

The streets were comparatively quiet, and the night air, blowing coolly upon them, was so refreshing that Flanders and Juan soon began to experience a lively optimism. An optimism so lively that they were inspired to sing the Toreador song from *Carmen*. They took Harris to his flat, and Juan, after a long search through innumerable pockets, found Min Cho-fu's address, which he had noted on the back of an envelope, and directed the driver to a street near Bubbling Well Road.

'I've thought over this matter very carefully,' he said. 'I've examined it from all angles, dissected it, and analysed it. And I foresee no difficulty whatsoever. I'm simply going to appeal to Kuo's sense of generosity. She's a very very generous girl, and she'll never dream of denying me such a favour as this.'

'But let me talk to her as well,' said Flanders. 'I'll fill her with a sense of power. I'll make her feel her beauty like Caesar's bullies, the wings of a hawk, a catapult in nonage. She'll look for conquest and the upper sky, she'll scour hedgerows to kill sparrows. Give me beauty enough and make it conscious, and the world's a taken city.'

'You're right,' said Juan. 'You're perfectly right. But it won't be necessary. We'll be quite frank and straightforward with her. I'm not going to exaggerate the difficulties of what we want her to do, I'm merely going to suggest, as cogently as I can, that we rely on her generosity to help us. In this case honesty's the best policy.'

'Yes and no,' said Flanders. 'Honesty alone is like filling a balloon with cold water in the hope it will rise. But let me puff upon her, let me blow her full of pride, and she'll carry us over the clouds.'

'Absolutely,' said Juan. 'It's an irresistible argument. That in conjunction with my simple logical presentation of the case will convince her of the necessity of it.'

'But feather your logic with poetry, give it wings, or it won't fly.'

'I shall, if that's necessary,' said Juan. 'I certainly shall. But a simple statement of fact will probably be enough.'

'Keep a little valiance in reserve, and the Sinologue's our ally!'

'You can depend on that,' said Juan earnestly. 'She's the most charming girl, and I'm extremely fond of her. I've known her for a long time, and we've never had the vestige of a quarrel. She'll be absolutely delighted to help you.'

Flanders, pushing his hat to the back of his head, and stretching his legs to make more room for his stomach, began to sing, with great animation but no apparent relevance:

> *'Golden slumbers kiss your eyes,*
> *Smiles awake you when you rise . . .'*

Juan came in at the second line, and when the driver stopped below Min Cho-fu's flat their voices, powerfully mingled, rose clear and strongly from the cab:

> *'Sleep, pretty wantons, do not cry,*
> *And I will sing a lullaby!'*

Flanders staggered slightly as he got out, but Juan, like a tree that shores up an old tower, supported him, and with hardly an interruption they continued their song. They climbed a broad flight of stairs to the first floor, and rang a bell. For the third time they apostrophized their pretty wantons – facing each other now, their heads thrown back, a world of stentorian tenderness in their voices:

> '*Sleep, pretty wantons, do not cry,*
> AND I WILL SING A LULLABY!'

Kuo herself opened the door, and stood unnoticed till the song was finished. Then Juan, with the last note still in his mouth, turned and saw her, and instant silence cut that rotund sound clean through its loud circumference. He held out his arms.

'My darling!' he said. 'I came back as quickly as ever I could, and I've brought a very old friend with me, Major Flanders. This is Major Flanders here. We've got something of the very greatest importance to discuss . . .'

Cold as a little breeze in frozen rushes, Kuo said: 'Then you had better come inside.' She turned her back on them, and led the way.

'Careful,' whispered Flanders. 'That's a bad weather report.'

'Not a bit of it,' said Juan, and went confidently into a room where Kuo, like a column of apple-green chrysoprase, stood waiting for them; where Miss Min, a little column of flaming porphyry, stood in the background; while Min Cho-fu, a dark huddle of grief, was weeping bitterly on the floor.

'Where have you been?' said Kuo.

'At the Club,' said Juan weakly.

'Why did you leave the monastery?'

'Oh, that was a long time ago.'

'I said why, not when.'

'Well, there wasn't a lavatory, for one thing . . .'

'I have been looking for you all day. I was very anxious about you, and also I needed you. For the first time since we came here, you could have been of some use. But you were not to be found. You have failed me, and now you are drunk!'

'I'm not drunk,' said Juan indignantly. 'Do you think I never sing a song unless I'm drunk? Absolute nonsense. I'm constantly singing.'

Like an icy spray, words suddenly spirted from the rosebud mouth of Miss Min. Chinese words, hissing like the salt fringe of a wave. Incomprehensible to Juan, their meaning was clear enough to her brother. He rocked in agony before that biting spindrift. He offered no defence, but hid his face in his hands. Juan himself was somewhat intimidated by the boreal ferocity of so shy and gentle a girl.

'We have two men in the house,' said Kuo bitterly, 'and both have failed us. There were two men on whom we relied, and neither was trustworthy. They failed us because they were morally weak, intellectually unstable, and they could not control their appetites.'

Juan made a poor attempt to change the conversation. 'You haven't met my friend, Major Flanders, have you? Flanders! I say, Flanders!'

But Flanders had gone. Silently, on cautious feet, he had fled from the scene of female wrath.

10

WHEN Min Cho-fu and Kuo Kuo returned from Nanking, it was Min who had in his possession the segment of bamboo containing Lo Yu's plan for the salvation of China. When Kuo left him, to hurry back to Juan, he was no more than half a mile from his house. The time was early morning, the streets were fairly empty, and there seemed no reason for doubting that he with his all-precious burden would reach home in safety. But on the way there, in that short distance, he was stopped by a girl he recognized. She came running from the pavement, towards his rickshaw, and when Min saw her he almost fainted with horror and delight.

Her name was Peony Sun. At one time she had been the loveliest and most famous sing-song girl in Shanghai. Her talent and her beauty were both unrivalled, and to their attractions she added the glamour of an eventful history. She had had her slim finger in politics. She had been the favourite concubine of a war-lord in Manchuria. A princely merchant in Hankow had loved her, and she had ruined him. She was witty and dangerous, the cause of scandal and despair. And Min Cho-fu, that mild and scholarly little man who lived with his sister, had once spent a night with her.

It had cost him a great deal of money, but little in comparison with the presents that Peony Sun often received. Why she had been so obliging as to let him make love to her was a mystery. She may have been amused by his devotion or touched by it; his love was a creed rather than a passion, it nourished and consumed him. But his sister was extremely angry when she discovered, as was inevitable, that for one night at least his love had been rewarded. She grudged the money he had spent on Peony, which was much more than he could afford.

Min did not see her again. In some obscure way her fame suffered eclipse, and a few months later she went to Tientsin. There, with less competition, she regained something of her former glory, but soon lost it again, and disappeared, if not from local view, at least from the general eye.

For several months no one had heard of her, and Min's surprise at seeing her in Shanghai was natural enough. His love for her woke again – it had indeed hardly slumbered – and was mingled with pity when he saw that she was tired and poorly dressed. He took her into the rickshaw beside him, and told the runner to go to a tea-house on the fringe of the Chinese City. He dared not take her home, where his sister would certainly refuse to receive her.

She told the story of various misfortunes, and said she had come from Tientsin to see her father who lived in Chapei. Her father was dying, and he had a lot of money which he had promised to her. But she could not get into Chapei, for there were soldiers there, and the bombs frightened her. She had a friend in Shanghai – a business friend – who had sometimes lent her money, but now she owed him a lot, and he would give her no more. And she was ashamed to visit any of her former lovers, and let them see how poor she had become.

But Min Cho-fu was faithful and sympathetic, not scornful of her poverty, but pitying it. He could only give her a very little money, he said, for he was in difficulty himself. But what was the other matter in which she needed help?

She would not tell him. But she must, she said, see her father before he died. Would he take her into Chapei?

That was a different matter. Min was not a brave man, and he had no liking for so dangerous a task. But the longer they talked, the stronger grew Peony's insistence that she must go there. Her obstinacy became fanatical. If Min would not go with her, she would go alone, she said.

Min was in a pitiful state of mind, but at last his love proved stronger than his fear. They left the Settlement by the great gate in North Honan Road, which at intervals was opened under a strong guard for the clamorous passage of refugees. – Refugees who came and went, ever restless, always reinforced. – The day was quiet. A few shots were heard, a few fires dully smouldered, but no seaplanes with loud cargoes flew overhead, for now the greatest activity was in Hongkew, an outlying district to the north. But Min was hardly in a condition to judge the quantity of danger they encountered. That might be little enough, but its quality was always the same, which was deadly. He was pitifully frightened, and breathed as they walked in deep gasps, as though he had run a mile on a hot day. But Peony was in a mood of sullen indifference to everything but the purpose of their journey.

They hurried along a cinder-black lane beside the railway, and turned into a neighbourhood of small mean streets that were deserted except for a few skulking figures. The wall of a ruined house collapsed behind them, and then they ran from a band of looters. They turned into a passage beside a pawnbroker's, and entered a small house that was the back part of the same building.

Peony's father was peacefully smoking. He showed no surprise at seeing them, and Peony, having saluted him with brief ceremony, at once took the pipe from his unresisting fingers, heated another little ball of opium, and greedily inhaled its fumes. She smoked four pipes in succession, and then, quite simply – for she was too lazily contented to speak otherwise – she told Min that this was what she had come for. She knew that the old man would have opium; being poor and out of favour, she had no other means of getting it; and therefore she had come to her father.

Min was in utter misery. His mind, from a considering of Peony's degradation, could pass only to realization of his own danger. Like a pendulum it had no rest, but swung between these extremes of unhappiness. He spent much of the day weeping, but there was no one to see his tears, for Peony and her father were in their paradise of dreams.

Sometime during the night he left them. It had taken great courage to resolve on doing this, to get up, and leave the comparative safety of their house; but once outside he had no more need of courage, for panic, like a gale of wind, blew him headlong through the streets. How he managed to reach the Settlement he could not properly remember, but he collapsed outside his own house, and lay for a long time helpless on the pavement.

When his strength returned, he realized at once that his sister would want to know where he had been all day – all day and more than half the night – and he tried to go in quietly so as to avoid her till morning. But in this he failed. She was waiting for him, and Min, in no condition to withstand close questioning, was subjected to a merciless cross-examination.

He was saved from the unpleasantness of being grilled by falling into the fire. He suddenly remembered the all-precious nostrum for China, the bamboo-hidden scroll of salvation, and hurriedly feeling for it, found he had lost it.

Neither his sister nor Kuo Kuo had any pity for him. They themselves were appalled by the mishap, and the measure of their sense of calamity was the measure of their unmercy to Min. Then Kuo, sending a servant to the monastery with a message to Juan, was told that he had disappeared. Her ill-temper was naturally aggravated, and Min suffered the more. He had little peace all day, and when in the evening Juan came – Juan in his fine exalted mood that did not last – he was compelled to listen to a re-telling of his moral frailty and criminal negligence.

'For of course,' said Kuo, 'he left the plan in that woman's house in Chapei.'

'He had it hidden under his clothing,' said Miss Min bitterly. 'And where else was he likely to undress himself except in that dirty place?'

Min, still rocking to-and-fro on the floor, said pitifully that not so much as a single button of his long gown had he unfastened. But his sister attacked him with such bitter scorn that his resistance dissolved like a shaving of copper in strong acid, and nothing was heard but the hissing of her corroding speech and the bubbling sound of Min sobbing.

'She says that once before he spent a night with Peony Sun,' Kuo explained, 'and gave so much money to her that for a long time afterwards they were quite poor. And a dog, she says, will always go back to look for the bone that he has buried.'

'Well, it's all very unfortunate,' said Juan, 'but there's no use bullying Min any more. I'm very glad that I thought of coming along to see you. . . .'

'Why did you not come this morning? Why did you leave the monastery without telling me where you were going?'

'Those are two rather foolish questions,' said Juan, 'that simply confirm the impression I had previously formed. Now listen to me, and instead of gloating over poor Min's little weakness, fix your attention upon the glaring faults in your own behaviour. That's a very beautiful dress you're wearing, Miss Min – had I anything to drink I would like to drink Kanpei to your talented dressmaker – but as it is, let us sit down and talk things over.'

'She will bring you some tea,' said Kuo.

'Any port in a storm, as the gourmet remarked when his aeroplane struck an Australian vineyard,' said Juan amiably, and drank several cups of the excellent green tea that Miss Min somewhat unwillingly made for him. He had recovered from the shock of Kuo's unexpected hostility, and he was pleased at having put a stop, if only a temporary one, to Min's punishment, whose unhappiness was distressing to see. Juan, indeed, throughout the recital of misadventure, had felt himself unable to be properly impressed by its gravity because of the pleasure he got from looking at Kuo and Miss Min. How delicious they were in their accurate Chinese beauty. Slim and pliant as ivory wands in their bright closely fitting dresses. Brilliant in their anger – and Min's flat was cheerfully equipped in the American style, the furniture and decorations, that is, being recognizably European in kind, but much smarter than anything to be found in Europe – and Miss Min's delightful little nose, now that he came to think of it, was really very like a nice cat's nose, low on the cheeks, and modest and straight. He had almost persuaded himself that the party was full of fun and charm, when he noticed the bright anger of Kuo's eyes, and hurriedly re-arranged his thoughts.

'As I was about to say,' he continued swiftly, 'you're crippled by conventional error. I dare say you believe in proverbs, and proverbs, to put it rather fancifully, are merely signposts to error. They lead you to the nearest mare's-nest, and that's all. Take, for example, such a statement as: *What's done can't be undone*. What nonsense that is. I could give you some very amusing illustrations of the ease of undoing things. But let us pass instead to that dreary quip, which is all the Latin I remember: *Pereunt et imputantur . . .*'

'What are you talking about?' said Kuo.

Juan made a gesture of disappointment. 'I was trying to demonstrate, by apt allusion and pithy instance, the folly of your pessimism, which appears to be derived from a study of the more dismal aphorisms. If you can't cure toothache, do you endure it, as the proverb recommends? Of course you don't. You get a new set of teeth, like Mr Fannay-Brown – but I haven't told you about him, have I? Well, then: since Min has lost this plan of yours, what you should do is to go and ask your old man of the mountain to give you another copy.'

'Lo Yu has gone back to his mountain, which is three hundred miles from Nanking,' said Kuo.

'Oh,' said Juan.

'Nor will he have a copy, for in China we do not think of such things.'

'Anyone who sets out to be the saviour of his country should have a good business training,' said Juan.

'And what will happen if, in the meantime, the Japanese have found the plan that my brother lost?' asked Miss Min.

'Now that's pessimism again. We have just as much chance as the Japanese of finding it.'

'My brother will not go back to Chapei. He says it is too dangerous.'

'He's probably right,' Juan agreed.

'He should be only too glad to sacrifice himself for China . . .'

'That wouldn't be any good either,' said Juan. 'If he sacrificed himself, the plan would still be lost. I'm all against sacrifice of any kind.'

There was a long silence.

'I shall go and get it,' said Kuo softly.

'I knew you were going to say that,' exclaimed Juan. 'It's just the kind of thing a woman would say. Sheer sentimental blackmail! Now I'll have to go, and I don't suppose the plan's there in any case, and even if it is there it probably isn't worth anything.'

The argument changed colour. Now it became combative through excess of kindliness, and generosity strove with rival generosity for mastery. Kuo reiterated her intention of going into Chapei, and Juan said he would assuredly permit no such thing. But for his part, he said, he'd be only too glad of a little excitement. They grew warm with the contest, and their warmth generated such mutual affection that they could barely stay out of each other's arms. Then the charming little Miss Min burst into tears and said they could remain where they were, for she was going that very instant to search for the plan. Where-upon Juan, moved extremely by admiration for her courage, embraced her with great kindness, and found her slim figure very adaptable to such congratulation.

Alone among them, poor Min was unmoved by this new enthusiasm. He sat on the floor and watched them in melancholy bewilderment.

II

JUAN had breakfast in bed. It was a very good breakfast, and Kuo and Miss Min waited on him. He ate fruit and fish and bacon and eggs, and drank a great deal of coffee, and enjoyed himself thoroughly. It was delightful to be a hero, and be served by such lovely creatures. Kuo was now wearing a slim dress the colour of a smoky pearl, and Miss Min's was the hedgerow hue of a pale celandine. Could heroism be assured of such rewards as these, it would become the most popular of all vocations.

He dallied with his breakfast as long as he could, for the thought struck him that this grateful anticipation of his gallantry and, if he survived, the subsequent acclamation, would be its only pleasant features. But he did not let such thoughts trouble him for long.

The upshot of their previous night's argument had inevitably been that Juan should undertake the retrieving of Lu Yo's plan. Min, who remembered very vividly his outward journey – though nothing of his homeward flight – was able to draw a map that showed the exact position of Peony's house, and Juan studied this carefully. Miss Min suggested he should disguise himself as a Chinese, but Juan thought that might lead to unnecessary embarrassment. He still had, he remembered, the cards that Harris had given him – the insignia of Messrs Gibbon, Kettledrum, and Dearborn, of the *Times*, the *Express*, and the *San Francisco Examiner* – which were inscribed in both English and Chinese; and though they would not protect him from a bullet or a bomb, they might, in the event of less serious trouble, entitle him to the respect of his captors.

Min was sent out to gather what news he could about the state of affairs in Chapei, and also to arrange, with a friend of his in North

Honan Road, that Juan should use his house as a stepping-stone into the debatable land beyond. But when he returned, his information was meagre and most of it contradictory. It was, indeed, impossible for anyone to give an accurate description of what was happening, and no one could plot the line of battle when much of the battle was street-fighting that might break out anywhere.

Juan, comparing a map of Shanghai with the plan that Min had drawn, and trying to collate the discrepancies of Min's latest information with both of them, grew rather bewildered. Let us suppose that Shanghai is London, he thought. Then the Whangpoo becomes the Thames, and the North Station is Euston. The Japanese are fighting their way from the east towards the London and North Eastern Railway, which unconventionally takes a turn down Euston Road. The Japanese hold the Temple – though Chinese snipers have been worrying them there – and they're pretty strong in Islington. Now the Soochow Creek's a broadish stream running from somewhere about Regent's Park to Waterloo Bridge, and the Japanese are patrolling several of the lower bridges on it. I've got to cross that, and get into no-man's-land from North Honan Road, which is roughly equivalent to Southampton Row. From there I must cross the railway where it goes down Euston Road, and look for a very obscure street in the neighbourhood of King's Cross, or where King's Cross would be if there were such a station in Shanghai. And meanwhile King's Cross is being raided by Japs and looted by Chinese, there's a lot of fighting about Gray's Inn Road, and casual bombing from the Angel to Camden Town. I'm going to have a lively time. I'd better write to my mother before I start, and tell her that if I die my wounds will be all behind.

Kuo Kuo, it was clear, was also worried. She had a long conversation with Miss Min, and both of them disappeared for an hour or more. When they returned, Kuo was wearing a dark blue padded tunic, blue trousers tight at the ankle, and soft black shoes. It was the costume of the lower classes that served, with little difference, both for men and women. She was going as far as Honan Road, she said, and she had dressed to be inconspicuous and able to run if that were necessary. Juan protested, but Kuo had made up her mind, and as he could not believe there would be any danger in the preliminary stage of his journey, he submitted without much argument. Kuo gave him another pistol, and Min presented him with a handsome walking-stick which, when Juan had politely accepted it, he found to be a sword-stick. He was somewhat embarrassed by this romantic armament.

They started about five o'clock, taking rickshaws as far as the Soochow Creek, which they crossed by one of the upper bridges. The streets were quiet. Somewhere beyond the North Station a Chinese battery was lazily in action but there were no seaplanes overhead, and the students, who for the last day or two had been noisily demonstrating, were apparently recuperating in private.

They dodged a party of Japanese ronin – the plain-clothes reservists – in the neighbourhood of Honan Road, and waited for a motor-patrol to pass before they crossed the road and slipped into the shop whose owner had been warned of their coming. It was a little shop that sold ink-sticks, and its small window was broken. But the proprietor was waiting for them, and led them by a narrow passage into a dirty yard, with a statue of Kwan-yin, the Goddess of Mercy, in one corner.

'Help me over the wall,' said Kuo.

'No, you've got to go home now.'

'I must come with you to the next street,' said Kuo impatiently, 'and then I can see that you take the right way. Hurry, Juan, hurry!'

Juan hoisted himself on to the wall, pulled Kuo after him, and dropped into another yard. From there, through a broken fence, they got into a dark alley and looked cautiously down a road that was apparently deserted, and empty except for a lost rickshaw and a dead coolie. Juan, in a voice more cheerful than he felt, said, 'Well, I expect I can find my way from here.'

Kuo did not reply, but suddenly, stepping into the road, began to run as fast as she could. Juan, after a second of startled immobility, pursued her with an angry feeling that his adventure, beginning in folly, would probably end in disaster. Kuo had a very pretty turn of speed, and she had covered a hundred yards before he caught her. Even then she would not stop, but struck at his outstretched arm.

'What are you playing at?' he gasped.

'This way,' said Kuo urgently, and pulled him into the opening of a lane. 'Ronin!' she gasped, and pointed to two squat figures who had come from a side-street into the road ahead.

'Very probably,' said Juan, 'but what sort of game is this?'

'You couldn't find your way alone,' said Kuo, and without giving him time to reply led him swiftly down the lane, across a narrow street, clambered over a pile of shattered masonry, ran up a stinking alley, and came out on a road in which a couple of bombs had dug ragged craters.

'This isn't the way I would have come,' said Juan.

'Then the ronin would have stopped you,' said Kuo.

'I'd have told them I was a journalist. How much farther do you think you're coming?'

'All the way.'

'Indeed you're not. You can't dictate to me like that.'

'I am coming to look after you.'

'Look here,' said Juan, 'have you ever been in Chicago? Have you ever run a cargo of liquor into Detroit? Let me tell you that your Chinese wars are simply the squabbling of children compared with what I've seen in America . . . What the devil's that?'

A rifle cracked, and as though it had materialized out of a conjuror's hat, a sprawling figure lay on the road ahead of them. They drew into a broken doorway, and presently, from houses that had seemed deserted, came men and women who half-surrounded the dying man, and watched his tortured movements. He wriggled and heaved, as though what hurt him was a stake that pinned him to the ground. Unmoving and pitilessly interested, the furtive spectators watched him die.

'We had better not go that way,' said Kuo.

The broken doorway in which they stood opened into a confusion of shattered walls and ruined houses. They scrambled over precipitous grey heaps of debris, and came into what had once been a little garden, full of the grotesquely weathered rocks that are the ornaments of a Chinese garden. They forced their way into a deserted house and emerged in a street parallel to that which they had left. There had been a miniature battle there, and the bodies of a dozen soldiers lay where they had fallen.

'I apologize,' said Juan. 'Perhaps I think too highly of American achievement. – Have you ever eaten shad roe and bacon? – But travel is broadening my mind.'

Cautiously they advanced, and presently came in sight of an elaborate barricade. There was a complicated entanglement of barbed wire. There was a rampart of sandbags with a coping of more barbed wire. There were the round black muzzles of two machine-guns.

'And now what can we do?' said Juan. 'Do you think they would allow Mr Dearborn of the *San Francisco Examiner* to cross their Hindenburg Line?'

'They will let us pass,' said Kuo, and calmly stepped into the middle of the road. Heads appeared above the barricade and they heard an excited chattering. I wish I had written to my mother, thought Juan, and with a desperate affectation of composure changed his step to keep in time with Kuo. The machine-guns were swung inwards till their muzzles stared straight at them. They heard a shrill challenge, to which Kuo in a loud high voice replied.

A young Chinese officer leapt over the barricade, with whom Kuo began a long conversation. She showed him several papers, which he examined with interest. After more conversation, now noticeably polite, he helped them over the sandbags and they found themselves in a company of grey-uniformed soldiers of the 19th Route Army. Kuo showed her papers to another officer, and there was more debate. Then they were offered tea, which Kuo politely refused, and a soldier was detailed to escort them over the railway line, some two or three hundred yards away.

'I take everything back,' said Juan. 'You must have some very useful friends.'

'I have a pass from General Wu Tu-fu, who commands the Tank Corps in Nanking,' said Kuo, 'and another from General Sun Sat-lo, who is one of the generals in Shanghai.'

They crossed the line, being impeded by nothing more than a dead camel. Its egregious brown shape, in the adjacent cinders of a railway, was to Juan a great surprise; but Kuo said it was probably a medicinal camel, one perambulated, that is, for the purgative quality of its milk. By the arousing of pity and fear, thought Juan, and by their consequent purgation, is tragedy made acceptable to the mind of man. But the camel had gone the wrong way about it, for purgation had preceded the fear and the pity, and the result was a stupid feeling of desolation.

On the far side of the railway was an amateurish block-house made of sandbags and sleepers, and their soldier escort, hailing its commander, called out a bespectacled young man who advanced towards them, perilously swinging a long Mauser pistol from his trigger-finger. He, a subaltern in General Sun Sat-lo's Shanghai army, was also impressed by Kuo Kuo's passports, but said he could give them no protection beyond the range of his guns. In the labyrinth of little streets ahead of them, he declared, there were perils more desperate than any they had yet encountered. The Japanese, what were they? Stupid little dwarfs from the Eastern Sea. But now, among these ruined streets, were striped tigers from the mountains of Szechuen; Chinese looters, freebooters, murderous thieves. He would rather encounter a company of Japanese Marines, new-landed from Yokohama, than a handful of his fellow-countrymen whose hearts had become wolves for plunder.

A theatrical young man, thought Juan, when Kuo had translated for him the subaltern's observations. But now both of them went forward with pistols ready, and as they turned each beggared corner they were conscious of a little disappointment when they saw nothing to shoot at.

Kuo, for the first time, made a mistake. They halted where a fallen house had blocked the road. Juan, looking at Min's plan, discovered they had taken the wrong turning. In consequence of this he felt a little surge of protective love for Kuo, and putting his arm round her drew her to him in the ruined street. She accepted his embrace without remark or opposition. Then they heard the crescendo roaring of a seaplane's engine.

'The aeroplane,' said Juan, 'our most triumphant invention, is the only vehicle that has no facilities for making love.' And he kissed her again.

But as he raised his head he saw, staring from a cracked window, a yellow face set in the lines of the laughing God in the monastery from which, but thirty-two hours before, he had so thankfully escaped. These battered houses were not yet wholly deserted, and such evidence of the outrageous fortitude of the human spirit, which could survive the desolation of war and play Peeping Tom on a battlefield, was curiously alarming. Juan with a compelling arm drew Kuo to the ruined pavement, and round the nearest corner.

'This is the way,' he said firmly.

They made one more mistake, turned and explored again, and found the shuttered pawnshop. There was a high-walled four-foot lane beside it. They went down the lane, and came to a wooden door ajar. They pushed it open. A tiny littered yard was the fore-court of two-roomed house, whose door was also open.

In the outer room, sitting on a wooden bed, was an old emaciated man whose bemused and gentle eyes were contemplating the pale picture of a grasshopper on a bending leaf. The room was bare, and faintly lighted from a paper window. Three scrolls, displaying fine penmanship, hung on the walls, and in a little red earthenware pot on a rough table grew a miniature pine tree. The old man paid no attention to them.

Kuo went into the adjoining room, and called to Juan. He followed her and saw, lying on a low bed, a girl with heavy eyelids, a pale oval face, and narrow chin. She slept without visible movement, and beside her, on the floor, were a pipe and the apparatus for preparing opium.

'Look for the piece of bamboo,' said Kuo. 'A length of bamboo about twenty inches. The plan is in that.'

But the little house was so naked it was easy to discover that Lo Yu's plan was not there.

'If Min lost it while he was running away, then we shall never find it,' said Kuo bitterly.

'I can't blame him for falling in love with Peony,' said Juan, looking thoughtfully at the girl who lay so placidly and dreamt of luxury and fantastic bliss. 'She must have been uncommonly pretty a few years ago.'

'She has ruined us all,' said Kuo harshly, and going into the other room, stared gloomily at the old man whose mind was in thrall to the picture of a grasshopper on a green leaf.

'There's another aeroplane,' said Juan, as the insect hum of a distant engine grew to a metallic roar above. 'They're firing at it,' he added, when, thrice repeated, they heard an explosive metallic cough.

Crrumph! said the anti-aircraft shells, and did no harm except to what was hurt already.

'God Almighty!' he concluded, and held Kuo tightly as the little house shook before a deafening roar. The indignant aeroplane had dropped its remaining bomb, which, exploding in the narrow yard, had so blown upon the outer wall of Peony's room that it overhung her like an inquisitive friend; and displacing a great fountain of earth and bricks it had blocked the only doorway of the house with a pile of invading rubble.

'Now we're here for the duration of the war,' said Juan, looking at the broken door and the avalanche that filled its space.

Peony woke and rose lazily from the bed. 'What was that noise?' she asked Kuo.

Kuo replied by questioning her about Min's visit, but Peony could remember nothing till she had smoked another pipe. Then she said, 'Yes, he came here. He used to be my lover when I was young.'

'Did he leave a section of bamboo containing a written scroll?' asked Kuo.

'He was my lover,' said Peony. 'Does the river ask the full moon to leave anything but the memory of its silver feet?'

She rose and walked slowly to the other room, where she sat on the bed beside her father. He, still intent upon his exquisitely drawn grasshopper, paid no attention to her; but Peony, who knew that he was dying, gazed at him with tender melancholy.

Already it was nearly dark in the little house, and Kuo, finding a couple of small lamps, lighted them and set one in each room.

'The only way to get out,' said Juan, 'will be to scrape that pile of rubble into the house. I can't push it away, because there's too much behind it. But Peony and her father may be annoyed if we fill their outer room with broken bricks and cobble-stones.'

'The plan is lost,' said Kuo drearily.

'It may not have been a very good one,' said Juan.

'Would Lo Yu have given us something of no value? He told me that by means of this plan China could be saved and regenerated.'

'Well, perhaps he was right. But what are we going to do now?'

'I do not care very much.'

Kuo sat herself on the bed in the inner room, nursing one leg and staring disconsolately at nothing. On the other bed were Peony, bemused by opium, and the old man, who was hypnotized by the imminence of death and a very good painting of a grasshopper. Juan felt as lonely as a recruiting sergeant among Quakers.

The situation, however, was by no means desperate. Their imprisonment was only nominal, for with an hour or two's work they could breach the rubble-filled doorway, or, if that proved unexpectedly difficult, a hole could easily be made in the flimsy and already shaken wall. But Juan felt that before starting on demolition of any kind, he should have the authority of the owner of the house; and neither the owner nor his daughter was in a mood for the discussion of practical affairs. Even the necessity for postponing a decision, however, was not really irksome; for though they were to force their way out at once, he doubted whether he or Kuo could find their way through the warren of little streets in the darkness. He sat down beside Kuo and affectionately pressed her hand. With no more encouragement than that she burst into tears.

It occurred to Juan, not for the first time, that patriotism was really a very great nuisance, for it either made people improperly arrogant or as touchy as a sore thumb. This was the second time within four or five days that Kuo had cried on his shoulder. A few weeks ago she had had no more thought of tears than a dolphin of drowning, but now she was as liable to grief as a child with bad teeth and a tin of toffee. What charming gaiety she had shown before they came to China! A lyric mood, clear and perfect as an old song. The mood of a summer morning, bright and cloudless, of the greenwood listening to its quire of birds . . . To the devil with politics, the queasiness and wrath of ambition, the vulgarity of conquest, and the bitterness of inferiority! The Chinese were right – the old Chinese – who said that man should enjoy the fruits of the earth and cultivate decent manners. They preached simplicity, which meant a glassless mind to the beauty and the benison of nature. They taught peace, which was freedom to live in the fullness of life. But how could the new Chinese obey such precepts, when they were harried on all sides by graceless arrivistes to whom the world was a kind of coalfield in which they dug for their ugly wealth, and fought and swindled each other for the right to dig, and darkened the green fields with slag-heaps and the black vomit of their chimneys?

'An ounce of civet!' cried Juan, jumping from the bed and leaving Kuo to regain her balance as she could. 'An ounce of civet to sweeten my imagination!'

'Have you got a pain?' asked Kuo.

'I had,' said Juan. 'For a moment I had. I entertained a serious thought, and that was a great mistake. For to think seriously is to wake anger, and to be angry is to burn for nothing. It is for me, at least, because I haven't the sort of nature to keep the fire going. What shall we talk about? If I were a poet I might tell you how beautiful you are, and that, if I did you justice, would be one of the most charming poems ever written.'

'There was a princess of my name who lived in the reign of one of the

T'ang Emperors, for whom Chang Hu made this poem: "When the Emperor sent for the Lady Kuo Kuo, she did not adorn her beauty, for that would have lessened it; riding to the palace in the morning, she just smoothed the little moth-wing of her eyebrows." '

'Now that,' said Juan, 'is a much prettier compliment than our tedious English habit of saying: "I could not love thee, dear, so much, loved I not honour more." '

'We do not estimate things in the same way as you. There was a Prefect called Liu who became famous, and is now remembered, because he loved wine and chrysanthemums.'

'Of course, we have our famous characters too, though at the moment I can only think of a regicide called Harrison. He was condemned to be hanged, drawn, and quartered, but no sooner had they disembowelled him than he got up and boxed the executioner's ears.'

'The English are very persistent,' said Kuo.

'We have a lot of even nicer characteristics, but we prefer to advertise our virtues, which is very stupid, because foreigners think they are merely the effect of our climate. We often go the wrong way about things. Teaching history, for instance. We make it such a dull affair, but really it's full of interest. Did you know that knickers were first introduced into England in the reign of Charles II? Now there's a significant fact.'

'He was a good king, wasn't he?'

'He was a very good king,' said Juan. 'Don't you think you ought to take that heavy tunic off? You'll be much more comfortable without it. – You're quite different from an English girl, you know. They're far more undulant. When Bacon said something about: "coming home to our business and bosoms," he was dealing, in England, with a very large reality. But though Chinese girls are pretty flat in front, most of the men are hollow-chested, so you maintain the essential difference.'

'They are hollow-chested because for centuries our ideal has not been physical strength but scholarship. But now it seems as though we would be better off if we had learnt to play games and be strong.'

Juan, smelling a return to politics, swiftly steered the conversation back to poetry, and having found that he could be very comfortable on the narrow bed, if Kuo lay there too, he listened contentedly while she cleverly paraphrased some agreeable verses. A good many of them described the plight of lovers who waited in vain for their distant or dilatory sweethearts. China, thought Juan, with its inability for keeping appointments, was probably very rich in poetry of this kind. But all the graces were at the mercy of efficiency.

'Though procrastination is the thief of time,' he said, 'punctuality is the abortionist of fancy.'

The smell of opium, which permeated the little house, grew stronger. Peony, a long slim pipe in her hand, had come to talk to them.

She was looking much better now, though her complexion still had a faintly greenish hue. But she was wide awake, and apparently inclined to friendly conversation. Kuo, with rather a bad grace, answered the conventional questions, and was formally polite in her turn. Juan was very sorry that Peony spoke no English, but Kuo translated most of what she said.

After a little one-sided gossip about Min Cho-fu – Peony was grateful for his escort – she asked what it was he had lost, and they had come to look for. 'You told me before, I think, but I do not remember what you said.'

Kuo described the precious piece of bamboo, and Peony shook her head. She had not seen it. 'But if it was valuable,' she said, 'perhaps the Japanese took it away.'

'The Japanese soldiers have been here?'

'Not soldiers, but a man I know, who came with two ronin.'

After another question or two, Kuo became far too excited to translate. 'Wait till we have finished,' she said impatiently, when Juan asked her what it was all about. But he heard a familiar name, repeated and again repeated, and he grew almost as restive as Kuo Kuo while he listened to the incomprehensible and exasperating dialogue.

At last he was allowed to speak. 'Was it Hikohoki?' he asked.

'Yes,' said Kuo.

'Good for Proteus! He gets around like the ghost of Hamlet's father.'

'We are now quite defeated,' said Kuo. 'The plan could not have got into more dangerous hands.'

'If Hikohoki has taken it, it's safe enough, and you'll be able to buy

124

it back. From what I know of him he'd sell anything that he didn't have to amputate. But tell me the whole story.'

It was, apparently, quite simple. Hikohoki had lent money to Peony, and when she returned to Shanghai she was still in his debt. She had come, as she told Min, to see her father, who was dying. But her father was in Chapei, and Chapei was a battlefield. So she had gone to Hikohoki, and asked him for help. But he refused her money, and refused to give her opium, which she needed even more. She lost her temper, and told Hikohoki that she could do without him. Her father, she said, had plenty of money and an abundance of opium. Hikohoki smiled and said he did not believe it. 'You can come and see,' she had boasted, and told him where her father lived. When she met Min she was nearly demented, but still too frightened to go into Chapei by herself. But as the day lengthened her craving grew, and by the time she had persuaded him to go with her, she was so desperate that she hardly needed his escort.

Peony thought it was early the following morning that Hikohoki arrived; but she could not be sure, she said with a charming sad smile, for she had rather lost count of time. He had two ronin with him, to guard him, and his manner had been very firm. He wanted the money she owed him, with appropriate interest, and he told her that unless she paid him immediately, she would immediately be arrested. And how could she suffer arrest, when her father was dying and she must stay with him? She knew where the bag of silver dollars was hidden, and she took what was needed. Hikohoki had not behaved badly. The interest that he asked was rather heavy, but he had not robbed her. He had, indeed, after counting and re-counting the money, been very kind. He had given her a bottle of cough-mixture for her father, and told her that if she needed a job at any time he would be only too glad to help her. Then, with polite wishes for her safety, he and his two gun-men had gone.

'It is a very suspect story, isn't it?' said Kuo.

'Suspect?'

'I mean that Hikohoki was not likely to go into Chapei merely to collect two hundred dollars. That motive was the cover for his real one. He discovered that Min had come here, having the plan with him, and followed at once, hoping to find him still here.'

'You're still shooting at a target that isn't there,' said Juan. 'I've told you a dozen times that Hikohoki isn't a spy or a Secret Police-man, but simply a good dishonest grafter.'

'Then why did he try to murder Colonel Rocco?'

Juan sighed, and assured her that he had done no such thing. Kuo listened with patent unbelief, but before Juan could answer more than five or six of her stubborn questions, Peony, with a languid air un-suited to the importance of the news, returned to say that her father had been asking who these visitors were, and what they had come for. Having been told their errand, he at once said that he had seen one of the Japanese pick up a short bamboo staff from the floor, and conceal it in his clothing. He had noticed and remembered the incident, because the piece of bamboo was spotted, and spotted bamboo, as everyone was aware, had acquired its spots through the dropping of the tears of the two wives of the Emperor Shun as they wept over his tomb in the land of Ts'ang-wu. He had always, said Peony, enter-tained a vicarious affection for the wives of the Emperor Shun.

'We must leave here at once,' said Kuo decisively. 'Hikohoki has the plan, and we must get on his track. We shall now go to any length to deal with him.'

'Then I suppose you want me to clear away all this rubble,' said Juan.

Peony had no objection to his filling the outer room with the block-ading stones, though she asked him first to carry her father to the other bed. He would die before morning, she said.

The old man was no heavier than a child. His eyes, half covered by their yellow lids, were clouded and apparently sightless; but still in his frail fingers he held his pale green picture of the grasshopper. He lay motionless on the inner bed, a little anatomy that waited at the bourne of life for death to catch him up.

Juan considered the business of clearing the blockaded doorway without enthusiasm. He had neither pick nor shovel with which to attack the heap of stones, and all he could do was to pull them away one by one. But while he was thoughtfully taking off his coat he heard, coming from outside, the sounds of an agitated scraping. Someone else was already at work.

Kuo became very excited and insisted that Juan should draw his pistol and hold it ready to shoot the intruder, who, she was already sure, was a member of the Japanese Secret Police. Peony, mildly interested, also waited to see who their visitor might be. One of their neighbours, she thought. Juan, though he inclined to Peony's view rather than to Kuo's, judged it prudent to put out the light. They waited in darkness.

The scraping in the stone-heap continued and grew louder. Presently, between the rubble and the top of the door, they could see a dark little ragged patch of sky. A few large stones were pulled away, and into the hole came the round shape of a head. It spoke in a thin creaky voice, and Peony replied. There was a brief conversation, and then the stranger began to dig as furiously as a terrier.

'His name is Wang,' said Peony. 'He is acquainted with my father, and he wishes to come in here so that he may effect an entrance to the pawnshop, which is part of this building.'

After several minutes of impatient digging, during which a great deal of rubble came down into the room, the energetic Wang had made a hole large enough to enter by, and he slid into the house like a sheep on a slope of loosened scree.

He was a cheerful little man with a round smiling face – Juan relighted the lamp and Mr Wang blinked in the feeble glare – and while slapping the dust off his clothes he began, very volubly, to explain to Peony the purpose of his coming.

He also had a dying father. Or, to be more accurate, a father who, after a long illness, had appeared to be dying. In the early days of his illness, when they had not thought it very serious, they had pawned his coffin, which in readiness for his death had lain in the house for several years, in order to buy medicine. But the medicine made the old man worse, and the need for the coffin became suddenly urgent. Deciding therefore that a dying man had no use for clothes, they pawned his whole wardrobe and with the money thus obtained redeemed the coffin. Then, to their surprise, the old man showed signs of recovery. Despite having had no medicine for a week, his appetite returned, and he grew rapidly stronger. He was now quite well again, and eager to be up and about. But all his clothes were in the pawn-shop, and the front of the pawnshop was heavily shuttered; the proprietor had fled. Mr Wang had found it impossible to force an entrance from the street, and would have been in despair had he not fortunately remembered that in the honourable abode of Peony and her father there was a trap that gave entrance to a loft that communicated with the upper floor of the pawnshop. Could he therefore so far presume on their kindness as to crave the use of that felicitous back-door? He did not mean to commit robbery in the pawnshop. He would, if he could find them, take only the garments originally belonging to his father; or alternatively such a mere sufficiency of attire as would enable a very tetchy old gentleman to leave his bed and walk once more abroad.

Peony had no objection to so reasonable a proposal, and Mr Wang pointed triumphantly to the trapdoor in the ceiling of the inner room. It was too high for him to reach without assistance, but Juan was willing to help, and Mr Wang, with many apologies for putting him to so much trouble, climbed nimbly on to his shoulders. The trap was secured with only a couple of nails, and Mr Wang soon forced it open, and disappeared into the loft.

Kuo was now in a great hurry to be gone, but Juan was beginning to worry about Peony. Her father was very near to death, and how could they leave her alone with a dying man, or with a corpse? But Kuo, intent on the pursuit of Hikohoki and national salvation, would certainly refuse to be delayed by any consideration so finical as that.

'It is still very dark,' she said, 'but perhaps we can persuade Wang to show us the way.'

Peony put a shred of cotton wool on her father's lips, a wisp of it in his nostrils. It lay motionless, for there was no breath to shake it. She began to wail, quietly, but with a shuddering intensity of grief. She took off the few pieces of worthless jewellery that she wore, and threw them on the floor. She loosened her hair, and bared her feet.

Juan's attention was distracted by a noise in the loft, and looking up he saw that Mr Wang was trying to force an enormous bundle through the small trapdoor. He had found a piece of red cloth, the size of a sheet, and with this he had made a great unwieldy pack of clothes of all kinds. But push and knead and shove it as he would, he could not get it through the trapdoor without undoing it. He was loth to do this, but at last accepted the necessity and poured into the room an innumerable shower of coats, vests, trousers, tunics, gowns, hats, and robes of ceremony; on top of which he presently descended with a charming but somewhat bashful smile. But discovering, a moment later, that the house had become a house of mourning, his expression immediately altered, and to Peony's small wailing he added his own cries of grief.

Nor was that all his sympathy, for searching the heap of clothes he found a very handsome robe of honour in which, to Peony's great comfort, he arrayed the body of her father. Then, with the air of a kindly man who has done his duty to others and must now think of himself, he began to bundle his loot together and wrap it in the red sheet.

Kuo asked him if he would be their guide out of Chapei, and Wang, having considered the request and put a price on his services, said he would willingly help them, but first he must take the bundle of clothes to his own house, so that his father, who was impatient to get up, might dress himself in the respectable style to which he was accustomed. He also stipulated that Juan should wear Chinese costume, for in the streets, he said, there were marauding bands who would shoot at sight anyone in European attire.

'And what's Peony going to do?' Juan asked.

Peony was persuaded to go with Wang. She put a pearl – an artificial one – in her father's mouth, and a branch of faded willow in his right hand. In his left hand she placed a handkerchief and a fan. Then she made a parcel of her pipe, three little pots of opium, the lamp and the dipper, and having taken the bag of dollars from its hiding-place, said she was ready.

Juan, in the meantime, had taken a long black gown and a little round hat from Wang's convenient bundle. He wore the gown over his own clothes, and felt somewhat tightly circumscribed till he had ripped a seam or two under the arms. The little black hat, the shape of Brunelleschi's dome, he put on with diffidence; but was somewhat reassured when no one laughed.

The gap in the blocked doorway had to be enlarged before Wang could get his bundle through it. Scrambling over the stones, the others followed him.

The bomb had dug a crater in the yard, and the wall of the adjacent lane had collapsed. Everything seemed black as a tomb at first, but presently their eyes grew accustomed to the darkness, and to the east they discerned – or so they thought – a weakening in the sky, a grey hand behind the curtain. A cold thin rain was falling, and a little snarling wind blew angrily through the ruined streets.

They had gone no more than a couple of hundred yards when suddenly, from the obscurity of a doorway, came two men who halted them with a rough challenge to Wang, who led the way. In another second they were hemmed against the wall by eight or nine figures, dimly seen, who came swiftly from the farther darkness.

Wang, in a good confident voice, answered whatever question he had been asked, but before he could finish his sentence, and without any warning, the two leaders struck him fiercely on the head and shoulders with heavy clubs that they carried. Wang stumbled and let fall his burden of clothes. Again and again he was hit. They hit him as he fell, and belaboured him on the ground.

Peony and Kuo were screaming loudly, and Juan was struggling to find, beneath unfamiliar clothes, the pistol that Kuo had given him. Before he could pull it from under his long gown, Kuo had drawn hers and fired it wildly in the air. Her first bullet did no harm to anyone, but narrowly missed killing Juan. He felt its passage like a hot poker thrust at his neck, and was deafened by the report. He ducked so hurriedly that he nearly fell. But Kuo's third or fourth shot must have wounded or badly frightened one of their assailants, who suddenly yelled with anger and threw a knife that hit the wall behind them with a clattering smack.

One of the leaders of the gang stooped for Wang's bundle, but Juan, who had now got his pistol free, fired quickly and hit him in the hand. He shouted with pain and fled into the darkness with a curious stumbling movement.

The others also retreated a little way, and Juan told the two girls to get into the doorway behind him. 'You'd better give me your pistol,' he said to Kuo. 'You can have my swordstick instead, but for heaven's sake don't stick it into me.'

Two of the gangsters – footpads, looters, or whatever they were – had pistols or revolvers. They opened a brisk but very inaccurate fire, to which Juan did not reply. They drew nearer, the whole crew of them, in a ragged half-circle. One of them stepped forward out of the ring, shooting as he came, lunging fiercely with every shot. Juan fired once, and shot him through the chest. He fell shrieking, and jerked about on the road. Juan fired again. His body shivered violently and lay still.

'It's very funny,' said Juan, – 'for God's sake keep your heads down!'

The gangsters had begun a bombardment more dangerous than bullets. Chattering like apes, they were throwing clubs, cobble-stones, and half-bricks. A club struck Juan on the knee, and with a roar of anger he went limping to the attack. The magazines of both his pistols were more than half-full, and aiming low, he opened rapid fire. The gang broke and fled, but still Juan fired furiously into the darkness, aiming wherever he could see a running shadow, and three or four times there came an answering cry of pain.

He returned to the doorway and handed his empty pistols to Kuo. 'Reload them both,' he said, and went to look at Wang.

Wang was dead. There could be no doubt about it, and Juan did not prolong his examination, for the little man's head was unpleasant to look at.

He took one of the pistols that Kuo had recharged, and told her to keep the other, but to put the safety-catch on. 'They've killed Wang,' he said. 'His father will have to stay in bed, I'm afraid. And that fellow's dead too. It's funny, as I was saying a minute ago, that I should come here to fight Japanese, and the only person I succeed in killing is one of your countrymen. But we'd better get a move on.'

'Peony's hurt,' said Kuo.

A stone had struck her on the head. She was faint and dizzy, but able to walk with assistance, and Kuo carried the small parcel of her belongings.

'Do you know if we're going the right way?' asked Juan.

Peony murmured something, and Kuo translated. 'She says we can get to Boundary Road and North Honan Road, where the gate is.'

'How often do they open the gate?'

Juan suddenly put up his pistol and fired at a sinister dark shape ahead of them. It did not move. He went forward cautiously, and saw it was the door of a house, broken away from its upper hinge and lean-ing forward like someone peering down the street.

'I'm taking no chances,' he said truculently. 'From now on I'm shooting first.'

In several places the whole road was filled with shattered masonry, and they had to climb over treacherous mounds of splintered stone and protruding rafters. Peony fell once or twice, and had to be lifted over the worst of the obstacles. But she did not complain and without hesitation directed them where to go.

Slowly it grew lighter. The ragged line of a broken wall was black against a dark grey sky. With a sort of timidity, a shrinking astonishment, the streets revealed their shameful disarray. A coolie lay dead beneath a heavy handcart he had been pulling. A cold vagrant breeze blew, with a run and a skip, a blood-stained felt hat along the pavement.

They came to the railway. There was rust on the disused rails, and one of them, torn loose by a bomb, rose like the neck of a swimming cormorant from the cindery track.

'The North Station can't be far away,' said Juan. 'They've probably got a couple of machine-guns covering the line.'

They halted irresolute, and waited a little while behind a heap of debris. Everything was quiet.

'Blast this bloody war,' said Juan. 'Look here, I'll go across, as slowly as I can, and if nothing happens, you follow. I don't suppose they can shoot straight anyway.'

With a hollow feeling in his bowels and a great temptation in his mind to duck and run, he walked leisurely over the line. Nothing happened. He waited for half a minute, while the pulse moderated in his throat, and waved to Kuo. She and Peony came as slowly, because Peony could not hurry, and reached the other side without an alarm.

On the dangerous side of the Boundary Gate there was a Chinese defence-system of sandbags and barbed wire, with grey-coated soldiers watchful behind it. But here there were too many other people for three dishevelled figures to attract attention. A crowd of two or three hundred Chinese were waiting under the huge steel-sheeted gate that closed the street to them. They squatted on the ground with small bundles beside them, or stood motionless, patiently waiting. There was a man whose only possession was a flute, and near him a fat woman with a bird in a wicker cage.

'We may have to wait a long time before they open the gate,' said Kuo.

'Are you sure it will be opened?'

'Yes, I think so.'

At the other side of the gate, watching the Settlement's frontier, was a company of Shanghai Volunteers. But how to communicate with them was a difficult problem. To push through the crowd and shout for assistance, hoping that a quick-eared sentry would immediately recognize an English voice and English words, was the simplest solution, but a dangerous one. The crowd of refugees, nervous under their passivity and easily moved to hysterical anger, might suddenly turn upon a foreigner. His unexpected appearance among them might start a panic in which anything could happen. And to sit down till the gate was opened, not knowing with certainty that it would be opened, was a prospect hardly more pleasant. They were too near the apex of the battle-line to wait for daylight with equanimity.

'I've got an idea,' said Juan, and fumbling beneath his black gown he found his pocket-book and took from it the three cards that Harris had given him. Then he looked for three half-bricks, which were easily discovered, and tearing strips from his handkerchief tied a card to each brick.

'We'll give Mr Kettledrum of the *Express* the first chance,' he said, and threw the brick over the heads of the crowd, over the gate beyond them, into the safety of the Settlement. A few of the Chinese looked at him in mild astonishment.

Mr Kettledrum failed to attract the attention of the Shanghai Volunteers. A minute later Mr Dearborn, of the *San Francisco Examiner*, described a parabola and landed not far from a disgruntled sentry who was suffering from a slight hangover.

He called the sergeant of the guard and said, with justifiable annoyance, that some illegitimate foundling of the Middle Kingdom was chucking meretricious stones at him over the incarnadined gate.

'Chuck 'em back,' said the sergeant, and was about to return to his early morning cup of tea when Mr Gibbon of the *Times* hit the sandbags behind him with a dull thud.

'Damn their bloody impudence,' said the sergeant, whose surprise was increased when he saw that the brick was bandaged with a strip of handkerchief.

'That's funny,' he said, and discovered Mr Gibbon's card. 'Go and look for the other one.'

The sentry returned with Mr Kettledrum's brick in one hand and Mr Dearborn's in the other.

'There must be three of them out there,' said the sergeant. 'These sons-of-bitches of newspapermen ought to be kept on a lead. Call the bloody guard, Charlie, we've got to open that blasted gate.'

Cautiously the gate was swung open, but half a dozen bayonets prevented the refugees, who with loud cries rose instantly and surged forward, from rushing into the Settlement.

'Damned if I see anyone who looks like a special correspondent, or even a reporter,' said the sergeant.

From the back of the crowd Juan shouted urgently.

'But I can hear them,' said the sergeant. 'Kick these bastards out of the light.'

After a little shoving, a little thumping of slippered feet with their rifle-butts, the guard forced a passage through the clamorous mob, and Juan, shouting again, caught the sergeant's eye.

'Who the hell are you?' he demanded.

'What the hell does that matter?' shouted Juan. 'Get this stinking coolie out of my way.'

'He's English all right,' said one of the guard.

'Take hold of these two girls and get 'em inside,' said Juan. 'I'll explain everything later.'

After a certain amount of scuffling the gate was shut again, and the mob howled dismally on the other side.

'Now,' said the sergeant, 'are you Dearborn, Gibbon, or Kettle-drum? What have you been doing, and who are these girls?'

Juan took off his long black gown and little black hat, and felt more comfortable. 'Can I speak to you privately?' he asked.

Side by side, talking earnestly – the sergeant obviously surprised and even showing signs of admiration – they walked up and down beside the rampart of sandbags. Then Juan shook hands with the sergeant, and returned to Peony and Kuo.

'Come along,' he said, 'we'll find rickshaws somewhere or other. Good-bye, sergeant, and thanks very much.'

'Now damn my eyes,' said the sergeant, 'he may be crazy, but he's certainly got guts.'

'What's he been doing?' asked the sentry with the hangover.

'There are three of them,' said the sergeant, 'all newspaper cor-respondents. They've only been in Shanghai for a week, and they've all adopted Chinese orphan girls. But two of the girls – the two we saw – had to go into Chapei to look for their dying mother, and sent word that they couldn't get out again. So Dearborn, Kettledrum, and

Gibbon threw dice to see who should go and rescue them, and this fellow lost. Anyway, that's the tale he told me, and he didn't look a liar, did he?'

12

JUAN had decided to return to the New Celestial, for Min Cho-fu's flat seemed overcrowded, though this was due rather to the emotional atmosphere than to the number of people there.

Peony had collapsed just before they arrived. Whether opium was the trouble, or delayed concussion, Juan did not know, but he suspected the latter and insisted that Miss Min should take her in and put her to bed. Miss Min was most unwilling to do this, and her brother did not help matters by succumbing to an emotion so extreme and complex that he had to shut himself in the bathroom, where he was very sick. But Juan carried his point by opportunely remembering that Peony was the only person who could find Hikohoki.

'He left the hotel on Monday,' he said, 'and we don't know where he went. But he told Peony to come and see him if she wanted a job, and presumably he gave her an address. So if you're going to look for him, your easiest way is to nurse Peony, and when she gets better she may tell you where he lives.'

Kuo instantly perceived the force of this argument, and Peony was put to bed.

'It's funny,' said Juan with a yawn. 'I only missed him by a few minutes. After leaving that wretched monastery, I mean. I went back to the hotel, and they told me that Hikohoki had just gone. If I hadn't got lost in the Chinese City I'd have seen him, and we might have saved ourselves a lot of bother.'

'You got lost in the Chinese City, and because of that you failed to see Hikohoki?'

'Yes. Didn't I tell you?'

'You got lost!' Kuo repeated. 'When you knew that every minute was valuable, you got lost! Oh, how stupid of you!'

'My dear girl,' said Juan, 'I didn't get lost on purpose, nor had I any reason to suppose that time was particularly valuable that morning. To lose one's way is something that may happen to anyone.'

'Not to a grown man,' said Kuo. 'A grown man shouldn't lose himself in Shanghai. It is too stupid, too paltry.'

Juan, who had anticipated praise and some display of affection from Kuo, in return for what he considered his creditable behaviour in Chapei, was very much taken aback by this unexpected rebuke. He saw no justice in it, and he felt very much inclined to answer hotly and at great length. But he controlled this foolish impulse, and merely said, 'You must be tired, darling, you'd better get some sleep. I'll go back to the New Celestial, I think.'

There were, he thought, too many conflicting emotions in Min's flat for him to find much comfort there. But in his over-heated room in the hotel he slept undisturbed till five o'clock; and when he woke he found on his table a letter that his room-boy must have brought in without waking him. It was from Mrs Fannay-Brown to remind him of his promise to drink some sherry with them that evening.

This suited his mood to perfection, for though he did not nurse any resentment against Kuo for her failure to appreciate his activities in Chapei, he nevertheless felt that he deserved some celebration of them. And to return to Min's house would be to invite disappointment, for Kuo Kuo would be thinking of Hikohoki, and the plan, and China's salvation; Min would be balancing like a tearful acrobat between love of Peony and fear of his sister; and Miss Min – a pretty piece if one could get her away from her environment – would be simmering like a retort full of hydrochloric acid and iron filings. No, a sherry party was the better place, for though Mrs Fannay-Brown might prove to be a tedious hostess, the law of averages would surely bless her with one amusing guest.

The Fannay-Browns lived not very far from Min Cho-fu, but on the other side of Bubbling Well Road, and in altogether superior style. A white-gowned butler showed Juan into a many-coloured L-shaped room where some eight or ten people were talking in loud, high-pitched voices.

Fannay-Brown shook him warmly by the hand, and led him towards Mrs Fannay-Brown.

She was a tallish, good-looking, untidily dressed woman, getting on for fifty, with protruding brown eyes and a long narrow chin. Her hair was brightly and artificially golden, and she wore a loosely flowing mauve dress that made a violent discord with every other colour in the room. Round her neck, and reaching below her waist, hung a rope of enormous pebbles of dull jade that rattled whenever she moved. At the moment of Juan's entry she was lighting a cigarette from the stub of another, and throwing away the wrong one, she advanced to meet him, the rope of jade swinging like an unskilfully handled lasso.

'How nice of you to come!' she exclaimed. 'I haven't seen a new face for donkey's years. Dullest place on earth, Shanghai, and what a time of year to arrive! Just like Liverpool. Lord Street on a cold rainy day. Nastiest climate on earth except Shanghai. Dicky always wanted to ride at Aintree, but he's not nearly good enough, of course. Still, he's better than most men, and he knows a pony. You ought to buy Chang. You're going to ride him, aren't you? But come and meet some of these people. Ronny, Joyce, Harriet, everybody: this is Mr Motley, who's just arrived from Brisbane. I always hope I'll die on a ship, so much less trouble. Sorry we haven't any other Canadians to meet you, ought to have thought of that before. – Edward, Alice, Ben: this is Mr Motley, just arrived from Canada. He's going to ride Chang on Sunday. Edward's a lawyer, he'll get you out of any scrape, nastier the better. Now sit down everybody – Dicky, get Mr Motley a drink and give me another cigarette, will you? – because Ronny wants to go on with his story, don't you Ronny?'

Ronny was a young man with heavy black hair, a sallow complexion, very dark eyes, a square chin, and a pale grey suit. He appeared to have been ruffled by the interruption of his story, and resumed it in a rather loud and peremptory manner. Juan, already surprised at being taken for a Canadian who had come to Shanghai from Brisbane – but he realized that ladies' geography was sometimes arbitrary – was still more astonished when he discovered that Ronny's anecdote was a highly ornamented account of his own escape from Chapei: which had become the rescue of three sing-song girls who were an American journalist's mistresses.

'I heard it from Robertson, who was down at Honan Road this morning, and got it from the sergeant who let them in,' said Ronny.

'Charming boy,' whispered Mrs Fannay-Brown. 'Ronny, I mean. Thinks he's artistic, but isn't really. He takes photographs of Shanghai by night, but wants to do naked girls. Not art, just repression, but he doesn't know it. Scotch, of course. Lots of them inhibited, that's why they work so hard.'

'The American was about the size of Carnera, and arrived with one of the girls over his shoulder, and kicking the other two in front of him,' said Ronny. 'All of them were dead-beat, according to Robertson, but simply devoted to the American, who'd used them to get some exclusive information.'

'When did this happen?' asked the trimly dressed, grey-haired, desiccated man who had been introduced as a lawyer.

'This morning,' said Ronny.

'I don't believe a word of it.'

'I knew he wouldn't,' whispered Mrs Fannay-Brown. 'Dear Edward. One of my oldest friends, but he's got a passion for perjury. Just like a lawyer. They hear so many lies, they don't know the truth when they see it.'

Ronny maintained that his story was literally true, and the grey-haired man began to summarize the law of evidence.

'Not worth listening to,' said Mrs Fannay-Brown, and from a table at her side took a small flower-painted black vase. 'K'ang-hsi,' she said. 'Lovely piece. Take any interest in porcelain? Ought to, when you're in China. Let you have this cheap. Far too much stuff in the house, don't know what to do with it all. Three hundred dollars, if you like it. Don't want to press you, but it's a bargain if you want it. Pictures, too. Lots of pictures. Good heavens, is Edward still talking?'

With the manner of one who puts an unanswerable point, the grey-haired man declared, 'The whole story is fantastic. I can believe, though not readily, in the devotion despite ill-treatment of one woman to a man. But the devotion of three women I cannot and will not credit.'

Ronny looked sulky, and helped himself to another drink. A brown-faced handsome girl, who had been introduced as Harriet, said cheerfully, 'I wish I could meet a man who'd the ability to make three good girls happy.'

'Concurrently or successively?' asked Mr Fannay-Brown with an ingratiating flash of his artificial teeth.

'Dicky's getting fresh,' exclaimed Mrs Fannay-Brown. 'Always have been ambitious, haven't you? But he's too good-natured, really. Anyway, sauce for the gander's sauce for the goose. Equal rights nowadays. Equal rights have given women equal opportunities.'

'Do you believe that, Mr Motley?' asked the handsome girl. She had a mole like a beauty-spot at the corner of her right eye, and well-cut humorous lips, as red as rowan-berries against the brown of her cheeks.

'Indeed I don't,' said Juan.

'Nonsense,' said Mrs Fannay-Brown decisively. 'Don't want to shock you, I don't want to shock anybody – you never know with a stranger, especially colonials – but if civilization has done anything at all, it's made the world safe for adultery.'

'Only for a man,' said Juan. 'Infidelity's a natural condition for a man, but for a woman it's artistically unsound.'

'The fellow thinks he's being funny,' muttered Ronny.

'Not so loud, dear,' said Mrs Fannay-Brown.

'Surely propriety is an aesthetic term,' said Juan, looking at the brown-faced handsome girl to whom he felt greatly drawn, 'and male polygamy is like surrounding a teapot with six tea-cups, which is a natural and desirable arrangement. But female promiscuity is like a tea-cup with six teapots, which is both absurd and unsuitable.'

'A very happy illustration,' said the grey-haired man.

'Naughty, very naughty indeed,' said Mrs Fannay-Brown. 'Very broad-minded for a colonial.'

'It isn't funny,' said Ronny.

'Hush, dear!'

Juan sat down beside the brown-faced girl, whose eyes were sea-gull grey and whose hair grew pleasantly to a widow's peak.

'You're being a success,' she said. 'Beatrice likes being contradicted. She talks so much herself that the sound of anyone else's voice is a positive thrill to her.'

'What are your favourite sensations?'

'Do you think I'm going to tell you that on one sherry?'

'Let me get you another.'

Like a sunflower over a garden wall, the bright gold hair of Mrs Fannay-Brown impended upon them.

'Dear Harriet,' she said. 'How well you're looking. Terribly pale and drawn the last time I saw you, but you're simply à *peindre* to-night. A little plumper, too, aren't you? As soon as I saw you I said to myself, "Something's happened to Harriet. She's having an affair!" – One of

139

these modern girls, Mr Motley. They're always having affairs, one after another, can't enjoy them properly, but still they go on. – Tell me, was I right?'

'No,' said Harriet. 'I've been taking calcium, that's all.'

'Very disappointing. I hoped you were going to tell me all about it. – Never take medicine myself. Always healthy. Sound as a bell, though I'm grey as a skate if I didn't dye it. – Are you interested in modern painting, Mr Motley? I'll show you some of our pictures, if you are.'

She led him towards a strange, pale, hybrid sort of painting. 'Nice, isn't it? Done by one of the younger Chinese artists. Such an unhappy boy, you can see it, can't you. And terribly self-conscious. I only bought it to please him, let you have it very cheap if you care for it. He's impotent, poor thing.'

Juan looked at the pale grey nude. A very uncomfortable nude, neither Chinese in appearance nor wholly European, but rather like a report on nudity by a Committee of the League of Nations. 'I don't like the way her thighs have collapsed,' he said.

'So they have, never thought of it before. Well, you don't want that, of course, though it would do for a present to someone. But it's too depressing to keep if you look at it that way.'

There were numerous pictures in the room, of flowers, and ponies, and bathing parties, and objects or events not very easy to recognize. Some were modern, some conventional, and some had fallen between two schools. There was also an abundance of pots, bowls, statuettes, rams' heads, masks, and bells, in bronze, brass, ivory, porcelain, and terracotta; together with a great disarray of books and expensively illustrated magazines and geometrically patterned carpets. If Mrs Fannay Brown intended to show him all her treasures, he must husband his critical resources, thought Juan. But her attention was not wholly set on art. She kept one eye on her guests, and suddenly leaving Juan before a good painstaking drawing of a polo pony, she hurried away to greet a new arrival.

Then she returned and loudly exclaimed, 'Tiresome man, but lots of money. Sold him a piece of *famille verte* the other day. You mustn't mind Ronny. He's a nice boy, devoted to me, but quite silly. That's probably the reason.'

'I haven't been rude to him, have I?' asked Juan.

'Of course you haven't. The other way about. But he's furiously jealous, can't bear to see me with anybody else, though heaven knows I'm not that sort of a woman. Too old for it even if I were.'

'Perhaps I'd better go away. I'll go and talk to Harriet, shall I?'

Mrs Fannay-Brown laid a hand on his sleeve. 'Don't be silly. There's lots of things I want to show you, and it's good for Ronny to be neglected. Nothing like neglect for a silly young man. Teach him to think. Come and look at this ram's head.'

Before they could leave the drawing of the polo pony, however, a loud genial voice in Juan's ear exclaimed, 'A lovely pony that. Beautiful manners, and fast as a flash. And she knew as much about the game as I do. More, in fact. Yes, more, poor old girl. But she crossed her legs one day, and came a fearful purler. Had to be shot, poor old Molly.'

'Poor old Molly,' repeated Mrs Fannay-Brown. 'Always trust Dicky about a pony. Best judge in Shanghai, aren't you, Dicky? Go and get Mr Motley a drink.'

'I've just brought him this. Now don't forget about Sunday, Motley. The Japs have been very decent, and definitely agreed to an armistice. So that's all right. And you're riding a pony called Chang. A China pony, of course, but better-looking than most of them, and a good deal faster. He knows the ground, too, and he'll go all day if you want him to. I don't know how long you're staying in Shanghai, but if you're thinking of buying a pony, you couldn't do much better than Chang. But it's too early to talk about that, of course. Come and ride him first, and see what you think of him.'

'Never thinks of anything but horses,' said Mrs Fannay-Brown as her husband turned away. 'Ought to bore me by rights, but he doesn't. Marvellous thing, love – call it love if you like, but it simply becomes a habit, doesn't it? Still, there you are. When he was ill last year I read Jorrocks to him for a month. Can't go farther than that, can you?'

'Do you ride too?'

'Good heavens, yes. Ridden since I was a child. Too old now, though. I get left in the lurch. Pots and vases more in my line now. But everything I see, get tired of it, and sell at half-price. Take that *sang-de-bœuf* jug if you don't believe me. Six hundred dollars, and then ask a dealer what he thinks of it. He'll give you eight-fifty on the spot. Not if you don't want it, of course. Harriet's a nice girl, isn't she?'

'Yes, I like her very much.'

'Normal, thank God. You never know nowadays. Look at that girl beside her. Pretty as paint and not a bit of use to anyone. I suggested psycho-analysis to her once, but she wouldn't hear of it, so I suppose the trouble's deep-seated.'

'She looks perfectly healthy.'

'Makes it all the worse for her, doesn't it?' said Mrs Fannay-Brown in a voice that showed she was losing interest in the subject. She looked round, in a rather puzzled way, at the other guests. 'Now I wonder where Ronny is? I won't be surprised if he's taken a pique and gone home. Just the sort of thing he'd do. He wants to take photographs of naked girls, but he hasn't the nerve to ask them, so he dances attendance on an old woman like me because I sympathize with him. Lots of trouble myself, when I was young. Silly, isn't it? He's got three different cameras, just in case, but he'll never use them.'

Juan caught Harriet's eye, smiled, and was gratified by her indulgent smile.

'But you must come and see my Näfl,' said Mrs Fannay-Brown excitedly. 'Most interesting thing I've got. Some people like it, others hate it, but no one's ever indifferent. You'll have to come to my own sitting-room.'

'To see your . . .?'

'My Näfl. Austrian, of course. I got it in Vienna. Don't you know his work?'

'Oh, yes, of course. No, I'm afraid I don't. It's well known, is it? I mean he is, is he?'

'Not so well as he's going to be,' said Mrs Fannay-Brown, and with dangerous leapings of her rope of jade, led the way.

Her sitting-room was an extravagant pink flaccidity of cushions and drapery on pale gold furniture, at which her mauve dress shouted defiance. 'We're right away from the rest of the house here,' she said. 'Just like a hermitage, or a monk's cell. You've got to have privacy, haven't you? Horrible thing to be married and live in a small house. All very well to sleep with a man, especially when you're young, but you don't want to sit about with him all day.'

'Privacy . . .' began Juan.

'You're going to say it's a luxury. Of course it is, the poor can't afford it, but the poor don't need it. They've lots of work and the King-

dom of Heaven. Tired out by the one, believe in the other, shilling
on a horse, and Saturday night at the pictures. Not nearly so bad as it
used to be.'

'I was going to say that privacy's like a diving-board: you shouldn't
stay on it too long.'

'You're perfectly right. Plunge right into everything, that's always
what I've done. The deeper you go, the quicker you come up. There's
nothing in life except what you bring to it, and if you spend all you
have . . .'

'You must live on charity.'

'Now you're just being obstructionary. A clever remark, but it
doesn't mean anything. You're trying to put me off and keep me talking because you don't want to buy my Näfl. I knew you wouldn't,
nobody ever does. But take a look at it, and tell me what you think of
it. *Jeune Femme Assise*, it's called.'

It stood on an easel beside an escritoire of tulip-wood with ormolu
mountings. It offered, apart from its strictly aesthetic qualities, an
unusual view of a young woman. The artist had apparently executed
it underneath a cane-bottomed chair on which his model was sitting.
Such features as were visible to him in that position he had painted
with academical fidelity, and the others, such as eyes, ears, and breasts,
he had collected, without reference to their anatomical position, in
the upper left hand corner of the picture.

'Yes,' said Juan reflectively, 'I think I see what he means.'

Mrs Fannay-Brown narrowed her eyes and stared hard at the
picture. 'Well, it's more than I do,' she said. 'All I know is that it's
good. Balance, colour, design, drawing, form: everything's good,
but hanged if I see any meaning to it. You're not a critic, you're a
thought-reader.'

'I'm perfectly certain that you're not.'

'Now what do you mean by that?'

'At the moment I think there's someone in that other room.'

'In there? Nonsense, that's my bedroom.'

'A servant, perhaps.'

Mrs Fannay-Brown opened the door into a rose-red bedroom,
and discovered against that glowing hinterland a pale and agitated
young man.

'Now really!' she exclaimed. 'This is too much, this is definitely going too far. Heaven knows I'm broad-minded, and I've listened to your repressions time and again, and told you what to do about them. But this is unbearable, quite unbearable, Ronny. My privacy, my feelings, my bedroom – all outraged, grossly outraged, and just when Mr Motley had refused to buy my Näfl but was certainly going to buy a bit of *famille rose* or peach-blow or something of the kind. I don't know what to say!'

'I wanted to brush my hair,' muttered Ronny.

'There's a hair-brush in the cloakroom downstairs, as you know perfectly well.'

'I don't like that one.'

'I dare say you don't, it's a disgusting brush and ought to have been thrown away years ago, but you could have put up with it for once. This silly behaviour, this childish jealousy, I shall never forgive. Now go in again and sit down and be quiet.'

Ronny stood sulky and stubborn, and Mrs Fanny-Brown indignantly closed the door against him. Then, largely and theatrically, she exclaimed, 'Pique! Pure pique, I knew it. All comes of brooding over his photography. I do a lot of brooding myself, but not about that kind of thing. Isn't that a lovely piece? Hawthorn ginger-jar, best thing I've got, worth a mint of money. You couldn't possibly afford it, and I'm not going to sell it anyway. But here's a nice little piece, paper-weight or something of the sort, tea-dust glaze. Pretty, isn't it? Let you have that for thirty dollars, simply giving it away. Here, put it in your pocket.'

Juan, incapable of further resistance, meekly gave her three ten-dollar notes, which Mrs Fannay-Brown threw carelessly on to a table. Then she said, 'Now run along and leave me to deal with Ronny. I'm going to talk to him like a Dutch uncle, Dutch aunty, something of the sort. Lots of unpleasant relations in the world, aren't there? So glad to have seen you, you must come again. I've plenty of things to show you, Ming, Sung, pictures, anything you like. Oh, wait a minute. How did you guess that Ronny was in my bedroom?'

'He breathes rather loudly.'

'So he does, poor boy. So used to it I never noticed. Adenoids, of course. Common in Scotland. That's the worst of Edinburgh. East winds, draughts, cold houses, no comfort, kilts, all that kind of thing.

Tonsils and adenoids, can't escape them. Poor fellow, perhaps it isn't his fault after all. Well, good-bye, do come back.'

Juan made an inconspicuous return to the L-shaped room – its shape facilitated an unseen entrance – and was presently talking to the brown-faced Harriet.

'So you've escaped?' she asked.

'I've been dismissed. I stopped to see if you would come with me.'

'I don't know. Have you bought anything from Beatrice?'

'A paper-weight.'

'You've got off lightly.'

'I'm generally lucky.'

'Do you think that's a recommendation?'

'No, just boasting.'

'Where's Beatrice now?'

'Rebuking Ronny, who turns out to be a cousin of the de Trops. But I must speak to Fannay-Brown before we go. I shan't be a minute.'

Juan wanted to know where the paper-chasers were to meet, and how he could get there. Fannay-Brown, as cordial as ever, immediately offered to pick him up at the Club and drive him out.

'No trouble at all,' he said. 'Only too glad you're coming. And I can promise you a thoroughly good ride on Chang. A grand-going pony, I wish I was riding him myself. If you're not in the first four home, I'll eat my boots and spurs. On Sunday morning, then, at eleven o'clock.'

An hour later, after drinking a Martini or two in the lounge of the New Celestial Hotel, Harriet consented to dine with Juan.

'That's splendid,' he said, 'but don't let me talk too much. I've been talking rather a lot already, haven't I? I'm still rather excited, and sometimes, in such a mood, I'm inclined to be a trifle verbose.'

'What are you excited about? Beatrice's bargains?'

'No, I've recovered from that. But I shot a man last night. I was in Chapei, and we were attacked by gangsters. I shot one of them in the chest, and wounded a couple of others.'

'And you have blood on your conscience?'

'I don't think so, but I've got this curious feeling of excitement.'

'Oh dear. Do you want to get drunk?'

'No, not a bit.'

'Well, take your mind off homicide, it never did anyone any good to think about it. After all, there have been thousands of people killed in the last few days; one or two more can't matter very much. What were you doing in Chapei?'

'It's too long a story.'

'I can listen.'

'Not profitably. How do you like Shanghai?'

'I don't.'

'I'll give you another chance: why are the Chinese so different from us?'

'That's easy. They've never been taught that God made them in His own image.'

'So they've avoided our particular kind of seriousness?'

'Yes; they've very little sense of tragedy – some of the younger ones have, but it's not native to China – because they don't feel our ingrown belief in the special importance of Man. Their world isn't as anthropocentric as ours.'

'That sounds very authoritative.'

'It's my business to say things that sound authoritative.'

Juan looked at her suspiciously.

'So you're not one of my devoted readers?' asked Harriet.

'God save us, are you an author?'

'Yes. Don't you like them?'

'I knew a girl once, who was writing a novel, and she took notes of every word I said to her and every movement I made.'

'We've got to live, you know. And it's a hard life for the modern hack. We work all over the world nowadays, not in Grub Street. I was in Harbin a week ago, and only got out by the skin of my teeth.'

Harriet's profession was the purveying of vicarious adventure to people whose circumstances or temperament made it impossible for them to enjoy any personal experience of antres vast or anthropophagi. She had a talent for writing, which had grown with practice; a taste for reckless experiment and distant scenery, which time was diminishing; and a very reasonable contract with a fairly good publisher. At twenty-eight she had walked across the Congo, the Kalahari Desert, and part of Cambodia; she had been the mistress of a Mexican general, a Rumanian poet, and a very good-looking American marine; and she had written several books in which she described – often quite truthfully – the peculiarities of the countries she had visited and the persons with whom she had associated. In spite of the exacting demands on her mind and body that a life so arduous had made, her constitution was unimpaired, and her mental attitude was healthy, humorous, and fresh. She was about to visit Bias Bay in company with a former pirate who had become a convert to the Christian faith, and amassed a respectable fortune; a project which everyone assured her was extremely rash.

'I fling my soul and body down for literature to plough them under,' she said, 'and every year I come up as green as ever.'

'But you can't enjoy things very much, when you're doing them deliberately to fill another chapter.'

'Oh yes, you can. You cut and dry your plans, but enjoyment comes of its own accord.'

Juan was disposed to see in this last statement an approximate truth. His own enjoyment had grown so imperceptibly, yet with such steady progression, that to have accounted for its nourishment in terms of food and wine and Harriet would have been possible only to the most inhuman intelligence. That Harriet was chiefly responsible for its production he readily admitted. But did Harriet behave so agreeably to everyone she met? Perish the thought. Their mutual benevolence was unique; between Harriet and anyone else there might have arisen a kindness of some sort, but a kindness that was subtly different and certainly inferior to this that now filled him with such pleasure. Harriet was a gallant creature. Lovely, bedworthy, and full of character. He was very fond of her, and detected a responsive warmth. Hence, of course, enjoyment. A bio-chemical reaction. But was it worth the trouble to find a formula for it? It was easier, and perhaps more amply true, to say that it came of its own accord. Putting the cart before the horse, he then decided that enjoyment was the most superlative kind of eye-opener, for now he could see that Harriet had such a catalogue of beauty as had seldom been entrusted to five and a half feet of female being. Her hands were slim and finely shaped; good. Her hair was brown and bright as a hazel-nut; excellent. Her eyes were candid and sea-gull grey, her mouth wide and well-shaped, her breasts as round and seeming-firm as demi-oranges; the world was God's great success. And who had ever seen a more agreeable waist, an ankle more trimly turned, a neater nose? The world went singing through galactic space.

'Let's go and dance,' he said.

There was, on the topmost floor of the New Celestial, a little ball-room where people, on a space inadequate for dancing, could never-theless circulate in a close embrace for which music provided the conventional alias. The orchestra consisted of a piano, two steel guitars, and a serpentine, green-gowned, husky-throated lady from the Philip-pine Islands.

The floor was even more crowded than usual, for all but two or three of Shanghai's innumerable night-clubs had been closed because of the war. – Through one of the windows the sky shone red as blood, and into the scarlet firmament leapt windy tongues of flame and foun-tains of bright sparks. All afternoon Chapei had been shelled and bombed, and now the squalid streets were burning like a palace. – There were forty two-backed dancers, swimming up the current of the steel guitars like elvers in a moonlit ditch, with pliant limbs and mutual come-and-go, who performed their ritual exercise in honour of new-born Aphrodite. The green-gowned lady from the Philippine Islands leaned over the piano, lavishly displaying her teeth and her tongue, the gulf of her bosom and the whites of her eyes, and sang more sweetly than honey, as sweet as saccharine:

> '*Kiss by kiss, you're making me care,*
> *Kiss by kiss, I'm falling in love with you!*'

Like seaweed in this compulsive tide, the double spines of the dancers swayed, their heads precariously balancing on toppling piles of vertebrae, their thighs in restless apposition.

> '*Wonderful child, I'm nearly wild,*
> *Love was a stranger to me.*'

sang the priestess of Aphrodite; an Aphrodite not born in the foam, in the fair-haired waves of the sea, in the brine and the desolate beauty of the ocean, but in the heavy black fields of America's Congo, to drowse an exile and to comfort slaves.

'This,' said Juan, having danced for ten minutes or more, 'is not what I want. I'm no snob, and I am not repelled by other people's idea of pleasure. But, at the moment, this is not my cup of tea.'

'Nor mine,' said Harriet.

They left the hotel and walked on the riverside of the Bund. The bridge that crossed the Soochow Creek was heavily guarded, but in the Creek there were still sampans tied side by side, and families living in them by the heat of a diminutive fire. The black water was striped with the reflection of flames from the red sky over Chapei, and in the night air was the bitter smell of burning.

Juan and Harriet turned and walked the other way. The Bund was almost deserted, but here and there, on a high sentry-box, stood a Sikh policeman muffled in his greatcoat. They could faintly hear the roar and crackle of the burning streets.

'I've no sentimental objections to war,' said Harriet. 'I only resent its dullness.'

'The poor alternative of kill or be killed?'

'The worse alternative of right or wrong; which is like walking with a patch on one eye.'

'War's degenerated,' said Juan. 'It used to be a craft, but now it's only a factory-product.'

'Yes; but don't let's get serious about the world. It's crazy, but I like it.'

'So do I. But I thought you hankered after melancholy and I was doing my best to help you. Where do you live?'

'In a very small furnished flat off Nanking Road.'

'Can we go there?'

'I suppose so. But . . .'

'The only choice for a sensible mind is to be in love or to laugh at things. Heads is Venus, and tails Voltaire, if you like to put it so. And I prefer Cyprian obverse, because too much laughter is rather sterilizing. Also I like the shape of your finger-nails, the sound of your voice, and the thirty-eight other parts of your whole perfection. So I think we ought to go to your flat.'

An amah, with a face like a shrivelled fruit, opened the door and let them into a small and not very comfortable apartment. Juan helped Harriet to take off her coat.

'You haven't even the excuse that you admire my books,' she said.

'Doesn't a female author like to be loved for herself alone?'

'Yes, terribly. But I'd like you to read my books as well.'

'I shall. All of them. But not to-night.'

'I'm not really used to this sort of thing. I mean so suddenly. I've generally had weeks and weeks to make up my mind, as well as the most serious attentions.'

'But you're only going to be here for a few days longer. And there's a war.'

'And you won't think that this is how I always behave?'

'No.'

'You said this afternoon that a woman should be chaste.'

'Rules of conduct only apply to people who have no standards of taste.'

'But what are your standards?'

'I love the loveliest when I see it.'

An hour or so later Juan said, 'It's just occurred to me that I only know your Christian name. So how am I going to buy your books?'

'One of them has a picture of me as a frontispiece.'

'I could find them more easily if you told me your name.'

'You'll have to get someone to introduce us,' said Harriet sleepily.

In the morning they were wakened by the sound of guns, and looked at each other in mild surprise.

'Your necklace goes well with the morning light,' said Juan idly.

'It was terribly dear, but it's very good jade. I got it in a shop called the Dernier Cri Antique Store, in Nanking Road.'

'They make their Ming on the premises?'

'They've plenty of rubbish, of course, but there are lots of good things too. You should ask for the proprietor if you go there. He's a little Japanese called Hikohoki.'

13

BEFORE returning to Min Cho-fu's, Juan went to the Dernier Cri Antique Store, and found it shuttered and tenantless. On several occasions the Chinese students had led angry processions down Nanking Road, and a good many of the Japanese shops there were similarly closed and deserted. It was very disappointing; but nevertheless he thought that Kuo would be glad to know where Hikohoki did business, or some part of his business.

Neither he nor his news, however, were received with any warmth. Peony had recovered consciousness soon after he left, and Kuo had not only discovered for herself the address in Nanking Road, but having gone there had found the shop abandoned. She was, therefore, quite unimpressed by his report, since it was both stale and profitless.

There was a faint smell of opium in the house. Peony was still there, and seemed likely to stay: for Miss Min, having been forced unwillingly to receive her, was now completely captivated by Peony's conversation and inexhaustible store of gossip, and had spent most of the previous day in her company. She had also determined to cure Peony of her addiction to opium, by gradually reducing her number of pipes. There was every prospect, then, that Peony would be well looked-after for several months to come.

Kuo was now the unhappiest member of the household. Indeed the only unhappy one, for Min, though not permitted to be alone with Peony, was allowed to go in and look at her some two or three times a day. But Kuo had nothing to distract her from thoughts of failure.

She could, of course, distribute the blame for failure. Min was most obviously culpable. Juan had not been faultless, and the office-bearers of the Conquering Youth of China had grievously disappointed her. Their organization, if it ever existed, had melted away, and they themselves had vanished. Some, it seemed, had gone into hiding, being romantically convinced that there was a price on their heads; others had joined rival societies; and two of them, immersed in debate about the meaning of the difficult word *chinch'ing*, had entirely forgotten the present crisis.

But for the first mistake, the eldest of the brood of errors, Kuo could blame only herself. It was she who had postponed the great attack that was to have been the vanguard of resurgent China. She had indeed postponed it for good reasons; because Lo Yu's plan promised something better – a policy of salvation instead of a call to arms – and because she had inopportunely remembered that Confucius had once clearly said that he would never entrust military command to a man who would attack a tiger unarmed, or cross a river without a boat, or sacrifice his life without regret. Confucius was right, of course; and she was still quite certain that Lo Yu's plan was what China really needed. But the plan was lost, and the Conquering Youth had melted like butter in the sun.

Perhaps she would have done better and done more had she led her thousand young patriots – but would they have followed her? – to an exemplary death on the guns of the invader. She had, at one time, seen quite clearly the necessity of sacrifice. It had then appeared a necessity far transcending the indispensability of a policy. And then she had hesitated, vacillated, partly because of something Confucius had said; though Confucius also said that the wise man does not vacillate, the man of natural goodness does not fret.

The deduction was obvious. She was neither wise nor naturally good, and therefore in desiring to save China she was presumptuous, since neither by sagacity nor by virtue was she fitted for so great a task. But how, loving China, could she be idle and do nothing to help it in its distress? How at a time like this could even the Superior Person, as Confucius declared, be calm and serene? Kuo found it quite impossible; and Juan suffered.

He, having been unfaithful, was eager to be kind; but Kuo would not let him. He would have liked to do something for her; but Kuo had no time for attainable desires. He was willing to sit and talk about anything in particular or everything in general; but Kuo's mind was busy with its own unceasing and profitless debate. They spoke a little about the progress of the war, and Kuo said there was great activity in Nanking. But even such a topic as that could not make her forget her own troubles. She asked Juan to stay to lunch, but without warmth in her invitation, and the meal was a poor scanty affair such as women eat alone. So Juan, having done his best, said good-bye and went to the Club.

He found Flanders there, as he had hoped; who had the grace to look ashamed. Juan had not seen him since they went, singing *Sleep, Pretty Wantons*, to Min Cho-fu's flat, and Flanders like a coward left him to face alone the anger of Kuo and Miss Min. But now, to cover his embarrassment, Flanders put on a manner of great heartiness and welcomed Juan somewhat noisily.

'God's my life and lord!' he exclaimed. 'I'm glad to see you! I've been looking for you these three days, and not a finger to be seen. I thought you'd been murdered or trepanned or gone home in the ship that sailed the other day. – She went down the river with shells dropping in her wake like boys pelting an otter. – Now what will you drink? There's no security in the world. None at all. What'll you drink, Motley?'

Anything, said Juan, that would take the taste of smoke out of his mouth. The wind had shifted, and Shanghai was covered with a dark brown roof blown thickly from the smouldering streets of Chapei.

'There's the stink of hell in the air,' said Flanders. 'The odour of greasy corruption. I was all but killed myself on Tuesday, and that would have made matters worse. I'd have basted the whole city, the Bund would have gone up in flames if my fat had run, and all the hungry mouths in the Orient, the whole forty million, would have gathered like paupers round a roast ox to suck the mere steam of it. But I escaped, thank God. I was standing near the Creek, watching the seaplanes going like seagulls in and out of the smoke, and dropping their excrement in the town. There were bullets going *whisss* here, and *whisss* there, and *ping* on the houses; and anti-aircraft shells bursting like a drum full of ruptured bagpipers. But I paid no attention to them. Not a scrap. And then I moved a little, and heard a groaning about my ankles. So I looked down and saw I was standing on an old Chinese woman about eighty years of age, with a wem on her right cheek. And that wasn't all. She had the whole family with her, her son and two grandsons, a grand-daughter suckling her six-weeks child, three or four tidy girls, a couple of gaping hobbledehoys, and eight or ten children playing marbles or piddling in the dark of my penumbra. She had the whole tribe, twenty-eight or thirty of them, taking shelter under the overhang of my belly. They were using me like a bridge or the side of a hill. If I'd stayed another hour, they'd have lighted a fire, and coupled and brought forth, and buried their dead in the shadow of my paunch. When I moved a step or two they all looked up as though the roof had come off. They blanched in the sun, and gibbered, and took to their heels, and ran. So I thought of my own danger, and came away too.'

'And I expect you disappeared quicker than they did.'

'Now what's at the back of that?'

'You're very good at disappearing. You vanished from Min Cho-fu's the other night like a cat going over Niagara.'

'And a good thing for you I did,' said Flanders. 'I can explain that. It was for your sake I went. For no other reason in the world.'

'You ran away. You said you could persuade Kuo to do anything you wanted, but when you saw the temper she was in, you cleared out and left me.'

'You're wrong, Motley. By God, you're wrong. I went because of a borborygmus, a great rumbling in the belly.'

'That wouldn't have worried me.'

'It would have deafened you. It would have filled the room with the noise of a mill-stream, the pealing of bells, and passing thunder. You may say a borborygm is common property, that all the world has heard a squeak and a running bubble in his neighbour's bowels, and thought no more about it. But here's a belly that gives more room than the majority. It's none of your penny cadenzas or pipings on a single flute when I begin, but the whole band of the Brigade of Guards. I took such a hullabaloo, I remember, last Good Friday, that Wagner himself could have made no better. There was wood and brass in it, a very good glockenspiel and a cor anglais. It was orchestrated. My duodenum declared the theme of vacancy, and a bassoon in the south-west corner made pretty play with that. Then the ileum comes in with its variation, and hunger's the new subject. There were fiddlers in my jejunum, tubas in my transverse colon. Modulations followed, development, decoration, counterpoint under the liver, and a double-bass on Poupart's ligament. They took hunger to the tonic, recapitulated, and finished with a coda like the death of a pig. It was better than Sir Henry Wood, and all who heard it stood up and cheered till they were hoarse.'

'You should have had it recorded,' said Juan.

'There was a man called Philpotts who made me a very good offer for gramophone rights, but I said no. There's unemployment already among musicians. Times are hard, competition ruthless, and I'm an amateur. I'll use no mechanical invention, I said, to take the bread out of anyone's mouth. And there was an end of it. But tell me what happened with the Sinologue. Did you handle her? Was she plastic? Did she come for sugar?'

'I had an uncomfortable half-hour, but I got the better of the argument at last,' said Juan; and briefly described his adventure into Chapei and its lack of success.

'So you've heard nothing of Sergeant Blow-fly, of that dog Rocco?'

'Nothing at all.'

'Rocco and Hikohoki,' said Flanders. 'I want one and you want the other, and if we had them both we could breed polecats. I could have told you about the shop in Nanking Road, if I'd thought it was any use to you. I've done business there myself, selling a few things that came into my hands in one way or another. Hikohoki paid little enough, but he asked no needless questions. He has a house, I've heard, outside Shanghai, but where it is I don't know.'

'He's a hard-working fellow.'

'With money in the bank. He's got money, Motley. That lovely word, and lovelier thing. I think of ten thousand pounds – no, five thousand – as a fine young man will dream of love, or a mountaineer of the top of Everest. Have you got money?'

'Very little. None of my own.'

'You need none in youth. Room for action is all youth needs to make it happy. But come to my age, and you want room to live; to be, and digest, and comfort your five senses, and count the sunsets; and a little money will buy you such a room.'

'Have you seen Harris to-day?'

'Harris? No! I want to see a free-handed millionaire who'll give me ten thousand pounds as I've given shillings, which were greater in comparison with my no-fortune, to blind beggars and stumping matchsellers. But charity doesn't grow with the store, and a million pounds are stuck tight together.'

'I heard this morning that Wu Tu-fu was coming down from Nanking, and I thought Harris might have some definite news about him.'

Flanders took off his spectacles, polished them, and replaced them on his fine fleshy nose. 'Does Sergeant Blow-fly come too?' he asked.

'I don't know. But Harris may have heard.'

'We'll wait for him. He'll be here before long.'

It was an hour before Harris arrived. He came in yawning, his hands in his pockets. His look of dishevelment was increased by a cigarette, sticking to his lower lip, that he did not bother to remove. 'As soon as this bloody war's over,' he said, 'I'm getting right down to steal Rip Van Winkle's record. Let's go to the bar. You get your drink quicker there, and I've got to be off again in ten minutes.'

Harris drank his whisky greedily, gulping it down. His face was grey, his collar dirty, and he had a sty at the inner corner of his right eye. But his mind was active, his spirit undiminished. He had no time to shave, but none to worry about not shaving.

'What's the news?' asked Juan.

'Upwards of a thousand casualties in the 19th Route Army; but they're holding on. There's nothing left of the North Station except a few broken walls. You should have seen it last night. Blazing like a bloody furnace, like a bloody great lantern. But they're holding on. The Japs can't shift them. They're damned good soldiers, those Cantonese. Have a drink?'

'What's moving in Nanking?' said Flanders.

'A whole lot,' said Harris. 'They've got four tanks for the Ever Invincible Tank Corps, and General Wu Tu-fu's bringing them down at the beginning of next week. I believe that's authentic.'

'There's an American called Rocco...'

'I know him. He used to be a gunman, and now he's Wu Tu-fu's Military Adviser.'

'A gunman, a bruiser, a sergeant in the American army, and a blow-fly into the bargain,' said Flanders.

'It's funny,' said Harris. 'Wu Tu-fu's a good man. Clever, well-educated, nice to talk to, and as honest as they make them nowadays. What he sees in Rocco I just can't understand, but he uses him for a whole lot of things. I suppose it gives him face to have a foreign adviser.'

'You haven't heard if Rocco's coming here with Wu Tu-fu?' asked Juan.

'No. But he's sure to. Do you want to see him?'

'I do,' said Flanders.

'What for?'

'To wring him like a dirty rag and squeeze ninety thousand dollars out of the tallow in his bones.'

'You can't do that under the eyes of Wu Tu-fu and the guns of the Ever Invincible tanks.'

Flanders leaned against the bar, a heel on the brass rail, his belly to the front like a round tower in the wall at Carcassonne; but when he folded his hands upon it, it looked like a barrel that he was straining to embrace. He frowned and muttered, and then as gruffly as he could, 'I'll take nothing to do with the tanks,' he said, 'nor with Wu Tu-fu, nor anyone but Rocco. The tanks are their concern, not mine. But let me have Rocco alone, Rocco in a quiet corner, out of sight and ear-shot.'

'I can't bring him to you on a plate,' said Harris. 'As soon as I hear that Wu Tu-fu's arrived, I'll be going out to see him; and if you like to come along on the chance of finding Rocco, you may; but that's all I can do for you.'

'It might be a good idea to tackle him in front of Wu Tu-fu,' Juan suggested.

'It's private business,' said Flanders testily. 'I want no audience for my private affairs.'

'What have you been up to?' asked Harris. 'What have you been selling? Guns?'

'Nothing of the sort.'

'A rubber estate full of nice dead trees? A mining concession that wasn't yours and can't be worked?'

'D'you take me for a swindler? Do you call me a sharper?'

'Not if it hurts your feelings.'

Juan looked at his watch. 'I've got to go,' he said.

'Same here,' said Harris. 'I've a date with the Japanese. I'm going to talk to them about their civilizing mission in Asia, and ask them to show me their new batteries at Hongkew Park and the Rifle Range. We've just time for a quick one, haven't we?'

They had another drink and said good-bye to Flanders, Harris again promising to let him know when the Ever Invincible tanks and their pair of generals should arrive. But Flanders was still surly, and with a small gesture of farewell he turned his back – a back like the gable of a house – and spoke imperatively to the nearest barman.

Harris and Juan put on their coats.

'Rocco's double-crossed him, has he?' said Harris. 'Well, Flanders ought to have known better. He's not exactly the white flower of innocence himself. He's been living on his wits ever since I've known him.'

'I like him,' said Juan.

'I've known better men that I disliked more. What are you going to do now?'

'I'm taking a girl out to dinner.'

'Got any more engagements in Chapei?'

'I hope not.'

'I heard about you from the fellows down at Windy Corner. They showed me the cards you chucked over the gate, and I remembered giving them to you. What were you doing?'

'Nothing very much. We nearly got into trouble, but not quite.'

157

Harris looked at him with speculation in his eyes. 'If you get hold of anything that's news – real news – you'll let me know?'

'I will,' said Juan.

They parted, Harris to talk disingenuously with a Japanese colonel, Juan to dine with Harriet. She was in very good spirits, and soon after dinner they returned to her flat.

14

JUAN spent the whole of Saturday with Harriet. He had become so fond of her that he was tempted to tell her about Kuo Kuo; but fortunately he had enough sense to restrain so foolish an impulse, remembering that even the most delightful young women were apt to be unsympathetic towards other young women, especially if they discovered they were sharing a lover.

It was natural, however, that he should want to talk about Kuo, for she had hurt his feelings badly by her neglect and indifference. She had shown, again and again, that she believed the welfare of China to be more important than a love affair. This, however, Juan might have forgiven – for his nature was essentially tolerant – had she been reasonably polite about it, and preferably apologetic. But she had shown not the slightest inclination to apologize. She was, it was clear, unaware that any cause for apology might exist; she was now, indeed, almost unaware that he existed. This blank indifference was very humiliating, and Juan could only comfort himself by realizing – which he did with ever increasing clarity – that politics were inevitably the enemy of human happiness.

Their love had been shipwrecked on the dangerous coast of China. So much was obvious, though the wreck had been gradual, the bark had not broken at once. On their first night in Shanghai, when he had lost his way after leaving the Mei-sum restaurant, Kuo had been anxious for his safety and glad when he returned. For a few deceptive hours her love had been richer than ever, and more generous. Her love for China, flowering in its native air, had embraced him also, because he had come to China with her. But that was a brief and illusory effect. Her patriotism had got into difficulties, the bloom was shed, and nothing left but an indigestible green fruit, whereon love and

Juan starved. Once or twice, indeed, she had shown him something of her old affection; when she returned from Nanking in the unwarranted flush of a triumph that did not materialize; and for a few minutes, when she admitted failure, in Peony's house in Chapei. But these were exceptional instances. They were eddies from an outgoing tide. It was very sad; and whenever Juan thought about it his mind played with these sad metaphors of shipwreck and falling blossom and the ebb-tide.

But fortunately he was never given to any great extravagance of regret. His nature was not envious, he was generally contented to be where he found himself, he inclined to believe that the unattainable was undesirable, and so far as women were concerned he was disposed to admit the good sense of 'If she be not fair to me, what care I how fair she be?' He was disposed to admit it; but he could not forget the idyllic months he had spent with Kuo in America. They had declared their love on the warm cypress-guarded coast of California; they had taken it to the mountain-walled orchards of Oregon; they had esteemed it the more by a lonely stream in the green solitude of Vancouver Island. And wherever they went they had lived under the blue sky and golden light of their happiness; which was a climate even more perfect than California's.

An idyll on the edge of the world; but they had crossed the sea, and the idyll had not survived the huge Pacific. It had gone sour, like a delicate wine that will not travel.

It would have been pleasant, after a melancholy fashion, to talk about it and discuss the vagaries and the vanished charm of Kuo. But pleasures are so frequently antipathetic and mutually exclusive that of all people the Cyrenaic must learn to select, and to practise renunciation; so Juan put away the temptation to tell Harriet about Kuo, and consoled himself by telling her more acceptable things.

Her small flat was stuffy and tawdrily over-furnished. – Its previous occupant had been another young woman who had left in a hurry to take up residence in a similar establishment in Manila. – But Harriet was not dependent on a domestic background to show off her complexion and her character; and Juan's constitution was too robust to be upset by the tastelessness of any household furniture. Indeed the insistent and rather untidy feminality of Harriet's flat was in welcome contrast, he thought, to the uncompromising masculinity of the Shanghai Club. Sometimes the world of men grew very tedious. Its self-importance, its ponderous surroundings, were like a dull play more dully acted. Female society, on the other hand, had the pleasing simplicity of a music-hall. And there were times when a good nimble girl who could sing a little, dance a little, toss her head, and do her stuff, was worth the whole company of serious playwrights of the last hundred years.

Juan, in a dressing-gown, lay on a yellow-cushioned day-bed and watched Harriet – in a dressing gown – who was brewing coffee in a percolator.

'In the extensive grounds of my father's house,' he said, 'there is a coppice of fig-trees grown from seeds that my great-grandfather picked from his teeth after breakfasting with the Prince Regent at Brighton.'

'Is that true?'

'Probably not. I was just thinking that if I were an author, like you, I might begin my first novel with those words. I should also write a short story, a love story, a simple little thing, very delicately told, and finish it with the consolatory sentence, "And then they were divorced and lived happily ever after." How often have you been in love?'

'Just this once.'

'Me too. Isn't it marvellous?'

'The worst sort of men for a girl to fall in love with are the conscience-stricken ones who say, "I leave it to you." They're often quite nice, but they're a terrible drain on your strength.'

'I don't like girls with a hare-lip or a devoted family. Otherwise I'm pretty tolerant. If I were a politician I think I'd be an anarchist.'

'I once knew a politician,' said Harriet. 'He was an emotional Socialist, but intellectually pre-Tory. He wanted to make love to me, but he was so awfully humble about it that he made me frightened. I thought his gratitude would be overwhelming.'

'Humility in love,' said Juan, 'is like poor relations at a wedding. They take up a lot of your time and only make you feel uncomfortable.'

'But arrogance – bone-headed male arrogance – is just as bad. There are lots of men who think that a girl is amply rewarded for taking off her skirt if they succeed in enjoying themselves.'

'Do you know any women novelists?'

'Dozens of them.'

'The kind that specialize in describing the tortures and agony of childbirth?'

'Yes. That's because they've got narrow pelvises. Or sometimes it's a sympathetic husband who's unhappily married to a narrow pelvis.'

'It must be fun,' said Juan, 'to be an author and to know these things.'

'I'd rather be a scientist. I would have been, if my father could have afforded to send me to the university.'

'Science,' said Juan, 'is also good fun. I remember reading that the universe will ultimately reach a state of complete disorganization, which will be the end of the world. Nothing more will happen, except that the universe will gradually swell. There, if you have the mind to appreciate it, is the fourth dimension of fun.'

'And the electron travels at a hundred and eighty-six thousand miles per second, and puts on weight all the time.'

'We do know a lot,' said Juan. 'Let's pool our knowledge.'

'I really don't know very much. Only gossip, and what I've seen. There was a paramount chief in Nigeria, when I was there, who had the most embarrassing kind of flatulence. So wherever he went he took with him a young man whose job was to take the blame for any noise that occurred.'

'The ancient kings of Egypt,' said Juan, 'hadn't nearly as much sense. They wouldn't drink wine, because they thought it was the blood of rebels who had fought against the gods. The rebels were killed, their bodies rotted, and out of them grew vines whose grapes contained a tincture of rebellious spirit. Therefore the kings were tee-total. Which seems to me absurd.'

'Once,' said Harriet, 'I got a little bit drunk – just lightly and super-ficially tight – in a bathing suit.'

'It's a delicious sensation.'

'It's like the realization of all romantic ideas about beach-combing.'

'It takes a good man to be a beachcomber. What do they do when they get toothache?'

'I suppose there's always a medical missionary somewhere about.'

'I suppose there is. Are you religious?'

'Not really. But I'd be much happier if I were sure, one way or the other.'

'Aristotle thought that God had begotten the world in a moment of absent-mindedness, and was ignorant of its actual existence. Like an eighteenth-century aristocrat and one of his bastards.'

'Don't let's talk about God or bastards. One's never quite safe from either of them.'

'Just as you like. Is there any more coffee?'

'Plenty. Are you going to get dressed before lunch?'

'I don't think so. We'll go out somewhere afterwards.'

'I'm not going to look at the war. It sounds horrible to-day.'

The irregular thunder of the Japanese bombardment was indeed almost continuous. Explosion followed explosion like links in a chain, each new crash entering the expanding echoes of the one before it. Then would come a frenzy of gun-fire, a thudding crescendo, intolerable to the ears. A little interval of peace might follow, but so brief that to the listener the air still seemed full of tumult, like a seashell that holds the roaring of remembered tides. Then, into that fancied vibration, more violence detonated, and echoes almost as loud would boom anew. While Harriet was still speaking a confusion of shell-fire jarred the window-panes and set the coffee-spoons chattering in their saucers.

The battle-front was now more definitely established. The Japanese had advanced into that part of Chapei which Juan and Kuo had so rashly visited, and their line was somewhat behind a continuance of North Honan Road on the other side of the railway. – A line from Judd Street to Camden Town Station, if Juan's comparison of Shanghai and London be remembered. – The Chinese were still in possession of Euston, though Euston was torn and shattered beyond recognition. They were still, with remarkable tenacity, holding a ragged position against the slowly extending attack, though their artillery was far inferior to the Japanese guns. And Chapei was still burning, and yet not wholly deserted despite fire and the dropping of countless bombs. When the wind blew from the smouldering streets it carried the smell of burning flesh.

So Juan and Harriet avoided the war; except the sound of it, which they could not escape. In the afternoon they went to see a game of pelota, which in Shanghai is called *hai alai*.

'Shanghai,' said Harriet, as they thrust their way into the crowd, 'is certainly hard-boiled.'

It was so hard-boiled, so tough and resilient, that war in its suburbs and snipers among its chimney-pots could not prevent it from amusing itself in whatever ways were possible. The cinemas were still open, and some twenty or thirty night-clubs had now reopened, while a crowd of more than two thousand people, most of them Chinese, had come to see the swift-moving pelota players, and to gamble on every match.

They were well worth seeing. Slim figures in gaily coloured shirts, they moved with rapid grace and hurled the ball from the long wicker *chistera* with fierce dexterity. The spectators were also worth watching. Plump and amiable, they were very different from the sinewy swift players and their rushing game. They betted eagerly on every set, and won or lost with seeming indifference. But neither players nor spectators could hold the attention of Juan and Harriet for very long. Deliberate entertainment was redundant to them, who had no need to be entertained; and a crowd was nothing but impertinent trespassers on what should have been solitude. They returned to Harriet's flat.

It was late in the evening when Harriet said, 'I'm going away to-morrow, you know.'

'You're not.'

'Yes, I am. The ship that takes my dirty little friend the ex-pirate to Ping-hai is sailing at midday, and I've got to go with him.'

'Forget about it.'

'And lose my chance of getting a close-up of all the pirates in Bias Bay?'

'We'll go somewhere else.'

'But Bias Bay is going to be the peak chapter in my new book. The bright light, the top of surprise, the real thrill.'

'Have you ever read any Byron?'

'I used to.'

'He's dated badly, hasn't he?'

'How?'

'You remember that he says: "Man's love is of man's life apart, 'tis woman's whole existence"? That makes him pretty grand-fatherly, doesn't it?'

'But I must go. I make my living by writing books, and if there's nothing exciting in them they won't sell.'

'Yes, I know. Byron's the mug, not me.'

'Well, you can't expect me to cry myself to sleep because of that.'

'No, of course not.'

'I don't want to go. I mean, I don't want to leave you.'

'That's nice of you.'

'It's because you've never had to do any work yourself that you don't understand . . .'

'Lovely Harriet, don't talk like that. Don't join the great sisterhood of sadistic Marthas whose chief joy is the necklacing of their men with the millstone of work. Work is the deadliest of the perversions. The natural instinct of natural man is to avoid work, and nothing shows more clearly the degeneracy of the modern world than the fact that work has become a social jewel, something to be sought with fervour, even a rarity, a prize for those who most closely resemble the ant, the pismire, the detestable insect that never raises its head.'

'That's all very well, but . . .'

'I know, I know. You can out-argue me at every turn. But I'm right, and you're wrong. I say work's a perversion, and so it is: everything except pure and voluntary creation. But it isn't recognized as a perversion because it isn't obviously destructive, and because its results are profitable. But no one who has worked for twenty years – and when I say worked, I mean laboured for hire – can either see clearly, hear with certainty, think straight, or feel ecstasy.'

'So you're serious too? That's the worst of men. All the nice ones have got some cock-eyed philosophy – anything from grouse disease to Fascism – that makes them fanatics at bottom. To hell with men!'

'I'm not serious! Your serious man is concerned with the welfare of his fellow-men, and I'm beautifully and purely selfish.'

'Then why did you come to China and get mixed up with Chinese Nationalists?'

'Who told you I had?'

'You haven't been so discreet as you think.'

'Well, I was experimenting with induced emotions.'

'O Juan, you are a darling!'

'That,' said Juan complacently, 'is the impression I have been trying to create ever since I met you.'

15

HARRIET was not to be moved from her resolution to seek adventure and a stirring chapter in Bias Bay. She woke early, and insisted that Juan should return at once to his hotel. She could not, she said, be bothered with him while she was packing, and she would not let him see her off.

Juan had only one argument with which to oppose her decision: the argument of their common pleasure. But in Harriet there was an element of puritanism – the modern shape of puritanism, that has transferred to work the sanctity which once belonged to the flesh – and her resolution was like adamant, on which Juan beat in vain.

But when they said good-bye her lips were hard for a different reason, and her fingers held his shoulders with desperate strength.

Juan returned to the New Celestial – that smooth abode of commercial luxury – in a mood of arrant and explosive unhappiness. It was so explosive that some of it was immediately vented in blasphemy; so unhappy that much of it escaped in a disemboguement like the breaching of a dam.

Then he found spurious consolation in a sort of romantic stoicism; a somewhat Byronic defiance and acceptance of unhappiness; a decision to wear his distress like a dark and lustrous plume. He saw himself as destiny's plaything, a shuttlecock in the hands of circumstance: and was perversely pleased with the idea.

To be jilted twice within a few days was a bitter thing, though his rival in one case had been China, and in the other the hot and resplendent muse of journalism. But bitterness might be a tonic. He would take it so. He would temper his solitary spirit in a cup of quassia. The thought of his solitude reinforced this intention. He was, he remembered, a wanderer over the face of the earth, and homeless – unless he chose to go home.

'Call me Ishmael,' he said, and with some difficulty got into a pair of very well cut jodhpurs. The Byronic disposition was dynamic, not static. To reveal his embittered but unbroken spirit he must go out into the world of men. Even his solitude – his inner solitude – would be intensified by company. He would keep his appointment with Mr Fannay-Brown and the paper-chasers.

He was relieved, however, when he met Fannay-Brown at the Club, to hear that Mrs Fannay-Brown had a severe cold and would not be able to accompany them. His inner solitude was so newly acquired, its rind was so young and thin, that he was doubtful whether it would have been proof against so energetic a talker. But he could stand the innocuous and not unamiable chatter of Fannay-Brown himself. Indeed he welcomed it, for its cheerful triviality made him realize more strongly than ever how far apart from ordinary humanity his unhappiness had taken him.

Fannay-Brown had a large Cadillac, and a very good Chinese chauffeur; so they drove rapidly out of Shanghai. The tall buildings and the splendid ones and the crowded and innumerable buildings were left behind them like a sediment, and they came into an area less thickly populated, where between the houses could be seen open stretches of pale green country. It was a windless day, with a raw mist in the air, and very quiet. The quietness was mysterious and even oppressive, till Juan remembered the reason for it. The guns had stopped firing. There was a little interval of peace, and one might almost think the sky was holding its breath lest its peace be untimely discovered.

Having discussed several of the more notable ponies that at one time or another he had owned or ridden, Fannay-Brown crossed by some verbal bridge, that Juan failed to notice, to the subject of his wife. Of her also he spoke with enthusiasm. There was indeed a definite resemblance between the way in which he described a hock with plenty of bone in it, and his manner of reporting the finer points of the mercantile Beatrice – though he confined himself, of course, to her intellectual equipment.

'She was very disappointed at not being able to come out to-day,' he said, 'but not nearly so sorry as I was. As I still am, if it comes to that. Heaven knows I'd go anywhere for a ride – desperately keen on hunting, even hunting paper – but I always say that half my pleasure's in listening to Beatrice's remarks about the other people. We go home after one of these paper-chases, and for an hour or more she'll describe what she saw and heard, and I'll sit and simply rock with laughter. Of course she isn't always kind in what she says, but that's the way with witty people. If you've got a knife, you want to cut something: that's natural. I always remember what she said about – well, perhaps I'd better not tell you his name. He came out with a parliamentary commission a year or two ago. Nice fellow, a bit dull, didn't ride, but we took him out to see the ponies, and when we got back I asked Beatrice what she thought of him. We'd a dinner-party that night, and everybody listened to her reply. – They always do, of course. – Well, what d'you think she said? As cool as ice, and right off the bat, she answered: "A liberal in politics, agnostic in faith, and not quite a gentleman." Pretty shattering, don't you think?'

'Very,' said Juan, 'very shattering indeed.'

'She's constantly saying good things. They're no effort to her. There was a man called Patch, for instance, who made himself conspicuous with a Mrs Hiploe, whose name was already pretty notorious. Somebody told Beatrice that Mrs Hiploe was going about with Patch, and Beatrice at once replied: "It's just what her reputation needs." Not bad, eh? Then there was a young man, rather an oafish fellow, who told her he couldn't read modern novels or modern poetry. Said they were all Greek to him. Said you needed a key to understand them. "Only the qui-vive," said Beatrice.'

It seemed that Fannay-Brown's horse-coping had become so much of a habit that he even spoke of his wife as though he were trying to sell her; but as he could not with propriety praise her withers and cannon-bones, he praised her wit. It was, thought Juan, a very charming tendency, and in the coruscation of Fannay-Brown's remarkable denture he descried the gleam of a kindly optimism.

Open fields were now visible through the windows of the car. Rough winter-fields intersected by ditches, hummocked with grave-mounds, and tufted with willows. They drove through a squalid hamlet. They passed some large houses with high-walled gardens, and crossed a black and muddy creek. Fannay-Brown continued to recite his wife's *obiter dicta*.

'... It was a big party, and there was a woman there who rather took the floor. Young, quite good-looking, stupid, and married to a hideous old man – very wealthy – who might have been her father. She was constantly making foolish remarks with unnecessary emphasis. But Beatrice took the wind out of her sails. Indeed she did. Somebody else – another foolish woman – said something idiotic, and this woman, wagging her finger, crowed, "Ah! But women never give themselves away!" Quick as lightning, Beatrice said, "Except to very rich men." Ha! You should have seen her – the other woman,

I mean. Absolutely collapsed. Hadn't another word to say. Look at all those cars, Motley. We're going to have a big turn-out.'

They joined a long procession of motor-cars that were discharging their occupants at the end of a muddy lane, and following the crowd, crossed a hump-backed bridge and came into a field where there was a multitude of ponies, grooms, paper-chasers, and spectators. Everyone seemed very cheerful, and on all sides Juan heard commendation of the Japanese for their sportsmanship in agreeing to an armistice. – The Chinese had consented to it simply because they wanted a chance to bury their dead. – Some ten or a dozen Japanese officers had themselves taken advantage of the truce, and were already in the saddle.

Fannay-Brown introduced Juan to several people, but gave him no time to talk to them, for he was in a great hurry to find his ponies. They were, like most of the ponies there, sturdy in appearance rather than fast; thick and cobby, with somewhat heavy heads and manes whose luxuriousness was evident despite hogging. One was mouse-coloured, and the other a curious faded orange. A Chinese groom, with a melancholy expression and a cast in one eye, was in charge of them.

'There!' said Fannay-Brown, with marvellous satisfaction in his voice. 'That's Chang there.' And he pointed to the orange pony.

'He looks strong enough,' said Juan.

'Oh, tireless,' said Fannay-Brown, 'absolutely tireless. Look at those shoulders. Powerful, lying well on the chest, there isn't a pony on the field with better shoulders. And look at the breadth of his loins. Look at the substance in them. You won't see a better pony in Shang-hai.'

'That's a nice animal over there,' said Juan.

'Curby hocks,' said Fannay-Brown promptly.

'There's a good-looking chestnut too. Almost as good as the girl who's riding him.'

'That brute with the great grass belly? He won't last a mile. But Chang's in beautiful fettle. Tip-top condition. I give you my word that if you're thinking of buying a pony, you won't do much better than Chang. Here, boy!' – he spoke to the groom – 'Lead him up and down. This master maybe going to buy him.'

Seeing his pony in movement, Fannay-Brown became almost lyrical in his praise. For springy pasterns, dilating nostrils, and large fetlock-joints he made such a rich encomium as would have flattered Keats's Madeline beneath the moon of St Agnes. He spoke of horses in general, and of breeding, touching on the Darley Arabian, Eclipse, Blair Athol, Bend Or, and Persimmon; he felt pretty certain there was a trace of Blood in Chang; and in any case there were flyers that the Stud Book had never heard of. Nor did he seek a prohibitive price for the orange pony. A very modest sum indeed was all he asked.

Juan grew somewhat alarmed as Fannay-Brown became more and more business-like. Unless he was careful, he felt, he would soon be the owner of a pony that he did not want and for which he had no use. So he pointed a depreciatory finger at Chang, and said in a very confident voice, 'He dishes his near-fore.'

Fannay-Brown was very surprised to hear this. Very surprised indeed. He watched Chang closely, and said he really didn't think so. No one had ever suggested such a thing before. But his assurance was weakened, and Juan, who knew next to nothing about horses, was very pleased at having so fortunately remembered a scrap of stable conversation he had once overheard. Before Fannay-Brown regained enough composure to refute the charge – for which indeed there was very little justification – they perceived that everyone but themselves and a Japanese subaltern, whose pony was evading him with singular dexterity, had mounted and formed a rough line in an adjacent field. They hurriedly got into the saddle and trotted after the others.

It soon became evident that Chang was a pony with a decided personality. The starting line was already a long one – the field was about eighty strong – but no sooner had Juan piloted Chang into a convenient gap than it extended by some ten or fifteen yards. The ponies on either side immediately recognized him, and sheered off to left and right, thus compelling their outside neighbours to side-step and ultimately, after a good deal of confusion, to lengthen the whole line. When the starter's flag dropped, Juan – on Chang – was in a conspicuously empty space.

Within fifty yards, however, he was riding knee-to-knee with a nervous young man on an eager, splay-footed, camel-necked dun. 'For God's sake,' said the nervous young man, 'keep that beast of yours out of my way.'

'I wish I could,' said Juan.

Then Chang bit the splay-footed pony in the neck, and went off at a tangent. It charged a narrow ditch, slowed and bunched itself for the take-off, and leapt it like an angry cat. By the time Juan had recovered his stirrups he was riding in embarrassing proximity to a lady in a very smart habit and a bowler hat, who rode with great elegance a tall spindly bay. She was, apparently, a lady of some local importance. Before the start Juan had seen her speaking to one of the five or six pink coats who glorified the dark-clad field. She had a high-bridged nose and very heavy eyebrows.

'Where the hell d'you think you're going?' she demanded, as Chang rubbed her spidery bay.

'Wherever my pony takes me,' said Juan a trifle breathlessly.

The trail of paper stretched clearly in front of them, over a black field and another ditch. To left and right, ahead and behind, were the eighty horsemen, the thudding of many hooves, the creaking of leather, the snorting of ponies, the earnest breathing of their riders, and their occasional imprecations. It was a gallant thing to see such furious action in the still Chinese air. From panting nostrils rose a livelier steam to mingle in the sluggish mist, and with flying clots of mud the patient earth leapt like a mackerel-quickened sea. Black soil and grey-green winter grass were cheered by scarlet coats, pink faces, and the many-coloured ponies; the sightless air awoke and wondered to hear the thunder of such cheerful cavalry. It was a glad courageous sight, made whole and reasonable by the single purpose of the riders, the single aim of all but one of the ponies.

For Chang had his own intentions. He was out to enjoy himself, not to hunt paper, and for the moment his enjoyment lay in riding-off the well-habited lady and her spider-legged bay. He had a mouth like iron and a neck so strong and self-willed that whenever Juan tugged at the near rein it curved like a scimitar to the off. With clownish delight and a resolute indifference to his rider, Chang so bored and thrust against the bay that presently they were all on the extreme right-wing of the hunt, and the lady's language had become repetitive and profane.

'God damn you,' she cried. 'Damn you to hell, and get to hell out of here!'

'That's all very well,' gasped Juan, 'but . . .'

'That bloody pony . . . blast your soul . . . why the hell don't you learn to ride?'

She struck furiously at Chang, but the orange pony merely tossed his head in a villainous sort of horse-chuckle, and rubbed closer than ever.

Juan, while not wholly sympathizing with Chang's behaviour, was yet conscious of a certain admiration for him. His independence of mind, and the steely strength of his neck were both remarkable, and the taut arc of his neck had a certain beauty. Quite suddenly Juan remembered the name – the horseman's name – for the disobedient muscle.

'It's his paxwax,' he shouted. 'It's dextro-rotary!'

This explanation seemed to infuriate the lady more than ever. 'Paxwax be !!! !' she screamed, and dealt a furious blow at Chang's head. The violence of this action, however, combined with an extra nudge from Chang, upset her balance and the last Juan saw of her was her well-booted heels in the air. She landed quite comfortably on squelchy ploughland.

Snorting with pleasure, Chang swerved sharply to the left and charged the tailing field. Fannay-Brown had told the simple truth when he said that Chang was fit to go all day, for he was clearly gathering strength with every yard, and Juan, perceiving there was little to be gained from trying to steer a course, sat back and rode him philosophically.

In front of them, riding laboriously towards another of the innumerable ditches that intersected the flat country, was the nervous young man on the splay-footed dun that Chang had already bitten. With great cunning Chang headed for exactly the same point to which the young man was riding, and his diagonal course brought him to the ditch half a length in front of the dun. He cleared it with another of his scalded-cat saltations, but the dun, balked at his take-off, stiffened his fore-legs and pitched his unhappy rider into three feet of cold water and oozy mud.

As though satisfied by this clever piece of work, Chang modified his pace, gave a little to the rein, and galloped with flattering docility in the paper-strewn wake of the hunt. Their diagonal course had lost them a lot of ground, and there were now only three or four people behind them. But forty yards ahead was the familiar figure of Fannay-Brown. He also had fallen, for his back was dark with mud, and he was flapping like a new-risen heron in his efforts to regain his place among the leaders.

No sooner had Chang recognized his stable-mate than he joined the race again. The tremendous working of his loins was suddenly like the plunging of giant pistons, and the forty yards lessened in as many strides to thirty, to twenty, and ten. Then he neighed his challenge, shrill though a trifle breathless, and Fannay-Brown, badly startled, looked over his shoulder.

'Get him by the head,' he cried.

'Sauve qui peut!' shouted Juan, and nerved himself for the shock.

But Chang, abruptly changing his mind, thought of something better to do. The paper-trail skirted a little group of grave-mounds – tall green barrows, made cheerful with a few willows – and swerving violently towards them he tucked his legs under his belly, went up and over, down and up again, and tossed his head with obvious disgust to find that Juan was still on top of him.

A road lay ahead of them. Chang scrambled up the bank, and cantered loosely – but with the bit between his teeth – along its muddy surface. He seemed undecided what to do next.

Juan, who had felt a little seasick during his passage over the grave-mounds, was thankful for an interval of level going. But not for long. The road was cut by a series of wooden bridges, their planks loose, greasy and hidden by mud. They rattled as Chang crossed, and he pretended to be frightened. At the next bridge he shot out his fore-feet, sat on his rump, and slid. Juan remained on the bridge, and Chang, getting nimbly to his feet again, walked casually away till he came to some grass, which he nibbled with an air of admirable indifference.

But he kept a wary eye on Juan, and showed great unwillingness to be caught. He would let Juan approach within a few feet, and then with a snort, a flirting of his big head, and a flyaway flourish of his hooves, he would leap or sidle away, and put another fifty yards between them. He led Juan along the road for perhaps half a mile, and then, with the mildest manner in the world, trotted quietly through a double gate that opened into a large and well-tended garden.

The house was in a lonely position, its nearest neighbour being several hundred yards away. It was well built in European style, and in the garden, of some two or three acres, was a flagstaff which drooped, in the still air, the sunrise ensign of Japan.

Though he realized that no one could quarrel with him for pursuing a loose horse, Juan could not help hoping that he would be able to get

Chang out of the garden unobserved. But Chang trotted quietly towards the front door and Juan followed with irritation and a certain feeling of anxiety.

The drive was horseshoe-shaped and led to another gate, which was closed. Chang turned, quickening his movements, and continuing across the lawn, cleared an empty flower-bed with easy precision. Juan, now very angry, was about to continue the pursuit when, running down the drive, he saw two squat, khaki-clad Japanese soldiers.

There was, he told himself, no possible cause for alarm. He, as an Englishman, had no quarrel with Japan, and Japan could have no quarrel with him, unless his very modest and trifling association with people of anti-Japanese sentiments had been noted and thought of any importance. Which was absurd to suppose. He began to explain to the soldiers his unwilling presence in the garden.

They spoke no English but indicated their desire that he should come with them. This he was not eager to do, but before he could make up his mind he saw a slim trim figure in civilian dress – presumably the owner of the house – come hurrying down the drive; and recognized Hikohoki.

He was smiling with evident but ambiguous pleasure. 'Mr Motley,' he cried. 'I am rejoiced to see you! I observed you from the windows of my indifferent library, and sent these two fellows to detain you. Come, let us go in and talk. I have much to say to you.'

Though he had always derided Kuo's belief that Hikohoki was a sinister and mysterious figure, Juan had not been wholly impervious to her ideas, and now his mind was suddenly filled with doubt and fear. In Shanghai, on neutral ground, he had been willing enough to meet Hikohoki. But here, in this lonely place, with soldiers at his command, it was a very different matter. Perhaps Kuo had been right – Hikohoki had certainly stolen Lo Yu's plan – and why, if he was only an insurance agent, the proprietor of a couple of night-clubs, and the owner of the Dernier Cri Antique Store, why had he soldiers to guard his house?

These and kindred thoughts came and went with little less than the speed of light; and Juan made up his mind

Taking a swift step he swung a left hook to the nearer soldier's jaw – a pretty punch that lifted the Japanese off his feet – and aimed a tremendous blow at the other man. But his right fist met insubstantial air, his forward movement was strangely accelerated, he rose abruptly from the ground, and somersaulted perforce over the soldier's right shoulder. Then, before he could recover his breath, he felt the extremely painful pressure of a thumb on his Adam's apple, an equally uncomfortable knee on his solar plexus, and an agonizing grip that threatened to break his wrist. Through the fog of pain that dimmed his senses, he heard the distracted voice of Hikohoki, and slowly understood that he was not merely pleading, with sorrow in his voice, for an explanation of Juan's assault upon his bodyguard, but reiterating with mournful prolixity his great friendship for Juan, his gratitude for some unstated kindness, and his desire to serve him.

So extreme was Hikohoki's agitation that he never thought of ordering Juan's release; but Juan, fortunately remembering a demonstration of jiu-jitsu that he had once seen at school, summoned enough strength to tap with his free hand on the ground, whereupon the soldier very obligingly got up, and courteously helped Juan also to rise.

Hikohoki continued to protest, to apologize, and proclaim his undying devotion to Mr Motley. Unceasingly voluble, he led the way to his house, and Juan, supported by the two soldiers, willy-nilly followed.

16

HIKOHOKI proved an expert host. His house was furnished in a happy blend of great comfort and good taste, and little more than an hour after succumbing to the jiu-jitsu expert, Juan was eating sole Cardinale, caneton en grenadin, and a cheese soufflé of superlative flavour and ethereal consistency. He regarded Hikohoki with a new respect. The sole, with its auxiliary prawns and mushrooms, had been exquisite; the duckling was a gastrosoph's darling; and the soufflé the most delicate of sensualities. Nor had these triumphs of collaboration between nature and the kitchen – between farmyard and the sea and the cunning benignity of man – gone unattended by wine. They had drunk a white Hermitage, a Château-Lafite, and a glass or two of Cockburn's port.

After the second glass Juan stated, without verbosity yet with agreeable addition to the mere skeleton of fact, his appreciation of a host whose gracious nature and savoir vivre were so admirably wedded as Hikohoki's.

'The home,' said Hikohoki, with comparable expansion, 'is the orbit of the soul, and it is my delightful ambition that my soul should have perfect surroundings whenever possible. In the world of commerce and affairs, of course, that is not possible. One must labour the earth and cull the fruit in the torrid heat of competitive trade. But in the home there should be only what may soothe the senses and expand the heart or soul. That picture of a mountain – it is by Hiroshige – cost me fourteen hundred yen, and this port wine was also most expensive. But I grudge no luxury either to my soul or to my guests.'

Juan found much to admire in these sentiments, and he thought of Hikohoki with growing affection; who had indeed done everything to make him comfortable. While his clothes, muddied by the fall on the bridge, were being dried and brushed, he had bathed and rested, and though Hikohoki could not give him a clean shirt – for his own were too small – he had offered Juan a very handsome tie to replace that which the jiu-jitsu expert had spoiled. It was a dark blue tie with a pale blue stripe, and Hikohoki explained that he had chosen it because in London he had observed that it was a pattern which appealed to many of the best people. Juan accepted it with proper reverence.

He had apologized for his attack on the soldiers by an ingenious fiction. In his youth, he said, he had had an unfortunate experience with some military men, and ever since then he had been liable to sudden and uncontrollable fits of violent stratophobia. Generally, of course, he could endure the sight of a uniform without turning a hair; but every now and then it filled him with rage and fear. Hence his ridiculous assault, for which he apologized most humbly.

Hikohoki begged him to think no more about it. The soldiers, he said, were rude uncultivated men who cared nothing for a blow. If Juan would enjoy another rough-and-tumble, they were at his disposal.

They exchanged some further courtesies, and passed the port. Hikohoki mentioned again his great indebtedness to Juan, and Juan begged to be told the reason for it.

Hikohoki was very much surprised. 'Had it not been for you,' he protested, 'I should have been a bereaved and hapless person. It cannot be that you have forgotten that night when our Chinese friends so treacherously began this accursed war? That night when you so bravely rescued the two Misses Karamazov?'

'But of course! They're your protégées, aren't they? Where are they now?'

'Where else but here? Thanks to you they are alive and happy, and eagerly anticipating the triumphs that await them.'

'I'd like to see them again.'

'You shall, Mr Motley. But meanwhile they are engaged in the daily regimen necessary for their forthcoming career.'

Having offered Juan a cigar, and very elaborate paraphernalia with which to cut and light it, Hikohoki presently ushered him into another room, furnished in European style, and artistically decorated in a shade of blue that was cleverly subservient to several very good colour-prints by Hokusai, Hiroshige, and other masters.

'It is a rare and respectable art,' said Hikohoki when Juan expressed his admiration of a deep blue bend – dark trees above it – of the Sumida River. 'In Japan we are all like Hiroshige. We can naturally be moved by him and feel with his art as if our own creation. You would undoubtedly be surprised if I told you what I had paid for that picture.'

But artistic conversation did not occupy them for long, Hikohoki being more eager to talk about the Sisters Karamazov.

'Are they not the most delicious of young ladies?' he exclaimed. 'They are so fascinately refreshing in all their habits. They are indeed a bundle of charms, and I am devoted to them. Their genius is also remarkable, though in need of certain trainings, and already I am making a plan for presenting them in the best theatres of London, Paris, and New York. They will enjoy an artistic triumph, and the pecuniary profits will be very great. That is a most satisfactory state of affairs when, by giving to humanity, like Hiroshige, something that is truly beautiful and of poetical essence, one can also make lump sums of money.'

Hikohoki, it appeared, was undertaking the education of Varya and Masha in the most serious and determined fashion. Having watched them closely and listened attentively to several of their performances at the night-club – before the interruption of the war – he had acquired a lively ambition and inordinate faith in their conjunctive talent; but he also perceived that their fashion of singing required radical correction, and they would be the better of a more extensive repertoire. He had therefore prescribed a very thorough course of training, and they were now working eight hours a day, under competent instruction, at singing, dancing, French, and exercises for beautifying the bust, fencing, elocution, and American wisecracking. When summer came they would also be taught swimming and fancy diving. There was no end, said Hikohoki, to their potential accomplishment, and when they were fully trained they would be an attraction unique in the whole world of entertainment. They would tour America and the capitals of Europe, and wherever they went he would be able to command a salary exceeding that of movie stars and prima donnas. He would, of course, give up all his other interests, and devote his whole life to the Sisters Karamazov.

'For too long I have been dissipating my energy in many directions,' he said, 'but now I shall concentrate and specialize.'

Though abundantly aware of the money-making power of Varya and Masha, Hikohoki's interest in them was clearly not limited to that. He was proud and fond of them, as proud and affectionate as their Uncle Georgy had been. Like a doting parent he told little stories about their clever behaviour and quaint remarks. Wiping a tear from his eye, he repeated, 'They are a bundle of charms. No, they are two bundles, and each is perfect. And it is to you, Mr Motley, that I owe their salvation from the flames and inconvenience of war.'

A little later, with many apologies, Hikohoki begged that Juan would excuse him. He had a most urgent business appointment, and he would be compelled to dine away from home. But he insisted that Juan should stay. The two Misses Karamazov were most anxious to see him, and their company at dinner would more than compensate for his absence. At present – he looked at his watch – they were taking a motor-drive. They had been confined to the house for several days, and fresh air was so beneficial, was it not? But they would be back in an hour or so, and broken-hearted if they found Mr Motley had gone.

Juan, who had nothing else to do, said he would be delighted to stay and dine with Varya and Masha.

'They are the two apples of my eyes,' said Hikohoki, and got up to go.

'By the way,' said Juan, 'there's a friend of mine who's very anxious

177

to get hold of that piece of bamboo you found in Peony Sun's house in Chapei.'

Hikohoki was genuinely surprised, and betrayed it by a poker-face. Till then his expression had been animated, his eyes kindly, his smile sincere. But now his smile became a mask, his eyes blank.

'I did not know that you were a friend of Miss Sun,' he said.

'I've met her. But the piece of bamboo is what I'm interested in.'

'It is only a curio. I bought it from Miss Sun.'

'How much do you want for it?'

'It is worth very little. I shall give you more better things if you are a collector of curios.'

'I'm not. But I should very much like to have the bamboo.'

Hikohoki shrugged his shoulders. 'If you want it, I shall make you a present of it.'

He went out and returned in a minute or two with a short thick piece of prettily speckled bamboo. It was about the size of a policeman's truncheon, carved on one side with a red-lacquered dragon, and sealed at one end with red wax. He gave it to Juan with a bland impenetrable smile.

'Peony said she'd never seen it,' said Juan. 'She was pretty thoroughly doped, but she'd have remembered selling it to you. Especially as it didn't belong to her.'

'I have made a mistake. It was her father who sold it. He is very old.'

'He's dead now.'

'Aah! We were not much acquainted, but it is always melancholy to hear of death.'

Juan turned the piece of bamboo and looked at the red dragon. He wondered if Lo Yu's plan were still in it.

'Would it be impertinent,' said Hikohoki, 'to ask why you so much wanted that simple thing?'

'It has a certain sentimental value. A friend of mine lost it . . .'

'Miss Kuo?'

'Yes.'

'There is a written scroll inside.'

'So I understand.'

'But I do not. I do not understand at all, either why she wants it

178

or how you knew that I had bought it. But you are my friend and benefactor, so what does it matter? Take it. You are satisfied?'

'Yes. And thank you very much.'

Hikohoki seemed reluctant to go. His face had lost something of its unrevealing calm, and his eyes were puzzled.

'I have heard that your friend Miss Kuo is a politician,' he said.

'She has some political interests. Many people have nowadays.'

'It is bad for business,' said Hikohoki, 'and in this country it is sometimes dangerous. I think you should not be a politician yourself.'

When Hikohoki had gone, Juan put the bamboo on a small table beside a very handsome bowl of Satsuma ware, and lay comfortably on a broad couch. He soon fell asleep, for after an emotional night he had had a strenuous morning and a heavy lunch. He slept soundly for a couple of hours, and woke to find the Sisters Karamazov looking down at him.

'Zdrástvitye!' they cried. 'How do you do, Mr Motley? We are so glad to see you again.'

'This is quite like old times,' said Juan.

'When we came to wake you up in that house in the Rue des Andouilles,' added Masha.

'Do not let us speak about that unrespectable place,' said Varya.

'It was a rather nice comfortable house.'

'But not at all suitable for people like us.'

'She is getting very refined,' said Masha.

'You're both looking very well,' said Juan.

They were smartly dressed in what were evidently new clothes, and their maquillage was skilfully designed to represent a healthy complexion not wholly unaccustomed to the open air. Their appearance was much less exotic than when Juan had last seen them, but their new conventionality threw into higher relief their essential anomaly. In dressing-gowns and the lavish rouge of night-club fashion their unnatural juncture had seemed little more than the device of some ingenious régisseur. They had the look of people in a cabaret, and a cabaret is not expected to agree with the appearance and behaviour of everyday. Their nonconformity was extreme, but not really incongruous. Their new clothes, however, had made a great difference, and the compagination of two girls so respectable, even dignified as they now appeared, was very impressive.

Juan now felt somewhat in awe of them; as though their double respectability must roughly equal the legendary respectability of a Victorian duchess. But they were infinitely more attractive than any duchess since Charles II chose his own, and if Hikohoki thought their figures needed improvement – even for a French audience – then he was more critical than Juan.

They sat down, very neatly, on the couch where he had lately been sleeping, and he carefully arranged cushions to suit their comfort. Varya accepted these attentions with an air of having long been accustomed to such politeness, and was not satisfied till Juan had brought other cushions and redisposed every one according to her liking; but Masha was all against putting him to any trouble, and begged him not to bother.

'I hear that you're having a very busy time,' said Juan.

'We are continuing our education,' said Varya. 'It is most interesting.'

'It is a beastly nuisance,' said Masha, 'I am being bored to tears.'

'I have always been very fond of culture, Mr Motley. Have you been reading many books lately?'

'I'm afraid I haven't.'

'We are also learning to fence. That is a very graceful exercise.'

'And my God!' exclaimed Masha. 'We are having exercises to increase our busts. Do you think that is necessary?'

'Hush, Masha!'

'Why should I hush? I am asking Mr Motley if he does not think that our busts are already O.K.'

'I do indeed.'

'Do you hear that, Varya? I shall tell Hikohoki that Mr Motley has a very high esteem for our busts without further alteration.'

'The subject,' said Varya primly, 'is not well suited for general conversation.'

'Tell me about your singing lessons,' said Juan.

'I do not mind being taught how to sing,' said Masha, 'but I do not wish to have any disturbance about my bust.'

'The singing lessons,' said Varya loudly, 'are most instructive. We are beginning again from the bottom.'

'Hikohoki is discontented with every part of us,' said Masha. 'He says we cannot sing, and that we have inferior bosoms.'

'He has a great admiration for you,' said Juan. 'He's not only extremely fond of you both, but he's quite sure that as soon as you've finished your training you're going to have a triumphal career.'

'He is very appreciative,' said Varya. 'Come now, Masha, you cannot deny that he has gone to much trouble for our happiness.'

Before Masha could reply, a servant came in with a double-decked wagon of decanters, bottles, cocktail-shakers, glasses, and ice. Varya, with the elegant despotism of a born hostess, told him where to put it, told him to turn out the overhead lights, to bring a table lamp, and put a log on the fire. Then she asked Juan if he would be so kind as to shake a cocktail for them.

'You are giving him too much trouble,' said Masha. 'Get up, Varya, and I shall do it. Get up, you lazy thing!'

'Not at all,' said Varya firmly. 'Mr Motley can prepare a cocktail much better than you.'

'She is putting on airs,' Masha explained.

'You do not know how to behave, Masha.'

Hurriedly Juan inquired what sort of a cocktail they would like, and without waiting for them to decide, began to shake up a mixture of gin, vermouth, orange-juice, curaçao, bacardi rum, broken ice, and everything else that came handy.

'I like a dash of absinth in mine,' said Varya languidly.

'I hadn't thought of that,' said Juan, and added wormwood to the mixture.

Its eventual colour was a pale and murky puce, and its flavour was deceptively mild. Varya offered her congratulations, Masha made room for Juan to sit beside her, and for half an hour conversation flowed without break or difficulty. Then Varya said they must go and dress for dinner, and though Masha protested and Juan said he proposed, for the best reason in the world, to dine in jodhpurs, she insisted on the convention and finally had her way.

Her back, as she left the room, was the very picture of a dignified and social back; but Masha looked over her shoulder and kissed her hand.

17

IT was, thought Juan, a difficult situation. It was the very devil of a situation. To decline an appeal to gallantry was humiliating, but one's own humiliation could be borne. A certain degree of resilience, something of the quality of a duck's back, a properly reticulated memory, an objective intelligence – any one of these was a good enough safeguard against undue mortification. So that was all right. But only so far as he himself was concerned. He did not know if Masha had equally sound defences.

He must not hurt her feelings. That was quite clear. But to refuse a young woman's offer of love, without wounding her self-esteem, was at all times a difficult operation, and in the present case the difficulty was very curiously aggravated.

In Masha's eyes the situation was ideal. Bacchus had removed all competition, and love might frolic as it pleased. Varya had dined a trifle too liberally, and so there would be no protest, comment, or interference from her. But to Juan the spectacle of Varya's narcosis was strangely inhibitory. He could not make love to Masha while her adjacent sister lay in a post-prandial trance, but neither could he explain his reluctance without aspersing their twin condition. And that would hurt her feelings even more than a blunt refusal of affection. It was confoundedly difficult. For ten minutes he had been talking as well as he could, but Masha was weary of talk and wanted more substantial entertainment. It was about as unmanageable a situation as he had ever been in.

The twins had come down to dinner in white evening frocks of the most sophisticated simplicity. Slim and supple in the chaste candour of their gowns, they had entered the room like a pair of swans, like tall lilies that no rude earth had smutched, like schooners immaculate on the bright ocean-edge of a dream. To call them lovely would be the most miserly of statements. A barebone parsimonious statement that did neither of them justice, and for the pair of them was pitifully inadequate. As the beauty of the Taj Mahal is by a miracle doubled in the long lagoon that lies in front of it, so was Varya reflected in Masha, and the perfection of Masha made doubly evident in Varya. Whoso looks at the Taj, in the clear coolness of an Indian morning – in that air that tells sweetly of green things, youth, and the springtime of desire – will of a certainty find in his heart a divine adultery, being now in spirit wedded to the white marble dome that floats in thin blue air, and a moment later enamoured of its sister dome that swims in cold green water. So, looking from Varya to Masha – like as two swans in a lake, save that Masha's hair was the mild gold of an old spade-guinea, Varya's bright as a new penny – Juan perceived that fidelity to either implied a bigamous devotion to her sister, and faith unfaithful would keep him doubly true.

Or, to be more accurate, it would if he were in a mood for so heroic a consummation. But to admit a new affection, even a single one, after having just said good-bye to Harriet, would be grossly ungentle. It was, indeed, unthinkable. It was more remote from possibility than squaring the circle or arson in the Thames. He was going to be a stranger to emotional adventures for a very long time to come. That was quite certain, and even such duplicated loveliness as the Karamazov sisters' would not make him break faith with his latest memory.

They went in to dinner, and Juan, despite his conviction of fidelity, could not help wishing that a greater interval of time had separated his leave-taking from Harriet and his meeting with the twins. They were beauty and its mirror; beauty underlined by its lovely equal; and to escape the lambency of Masha's eyes was to encounter the soft brilliance of Varya's.

Their behaviour, fortunately, fell short of the perfection of their appearance. Varya's temper had again been ruffled, and Masha did nothing to improve it by declaring that her ill-humour was due to the redundancy of her underwear.

'She is now become so very refined,' she said, 'that she is wearing knickers. And naturally, in a smart gown like this, they make some wrinkles.'

'It is not possible to be truly fashionable unless you are proper underneath,' said Varya.

'You are now talking like a snob,' said Masha.

'And you are a sans culotte!'

'She will soon be telling you,' said Masha, 'that our Uncle Georgy had once the honour of being addressed by the Grand Duke Nicholas. The Grand Duke said, "Get out of my way, old man."'

'Masha,' said Varya, 'is at heart quite a Bolshevik.'

'Let us avoid politics,' said Juan, 'especially at the dinner table. I would sooner be a dog snarling over a bone than talk politics at dinner. Tell me instead about Hikohoki or your Uncle Georgy. The best of all conversation is gossip, don't you think?'

The atmosphere soon became friendlier, and argument was amiably reduced to the exchanging of anecdotes. In several ways, however, Varya continued to reveal her social aspirations and her affinity with the upper classes.

'In Russia, before the Revolution,' she said, 'the wealthy people were much addicted to wine. It is also a great favourite with me.'

She substantiated this proud utterance with sherry, hock, champagne, and brandy, and towards the end of dinner she wore a sleepy whimsical little smile. She mentioned the interesting fact that in the eighteenth century one of the most generous benefactors of the Bogoroditski Convent, in Kazan, had been a Count Karamazov. An ancestor, of course. Thereafter she contributed nothing to the conversation, except to give instructions that the brandy should be taken through to the drawing-room. But from her dreamy smile and the far-away happy look in her eyes, it was easy to deduce that she was enjoying very good company in the most superior kind of environment.

In the drawing-room, on the broad couch beside her sister, she fell fast asleep. But even in slumber her demeanour was admirable. Her head drooped a little, but she retained her smile and her breathing was gentle as a child's. Her behaviour, though admittedly negative, was otherwise beyond criticism.

Masha's behaviour, on the other hand, was regrettably positive. She wanted Juan to make love to her, and she made no bones about saying so. And Juan, for one reason or another, found the situation little to his liking and difficult to manage.

He discovered the solution almost by accident. Helping himself to a little more brandy, he inadvertently poured far too much into the large round glass, and was perturbed by the thought of wasting it. Then it occurred to him that the generous surplus might be put to a good and proper use, and with a sigh he said to Masha: 'I suppose you're fond of gambling?'

'Of course,' she said. 'I will make bets and wagers on anything at all.'

'I bet you ten dollars you can't drink this brandy at a gulp.'

Masha looked at it doubtfully.

'I'll make it twenty dollars.'

Masha still hesitated.

'I thought so,' said Juan. 'You're not really a gambler. You're only pretending to be one. I wish Varya was awake. She could do it.'

'I am a much better gambler than Varya.'

'It doesn't look like it.'

'Give me the glass.'

She drank it easily enough, gasped a little, and wiped a tear from her eye. 'There!' she said, triumphantly.

'That was very clever,' said Juan, and gave her two ten-dollar notes. He stooped and kissed her lightly on the forehead. It was a valedictory kiss.

With a trifling excuse he left the room, and when he returned, ten minutes later, he found Masha also sleeping. It was a shame, he admitted, but she would be none the worse except for a slight headache in the morning. And a headache was better than wounded vanity.

He thought he had better make the unconscious twins more comfortable, for Masha lay somewhat clumsily against her sister. Putting his hands under her shoulders he tried to thrust her farther on to the couch, but she slid down again. Then he attempted to lift her from the knees, but it was difficult to maintain his balance, and Masha rolled somewhat heavily towards Varya. This unfortunate mischance dislodged Varya, who began to slip, quite gently, from her nest of cushions. Juan made a hurried grab at her, but by a piece of undeserved ill-luck her descent was suddenly accelerated, and his hand caught the top of her dress and ripped it open from bosom to waist. The two sisters now lay on the floor, but their fall had not wakened them. They stirred a little; Varya smiled, and Masha blew the prettiest little bubble imaginable; and heavy slumber again descended on them.

It was now comparatively easy to arrange them in a comfortable position, and having straightened them out, Juan put cushions under their heads and covered them with a convenient piece of brocade. Lying there together, so lovely and so innocent, they reminded him of a pantomime he had seen at the age of six or thereabouts. He and his brother Noel and his sister Rhea and his mother had sat together in a box, and Noel and Rhea, though both were older than he, had barely concealed their tears when the Babes in the Wood resigned themselves to the mercy of the elements. To Juan their emotion had seemed ridiculous, but the spectacle of Varya and Masha made him remember it with lenience.

It was a pity that Varya's dress had been torn. It had probably cost a lot and Hikohoki might not be too pleased by the necessity of buying her a new one. Hikohoki . . .

'My God!' said Juan.

He had suddenly perceived the awkwardness of his position. It was worse, much worse, than his earlier predicament. It was an appalling situation, and the prospect of explaining it to Hikohoki was enough to daunt anyone. It completely daunted Juan. He had been left alone with the sisters – those bundles of charm, twin apples of Hikohoki's doting eyes, and his most expensive investment – and the result of their evening together was that Varya and Masha lay unconscious, Varya's dress was torn to the waist, and tightly clutched in Masha's hand were two ten-dollar notes.

'Oh, my God!' repeated Juan.

The knowledge that his conduct had been scrupulously honourable did little to comfort him. There was nothing in the evidence to suggest honourable behaviour, and the infatuated Hikohoki could not be expected to disregard all he saw for the sake of what, by patient listening, he might ultimately hear. There was only one thing to do, and that was to clear out immediately. It would be easy enough to explain everything in a letter, and meanwhile Hikohoki must think what he liked.

It was fortunate that Juan had made inquiries about the situation of the house and its relative position to the main road from Shanghai. He knew how to get back, and though he did not relish the thought of walking seven or eight miles in the dark, when the whole neighbourhood was suffering from the disturbing effects of war, he preferred the slight possibility of other danger to the certain embarrassment of facing Hikohoki.

He pushed another cushion or two under the twins, and tucked the brocade more securely round them. Then, very quietly, he opened a window and dropped into the garden. The night was dark, but not impenetrably dark.

He moved slowly and cautiously towards the gate, fearing that one of the soldiers might be on guard. But a careful reconnaissance showed that the coast was clear, and with great relief he got on to the road and began to walk briskly in the direction of Shanghai.

18

THE dark road was deserted, and the loneliness of his journey was uninterrupted save by two motor-cars. Warned by their headlights and fearing each time that Hikohoki might be the driver, Juan crouched in a ditch till they had passed. He saw nothing else. No bandits, footpads, or marauding soldiers interfered with him. The night was frosty, and little ridges of frozen mud crackled under his feet. A stinking hamlet through which he passed was empty as a buried city. Not even a dog came out to bark at him. The strength of the wine he had drunk at dinner was soon spent, and he felt very tired. He grew somewhat depressed, and thought, not of the twins, but of Harriet. The road was long, and when he grew weary of thinking about Harriet he considered the tediousness of walking. It was a poor alternative, and he came to the conclusion that he had probably drunk too much.

On the outskirts of Shanghai he was challenged by an English voice. It was a cheerful sound in the darkness of China, and the sight of a small detachment of Regulars, sitting at ease round a brazier in a sandbag redoubt, was also comforting. The sergeant in charge was sympathetic when he heard that Juan, having fallen off his horse, had been chasing it all day.

'A nasty animal, the 'orse,' he said. 'I never see one without thinking, Thank God for progress. All my people are in the garage and cycle business. You'd better 'ave a cup of tea, sir. You must be tired after all that walking.'

After a cup of strong tea, Juan felt better, but discomfort, both mental and physical, again assailed him when he at last arrived at his hotel. For a long time he could not sleep, and twice during the night he woke with a curious feeling of anxiety and dissatisfaction. But not until the morning, when he was shaving and the Japanese guns were again registering on the ruins of the North Station, did he realize what had been worrying him, and remember his most grievous blunder.

He had left Lo Yu's plan, in its dragon-painted bamboo case, on a small table beside a bowl of fine Satsuma ware in Hikohoki's country house. And now the war had started again, and the house was beyond the frontier, and once more the plan was lost. To tell Kuo that he had held the salvation of China in his hands, and confess that he had forgotten to bring it home, was going to be very difficult and thoroughly unpleasant.

The sly thought came that there was no need to tell her. Kuo knew nothing about his meeting with Hikohoki, and in all probability would never know – unless he told her. He was tempted to let her remain in ignorance. It would save a lot of trouble.

Before he had finished shaving, however, he realized the impossibility of silence. Kuo's heart was set on regaining the plan – to her it was of infinite and irreplaceable value – and to deny her news of it would be unforgivable. He must confess to losing it. He would have to admit his inefficiency, his futility, forgetfulness, unpardonable folly, his dismal hebetude, and anything else that Kuo might charge him with. She would probably accuse him of more than folly, of worse than futility. She had been angry enough when, in the Chinese City, he had lost his way; it was difficult to imagine how angry she would be when she learnt that he had lost Lo Yu's plan. He must brace himself for a really horrible half-hour.

He ate a hearty breakfast and under the stabilizing influence of food discovered that things were not so bad as he had thought. In the first place, though he told Kuo where the plan was, there was no need for him to explain that Hikohoki had given it to him and he had forgotten to take it away. That would help no one. And in the second place he could avoid actual contact, and most of the dangers of cross-examination, by using the telephone. The telephone was a very mitigating instrument.

He put his call through and waited with a reasonable degree of confidence . . . 'Juan speaking. How are you, darling? . . . No, I'm not being flippant, only polite. As a matter of fact I've got some very important news. I've found Lo Yu's plan . . . Well, wait a minute and I'll tell you . . . No, I haven't actually got it, but I know where it is . . . I'm going to, if you'll give me time. It's in Hikohoki's country house, about eight or nine miles away. I'm quite sure that he hasn't made any use of it, and I don't believe he knows its value . . . What? . . .

But there's no need for that. I can tell you everything from here, and I'm rather busy this morning . . . What? . . . Oh, all right.'

Kuo had insisted on his coming to Min Cho-fu's flat immediately. She had supplemented insistence with an emotional appeal. She had fortified her appeal with a brief reference to their mutual affection. And Juan, though reluctant, had agreed to go.

In the cab that took him to Min Cho-fu's he considered a variety of ways in which he might be greeted, but he failed to anticipate the sight that awaited him.

There was a certain disorder in the flat that accentuated the trim smartness of the two young officers there. Though hardly so well-tailored as an English uniform, their tunics and breeches were decently cut, and among soft civilian furnishings their polished belts and re-volver-holsters gave them an aggressively military air. One of them, who had seemingly had difficulty with his belt, was being assisted by Miss Min, who knelt beside him and wrestled with its buckle and tongue.

To his great surprise Juan recognized Kuo in this unfamiliar and unexpected attire. Though it did not suit her, it transformed her into a better-looking subaltern than was usual on a Chinese parade-ground, and she wore it without embarrassment. Her manner, indeed, was as soldierly as her uniform, and Juan felt sure that when he spoke to her over the telephone, she had not yet put on her breeches. She had been, for a moment or two, so entirely and successfully feminine that he had almost heard the emotional susurrus of her petticoat. It was only within the last few minutes that she had hardened her heart and her legs with those sternly martial trappings.

Before he could inquire the purpose of her disguise, she brusquely ordered him to tell her the whole story of his discovery of the plan. He, with responsive coldness, said he had gone paper-chasing; his horse had bolted and thrown him; pursuing it, he had come by accident to Hikohoki's agreeable residence, where in the course of conversation, he had mentioned his interest in Lo Yu's plan, and Hikohoki had shown him the piece of bamboo containing it.

'Why,' said Kuo, 'did you not bring it away with you?'

Juan looked at the polished holster, so prominently attached to her belt, and thought a little dissimulation would be more tactful than the naked truth.

'It is sometimes,' he said, 'considered ill-mannered to help yourself to other people's property.'

'The plan is not Hikohoki's property,' said Kuo, and spoke in Chinese to the young officer, to whom Juan had not been introduced. They had a brief discussion and Kuo inquired where Hikohoki's house was situated.

Juan told her, as well as he could, and said in a friendly way: 'It's a pity it's out of bounds. I'm afraid you won't be able to pay him a visit till the war's over.'

'Did you learn anything about his present activities in espionage?'

'My dear, I've told you a score of times that Hikohoki isn't a spy. He used to be an insurance agent, which was almost as reprehensible, but he's given even that up now. He's rather a nice little man.'

Kuo had another conversation with her fellow-officer, and Juan exchanged a few words with Miss Min. Then he asked Kuo the reason and purpose of her military attire.

'I have been given a special commission by the Generalissimo,' she answered proudly. 'I am going to play my part in the defence of China.'

'I promised,' said Juan doubtfully, 'to do something about that myself.'

'Are you still eager to fight?'

'Well, I'm quite willing, if you want me to. It might be a bit ostentatious to say that I was eager. But if there's anything I can do in a modest way . . .'

Again Kuo spoke to the young officer, and presently told Juan that his proposal would be considered, and if his services were required he would be duly informed.

'That's splendid,' he said, referring rather to the postponement of his offer than to the possibility of its acceptance. He turned to Miss Min: 'How is Peony getting on?'

'She is much better,' said Miss Min, in her soft whispering voice. 'We are very fond of her, and it is nice to have her here.'

Kuo put on her military cap, and prepared to go. Juan would have liked to stay and talk to Miss Min, and possibly to Peony, but Kuo, giving him no chance to loiter, ushered him firmly out.

'I'm sorry about the plan,' he said. 'I wish I had brought it with me.'

'One cannot do more than one's character permits,' said Kuo;

and before Juan could decide whether he had been forgiven or insulted, she bade him good-bye.

'Good luck,' he said.

Kuo gravely saluted.

19

JUAN spent the rest of the day in dullish idleness. He went to the Club and played a game of billiards with a hearty young man who, for the last year or so, had been commanding a gun-boat on the upper reaches of the Yangtze. He looked at the papers and the illustrated weeklies, and found a mild entertainment in contrasting the news of world-wide unrest and violence with the inanimate elegance of Society at its fashionable restaurants and First Nights. Then he began to write a letter to his mother, but did not finish it because he could not decide how to answer her often-reiterated question, 'When are you coming home?'

In her last letter she had tried to force a decision by enclosing the money for his fare. They had become very wealthy, she said, for Sir Hildebrand had retired from the Civil Service and been made a director of two Banks, three Investment Trusts, and several Limited Companies. His character, she added, had undergone a curious change as a result of prosperity. 'He is now convinced,' she wrote, 'that this is the best of all possible worlds, and he spends four evenings a week playing with a model railway that he has built in the library. I suppose his brain is softening, as his father's did, but he is very happy and making far more money than we can spend. Noel has resigned his commission and is also going into the City. He says the Stock Exchange offers more scope than the Rifle Brigade, and perhaps he is right. But I dislike him so much in a bowler hat. Rhea is also a disappointment. She is a model of virtue, dresses worse than ever, and her baby has two disgustingly superior nurses and a voice like a guinea-fowl. So I wish you would come home, for life has become very dull now that I have no need to worry about my bridge losses.'

He would probably go home before very long, thought Juan, but he was unwilling to commit himself to any definite date. He disliked the making of plans and their regimentation of behaviour, preferring by far the fluency of spontaneous movement. He could hardly leave China, moreover, without coming to an understanding with Kuo. A friendly understanding, if possible; but at present that would be difficult, for though she had practically discarded him as a lover, and no longer attached any importance to his collaboration in her nationalist ambitions, she would probably denounce his suggestion of going home as rank desertion. Everything would be very much easier if only the war would come to an end; but unfortunately there was neither hint nor sign of a conclusion. There was, of course, no need for him to make an immediate decision, or even to seek an early settlement with Kuo. In time the problem would solve itself, or disappear from view; and the pendant difficulty of how to answer his mother's question could be dealt with by not answering it. To postpone the arbitrament, to await the pointer of circumstance, and for the present to submit to the flux of events, appeared not only the easiest but the most sensible decision.

He played another game of billiards, ate a light dinner, went early to bed, and slept soundly.

In the morning he was wakened by the summons of the telephone. It was Harris who wanted to speak to him, and Harris had important news. General Wu Tu-fu and his Invincible Tanks – all four of them – had arrived in Shanghai, and both he and Rocco would be at General Sun Sat-lo's headquarters at noon. Harris had arranged an interview, and if Juan and Flanders wanted to go with him, he could take them. He was leaving at eleven, and he would meet them at the Club. But if they weren't ready by then, he couldn't wait.

He rang off, and Juan, having telephoned to Flanders and told him the news – he was audibly ill-humoured at being fetched from his bed – dressed without more delay and breakfasted in some haste.

He met Flanders in the reading-room at the Club, and was much surprised by his manner and appearance. He sat on a leather couch, his legs thrust out, his great paunch rising above them like the round hill of Morvern, his hands on the seat of the couch as though he were about to lever himself up, but had not yet nerved himself to so much labour. His chin, on double rolls of good firm fat, was sunk on his chest, his mouth was petulant, his eyes behind their gleaming spectacles were angry and perplexed. When Juan came in he was greeted by a muffled and rumbling voice that growled, 'It's raining.'

'Quite heavily,' Juan agreed. 'It must be horrible to be at war in weather like this.'

Flanders grunted again. 'They've got umbrellas. All Chinese soldiers have got umbrellas.'

'Harris is coming at eleven,' said Juan.

'The fellow's killing himself. Work and drink. He can't stand both of them.'

'It's very good of him to take us to see Wu Tu-fu.'

'Who wants to see him? I've seen thousands of Chinamen.'

'But you want to see Rocco, and I want to see Rocco's reaction when he sees you.'

'Have they brought the tanks here?'

'Yes. Harris said he thought they were going to take them into action almost immediately. I'd like to see a tank attack.'

'Seen it again and again. There's nothing in it.'

'A bit liverish this morning, aren't you?'

'Nothing of the sort.'

'I expected to find you roaring like a forest fire to get hold of Rocco.'

Flanders heaved his huge body forward – his fore-arms stiffened, his paunch impended – and sitting upright and looking seriously at Juan said: 'The trouble's this: I'm too sensitive, Motley. I've a sort of delicacy, I shrink from the brutality of commerce, and to quarrel about money is a thing I've never liked. It's distasteful, do you see? The whole business of chaffering and bargaining is foreign to my nature. I was meant for other things, and peace and philosophy, and sitting quietly in a corner.'

'But you can't sit in a corner till after you've dealt with Rocco. He's robbed you of seven thousand pounds.'

Flanders groaned. 'More than that. Of seven years, and my old age in Gloucestershire.'

'Well, what are you going to do about it?'

'If I could see Rocco . . .'

'You're going to see him. Harris is quite sure he'll be there.'

'With an audience about him, with Wu Tu-fu and an army at his back! I want to see him alone. If I had him alone I could talk to him.'

'But having an audience isn't going to suit Rocco. He's the swindler, and swindlers like a quiet life as much as you do. You still have the counterfeit money he gave you? Well, there's half your evidence, and the other half is the tanks. You sold them four tanks, and got bad money in exchange. Your case is complete, and neither Rocco nor Wu Tu-fu can dispute it.'

Flanders, wrestling with some private anger, had no words to express the turmoil of his thoughts. With a furious gesture he tousled his thick grey hair till it stood like tufts of benty grass. Then he exclaimed: 'Come and have a drink.'

'It's rather early, isn't it?'

'Come and have a drink!'

Under the impulse of some tremendous decision, he rose gigantically from the sofa, and striding into the bar addressed the little group of unoccupied and listless attendants in the voice and manner of a squadron-leader bidding his Lancers to charge the guns. 'Brandy and ginger-ale!' he commanded, and the air was filled with the thought of thundering hooves, and the menace of a long line of spears.

He emptied his glass in two gulps, and loudly smacked his lips, as though to symbolize the clash of cavalry and the waiting batteries.

'I'll come,' he exclaimed. 'I'll not lose my pension without a fight for it.'

'Good,' said Juan.

At that moment Harris appeared, tired and brisk, untidy and alert, his hat on the back of his head and his waterproof flapping open. With his handkerchief he dabbed blood from his chin, where he had cut himself shaving, and nodding to Flanders and Juan, told the nearest barman to give him a Horse's Neck.

'All ready?' he asked.

'All ready,' said Juan.

Harris finished his drink. 'Let's go,' he said.

In the vestibule, where coats were hung, Flanders paused irresolute, his ulster half-on, and said: 'I've forgotten something. I'll be back in a minute.'

'Where has he gone?' asked Harris.

'To have another drink, I expect.'

'Isn't he feeling well?'

'He didn't want to come with us. I think he's frightened of Wu Tu-fu.'

'He is, is he? Then I know what he's been up to,' said Harris. 'But Rocco got the better of him.'

'I'm looking forward to their meeting.'

'So am I.'

'And my sympathies are with Flanders.'

Harris looked at Juan with speculation in his gaze, and was about to ask another question, when Flanders returned with a certain moisture on his lips and in his eyes, a protrusion in one pocket, and the expression of a man well pleased with his own sagacity. He patted the protrusion and muttered confidentially, 'Emergency rations. Trust an old soldier, eh?'

They got into the car that was waiting. Flanders and Juan sat in the back, Harris drove, and beside him was a young Chinese journalist who was to act as interpreter. They left the portentous architecture of the Bund and turned into the busy traffic of Nanking Road. The black waterproof hoods of the rickshaws glistened in the rain, and the many-coloured banners with their gold or scarlet ideographs hung heavy and motionless. As though both sides had been disheartened by the dreary weather, there were no sounds of war. The guns were silent, and the ordinary noises of traffic seemed louder than usual; the iron screeching of tram-cars, the grunting shout of rickshaw-pullers, the scream of a motor-car's tyres and the blare of its horn, had acquired a tone of triumph or complacency.

Driving through the endless streets – innumerably intersecting, parallels beyond counting – Juan felt curiously abashed by the magnitude of human effort and its manifest absurdity. To work so hard and so long for no better purpose and to no wiser end than the building of a huge and ugly town was obviously a perversion; and to go to war in order to acquire a dingy segment of such a town was stark insanity. What could be more wildly idiotic than to fight and die for the conquest of a patch of hideous buildings rich in dirt and disease, for a new burden of responsibility, and dubious wealth that would be spent only on producing yet more ugly streets, dirt, disease, and tedious liability? Much of the world – most of it, perhaps – was certainly mad, and Juan, though thankful to have so far escaped the contagion of its grosser lunacies, was momentarily perturbed by their nearness and immensity.

But Western civilization had not wholly destroyed the native life of China. Even in the busiest areas it stubbornly persisted, for at the corner of a modern street would be a dirty little eating-place, with

195

steam rising from two cauldrons, a plate of pale anonymous food, another of brown bean-curd, or stinking fish; while back-to-back with office buildings would be a bright display of joss-papers and silver tissue money for the dead. – So in many parts of London there was the remnant of an ancient hedge or a drooping untidy tree, the last relics of some village that the great town had swallowed. – They passed a temple whose courtyard was crowded with refugees, and came into narrower streets and a poorer neighbourhood. They were stopped and questioned by soldiers at a cross-roads guarded on all sides by ramparts of sandbags and barbed wire.

Under a sky like dirty wool, over rougher roads and between squalid buildings, they approached a group of cotton-mills and a filthy hamlet of wattled huts. These wretched buildings, their walls of dark matting daubed with mud – built on the mud and fluttering in every wind – were crowded with dark-clad coolies and children half-naked, half patched in rags. A little farther on was a bend of the Soochow Creek, muddy-sided, spanned by a rickety bridge. They crossed and looked down at two sampans, matting-roofed, in which were half a dozen fat red-faced boatmen and their families. The road grew worse, and the wheels of the car churned loosely in the mud.

'We'll have to get out and walk,' said Harris. 'It's lucky the rain has stopped.'

They walked for about a mile, Flanders complaining volubly of the heavy going, and came in sight of what seemed to be a small and well-fenced plantation of young trees. It was ostentatiously guarded, on the side they were approaching, by numerous sentries and two machine-gun posts.

'Sun Sat-lo's a bit of an aesthete,' said Harris. 'That's why he's chosen a nursery for his headquarters. It's several miles behind the line, and that's another advantage. We'll probably find him talking to the gardener about conifers and cryptomerias. You and Flanders had better have cards, by the way.'

He took out his well-filled pocket-book, and selecting two visiting-cards gave them to Juan and Flanders.

'You're the *Manchester Guardian*,' he said to Juan, 'and Flanders is the *Christian Science Monitor*.'

They were halted by a sentry, to whom Harris showed his pass, and after some delay they were admitted to the nursery. A little breeze sprang up as they entered, and rattling the orderly thickets of young trees, blew from their stiff leaves a miniature storm of gathered rain-drops. As Harris had guessed, General Sun Sat-lo was talking to the gardener, a shrivelled old fellow in a long blue gown, and with them was a tall soldierly man, rigid of carriage, smoking a cigarette in a long holder. A little distance away, mute and decorous, was a group of eight or ten staff officers.

'That's Tsai Ting-kai, who commands the 19th Route Army,' said Harris. 'There must be something important going to happen.'

General Sun Sat-lo was a tall thin man with a scholar's face and abstracted expression. He was well-dressed, and distinguished by a thin black moustache that drooped slightly beyond the corners of his mouth. Juan found it difficult to believe that this was the ardent visitor to the *maison à gros numéro* in the Rue des Andouilles of whom he had heard from Masha and Varya.

Sun Sat-lo greeted them cordially, and apologized through the interpreter for his inability to speak English.

'I have been receiving instruction in the training of youth,' he said, and pointed to a small stone-pine whose branches, twisted round with wire and pegged to the earth with fifty strings, were being taught to grow in a certain pattern. 'Nowadays,' he added with a pleasant smile, 'gardeners are the only people in China who can command obedience.'

'They have certain advantages,' said Harris. 'They aren't troubled by doubt, and they know that the proper thing for a tree is to be ornamental.'

'Whereas the leader of men has innumerable difficulties, since the better kind of man is not like a vessel designed for a single purpose,' said the General.

Harris replied, 'There are three hundred odes, but they all teach the same lesson: avoid evil thoughts.'

Again the General smiled. 'If we tire of discussing the war,' he said, 'I see that we can amuse ourselves by talking of sylviculture and Confucius.'

He took Harris by the arm and led him into the main room of the gardener's house. This was a long bare apartment, furnished for military occupation with a couple of trestle tables, a chair or two, some benches, a stove in one corner, and maps on the wall. Beside one of the tables stood a plump and disconsolate officer in shabby uniform, whose wrists were manacled; two soldiers with rifles and fixed bayonets; and another officer, bespectacled, untidy, and fat. General Sat-lo sat down, and lifting a file of papers from the table read what was evidently a report of the prisoner's misconduct. He asked a question, to which the prisoner unhappily replied, and on another document inscribed his signature. The prisoner was led out.

Harris's interpreter whispered discreetly, 'He stole five telescopes and tried to desert, but they caught him and he is going to be shot.'

General Tsai Ting-kai, standing by the stove in the corner, had paid no attention to this brief episode. As soon as the prisoner and his escort had gone, he exchanged a few brusque sentences with Sun Sat-lo, and left. Thereupon Sun, in the friendliest manner, told Harris that he was now at his service, and Harris began to ask a number of questions about the disposition of forces, the unity of the Chinese command, its relation to Nanking, and the prospect of restricting hostilities to their present area. Sun Sat-lo was by turns disarmingly frank and blandly non-committal; he had taken a liking to Harris, and the interview promised to be a long one.

Juan and Flanders, as representatives of the *Manchester Guardian* and the *Christian Science Monitor*, pretended to pay close attention to this laboriously interpreted conversation; but Flanders grew more and more restless, and Juan's mind also began to wander.

Before coming into the house Flanders had managed to drink a surreptitious mouthful from the bottle of brandy with which he had thoughtfully provided himself, but his tongue was dry again, and his heart was again doubtful. Two or three times, when he heard footsteps outside, he looked quickly over his shoulder and nerved himself to encounter Rocco and Wu Tu-fu. He frowned and muttered; but Juan took no notice of him, for he was looking with great interest at the maps with which the opposite wall was lavishly decorated.

Immediately in front of him was an Admiralty chart of Hong Kong. Unfortunately it was upside down. On one side of it was a large map of Brighton and Hove, on the other a pictorial plan, torn from a guide-book, of America's Golden West. Unless Sun Sat-lo and the Generals associated with him were bent on world conquest, it was difficult to perceive any relevance in this strange assortment of cartography; but possibly the maps served to impress the General's less sophisticated colleagues, and perhaps they helped him to maintain a useful sense of proportion.

While Juan was still pondering the contingent effect of Brighton and Hove on Chinese strategy, there was a loud-voiced commotion outside, the door was thrown open, and in stumped a bulky figure in British uniform, gorgeous with medal-ribbons and red Staff tabs, who, having hoarsely shouted 'General Wu Tu-fu!' came noisily to the salute.

General Wu Tu-fu was a plump smiling little man who came in very neatly and quietly, and from his expression appeared to think that he had made rather a good joke by sending Colonel Rocco to announce him. He was followed by a staff as numerous as Sun's, and the room grew somewhat crowded. He greeted Sun Sat-lo, and immediately began a very animated discussion.

Rocco, meanwhile, had caught sight of Flanders. His right arm lost its rigidity, but for a long time, as though he had forgotten all about it, remained in the saluting position; and his mouth opened like a burst plum. He was a striking figure in his Staff Officer's uniform. His service cap, with its heavily gilded peak, was perhaps a little too big for him – it appeared to lean heavily on his rather prominent ears – and to a critical eye the primrose hue of his generously cut breeches might have seemed unnecessarily bright. But his mahogany-tinted boots were magnificent, and his tunic was cut with the opulence that is permitted only to officers of exalted rank. His two rows of medal ribbons were handsome enough for anyone, and his Sam Browne belt, with double shoulder-straps, impressively supported a holster at each side. Not for nothing had he learnt gun-play in America.

When he had recovered something of his composure, he used his right hand – still loosely saluting – to scratch his protruding ear, and assuming a smile of ghastly geniality tiptoed creakily towards Flanders.

'Well, for Christ's sake!' he whispered. 'Say, I never thought I'd see you out here. How's every little thing?'

Huge, red-faced, and menacing – but with a wary glance at Wu Tu-fu – Flanders muttered fiercely, 'Come outside!'

'Why, Major, there's nothing I'd like better. But I'm in attendance on the Big Shot, and he may want me any time.'

'You're a cockatrice!'

'Now keep it clean, Major.'

'You're a thief and a swindler and a cart-horse dressed up like a three-hundred-guinea hunter!'

'Ah, quit riding me. I don't understand what you're talking about anyway.'

'Then come outside where we can speak plainly.'

Rocco shook his head, and whispered, 'I tell you, it can't be done. I'm indispensable, see? The Big Boy would never forgive me if I left him to handle a conference alone.'

'What do you think he'll say when I show him these bogus notes you gave me?'

'Bogus notes? Now you sure have got me guessing, Major. I don't know what you mean by bogus notes.'

Flanders thrust his hand into an inner pocket and pulled out the thick packet of worthless paper for which he had sold his four tanks.

'Look at that,' he muttered. 'As false and counterfeit as the ribbons on your tunic.'

'Put it away,' hissed Rocco. 'You don't want to interfere with the course of the conference, do you?'

'I'll interfere with the whole course of Asia unless you come out and talk as man to man with me.'

The sight of Rocco's embarrassment had filled Flanders with confidence, and the strain of talking in a whisper had made his face uncommonly red. Peremptory, flushed, and inflated, he was an impressive figure, and Rocco's resistance collapsed.

'It's irregular,' he grumbled, 'but I'll do anything to save trouble and oblige a friend. We'll slip out quietly, see?'

With heavy but careful movements Rocco tiptoed to the door, and Flanders with elephantine caution followed him. None of the Chinese paid any attention, but Harris whispered to Juan, 'Do you want to go with them?'

'Better leave them alone,' answered Juan. 'They'll come to terms more easily if they've no opportunity for showing-off.'

Harris nodded, and beckoned Juan into a corner. 'You understand what's been happening?' he asked. 'The Japanese threw out a salient from Hongkew, and developed a new attack from there. That means they've pushed their front well out into open country, and they've moved forward from the extension, which is their right wing. Yesterday, they captured a village called Nanyang – there was no opposition – and dug themselves in on a line south-west of it. They're holding that line in strength, and preparing to advance again. But Sun Sat-lo wants to attack at once and drive them back from the Nanyang line.'

'Using Wu Tu-fu's tanks, I suppose?' said Juan.

'That's the idea.'

'I hope Flanders gets paid for them first.'

'It was Flanders who sold them, was it? I guessed as much. But where did he get them?'

'They were built in Japan and smuggled into Shanghai by a little man called Hikohoki. We met him, you remember, in Chapei the night the war started, and I've had quite a lot to do with him since then.'

'You've got mixed up with some queer people, haven't you?'

'They're all right.'

A moment or two later Harris asked, 'Is that Flanders's voice or Rocco's?'

From somewhere in the garden had come an agonized bellow, twice repeated. A bellow with a dying fall, at first enormous and rotund, but dwindling to a faint flute-like note of pain. It startled the two generals, their aides and other officers, who rose with questioning glances and hurried to the door, whither Harris and Juan preceded them.

About fifty yards away, on a broad grassy path between two groves of youngling trees, was a group of soldiers who watched with great enjoyment a spectacle of some brutality. Colonel Rocco, his face almost black with congested blood, lay helpless on the ground while Flanders sat astride of him, and, as though riding a horse, jogged up and down with a precise and regular motion. At each descent a sound of anguish came from Rocco's purple lips, but now no louder than a little whistling groan; for there was no breath left in his body.

'That sort of thing must be very bad for discipline,' said Juan.

'Very bad indeed,' said Harris, and pushed one of the soldiers aside to get a better view.

But the two Chinese generals, attracted by the unusual nature of the spectacle, were apparently blind to its subversive nature, and they also became interested spectators.

'Who is the very fat man?' asked General Wu. 'And why is he riding upon my Military Adviser?'

'I am told he is the representative of the *Christian Science Monitor*,' answered General Sun, 'but the reason for his riding upon Colonel Rocco I do not know. From his silence, however, and his great activity, I infer he is familiar with the Confucian precept, that the Superior Person is modest in speech but liberal in performance.'

20

NOTHING but exhaustion – the exhaustion of Flanders – saved Rocco from a humiliating death. Flanders rode him till he was almost as breathless as his victim, and when at last he got up, Rocco lay comatose and visibly flattened. He was carried inside, his clothes were loosened, and Juan, having borrowed Flanders's brandy, poured restorative doses down his unresisting throat. Rocco did not immediately recognize him, but the first flicker of returning consciousness brought recognition of the bottle, which he seized with tremulous hands and would not release.

General Wu Tu-fu, in the meantime, had politely inquired in what circumstances and for what reason Flanders had so curiously assaulted his Military Adviser; and Flanders, seizing the chance to tell his story without interruption from Rocco, explained that it was he who had procured the four tanks which General Wu now commanded. He had had great difficulty in getting them – they were made in Japan – and but for his influence with the Japanese he could never had done it. And then, after all his expense of time and money and trouble, Rocco, by means of counterfeit money, had swindled him out of the agreed price. He produced the fraudulent notes, which the generals examined with interest.

'So to relieve your feelings you knocked him down and sat on him?' suggested Wu.

'I knocked him down – or rather I took him round the neck and leant my weight on him, so that he fell – because he denied that these were the notes he gave me. He said he had given me good money, and I was using this spurious paper to get a double price.'

'And is that suggestion true or false?'

'As false as fortune-telling. My friend Motley will tell you I was going home, my passage booked, and I might have been half-way there by now. But the money I was to live on lost colour, my fortune ran out through a hole in the bucket, and I had to stay in Shanghai like a ship on a reef. Poverty I plead guilty to, but neither falsehood nor larceny.'

'You are not, however, the correspondent of the *Christian Science Monitor*?'

'No.'

'And is your friend Mr Motley a genuine representative of the *Manchester Guardian*?'

'I'm afraid not,' said Juan, 'but I was very anxious to see something of the war . . .'

'Are you going to try and sell aeroplanes to me? No? Then that is all right. I am pestered by people who want me to buy aeroplanes. It used to be missionaries who worried me, but they were not nearly so difficult. One could always get rid of them by consenting to be baptized – I have been baptized at least five times – but the aeroplane-sellers are much more persistent.'

Despite the humiliation of his Military Adviser and the disclosure of his criminal behaviour, General Wu's demeanour was as calmly genial as when he had first appeared. He spoke perfect English, with a slightly metallic tone, and his round face, which was quite hairless except for a few almost invisible bristles where his eyebrows should have been, wore constantly an expression of benign amusement. General Sun, having learnt from the interpreter the nature of the dispute, had shrugged his shoulders, and seating himself at a table began to write, in beautiful square characters of the kind known as *Li*, a brief poem on the mutability of the human heart. His G.S.O.I., D.A.D.M.S., D.A.Q.M.G., and A.P.M. – or their Chinese equivalents – watched him with serious and silent admiration.

Rocco had by now sufficiently recovered to sit up, but his face had the mottled appearance of a piece of brawn, and his eyes were dazed like a sleep-walker's. He shuddered and took another long swig from Flanders's bottle of brandy, and shuddered again. Then, apparently with a memory of his old days in the ring at the Garden, he staggered across the room and, taking Flanders warmly by the fist, exclaimed: 'It was a swell fight. Tell 'em I enjoyed every minute of it.'

Raising his clasped hands, in the way that boxers do, and waving them to an imaginary audience, he returned to his corner, and sat there lost in thought.

General Wu tried to persuade him to reply to Flanders's charge of uttering counterfeit notes, but Rocco's explanation was so incoherent that it would bear no meaning of any kind.

'His brain may have been affected,' said General Wu. 'Did you by any chance sit upon his head?'

'I went no higher than his brisket,' said Flanders.

'Perhaps he will get better in time. It is a pity he is disabled, however, as I wanted to explain to General Sun Sat-lo the equipment and design of our tanks. But possibly you can do that? Your knowledge of them may be even more extensive than Rocco's.'

'They're light tanks,' said Flanders, 'bullet-proof and warranted against penetration, splash, flaking, and shearing of nuts and bolts. Their speed across country is ten miles an hour, they'll cross a six-foot trench, a river four feet deep, climb a slope of forty degrees, and crush a tree six inches in diameter. Their range is a hundred and twenty miles, and their armament .303 Vickers machine-guns.'

The interpreter translated this for the benefit of the two generals, and Sun Sat-lo made a suggestion with which General Wu at once concurred.

'My colleague,' he said, 'has expressed a desire to see the tanks, and as they are no more than a mile away, I have taken the liberty of telling him that you will come with us and demonstrate their mechanism. For I myself have only a nodding acquaintance with them.'

Flanders winced and started like a cow in summer with the gadfly on her. 'No, no,' he stammered, 'take an expert – I'm no expert – you need an engineer, a man who knows the inner parts of machinery. I'd be no use at all, but worse than useless, for in all innocence, I'd mislead you. I know nothing of tanks, less than a babe unborn . . .'

'But you have just described them with a very fluent exactitude.'

'Out of book-learning only, mere pedantry. Set me beside a tank itself and I'm lost. I could neither tell which end goes first nor how you enter nor the tactics of their employment.'

General Wu was manifestly surprised at the vehemence and agitation of Flanders's manner. 'The tanks,' he said, 'are still a long way from the front. There will be no danger in going to see them.'

'Danger? Danger's my shadow,' exclaimed Flanders. 'It's followed me all my life, and I take no notice of it. But tanks are a different matter. I tell you I'm innocent as a pullet's egg about them, and my left knee's so stiff I can hardly walk. To go a mile would kill me.'

'Either you are excessively modest, or you have some private reason . . .'

'No reason at all but simple incapacity. There's Rocco, though; lively as a sparrow again; take him, and I'll go back to Shanghai.'

Rocco, indeed, having straightened his tie, buttoned his tunic, and swallowed half a bottle of brandy, was looking much better; but his recovery was more apparent than real. He had been listening solemnly to the conversation, and now, approaching Flanders with great care, he said, 'So you're going back to Shanghai, Major Flanders?'

'Yes, I am.'

With an unexpected lurch, Rocco caught Flanders by the hand – then swaying to the right he clasped the nearer hand of General Wu – and in a hoarse Italianate tenor and his gunmetal accent, with much emotion, began to sing:

> *'Home to our mountains, let us return, love,*
> *There in our young days peace had its reign;*
> *There shall thy sweet song fall on my slumbers,*
> *There shall thy lute make me joyous again!'*

General Wu disengaged himself. 'My Military Adviser is not yet himself,' he said, 'and so again I must ask you to accompany us.'

'My knee . . .'

'I can lend you a walking stick.'

'But I have urgent affairs in Shanghai . . .'

'Your only hope of regaining the money, of which you say you have been cheated, lies in my goodwill, Major Flanders. And if you refuse to come and explain to General Sun Sat-lo and myself the mechanism of the tanks which you have sold me, then I must tell you frankly that you will lose my goodwill.'

Flanders scratched his grey hair and shuddered at some secret thought. Then, with a visible effort, he nerved himself to outface the danger that his imagination saw so clearly, and to trust to his luck, in which he no longer believed.

'If you put it that way,' he said, 'and ask me to do you a favour –

I take it that was your meaning? – then I have only one answer. I'll come. I don't like to be driven, and I can't be bought; but if you appeal to my good nature, then my nature's to say yes. Forget the rest; I'm with you and ready to go.'

Wu Tu-fu and Sun Sat-lo, with their numerous staff, and Harris and Juan, all set out to inspect the tanks. Rocco also accompanied them. Observing a general movement he exclaimed in a loud voice, 'Step on it, brother!' and obeying his own command revealed the old soldier's faculty of suddenly appearing sober when the need arose.

They left the nursery by a path that took them into a road sheltered on one side by a low bank. The two generals walked together, and Flanders so contrived it that several other officers were a barrier between himself and Juan and Harris. Rocco, walking in a very stiff and military fashion, brought up the rear.

Every few yards they passed a group of grey-uniformed soldiers, most of them idle, but unaware of idleness; for those who did nothing at all were doing it with the utter indifference of beasts in a field, and those who were more busily inactive were volubly talking in a high-pitched clattering tongue, or gnawing gobbets of strange food – sitting with rounded shoulders over a small bowl of rice – or earnestly chewing dried melon-seeds.

The tanks, guarded on all sides by a line of soldiers, were heavily camouflaged with winter branches and boughs of willow. Their armour-plated sides shone dully, like a sunless sea, and their characteristic shape, with their slanting stern and blunt raking bow, gave them a ponderous and menacing appearance. Their function was single and unmistakable, and though they were a triumph of modern invention they curiously suggested a brood of primeval monsters. Beneath their untidy thatch of willow-boughs their smooth brutality was prehistoric in its sterile malignity, like dinosaurs in a jurassic wood; but the ingenuity and strength of their mechanism was the last word in civilization – or as near to the last word as could be expected in China. Impervious to rifle and machine-gun fire, armoured against shrapnel, they could trample a thicket of barbed wire, stride across trenches, shatter stone walls, and all the time at ease bombard the enemy. The simplicity of their name was a tribute to the contemptuous simplicity of their tactics. If there were difficulties, they ignored them; if there was opposition, they crushed it; and to the generals and all their subordinate officers, to Harris and Juan, it seemed as though China's armies, led by these mighty engines, could hardly fail to triumph.

The roof of willow-branches was removed from the nearest tank, and General Sun Sat-lo examined it with interest. Wu Tu-fu, wearing a happy proprietorial smile, accompanied him in his circuit of the monster, and prodded its steel sides with a stick as though he were a farmer at a sale of fat stock. Flanders watched them with ill-concealed anxiety. Then Sun Sat-lo asked a question about their mode of propulsion, and General Wu, having translated it, invited Flanders to explain in detail the transmission of power to the revolving tracks.

'That's very complicated,' said Flanders.

This information was immediately amplified by Rocco, who – with the voice and manner of one crying: 'Walk up, ladies and gentlemen! Walk up and see the Bearded Lady, the Two-headed Calf, and the Fattest Boy on Earth!' – recited: 'in the Vickers machine-gun there are three types of fouling and three principal stoppages. After firing, the gas-affected parts must be thoroughly cleaned, and always remember that the sear is a safety device. If the roller breaks during firing, what stoppage occurs and why?'

'Thank you very much,' said General Wu; and told his fellow general that the mechanical details were unfortunately beyond his comprehension.

'Is the armouring proof against fire from point-blank range?' asked General Sun.

Wu Tu-fu repeated the question, and Rocco in a stentorian voice declared: 'The armour-plating of this tank is guaranteed unpenetrable and will deflect rifle or machine-gun fire at any range. It is composed of one-inch toughened steel, and is also proof against shrapnel. But what you don't see, you can't believe, so I will now shoot the works.'

From his twin holsters he pulled his two revolvers, and pointed them at the tank. But before he could fire Flanders had caught his nearer wrist, and shouted imperatively, 'No, Rocco, no!'

'But why not?' asked General Wu.

'Because there's no sense in destruction.'

'But the tank is bullet-proof...'

'That's what I mean. The bullets will ricochet, bounce away from it, and fly back at us. We may all be killed, so put away your pistols, Rocco, and tell us more about the sear and the stoppages.'

'If we go back some twenty yards, however, there will be no danger of a ricochet.'

'You never can tell. If you want my advice, I say no shooting. Leave that to the Japanese.'

'Colonel Rocco will fire from twenty-five yards,' said General Wu, 'and I cannot doubt that we shall all be perfectly safe if we stand behind him.'

Flanders, with a gesture of despair, turned away and muttered to himself, 'I should never have come. By God in his solitude, I should have stayed at home. This shooting will be the death of someone.'

He stood a little way apart, his shoulders hunched and his hands deep in the pockets of his ulster. Rocco, having stepped the distance, turned towards the tanks and stood in a swaggering attitude, his feet wide apart and his chest out. He had a revolver in each hand. With a violent movement, as though he were punching the air, he fired, left and right. At the sound of the two shots all the soldiers who were guarding the tanks turned their startled faces towards him, and little groups and clusters of soldiers, whose presence no one had suspected, leapt up, staring, and in high-pitched voices made excited comments.

'We will now go forward and give the target the once-over,' said Rocco, 'and we'll be tickled to death to find that those bullets haven't done it no harm whatsoever.'

Rocco staggered slightly as he led the way. The spectators, having examined the tank, were much impressed by its quality of resistance. Its plating was quite unmarked.

'Would you fire two more shots?' asked General Wu. 'And please aim just there.' He pointed to an intersection of rivet-lines in the centre of the turret.

Rocco, assuming a truculent expression and a pose of yet more extreme bravado, fired again. Immediately there came a loud shriek from a soldier at the left-hand corner of the perimeter-guard, and a frightened howl from another in a little group of onlookers who stood far away on the right. The former soldier stooped and clutched his ankle, and the latter clapped his hand to a blood-stained ear. Rocco had missed rather badly to begin with, but he was now getting closer to his target.

There was, however, no ill-feeling. The wounded soldiers at once became objects of great interest, and their comrades, crowding round them, were evidently struck by the humour of the situation; for on all sides rose shouts of happy laughter.

Ignoring both Rocco, who had the grace to appear embarrassed, and his victims, whose howling could be heard above its circumference of laughter, General Wu drew his own pistol and fired several shots at the target he had indicated. Then he walked forward alone, and stood for a long time, motionless, looking at the result of his shooting.

'Come and see what's happened,' said Harris, and he and Juan joined Wu Tu-fu beside the tank.

He had fired four shots, and within a space that a plate could have covered were four neatly-punched holes. The bullets had gone right through the armour-plating; which on inspection proved to be wood, about an inch thick, covered on each side with tin. The rivets, though their heads were genuine steel, were merely glorified drawing-pins.

'Looks like we got into something up to our necks,' said Rocco.

Juan whispered to Harris: 'We'd better get hold of Flanders and go back to Shanghai as quick as we can.'

'Flanders is on his way there now,' said Harris.

With the casual air of one who was walking merely for amusement, Flanders had already put two hundred yards between himself and General Wu, and he was beginning to lengthen his stride. But Wu, turning a moment later, shouted an order, which was repeated and again reiterated by all the officers who had accompanied him, and like a flock of pigeons rising from the stooks a grey crowd of soldiers set out in pursuit.

In a few minutes Flanders was brought back, indignant at being surrounded by bayonets and chattering coolies, but also frightened and somewhat breathless; for he had been compelled to hurry.

General Wu was no longer smiling. His lips were closed in a narrow line and his eyes were cold as a lizard's. He pointed to the bullet-holes in the tank and said: 'You have complained of receiving fraudulent notes in payment for these tanks. But now it appears that the tanks themselves are fraudulent.'

Flanders tried to simulate astonishment on seeing such damage done to armour-plating by a mere pistol; but his pretence was unconvincing. Then he blustered, and said that in commerce the first commandment was *caveat emptor*. Wu Tu-fu grew visibly angry, and when he spoke, there was a harsh tremor in his voice.

'You are in Chinese territory,' he said, 'and China is at war. Our enemies are the Japanese, and on your own admission you procured these tanks by means of your influence with the Japanese. That is to say, you deliberately, and in collaboration with the Japanese authorities, supplied me with worthless armaments in the expectation that our enemies would thereby reap a military advantage. You have shown yourself hostile and treacherous, and I am justified in ordering your arrest.'

Before Flanders could reply, Wu Tu-fu had turned away and was walking with a quick nervous stride in the direction of General Sun's headquarters. But when he had gone a few yards he stopped, and summoning one of his officers, said to him in a voice which he could scarcely control, 'You will also put under arrest Colonel Rocco and Mr Motley.'

21

FLANDERS and Juan, having returned to the nursery under the alert but untidy guard of several officers and about twenty soldiers, were confined in a greenhouse. Rocco, under a separate escort, was detained elsewhere until he had been questioned by Wu Tu-fu.

The choice of a greenhouse for the place of imprisonment appeared to be a deliberate refinement of cruelty, but it was really due to the fact that in the small group of over-crowded buildings there was nowhere else available for them. It did, however, increase their discomfort, for there was always a double row of soldiers staring at them in solemn wonderment, the inner rank with their noses pressed whitely against the glass, the outer rank leaning over their comrades' shoulders. The greenhouse was empty except for a hank of bass and a few dozen flower-pots on shelves from which the paint was flaking. In this transparent cage, Juan, leaning against the door, preserved an admirable composure; and Flanders, striding to and fro, was now furious and now intimidated. At one moment he would stop and glare at the flattened faces of the soldiers, at the next he would lurch into movement with the head-sunk heavy-shouldered gait of an angry bull.

Suddenly he picked up a flower-pot and threw it at a large pock-marked face that was peculiarly irritating in its patient and witless curiosity. The flower-pot crashed through a pane of glass but missed the coolie, who, with a quickness not to be expected in such an oafish creature, had ducked in time. There was a shrill and wrathful outcry, but in a few seconds the crowd settled down again to its dispassionate watch.

'You shouldn't have done that,' said Juan. 'It'll be cold when it gets dark, and there'll be a nasty draught.'

'You don't think we'll have to stay here all night?'

'I expect so.'

'But by God in his three hypostasies, we're British subjects. We can't submit to bilboes and a Chinese clink.'

'I don't see what else we can do. In any case, I've got far more to grumble at than you have. You've earned your imprisonment – on a rough estimate, you've earned about three years – but I'm guilty of nothing but curiosity and keeping bad company.'

'If it hadn't been for you I'd never have come here.'

'I didn't know that your tanks were only a clutch of biscuit-tins. You'd told me that you wanted to see Rocco, and I wanted to see what happened when you met him.'

A minute or two later Flanders spoke with more confidence. 'Harris'll turn the key,' he said. 'They've got nothing against him, and he'll go back to Shanghai and raise such a whirlwind of protest as will suck us out of durance on the very instant.'

'There's going to be a storm of some kind,' said Juan, and looked up through the glass roof at a swiftly moving sky. Throughout the afternoon there had been a coy uncertain wind that blew fitfully against the shapeless clouds, and whirled with spasmodic violence among the walls and heavy curtains of mist. Now it was blowing in earnest, and the sky was like a bundle of tattered ribbons straining to the north. Between the strips of cloud the lift was a pale and dusky blue, the shadow of night already upon it, and the earth-bound lower winds were noisily combing the shuddering plantation of young trees.

Flanders continued to speak hopefully about what Harris could do, and how soon he might be expected to do it. In the middle of his hopeful prediction, however, the row of faces that surrounded the greenhouse was suddenly removed, and the watchful soldiers turned to look at a new spectacle. This was Harris and his interpreter, who had also been arrested, and were now approaching the greenhouse with a small but self-important escort.

The door was thrown open, and Harris and his Chinese colleague were thrust inside.

'You've come to join the gold-fish?' said Juan pleasantly. 'And what's your crime?'

'Folly,' said Harris. 'Mere folly. I laughed at him, and I shouldn't have done that, because I know just how he's feeling. He's lost a lot of face, and he's naturally in a blazing temper.'

'What happened?' asked Juan.

'Well, I began by reminding him that you were both British subjects . . .'

'Didn't I tell you so?' exclaimed Flanders. 'There'll be storm and fury in the Empire when they hear of this. You can't twist the Lion's tail and hope for a ripe old age.'

'Unfortunately,' said Harris, 'General Wu doesn't seem to have a very high opinion of the British Lion. He thinks it's rather tired at present, and not so good at roaring as it used to be. He's also of the opinion that you've forfeited all right to protection by the British Government, and though I said what I could in your defence, I didn't make much impression, except that I convinced him you had nothing to do with the Japanese, or the Japanese with you. I told him that profits were your vital interest, not politics, and you were simply an unsuccessful business man. That's right, isn't it?'

'I cut my own belly timber; there's no charity keeps me. I must live, mustn't I?'

'Wu Tu-fu doesn't think so, but I suppose it's natural you should differ. Well, then I tried to persuade him that Motley had nothing to do with your blasted three-ply tanks, but he was so angry he wouldn't listen to that either. So I thought I'd shift the storm-centre on to Rocco, and I told him that Rocco was really the one to blame. He was Wu Tu-fu's agent, and it was up to him to see that the tanks were good before he took delivery. But instead of that he bought them for ten dollars' worth of phoney notes and pocketed the price of four right and proper tanks that he'd drawn from Wu. But that didn't do much good. Wu said he was going to deal with Rocco, and didn't need any suggestions from me. He's going through the hoop now.'

'Then let him shoot Rocco and be done with it,' said Flanders.

'And why should you go scot-free? Rocco got you into a hole, but you and your fretsaw models have got us into a hole, and I tell you again it *is* a hole.'

'The tanks would do well enough,' said Flanders. 'If you bring tanks into a battle, it's their moral effect you rely on, and the moral effect is in their appearance, not in their plating.'

'Then you'd better volunteer to drive one.'

'That's *ad hominem*,' said Flanders. 'I hate your *ad hominem* arguments.'

'I bet you do.'

'I still don't understand why Wu ever had anything to do with Rocco,' said Juan.

'Face,' said Harris. 'He got a lot of face through having an American, dressed up as a colonel, for his Military Adviser. There's nothing a Chinaman won't do to gain face or save it – we had an argument about that once before; do you remember? – and it's because Wu has lost face, and is going to lose a lot more when he can't send his tanks into action, that he's in such a boiling rage at present. Not because he's been swindled – he's probably used to that – but because the result of the swindling will be the diminution of his precious face. If it was only a matter of swindling, we could buy or bribe our way out, but as it is we're in a regular hole, and Wu, in the state he's in at present, is liable to act without thinking of the consequences. My God, he's put *me* in prison, a newspaper man! That shows the frame of mind he's in.'

'Why did you laugh at him?'

'I just couldn't help it. We'd been talking about Rocco, and there was a sort of embarrassed silence after that, and in the middle of it, Sun Sat-lo, who'd been sitting there like an image made of butter – you wouldn't suspect him of frolicking, would you? But he's a great man for the ladies in his spare time – well, Sun Sat-lo began to talk about willows, in a slow meditative voice, and Lin translated for me as he went along. He said: "The characteristic feature of a willow is that its branches hang down. If they didn't hang down, it wouldn't be a willow. And in order to sway prettily in the wind, its branches must be long. For if they didn't sway, there would be no point in their hanging down. In a similar fashion a man who is a criminal must perform criminal acts. Otherwise he wouldn't be a criminal. His criminal acts, moreover, should be large and monstrous, or else we should not have the pleasure of observing them and being thoroughly shocked…" Not bad for a general on active service, was it?'

'But the idea of Rocco as a sociological willow undid you?'

'That, and the picture of Sun being philosophical and imperturbable while Wu Tu-fu was bristling like a panther's whiskers. I laughed like hell, and the next thing I knew was the escort coming.'

'And what are you going to do now?' asked Flanders.

Harris spoke to his interpreter: 'Go and talk sweetly to the sentry, Lin. Tell him we want a lamp, and promise him half a dollar if he brings one.' Then he said, 'I'm going to play a game of Miss Milligan. I haven't had time for patience since the war started.'

He took out a case that held two small packs of patience cards, and clearing a space among the flower-pots laid them out on one of the dusty shelves. Presently a small smoky lamp was brought, and by its uncertain light Harris calmly continued to assemble his suits and sequences.

'Does your editor ever get worried about you?' asked Juan.

'No. He's pretty phlegmatic.'

'But he must be expecting the story of your interview with Sun and Wu, and when you don't get back with it, he'll send someone to look for you, won't he?'

'I had a day off to-day. If there's a battle to-morrow I've got to cover that, but the interview was on the side. I fixed that myself, and no one'll start looking for me till about the time of evening drinking to-morrow. I could do with a drink now. I haven't been teetotal for so long since I was a young man with boils and ambitions.'

Five minutes later Juan said, 'There's somebody coming to see us.'

It was, however, not a visitor but another prisoner. Rocco, having submitted to examination by General Wu, had been sent to join them. He came in with a slouching gait, and his hands in his pockets. His eyes were furtive, but in his bearing there was a certain defiance. His belt and holster had been removed, and the top button of his tunic was unfastened. He looked something like a boxer going into his familiar pub after losing a fight that all his friends had backed him to win; and something like a suspected burglar in a police station.

'Well,' said Harris cruelly, 'have you had a nice party with Wu Tu-fu?'

'Where's my money?' demanded Flanders.

'Forget it,' said Rocco sullenly.

'I'll as soon forget hunger and thirst.'

'Well, I'm going to tell you something. If you've been flim-flammed, so've I. You thought you were going to play Wu Tu-fu for a sucker, and I thought I was going to play you for a sucker. And maybe we were right. But now we're the suckers, and he's laughing. I know tough guys. I've tangled with 'em plenty, but that little Chink would knock 'em all for a loop. D'you know what he done? He goosed me. Before I knew what they were at, a couple of his strong-arm guys grabbed a hold of me and went through my pockets with a comb.'

Flanders threw back his head and let fly a thunder-clap of echoing laughter.

'But how much money were you carrying?' asked Juan.

'I was carrying plenty. I'd Chinese and American and English money, just in case.'

'Just in case Wu Tu-fu wanted it back?' asked Harris.

'Ah, stop crabbing. I told him it wasn't his – well, not all of it anyway – and all I got was a dead pan. Then I said it was money I'd earned. I'd been his Military Adviser for six months, and I'd been saving my salary. Was there anything wrong in that? So then he said he'd give me what I deserved, and he gave me five hundred Mex. Boy, was my face red? And did I give him the razz? I certainly did. And then I came out on my ear. I'll say those Chinks are tough.'

'But you still have the five hundred,' said Juan.

'Sure I have.'

'Then we'd better play poker. We've got to pass the time somehow, and I hate to see Harris being unsociable with two packs of cards.'

'They're rather small, and we haven't a table.'

'They'll do; and we can make a table out of that broken shelf and four flower-pots.'

'D'you want me to sit on the floor?' said Flanders. 'I'm not built for informal postures.'

He sat fairly comfortably, however, with the balcony of his paunch in front of him, his back to the door, his legs thrust out, and one end of the improvised table between them. He took the first pot with a pair of aces and crowed with delight.

For some time after that, Lin, the interpreter, won steadily, and Rocco, counting his remaining money, began to grumble. Then, after a dull patch when no one had any cards worth betting on, Juan, on a pair of sevens, opened with five dollars. Rocco and Flanders came in, and Juan raised them another five. Flanders, who was playing with great caution, threw in three fours, and Rocco, after another couple of bets, decided that a small straight wasn't good enough, and let Juan take the pot.

'Bluff?' asked Harris.

'I held some useful cards,' said Juan.

'I wish I could get a break,' said Rocco.

'I think he was bluffing,' said Harris.

Two hands later Juan again opened with five, raised it another five, and five again. Harris stayed in, called him, and found him with five rags to the queen.

'I knew it,' said Harris. 'Bluffing all the time.'

'I never seen such lousy cards,' said Rocco. 'Why the hell can't I get a break?'

'You should have called him,' said Harris.

'How was I to know he was bluffing?'

'He's always doing it.'

Juan drew a pair of knaves, and then three aces. Rocco opened with two dollars, and Juan said, 'I'll make it five.'

Flanders, holding a pair of tens, exclaimed with great confidence, 'I'll see that.'

'I'll raise it five,' said Harris.

'Another five,' said Lin.

'All bluffing, eh?' said Rocco. 'Well, I'll see you.'

'I raise it ten,' said Juan.

'You can't shout against thunder,' said Flanders, and threw in. But Harris and Rocco stayed in the game till the pot was like the till of a London pub on Saturday night. Juan complacently showed his hand. 'It's full, and it has bullets on the roof,' he said, and collected his winnings.

'Read 'em and weep!' said Rocco.

'Well, you never know,' said Harris philosophically.

The following jack-pot went to Rocco, but there was little money in it.

'It's only the breaks that count,' he said.

Then Juan added a club to four spades, and decided to try another bluff. It was successful.

'He can't go wrong,' said Harris.

'It's a very good game, if you play it properly,' said Juan. 'It's like Flanders's theory of a tank attack: it isn't what you hold that counts, but the moral effect of what you do.' He threw his cards down carelessly, face upwards, and Harris looked at them.

'I'll be damned!' he said. 'Well, maybe you're right. If you can win a pot with a bobtailed flush, you ought to be able to go into battle in a plywood tank.'

'That's just what I was thinking. I suppose your tanks go, do they?'

'They've been to Nanking and back.'

'And there are proper guns in them?'

'Vickers machine-guns.'

'I have a distant memory of being taught the use of a machine-gun in my O.T.C. at school,' said Juan. 'A classical education, say what you will against it, is bound to be useful in the end. What about you, Harris?'

'In the year of grace 1917,' said Harris, 'I was machine-gun officer in a battalion of the Northumberland Fusiliers.'

'And Rocco has played with gats, rods, and tommy-guns from birth. Don't you think we might try it?'

An expression of extreme solemnity descended, with various effects, on all their faces; but no one answered him.

'Harris says we're in a fairly desperate situation,' said Juan, 'because Wu Tu-fu, in the state of mind he's in at present, is liable to act without thinking of next day's headache.'

'He's madder than hell,' said Rocco.

'So we might as well take a chance in the tanks. There are four of us here, not counting Lin, and if we offer to take the tanks into action, we'll save Wu's face, discount his madness, and – well, trust our luck to moral effect and a bobtailed flush. I think it's a better bet than waiting to be called.'

'I believe you're right,' said Harris slowly.

'Looks like gun-play to me,' said Rocco.

'Well, I've little to lose,' said Flanders, 'and a poor man's a better soldier than him encumbered with a fortune. I'll go with you, and God forgive me for folly.'

'Lin,' said Harris, 'you'd better go and talk to Wu. You know what to say?'

'I am to say that you four gentlemen have volunteered to ride in the tanks in the battle to-morrow morning, in order to demonstrate their moral value.'

'That's the idea.'

There was little conversation during Lin's absence, and though they played another few hands of poker, no one bet with any enthusiasm. Juan stuffed some pocket-handkerchiefs in the hole in the glass that Flanders had made, and the last of their spectators – it was pitch-dark outside – removed his white face from the window.

Lin returned.

'Well?' said Harris.

'General Wu Tu-fu has instructed me to say that he accepts your offer, and for those who survive there will be no further unpleasantness or imprisonment.'

'So that's that,' said Harris.

22

THE wind blew boisterously out of the south. It had torn from the sky its shabby lining of mist and cloud, and racing through the pale blue heights of the air were the tattered shreds of its pellicle. The young trees in the nursery bent indignantly, all one way, and their stiff leaves chattered as their tough twigs beat upon them. Bright in the contrary movement of the sky, in that cold and swift immensity, the winter sun shone like a naked runner, and in its sparse radiance the sapless fields put on a livelier hue.

Of the prisoners in the greenhouse Juan was the first to wake, for Flanders, stirring in his sleep, had rolled on to his back and come near to overlaying him. With some difficulty he pulled himself from under that warm bulk, and sitting up surveyed his slumbering companions. Harris, in the morning light, lay like a corpse with the blanket to his chin, and Rocco's vivid face, paler in sleep, was the bloodless colour of old stained glass. Of Lin the interpreter, who lay between them, there was nothing to be seen but an irregular hummock under his blanket. But Flanders asleep was a noble sight. He lay like a bull seal ashore with his seraglio, his great size dwarfing the others, and repose had given to his huge red face a fat serenity out of which his nose, freed from his spectacles and seeming the larger, rose as if it were a monument to the triumph of his spirit and digestion. There was warmth about him, a radiation from the slow furnace of his body, but beyond the compass of this benign thermogenesis the air was bitter-cold; and when Juan sat up he shivered as though he had come out of a heated room. He was glad to lie down again, and once more in a tropical latitude he contemplated with a mixture of excitement and foreboding the dangerous business to which he had committed himself.

There were sounds of activity outside, and through the misty panes of the greenhouse Juan could see dim figures moving to and fro.

Presently the door was opened, and one of Wu Tu-fu's Staff Officers came diffidently in. He appeared uncertain as to how he should address the dormant prisoners, but the cold wind that entered with him solved his difficulty. One by one they woke and sat up, yawning and shivering, and Flanders, stretching gigantically, exclaimed: 'Who wouldn't roll with pleasure in a sensual sty? I saw my image in a pool of the Severn last night, but wind ruffled the waters. Ask the yellow man what he wants.'

Lin, still dazed with sleep and his black hair falling untidily over his face, struggled to his feet and addressed the visiting officer. They were very polite to each other, and then Lin explained: 'He has come to say it is time for us to start. They are waiting to begin the battle.'

'I'll not go without breakfast,' said Flanders. 'Tell him my answer's a *nisi prius*, for the sides of my belly are flapping like shirts on a line, and I shan't budge till I've wedged them apart with a Dover sole, three rashers of bacon, as many eggs, a couple of kidneys, and a quart of coffee.'

'I don't want nothing but a beaker of orange-juice and some corn-flakes,' said Rocco.

Flanders snorted contemptuously. 'I start the day with an appetite, you with stenosis. Leave orange-juice to spinsters. Are you worried about your complexion? I've a stomach to fill, but you've nothing more than a diverticulum in your gut that you flush with the squeezings of fruit and call it a meal. What's the upshot, Lin? Will he send us breakfast?'

'He says he will do what he can, but they are in a great hurry to start the battle.'

Flanders was in high spirits, but Harris looked cold and miserable. He shivered and said: 'I suppose this is the last time we'll have the discomfort of waking and getting up in the morning. Well, I've always hated it.'

'Ah, give him a Bronx cheer!' said Rocco.

'I wish I could have a wash,' said Juan.

'You want soap and water?' said Flanders. 'Then you're a fop and a nancified civilian. Dirt's the wear for soldiers. There was never a good soldier in history, from Hannibal at Trasimene to the troglodytes at Passchendaele, who wasn't glazed with dirt and stinking with sweat and lousy into the bargain. You can tell a hero a mile away by his smell and his scratching in the armpits, but cleanliness never got nearer to a battle than divisional headquarters. By the nonage of God, I'm young again! It's poverty that's done it, and going sober to bed. There's a penn'orth of virtue in sobriety after all.'

A soldier came in with five little bowls of thin gruel such as they had supped on, and set them down on a shelf.

'There's your Dover sole and your kidneys and bacon,' said Juan.

'Give it to Rocco,' cried Flanders in a rage. 'There's nothing but a horse could go to war on that.' But in case anyone should take him at his word he seized a bowl, and having sucked down the gruel in three gulps, assiduously scoured it with his tongue.

The officer who had wakened them returned and waited uneasily till they had finished their meal. Then he requested them to follow him, and led them out of the now deserted nursery. The lively coldness of the blustering wind was better than the stagnant chill of the greenhouse, and even Harris began to look more cheerful.

Between the nursery and the village they passed a battery of small field-guns, numerously attended, in gun-pits that were placed with advantage behind a little greenish crest. They looked fairly efficient, and their gunners, though there seemed an unnecessary number of them, had a quiet and well-disciplined appearance. The village itself was crowded with soldiers. They thronged the muddy lanes, grey swarms of men clutching their rifles, vacant of face or chewing a last handful of food with the brutal indifference of cattle in the butcher's yard. At the far end of the village were the tanks. They still wore much of their lavish camouflage of willow-branches, but now they were on the road in line ahead, and their drivers stood beside them.

Behind the farthest house stood the two generals with nearly thirty of an attendant staff. An attempt had been made to excavate a dug-out for them, but the hole had filled with water and been abandoned. General Sun still wore a look of mild amusement and academic interest, as though he were about to watch a curious experiment with which he was not intimately concerned; but General Wu's expression was stern and nervously important. Rocco saluted him with such a violent movement that had he misjudged the ambit of his hand he must have stunned himself; and General Wu, responding somewhat coldly, requested them to board their tanks.

At this sudden and immediate prospect of action, Juan became very much alarmed, and Flanders and Harris both expostulated loudly. They insisted that they must first see the ground over which they were to advance. They wanted to know what distance they must keep, their targets and objective, their orders in case of breakdown, the disposition of the infantry, the arrangements for support and covering fire, and so forth. Flanders in particular was indignant at the idea of an amateur and extempore battle, and was beginning a dissertation on the whole art of war when General Wu interrupted him.

'The drivers of the tanks,' he said, 'have reconnoitred the ground. They have their orders and they know their objective. Your duty is simple. It is to demonstrate the moral value of the tanks.'

For a moment or two they were all silent. Like a respectable cashier whose embezzlement has brought him unhappily to the dock, they felt their position keenly, having heard it so coldly and tersely defined. Then Flanders exclaimed: 'Not a foot do I move till I've seen the ground,' and very coolly taking a pair of field-glasses from the hands of an officer who stood nearby, he left the shelter of the house and beneath a tree that grew in the angle of a bamboo fence began to study the landscape. Juan and Harris joined him, and in turn looked through the glasses.

The view was comparatively peaceful. To their left, about a mile and a half away, was the little village of Nanyang, which was the extremity of the Japanese line. The naked fields fell in a scarcely perceptible slope to the north, and between Nanyang and Hungpo the country was diversified only by several ditches, some grave-mounds, and a narrow creek that guarded Nanyang and approached in a gradual curve the right of the Chinese position. On the far side of the creek and roughly parallel to it, the Japanese had built a series of redoubts, each one consisting of some perfunctory barbed wire, a rampart of sandbags, and a shallow trench. Behind the redoubts were several large working parties, leisurely digging what appeared to be communicating trenches. There were no guns in sight, though a battery might be concealed by the village, and it was clear that the Japanese were neither expecting an attack nor aware of the concentration of Chinese troops. Far away to the right the sky was dark brown, where the strong wind tore the persistent pall of smoke from the ruins of Chapei; and they listened to the dull sound of the guns that still shelled, without noticeable success, the heroic entrenchments of the 19th Route Army.

'If the tanks were any good it would be a walk-over,' said Harris.

'If they were made of brown paper we'd do it,' said Flanders. 'By God's first Saturday night, we'll roll up that flank of theirs like a length of drugget and throw it back on the shelf. We'll take them napping and hammer them before they wake. What d'you say, Motley?'

'It looks as though it were going to be a more agreeable battle than I expected.'

'The very luxury and quintessentialized refinement of war,' said Flanders. 'The image of fox-hunting without its guilt and only twenty-five per cent of its danger. We're ready,' he told Wu. 'The imminent deadly breech is no more than a garden gate, and danger's the yapping of the vicar's pug. Tell your men to cut walking-sticks and be of good heart.'

'Before you start,' said Wu, 'and in case I shall not have another chance to do so, I should like to discharge my debt to you. The tanks, though their value is small, are worth something, and you have not been paid for them. Five hundred pounds would be a fair price, I think, and as Colonel Rocco had provided himself with some English notes, I can pay you now.'

At the sight of Bank of England notes – five of them, each bearing the magnificent inscription of £100 – Flanders fell silent. He took them reverently, held them up to the gaze of the wintry sun, kissed them, and put them in his pocket-book that was still bulging with Rocco's worthless money. He sighed profoundly, patted the rich protuberance of his pocket, and half forgot his present surroundings in thoughts of Gloucestershire.

Harris and Rocco, in the meantime, had been arguing with Sun Sat-lo and the colonel commanding the battery of field-guns about the use of artillery. They said, very sensibly, that their hope of success lay in surprise, and that a preliminary bombardment would merely warn the enemy of what was coming. But the colonel maintained that a battle without artillery was no battle at all, and he insisted that as he had gone to so much trouble in bringing up his guns in the darkness, and had found so excellent a site for them, he was entitled to fire them; while Sun Sat-lo was of the opinion that his soldiers would enjoy the noise of a bombardment, and might not be willing to advance without it. They were far more frightened of devils than of the Japanese, he said, and devils were notoriously susceptible to noise. A simple exposition of the tactical advantage of surprise was of no weight against such arguments as these, and Harris retired defeated. Juan had just discovered that his tank was the one which had been used as a target on the previous day, when with the roar and multiple crash of nearby thunder the battery opened fire.

The guns were well served, and they could hardly hear themselves speak; but there was a great deal of shouting and gesticulation when it was found that Flanders was too fat to get into the turret of his tank. He stuck in the round opening like an egg on a liqueur glass, and grew purple in the face as he tried to thrust his way in. Then a portion of the roof collapsed, and he went down with a jerk, surrounded by bent and buckled tin.

Juan got into his tank, and bolted down the lid of the turret. The driver was already in his place, and the engine was running. There was a smell of oil, and the wind blew coldly through the holes that Wu Tu-fu's experimental bullets had made. Juan, for a moment, experienced a feeling of panic at being narrowly confined. A thick belt of porous rubber surrounded him, to protect his ribs when the tank was travelling over rough ground, and the turret-lid was lined with rubber lest he should be thrown up against it and stunned. He was imprisoned in a travelling oven – the small interior was already growing

223

warm despite the draught through the bullet-holes – and nervously he wished himself out of it, and safely out of present danger in the comfort of another day. Then he looked through the slot in the turret at Flanders's tank in front, and saw that it had acquired a curiously rakish appearance. Its badly buckled turret leant sideways at a drunken angle, and its lid was loose. It looked like a late-night reveller, a seaside tripper. Its unsoldierly dishevelment was reassuring, and Juan's momentary panic dwindled to a feeling of intense impatience. He wanted the guns to stop firing and the tanks to start moving. Movement would release him from the feeling of confinement. He swung his machine-gun, and restlessly fingered the long belt of ammunition.

At last, after what seemed interminable waiting, he saw that Flanders's tank was slowly going forward. He heard the harsh grinding of gears, he felt a lurch and a bump, and realized the attack had begun.

Wheeling right, the tanks left the road and advanced in line ahead. They crashed through a bamboo fence and wheeled right again. Number Four – Rocco in command – turned left and stopped. The others rolled on, stopping at intervals of a hundred yards and turning to their front. When Flanders came into position on the right they advanced again, slowly and in line.

The infantry debouched from the village in four untidy close-packed columns and followed the tanks. The battery ceased fire, the pace of the tanks quickened, and the following troops, shoulder to shoulder and treading on each other's heels, broke into a shuffling trot. Sun Sat-lo had established machine-gun posts on either flank. Both were well-placed among convenient grave mounds, and that on the right, because of the diagonal course of the Japanese line, was almost in a position to enfilade it. They opened a hot but not very accurate fire on the enemy's redoubts.

It occurred to Juan that he also had better start shooting. He set his sights at fourteen hundred yards, aimed at the nearest redoubt, and let off a short burst. Almost at the same moment two bullets pierced the turret-wall above his head and tore ugly holes in its tin lining. The Chinese bombardment had done very little damage to the Japanese position, but by advising the enemy of coming danger it had brought them all into their trenches, and their machine-guns, despite constant fire from the Chinese flanks, were being served with haste and zeal. With too much haste, perhaps, for their shooting was wild. But there were several casualties in the closely packed columns of infantry, whose officers promptly ordered them into an extended formation. The pace of the tanks quickened again.

Juan, who was now tremendously excited and very angry with the Japanese machine-gunner who had given him such a fright, was firing with the utmost enthusiasm. Because of the lurching movement of the tank, however, he found it very difficult to take an accurate aim, and in spite of his enthusiasm he could not believe that he was causing many casualties among the enemy. He put in a new belt of ammunition, and wriggled out of his coat. The air in the tank was stifling. He was sweating profusely and nearly deafened by the iron stammer of his gun and the roar of the engine. The tank heaved and slithered, and Juan fired wildly into the air. He steadied himself, and took aim again. The redoubts were coming rapidly nearer, and he reduced his sights. Bullets struck the tank and missed him by inches. Through a corner of the slot in the turret he could see the village of Nanyang. Suddenly a small tight cloud appeared above it, then another, and two more. There were field-guns behind those innocent houses and winter-weary trees, and the battle was not to be so easily won as Flanders had thought. – Then stiffen the sinews, summon up the blood. – With beautiful disregard for the rights or wrongs of the cause for which he was fighting, and with never a thought of the circumstances that had brought him into battle, Juan, in his hot and stinking tank, was filled with a fierce and concentrated determination to reach and ride over and destroy the sandbag fort at which he was aiming. He could see his rival gunners now, and held his breath as he fired.

Less than a hundred yards ahead was the creek that had looked so small from Hungpo. It was, indeed, not large; but bigger than it had appeared. Its sides, of black mud, were perhaps five feet deep, and fell at a steep slope to a bottom about seven feet broad. But that was the kind of obstacle that a tank could take in its stride. There would be a dip and a heave, a forward lurch, and they would be on the other side. Juan fired a last burst at his chosen target, and braced himself for the shock.

For the fraction of a second the tank balanced on the slippery edge of the creek, its forepart in the air. Then it fell forward, slid down the muddy bank, and entered the shallow water with a great splash. It lifted its nose and essayed to climb the farther side. Its revolving tracks churned the soft mud and thrashed the water like a paddle-steamer. It rose a little, and then as though disheartened slid backwards. The water came in, rising to a depth of several inches on the floor, and with a last indignant cough the engine stopped.

In a fury of frustration, Juan threw open the turret and clambered out. As he rose for an instant above the level of the bank he heard the angry *whiss* of bullets, and ducked and came down into the water in a great hurry.

The other tanks had all failed to cross the creek. Two of them, having toppled over, lay on their sides, and Juan hurried to help Flanders, who was struggling desperately half-in and half-out of his crumpled turret, and likely to tumble headlong into the water. His face was bedewed with sweat like summer grass in the morning, and the veins stood out on his forehead. He laid his hands on Juan's shoulders, and with a prodigious effort hauled himself free. Juan's legs bent and he staggered as Flanders's weight came on him. Then they stood together, knee-deep in the creek; and Flanders said: 'The moral value of my tanks is written down. Well, I never thought much of moral values anyway.'

Panting and gasping, the horde of infantry came with a rush into the safety of the muddy ditch. They tumbled down the slippery bank, they leapt into the water, and crowded round the disabled tanks. They filled the creek, shouldering each other and scrambling for room to move. Their grey uniforms were splashed to the shoulders with black mud, and a babbling excited noise competed with the nervous stammer of machine-guns. On the field behind them lay a score of bodies, some of them motionless, and others still horribly alive.

'Do you think there's any chance of getting these fellows to go over the top?' said Juan.

'Come and see what Harris and Rocco are doing. The tanks are driftwood, but we could salvage the guns if we knew enough Chinese to give an order.'

They began to force their way along the creek, thrusting themselves laboriously through the mass of soldiers, and came presently to where several officers were reorganizing their men and encouraging them to continue the attack. One of the officers was slim and girlish in appearance. He was wildly gesticulating, and with passion in his voice exhorted the unwilling coolies to follow him. He clambered half-way up the bank, and turned, his head and shoulders above the top of it, so that Juan saw his eager profile, and recognized Kuo Kuo.

Another officer scrambled up the mud, and among the men there was a tumultuous movement as about thirty of them pressed forward. Kuo went over the top, and the little company of volunteers, struggling up the slimy bank, followed in a gallant confusion.

Juan, caught in a press of soldiers, made a violent effort and got free. There was a small space about him, of black uneasy water, and in front of him the slope of mud, scored and scalloped as though by cattle at a drinking-hole. He dug his hands in the bank and heaved himself up. Bullets went hissing over his head.

The attack had crumpled almost as soon as it began. Eight or nine of the soldiers lay dead or wounded, and the rest were tumbling back into the creek. Kuo stood, half-turned towards her retreating country-men, with her arms stretched out in an attitude of appeal or despair. She carried, absurdly enough, the sword-stick that Min had once given to Juan; and the light played on its thin blade like a thread of quicksilver.

Crouching low, Juan ran towards her and caught her round the waist. She cried to him to let her go, and struggled fiercely; but he dragged her back to the edge of the creek, and they slid together down the black mud.

Kuo still fought to release herself, but Juan held her firmly. 'I'm not going after you again,' he panted. 'I'm not a hero, and you're not really a soldier. So you'd better stay where you are.'

23

Kuo grew a little calmer; or perhaps it would be more accurate to say that her excitement changed its colour. For a second or two she was sullen, fighting against Juan's restraining hands. Then she stopped struggling, and her face became eager again, as when Juan had seen her climbing out of the creek. Her eyes shone with the light of an exalted mind, her lips parted in glee. The noise and danger and con-fusion of the doubtful battle were forgotten in her consciousness of a greater triumph. 'Juan,' she exclaimed, 'we have got the plan!'

Juan shivered and wiped his muddy hands on his trousers. He was still in his shirt-sleeves, he was wet to the waist, and the wind was cold. 'Good,' he said. 'How did you get it?'

'I took twenty soldiers and went yesterday to Hikohoki's house. I found it easily, because you had told me very clearly how to get there. Then we fought with the guards, and went in. Hikohoki tried to run away, but we caught him and I found the plan. I have given it to General Sun Sat-lo, who is sympathetic and knows all about it.'

'And what became of Hikohoki?'

'We brought him back. He is our prisoner, and he will certainly be shot. But that does not matter . . .'

'It matters a great deal,' exclaimed Juan angrily, and was nearly pushed off his feet by a sudden wave or flux in the throng of idle soldiers. He realized the impossibility of persuading Kuo, in such a situation, that Hikohoki was less guilty than she so stubbornly believed; but he was none the less perturbed to think he was largely responsible for Hikohoki's present danger, and hotly impatient of the various circumstances that made him powerless to help him – circumstances so incontestable and various as a battle-field from which there appeared no exit, and a female mind so wholly convinced as to leave no entrance. Irritably he shoved a couple of soldiers out of his way, and saw that their surging movement was due to Rocco, who, forcing a path down the creek, was driving the more timid ones before him.

Rocco had risen to the occasion. His compact and bulky body was the very picture of indomitable strength and brute courage, while his face had acquired an even livelier coloration than was normal to him. Its red was brighter than ever, and his blue unshaven chin was like thunderclouds on a sunny day. Nothing in the animal kingdom was more gaudily hued save possibly the hinder parts of a baboon; and nothing in the world of animals could equal the fierce determination of his eyes. Rocco was going to fight, though he fought alone.

'I got the guns outa those tanks,' he said, 'and a coupla guys can shoot one of them, and I'll handle the other. Who's goin' to take this bunch of yellow-bellies over the top?'

'I shall,' said Kuo.

'Nonsense,' said Juan.

'They won't stir till darkness falls, and then they'll bolt for home,' said Flanders.

This appeared to be the opinion of several officers who had gathered round their English allies. Some of them were angry at the troops' obvious reluctance to leave the safety of the creek, and others acquiesced in it. Kuo spoke to them with voluble and shrill emotion, insisting on the necessity of immediate attack; but none of them gave her any hope of such a possibility. From the attitude of the soldiers, indeed, it was clear that nothing short of a miracle would persuade them to leave the miserable security of their ditch. They stood there, crowded together and knee-deep in water, like cattle in a storm, huddled for shelter in the lee of a wall. They had even stopped talking. They simply stood with their backs to the roaring wind and their faces to the black slope of mud. And meanwhile the Japanese artillery in Nanyang was engaged in a casual duel with the Chinese battery in Hungpo, the machine-guns on the Chinese flanks were intermittently firing at the Japanese redoubts, which on occasion returned a dangerous and stuttering answer. If there was discomfort in the slimy creek, there was urgent peril everywhere else; and the soldiers, having been used to discomfort all their lives, naturally preferred that with which they were familiar.

Juan, suddenly remembering Harris, asked where he was.

'He broke his ankle when the tank went over,' said Rocco. 'I pulled him out, and he's sitting on top of it now, nursing his lame leg and shooting off his mouth.'

'I'll go and see him,' said Flanders.

'Wait a minute,' said Juan, 'I've got an idea.'

Like cockcrow in the dark of the night – the scarlet-throated ringing cry that heralds an unsuspected dawn – a gorgeous and fantastic thought had trumpeted in his mind. A lovely and preposterous thought, wild as an untaught setter on the hill, more extravagant than a sailor home from sea. The very jewel of a thought, imagination's Kohinoor, and serviceable, he knew it – he lifted an eye to the heavens, and saw the goose-feather clouds fly north at forty miles an hour – serviceable, he would swear, and the only thing on earth to lift these cattle-sullen soldiers from their muddy sanctuary.

'Go back to your guns,' he said to Rocco, 'and shoot everything you've got.' He turned to Kuo: 'You told me once that you could handle a machine-gun; so you can go and help him.'

'But . . .' said Kuo.

'Don't argue. I'm in command here. Flanders, give me the money you got from Rocco.'

'What's the use of paper? Do you want to cover jampots?'

'Don't talk. Give me the money.'

'He's light-headed,' said Flanders, 'shell-shock and hallucinations.' He produced his pocket-book. 'Dementia praecox and a last summer's calenture,' he added.

Juan took out the great wad of notes, and detaching a handful held them up and shouted to the surrounding soldiers. They looked at him in vacant wonderment. Then they saw the money, and crowded round him, stretching eager and dirty hands towards it. – From the left came the ear-splitting stutter of rapid fire. Rocco's guns were in action. – Juan taunted the soldiers, holding the money out of their reach. They chattered and cried loudly in their excitement, and pressed closer upon him, so that he became the centre of a tight swarm of coolies. More and more added themselves to the clamorous circumference, and from all sides rose a forest of frantic arms and clutching fingers. Then Juan tossed the fistful of notes into the air.

The wind took them. The flock of false money rose high above the creek, and was blown towards the Japanese redoubts.

Howling with greed and screaming with anger, the soldiers started in pursuit. Up the bank they went in a fierce chaos of legs and arms and irrelevant rifles – mud flew in fountains from their desperate feet, and seven who lost their balance fell all their length in the creek – over the top they bundled, and headlong ran with the wind behind them. Neither rifle-fire nor machine-guns could stop them. Leaping into the air and chasing the flying notes – blue pigeons in the breeze – they had never a thought for bullets or for death, never a thought for anything but the wealth that fluttered so near yet ever out of reach. Money that motivated the proud life of Western cities could hardly fail to motivate a few hundred indigent Chinese. It could pull away the most respectable people from virtue and beauty and their first love; could it not pull an ignorant coolie-army out of a muddy ditch?

As soon as he saw that this wild pursuit had begun, Juan ran splashing down the creek, shouted again, held up another sheaf of counterfeit money and gathered round him a second throng of poverty-bred cash-hungry soldiers. Them also, by the near display of apparent wealth, he goaded to desperate desire, and flung their hope of fortune to the wind.

Straight for the Japanese redoubts, dipping and tossing in the furious air, blew the fluttering notes; and quick-foot after them, brandishing their arms and yelling like devils who had seen the gates of hell fly open – sailing on the wind were their hungry dreams of love and comfort and security – maddened by the sight of a mandarin's wealth, the soldier-coolies raced like maniacs to capture it. If money had wings, their legs were tireless, and nothing on earth could stop their frenzied hunt. But the wind blew the paper over the Japanese lines, and so the irremissible pursuit became an irresistible attack.

Now all along the line the troops were alert and restless, having caught the infection without knowing what it was; and when for a third time Juan flourished his worthless money, he was almost torn to pieces, so wolfish were the surrounding coolies. Their faces like yellow platters were narrowed to a hungry snarl, their arms were writhing tentacles. He was blown upon by rank breath. He was enveloped by a mouldy and acrid stink, by thin convulsive bodies. A wild succession of faces leapt ceaselessly to the level of his eyes, and when the notes flew upwards, such a yapping and a baying broke out that all the hounds in the hunting shires could scarce have equalled it. Poverty had been these soldiers' lot, and hunger and unwilling abstinence; but now the air was full of fatness and delight. The capering notes were more wanton in their movement than the slender girls they could buy, they rose like the steam of the baked meats they could purchase, they flirted with the wind that a rich man's house would set at naught. Wealth and its bright companion dreams is the moon to suck humanity to sea – crossing great reefs and miles of clogging sand – and what shall cut the drag-ropes of the moon? Not guns or the taut little men from Japan. The enemy's redoubts were trampled flat, his soldiers thrust aside – stuck through or brained in passing – and the furious Chinese went on.

A little weary, having seen and spent so much energy, Juan gathered the last of the soldiers, and baited them with the last of the money. They howled and clamoured and fought to snatch it; for a moment he held them off, till their excitement should rise to madness, and above the high din of their voices he heard a full-throated shouting. It was Flanders, coming down the creek, and loudly calling to him.

Juan tossed up the remaining notes, the coolies' crying rose to a wilder sound, they scrambled out of the ditch, and joined the victorious attack.

Flanders, trampling the muddy water, his eyes and mouth agape, hoarsely exclaimed, 'God's mercy, my viaticum! What have you done with it, Motley? Where's my porterage, my bridge to England?'

'What's the matter?' said Juan.

'Money,' said Flanders, gasping. 'Loaves and fishes. Where's my competence?'

'But it wasn't worth anything. They were the notes that Rocco gave you....'

'And reality as well – Wu's payment – five hundred pounds....'

'Good God!' said Juan.

'You've thrown it away?'

'Yes. Everything you gave me.'

As though his bones had gone soft and were no longer capable of supporting his great weight, Flanders, standing in the sluggish creek and staring at Juan, seemed to lose bulk and substance. His face grew pitiful beyond belief, his mouth fell open, and his reddening eyes filled with tears. Then, with a sound that started as a groan and rose to a bellow of pain and fury, he stooped to pick up a rifle dropped by a soldier as distraught as himself, and with a gigantic effort heaved himself up the muddy bank. For a moment he surveyed the altered scene. Then, shaking his rifle as though it were a little sick, and still uttering strange cries, he went galloping, with ponderous gait and astonishing speed, in the wake of the attack.

At first a very proper sympathy and decent feeling kept Juan from laughing. But laughter was like an acid that soon dissolved such soft metal, and presently his sobriety vanished and from all over his body, as it seemed, there started small tides and currents of mirth that gathered and grew stronger and clamoured for release; and found it in peal after peal of merriment. He laughed and could not stop, and still laughing, he began to walk back along the creek. It was empty now, except for the foundered tanks, and, some distance away, a group of three people, who were Rocco and Kuo and Harris.

Juan decided that it would be easier to leave the creek and walk on firm ground. In places the bank had been scooped out and broken down by the urgent feet of the soldiers, and by such a declivity he climbed to the level of the fields, and beheld with amazement the victory won by a few dollars' worth of bad money. As though a hurricane had swept it, the greater part of the Japanese line had been not only conquered but demolished. Redoubts had fallen, their guns were dismounted, their defenders were dead or still running. Barbed wire had been no more hindrance to the Chinese than two loose strands to a sheep, and trenches they had taken in their stride. Feet had been the primary weapons, feet in the service of desire, and the greater number of those killed were trodden to death.

And the hunt continued. All over the countryside were the eager unsatisfied soldiers, erratic groups and darting individuals, who still pursued evasive wealth. Conspicuous by his size was Flanders, roundly running here and there, and brandishing his rifle, like an elephant chasing butterflies; now breaking into a cluster of agitated coolies – scrambling over their capture as sea-gulls for offal – and then trundling farther afield where a flutter of paper shone white in the sun.

Except for the village of Nanyang, the Japanese defence had utterly collapsed. When the centre was over-run, the flanks had fallen back, and though many survivors had found their way to Nanyang, the village was seemingly in a state of panic, for its guns were silent and there was no visible activity to suggest a counter-attack or even organized resistance. Victory was well-nigh complete.

Seeing all this, Juan's laughter became, with only the slightest pause for astonishment, a feeling of great and fantastic triumph. Waving his hand to Kuo and to Rocco, who were standing by their guns, he danced a lively and exaggerated jig on the soft Chinese earth, and shouted unnecessary encouragement to the conquering troops. Then he began to run, and stopped again for no better reason than a sudden desire to sing. An irrelevant memory of Harvest Thanksgiving had come to him, and he started to sing that glorious, rousing, exultant hymn:

> '*We plough the fields and scatter*
> *The good seed o'er the land. . . .*'

But unhappily, before he had sung more than a couple of lines, he felt in his right thigh a blow of such shattering and indescribable violence that he fell headlong to the earth, where he lay half-swooning with pain and clutching feebly at the trampled grass.

For no better purpose than a desire to celebrate victory with some cheerful noise, the Chinese machine-gunners on the extreme right had fired a few jubilant and undirected shots, one of which, by the infelicitous irony of accident, had struck Juan. The bullet went through the thick muscles on the outer side of his thigh, touching the bone as it passed, and before this awful invasion of pain Juan forgot all his laughter and triumph, and clutched at the muddy earth for comfort.

24

HE returned to consciousness in a curious and undignified position. He hung head-downwards over Rocco's shoulder, who with a rolling and uneasy movement was striding briskly across the fields. Kuo walked beside him, and held one of his dangling hands. As soon as he opened his eyes and began to speak, somewhat incoherently, she answered him with obvious emotion and great volubility. She told him with much repetition that he had no need to worry, that victory was theirs, and his recovery would be rapid.

She and Rocco had seen him fall, and gone at once to his assistance. Rocco, being totally unimpressed by a bullet wound, was very helpful. He had ripped open Juan's trousers and bandaged the double wound with handkerchiefs and a torn shirt – not his own, but Juan's which was ready to hand. No major artery had been cut, and the bleeding was checked without much trouble. There was more difficulty in knowing what to do next. Two Japanese, who had come in and surrendered, had been sent off with Harris; and there were no other soldiers in the vicinity who might be impressed as stretcher-bearers. Rocco was very properly unwilling to leave his guns; but Kuo persuaded him at last to abandon them and take Juan back to Hungpo. A fireman's lift was not the ideal carriage for a man so wounded, but in the circumstances it was the only one available.

Juan found it almost impossible to listen to Kuo. Waves of pain swept over him, and after them he would sink into a trough of semi-consciousness. In a vague and misty fashion he knew that she was sympathizing with him, and that her sympathy was intermitted with reflections on the magnitude of their victory. She appeared to think that a proper realization of China's triumph would assuage the agony of his wound; but Juan did not find it very helpful. She also spoke a great deal about Lo Yu's plan. This again was to comfort him, for he could not fail to derive satisfaction from knowing that at last it was safe in their possession. Or so Kuo thought. But Juan found Lo Yu's plan irrelevant, and quite incapable of compensating him for his present pain.

He fainted again before reaching Hungpo, and when his senses returned he was lying on a table in a house in the village. There were several people in the room. Kuo was there, and General Sun. They were talking together in Chinese – the incomprehensible sounds were sharply irritating – and Kuo was distressed. All the eagerness had vanished from her face, and its lines were woe-begone. As he watched her she appeared alternately to grow and diminish, like Alice in the Rabbit's house. At one time she filled his vision and her face came nearer, so large that its outlines were blurred and all he could see was her parted lips and tremulous chin. Then she receded and dwindled to the size of a doll in a corner, its outlines sharply clear, and in one hand she held something the size of a pencil, which was the lacquered bamboo containing Lo Yu's plan.

Juan could not understand why she should be unhappy, when but a little while before she had been so full of joy; but her grief infected him, and he grew more sorry for himself. He moved on the table and a swift current of pain raced upwards from his leg. He groaned and bit his lip, and forgot everything but suffering and thirst.

25

Two weeks later Juan lay, not unhappily, in a hospital bed. For several days his discomfort had been extreme, for the bullet had chipped his femur, necessitating the removal of two or three tiny splinters of bone, and the keeping open of the wound with a drainage tube. But now the tube had been taken away, the wound was clean, and healing rapidly. The pleasant feeling of returning strength made even the most trivial activity delightful, and had it not been for the disastrous collapse of all Kuo's hopes and projects, he would have been perfectly contented.

She had come to see him two days after his admission to hospital. She had been allowed to stay for only a few minutes, for he was in no condition to receive visitors. Nor indeed was Kuo very able to pay such a visit. She had come to say good-bye, she said, and to ask his forgiveness. For she had brought him to China on a fool's errand.

'I've had a splendid time,' said Juan.

She bent and kissed him. 'I wish we could have stayed in love.'

'What are you going to do now?'

'I am going home. To my father's house. He did not want me to go away, and he is glad I am coming back.'

'But the plan . . .'

'There is no plan.'

'But what has happened?'

Kuo shook her head. 'I have failed in everything. I wish I had been killed.'

'Don't be silly. It's unpleasant enough being wounded; it must be horrible to be killed.'

'I was too much in love with you, and then not enough.'

'I didn't find it too much.'

Kuo was silent. Then she said, 'I mustn't stay. They told me you were not to be worried. Juan . . .'

He had heard nothing more of her till that morning, when a letter had arrived, a long letter, and a small parcel with it. He opened the parcel and found the piece of lacquered bamboo, which had been the cause of so much trouble. In it was a long scroll inscribed with Chinese characters – Lo Yu's panacean plan – and an English translation in Kuo's handwriting. The translation was entitled, 'Precepts for the Individual and Good Counsel for Government.' It read as follows:

'The rivalry of honourable men is the source of evil and discomfort. But if you do not exalt virtue, there will be no incentive to rivalry.

'Greed is the fountainhead of evil activity. But if you are careless of that which others covet, they will soon cease to envy you.

'If the government does nothing, the people will have no cause to defy it. But for every new law there is a new transgression of it.

'Do not discuss their unhappiness with the people. When they become dissatisfied with their life, they are also dissatisfied with their government.

'Whoever will govern the people well, must first learn to govern himself. But who is so foolish as to cut himself off from immoderate delight?

'Where an army has lain, brambles and nettles spring up. If the enemy comes with a great army, and you summon a great army to resist him, there will be two armies, and therefore twice as many brambles and nettles.

'If you are greatly concerned with the idea of good, you must be equally concerned with the idea of evil. And that will be a grief to your mind.

'A house without windows is bound to be uncomfortable. A nation without weaknesses is intolerable.

'If the government is neither benevolent nor righteous, the people will seek comfort in their own homes. Filial piety is much to be desired.

'It is foolish to formulate your wishes and ideas too precisely. Exactness of knowledge breeds fluency of speech, and too great a fluency is quite as unpleasant to the ear as stammering.

'There can be no destruction without action, and it is only the action of time that makes comely ruins. To abstain from action is therefore to abstain from the ugliness of human destruction.

'Be pliant and tender. Rigidity is the characteristic of death. It is foolish and disagreeable to others to live in the likeness of a corpse.

'If you admire virtue, do not seek to acquire it for yourself, for then you will lose sight of it. Be content to admire it in others.'

This was the plan on which Kuo had set all her hopes, for which she had plotted, and prayed, and sought in vain, and gone into danger, and lost her sleep. It was on such insubstantial aphorisms as these that she had depended for the salvation of China and the defeating of Japan. Some of it, thought Juan, smelt vaguely of Taoism, but much of it seemed to be a curious kind of meta-Taoism, as though a cynic worldliness had overlaid the other-worldliness of Lao-tzu. The old hermit, Lo Yu, must be an interesting person, a sort of transcendental boulevardier, or sophisticated mystic. But whatever he was he was certainly not the teacher of national regeneration, if regeneration were looked for within a lifetime; though in a brace of millennia his refinement of laisser-faire might bear some pretty but unfattening fruit.

Poor Kuo. Her misery was plainly reflected in her long and dreary letter, where self-reproach stood side by side with gloomy comment on the political situation, and reminiscence of their happiness in America. It was finished off with a dismal little poem:

The evening sky is as green as water,
Over the marshes a white egret is flying.
But there is darkness under the broken city wall,
And I am afraid to go back to my empty room.

Then, in a postscript, she added: 'There is an aerodrome not very distant from here, and if I can obtain my father's permission I think I shall study to become a pilot. In the modern world it is everyone's duty to learn to fly.'

So her spirit, though badly bruised, was not broken, and she would probably find comfort in the excitements of aviation. She did not mean to sit like Patience on a monument, pining in thought, but to ride the impalpable sky and canvass the clouds for new opinions. The whirligig of Time brings solace as well as revenge, and Juan, philosophizing in this manner – in which indeed he claimed no monopoly – was almost as much relieved as he hoped Kuo would be; for the right of a discarded lover to alternative happiness had always been a primary clause in his doctrine.

He wished, however, that she had said something of Hikohoki. He had heard nothing about the fate of the little Japanese subsequent to his arrest for an offence of which he was certainly innocent, but for which he had probably been executed. Justice on the battlefield was often summary; and so was injustice. Hikohoki had presumably been accused of espionage, the theft of Lo Yu's plan, and the attempted murder of Colonel Rocco; and though the plan and Rocco had alike been discredited, the gravamen of all the charges was Hikohoki's nationality, which nothing could alter. Perhaps he had been shot before Lo Yu's plan was examined. The fact that Kuo said nothing about him might well be interpreted as reluctance to mention this fatal consequence of her stubborn misconception of his activities. The longer Juan thought about it, the more plausibly did this possibility become a probability; and a very distressing probability.

Neither Flanders nor Harris had been able to learn what became of him. Harris, who was in the same hospital as Juan, had naturally had no opportunity for personal investigation, but many of his newspaper friends had been to see him, and none of them could give him news of the unfortunate Hikohoki.

Juan recovered his composure by means of the morning newspaper,

238

which, in common with most newspapers, had the comforting faculty of reducing any lonely and individual misfortune to its proper proportions by providing for it a background of various and lurid horror, which, catastrophic though it might seem to the uninitiated, would be forgotten by the following day and was in the opinion of the City Editor of rather less significance than a change in the bank-rate. The day's news included such reports of the war as left no doubt that China's heroic effort was nearing an end. – The success at Nan-yang, of course, had been merely temporary. The village of Nanyang had not been captured, and the far-scattered Chinese had been routed by bombing-planes and a well-organized counter-attack. – But though a Japanese victory was in sight, it was unlikely to be the cause of much rejoicing in Tokyo. The Chinese had shown a wholly un-expected power of resistance, and whatever might be the terms of peace, the honours of war would go to the 19th Route Army and the other troops engaged in the defence of Shanghai.

A little later in the morning Harris, in a wheeled chair, came in to see Juan and exchange amiable gossip about the state of their injuries. Thanks to the breaking of his ankle and a couple of weeks in bed, Harris was looking several years younger, a great deal healthier, and very reasonably tidy. His accident, he protested, had given him a new lease of life. It was the luckiest thing that had ever happened to him, and so far as he was concerned Flanders's wooden tanks had served a noble purpose. 'And I'd break the other ankle to see those coolies going over the top again,' he said.

'No. I think once was enough.'

'Anyway, you won the battle, and it stayed won long enough for us to get out alive.'

'The handsomest bit of the picture was Flanders going over. I'm still sorry about throwing away his good money, but it was a stirring sight to see him chasing it.'

'He was lucky, too. He got some of it back.'

By the greatest good fortune Flanders had retrieved two of the £100 notes that Juan had flung to the wind, and this unexpected piece of luck had so delighted him that he had scarcely complained about the loss of the other three. He told, indeed, the tale of his hunting so proudly, with such magniloquent phrase and extravagant exploits, that it nowise suggested a mere recouping of losses, but seemed rather

239

a piece of inspired and gallant buccaneering. Heads had been knocked together, Chinese and Japanese pellmell; parapets had vanished like sand in the storm of his progress; panic had infected the scattered remnants of both armies at the sight of his wrath; and in the end they had all made submission and brought him, as it were tribute, their garnering of wind-tossed notes, from which he had graciously accepted those that were of any value. This was the story he told; and but for the arrival of two Japanese aeroplanes, he said, which took him for a certain strategic eminence that was clearly marked upon their maps, and therefore began to bomb him, why, he had stayed till the other three hundred pounds were brought in. But let the Chinese keep it, he added. They deserved something for their trouble, and three hundred pounds, if fairly divided, would give them all a fine holiday and a redoubtable hangover.

But Flanders was still unhappy about what seemed, in his gloomier moments, the necessity of ending his days in Shanghai. He now had, it was true, ready money with which to pay his passage to England, and he admitted the possession of a few hundred pounds in the bank, and a bundle of depreciated mining shares. – His protestation that Rocco, by his swindling, had left him destitute, had been a mild aggravation of the literal truth. – But how could he retire on so meagre a capital? And what chance was there of his finding pleasant and decently remunerative employment in England? None, none at all, he said. In Shanghai he could find something to do, he could scrape a living, but in England he would starve in a year. They would find him gnawing turnips in a field, with a snare of tying-string set for partridges, and take him to the poor-house, where he would dwindle and die. England was a kind of paradise for the rich, but hell for the poor. No, he dare not risk it. . . .

'And what's happened to Rocco?' asked Juan.

'He's blown. He's gone up north,' said Harris. 'Some of the boys were in last night, and they told me he'd been hitting it up pretty freely for a few days, and then gone off to Tientsin. He's teaming up with some new general in Hopei or Chahar. He'll look after himself all right.'

'I've never told you what happened at Egret Island, have I?'

Juan began to describe the disastrous termination of his visit to Red-eye Rod Gehenna's secret island on the Atlantic coast of America, when Red-eye and Rocco and Wonny the Weeper had returned to it so unexpectedly. But he had scarcely begun the story before there came a battering at the door, and Flanders appeared, red as a harvest moon and jovial as harvest home, followed by a servant from the Club, who carried a basket laden with straw-clad bottles.

'*Nunc est bibendum!*' cried Flanders, with a ripple of fat laughter in his voice and his eyes shining like sapphires in his red face. '*Nunc pede libero* – but I'd go through the floor if I danced. I'd be down like a sheep-stealer off the tail of a cart. And *absit omen*, for the charity of God has given me lambs to deal with. Lost lambs, and I'm their shepherd. Pull the trigger, boy, out with the corks! I'm going home, Motley! Harris, I'm going home! *Nunc est bibendum. Trinc!* if you've no Latinity – scholarship's dead and all good girth of being's rare enough – but I'll do it in German or any tongue but Kaffir, which is hiccups before the deed. Fill the glasses, boy, and here's to Gloucestershire and my going down where I should, with the setting of the sun on Severn!'

The glasses were filled – Flanders had brought champagne glasses as well as wine, and the bubbles rose joyously in their hollow stems – and Harris and Juan, with the proper congratulations and some evidence of surprise, drank very willingly indeed.

'So you're taking a chance?' said Harris. 'You've decided to go?'

'Neither chance nor decision,' said Flanders, 'but the large white hand of Providence. God's clapped me on the shoulder, and my declining years are made glorious. – Fill the glasses, boy. Wine in the morning's like youth at a fair. Drink hearty, there's more in the basket. This'll mend your bones with the sun's own strength. – I've been given a new trade. Othello's occupation's come at last, the black ram that he was. A position of trust, of responsibility, a teacher of morality. That's my function now. A power in the demi-world, and money to keep it up, and to live in Gloucestershire.'

'Somebody's given you a job?' asked Harris incredulously.

'A job?' roared Flanders. 'Mechanics find jobs, and befoul themselves with muddy fingers. I've been entrusted with a mission, I've been given a career.'

'But what is it?'

'Did you ever hear of the Honourable Adeline Pippin?'

'No,' said Harris.

'I think so,' said Juan.

'A notable woman with a face like a sheep and exalted morality. She married my uncle, Tredwell Flanders, of Chuffe Manor in Gloucestershire. . . .'

'I know it,' said Juan.

'He's ninety-four and a monument to the tonic properties of salmon-fishing and literature. From February to September he's on the river, and from October to January he reads *The Decline and Fall of the Roman Empire*; and this has been his habit for seventy years by the testimony of all who've known him. But my Aunt Adeline was given to good works and died at forty-eight of a patent remedy for stone, leaving three hundred thousand pounds, which was her private fortune, to the founding of the Adeline Pippin-Flanders Memorial Home for Fallen Women, and gave the bestowal of its governorship to my Uncle Tredwell.'

'But you don't mean to say . . .'

'You the governor of a Home for Fallen Women!'

'The previous incumbent,' said Flanders, 'was a weakling. I am his successor. Boy! Fill the glasses. *Nunc est bibendum; nunc pede libero pulsanda tellus.* If the floor were stout enough, I'd dance like King David in his pride.'

26

ALL day the ship had over-lurched the hollows and hills of a greenish-grey sea that was ribbed with stormy white. Now the sky was dark and the wind blew colder. For a little while a moon, chill widow-white, had mitigated the overwhelming gloom, but when the moon vanished the night was black and without form.

At intervals of three or four minutes a cat belonging to one of the stewards wailed hoarsely for an impossible lover. A few miles away lay the coast of China, lay Wen Chan-fu and Lot sin Bay and the infinitesimal island of Pe-shan. Beyond all doubt there were cats ashore, stout Toms with taut whiskers and yellow eyes, that would have comforted poor Tib. With curving back and tail in the air they stalked the odorous lanes, and turned from riper smells to snuff the sea. The salt estranging sea. She howled again, poor cat. The sea is love's old enemy, and those who weary of their love by instinct board a ship.

Feeling melancholy also at leaving China, but for reasons less simple than the cat's, Juan shivered on the dark windy deck, pivoted on his crutch, and went to look for warmth and company.

In the lounge Flanders was drinking whisky and soda with two bony, boisterous, high-coloured American spinsters. Flanders had no regrets. He was telling the Americans that life began at sixty, and cracking tremendous jokes to show them what he meant by life; and the American women, whose tongues were nimble as pelota players, glossed all he said with pungent observation. It was a noisy party, and when Juan joined them they called for more drinks and settled down to talk till midnight.

In the morning the sun shone mildly on a sea like pale green watered silk. The distant land was a bright shadow the colour of apricots, and like crescent moons on the water were painted junks, white and red and blue, with red and white pennants. The air was a little warmer, the sea was smooth, and Juan on his crutch walked cheerfully up and down the promenade deck. Then, leaning against the rail, he looked down at the ceaseless patterns of the cloven water, and felt on his hands and face the exhilaration of sunlight and the gentle breeze.

In this charming idleness he heard behind him a polite and propitiatory hissing, a sharp indrawing of breath, and turning he saw, to his very great surprise, Hikohoki.

'Hikohoki!' he exclaimed. 'My dear fellow, I'm glad to see you. How did you get away? What are you doing here?'

'I am rejoiced to see you, Mr Motley. But you have had an accident? That is a great mishap, and I trust you were well insured against temporary disability?'

'Never mind about that. Tell me what you've been doing. What happened after you were captured and taken to Sun Sat-lo?'

Hikohoki sadly shook his head and sighed profoundly. 'That was a most dire miscarriage, and very prejudicial to me.'

'Yes, I know.'

'I have suffered a great loss, Mr Motley.' Hikohoki's lips trembled, and he dabbed his eyes with a large pink-spotted silk handkerchief. 'I was condemned to be killed. They were going to shoot me to death because they said I was a spy, and had stolen a trumpery curio, and en-

243

deavoured to murder the American, Colonel Rocco. But all that was a tissue of lies, a holus-bolus of prevarication, and very unfair besides. I was innocent as a lamb in its mother's uterus. But I am Japanese, and that was enough. They were resolutely determined to kill me.'

Juan was uncomfortably silent, for he could not deny that he had been partly responsible, though indirectly and unwillingly, for Hikohoki's late predicament.

'I was in terror for my life,' said Hikohoki.

'And how did you escape?'

With an expression of the utmost sadness, Hikohoki said, 'I was compelled to effect a bargain with General Sun. As one of your poets has said, while there is life there is hope. And also it has been rather generally remarked that life is sweet. There is my excuse for what I did, so I trust you will not unduly condemn me.'

'I'm sure I shan't.'

'The General is a man of great literary gifts and curiosity. For a Chinese he is remarkably in the swim with cultured ideas, and like ourselves it is his hobby to spend much of his time in the society of young ladies. I informed him about the two Misses Karamazov, and he was highly interested. He said he would be very much pleased to become their protector.'

Hikohoki sighed again. 'He is a kind man and he will be good to them. But they were such bundles of charm. They were the apples of my eyes!'

'You gave them away?'

'I made a bargain with the General,' said Hikohoki. 'He acquired the Misses Karamazov, and I retained my life.'

The many-pointed sea sparkled in the sun, and a junk like a huge brown butterfly slid smoothly over the little waves. A steward with a brass gong came out of the saloon and beat a loud summons to lunch. He walked forward and beat it again. They heard it sounding in the smoking-room, the veranda café, the music-room, the writing-room, and in the long corridors of the ship.

'Shall we go down to lunch?' said Juan.

'Unhappily I cannot accompany you,' said Hikohoki. 'I am only second-class.'

In the afternoon Juan had another conversation with him. Neither of them referred to the Sisters Karamazov. Hikohoki said he had wound up all his affairs in Shanghai, and was leaving it for good. Conditions there were too unsettled for a business man, so he was going to Hong Kong, where, in the peace and stability of a British Colony, he hoped that by unremitting industry, and the assiduous employment of such talents as he possessed, he would be able to make a respectable livelihood.

'Tell me,' said Juan, 'about your dealings with Rocco. The trouble started – your part of the trouble – when you went to Rocco and told him he was paying too much for Flanders's tanks. Now why did you do that? Were you going to get your cut of anything he saved?'

Hikohoki was very much shocked at this suggestion, and with a great deal of anxious hissing protested his entire innocence of any such intention.

'That would be entirely unethical and contrary to the best commercial practice,' he said. 'My connexion with Colonel Rocco was wholly confined to legitimate business. It was my ambition at one time to take an interest in the game called hai alai. You have seen it, perhaps? It is nice to watch, and there is at least a fortune to be made out of it. So then I thought that Colonel Rocco would be an ideal individual to manage my hai alai establishment, and I suggested he should leave the employment of General Wu for this purpose. But he demanded such a fat initial premium that I was quite taken aback, for to pay such a sum would have crippled me. But fortunately I remembered his agreement to purchase four tanks from Major Flanders, so I gave him certain information about them that would, by enabling him to reduce his price, be as much value to him as the inordinate premium he had demanded. That was a good business transaction, Mr Motley, and you cannot complain that a business man should act in a business-like fashion. It is with business that we grease the wheels of civilization, and purvey its manifold benefits to struggling humanity.'

'I see,' said Juan. 'And you weren't a spy, of course?'

Hikohoki smiled. 'That was only your friend Miss Kuo's imagination. I have had many irons in the fire, but spying was not one of them. I am a loyal servant of my Government, but not in any official capacity. As a young man, indeed, I was in the Consular Service, but I left it because it did not offer much scope to my redundant activities.'

Hikohoki got off at Hong Kong, and Juan went ashore there to marvel at such solemn respectability established in a landscape so undisciplined and lovely. There were parts of the city that looked like an extension of Leadenhall Street. Its pillars and grey pilasters spoke of high finance. It advertised the gravity of imperial commerce. The long harbour was crowded with shipping, and from shore to shore innumerable sampans sped, that sturdy well-fleshed Chinese women sailed or rowed. Less muscular than this maritime gynaeocracy, but not less vocal, were the wives of well-paid civilians and of less-well-paid naval officers, who went shopping in splendid shops or conferred upon affairs of moment in the lounge of a fine hotel. And in the Hong Kong Club, among the prosperously large and dignified citizens of Empire, in furniture of imperial magnitude and in semi-ecclesiastical gloom, Juan and Flanders drank a notable drink – one of the many that the servants of Britain Overseas have invented for the comfort of their unceasing labour – called a gin-mash.

'And now,' said Flanders, 'we're in British waters. From here to Aden's like an English stream, and when we set foot ashore we're on English ground.'

They sailed south, over rougher seas but into warmer weather. They passed the great island of Hainan, like a stone in the throat of the Gulf of Tongking, and in shoal water the many and perilous Paracel Islands. Then, past other islands, they came to Singapore, where the shipping of half the world lay tidily in a great harbour, as green and lovely as Killarney. And in Singapore, in the spacious forecourt of Raffles' Hotel, Juan and Flanders drank a notable drink – one of the many that the builders of Empire have devised for the mitigation of their unfailing toil – called a gin-sling.

'We're round the corner,' said Flanders. 'The sea runs home, and we run with it, like spring salmon to the Severn.'

Sumatra was no more than darker clouds and hills in the sky, but over smiling seas, seas eyebright and deep lupin-hue they sailed in the sun; and Flanders, stretched on a long chair that the carpenter had reinforced for him, his great legs and arms asprawl, a pretty sheen of sweat on his face, would talk of the sultanate to which he was return-ing. There was no one so good, he said, at the laundering of shirts as a plump Magdalene of some thirty-two or four, while the prettiest of his frail captives would wait at a table, and from the rest he would choose a choir and have them taught Elizabethan songs. They would sing, 'O love, they wrong thee much,' and 'Among the leaves so green

O'. He would have them make ale and cider, and their uniform would be white and green. Once a day he would discourse to them on the moral life, and after supper there would be games and dancing. 'I'll show them,' he said, 'that true pleasure lies not in promiscuous entertainment on the streets, but in a spacious and well-ordered house.'

At Colombo Juan threw away his crutch, and more passengers came aboard. They turned northwards and ran parallel with the coast of India. Pricked on the chart, their noon position showed every day a hundred-league stride past the sun-gold, palm-green towns of Trivandrum and Cochin, of Calicut and Mangalore and New Goa. Then, in the islet-studded harbour of Bombay, the ship slid slowly past the Gateway of India, and from under it – or from the Taj Hotel behind it – came the leave-taking, homeward-bound Sahibs and their families; bankers and box-wallahs, planters, civilians, and men from the Forests, builders of roads and bridges, teachers, judges, and lean brown soldiers from Pindi and Quetta and the Afghan border. Now the ship was full, and the westering sun gilded her path before her.

How brave a thing is a ship in deep waters! Marshals and scarlet Caesars have won their victories on the land, but all are petty skir-mishes when set beside the sailors' conquest of the sea. Read in the Greek Anthology the epitaphs to fishermen whom coastwise storms had drowned; read of Leif Ericsson, Vasco da Gama, Magellan, and think of their anonymous crews; read of Frobisher and Hawkins and Drake, and remember their ships that did not come home; read of East Indiamen, clipper ships, the schooners of Nova Scotia, and be glad of the indomitable men whose partners in their business were the trade winds, and who drove their ships – masts groaning and the frozen sails rebellious – through the enormous seas about Cape Horn. These were the greatest conquerors the world has known, and the fruits of their victory are beauty and ease in the midst of the sea they have tamed. Sleep softly, eat richly, and watch the dark blue fields of ocean spring into fountains of crystal that scatter the bright waves with foam. See, when islands appear, to the one side, under parallel lines of flocculent small clouds, a tall profile the colour of helio-trope; to the other a confusion of wilder heights and cold shadow, but with yellowish light on the mountain-tops and a cloud like an Indian canoe sunk on three blunted peaks. And then, when the sky grows dark and the moon is small and luminous, when the solid clouds are become soft and spacious, lean from the rail and watch the silver ripples that shine like a society of silver jelly-fish in the dense white overthrow of the ploughed sea. This beauty is the fadeless laurels of the sailors' victory.

Thinking such thoughts as these – for he was daily growing more excited, and his mind was so full of many things that some of them could hardly fail to be splendid – Juan walked the long decks, and re-covered his strength, and filled his lungs with the bright salt air. Then he talked with the soldiers coming home from India, and drank pink gin with them, and the days passed swiftly.

And one day, when he had been thinking idly about the nature of England and the character of the English people – because the voyage had shown him so much of their greatness and so many of their triumphs, yet he could not conceive them as deliberate conquerors like the Romans of Imperial Rome – on this day he went into the smok-ing-room, alone, and asked a steward to bring him a little gin and tonic water.

It was the hour before lunch, and the smoking-room was full. He sat at one side of the room, on the edge of the crowd. Occupied as he was with an unwieldy and perplexing thought, he found the noise and chattering of the other drinkers – of pink or yellow gin, of lager, of gin and tonic, or John Collinses, or even lemon squash – a trifle irksome and disconcerting. He fidgeted in mild annoyance at the clamour of so many lips and teeth and tongues. And then he began to wonder what the innumerable sound was like.

The longer he listened to it the more compellingly it suggested something definite, but something so unlikely that he could not bring the similitude into his head. . . .

He found it at last, however. It was the noise of many birds. There was the underlying sound of starlings in a shrubbery but that was varied by sharper and by sweeter notes. There was the swift and cheer-ful scolding of blackbirds on a lawn. That was very clear. A thin but definitely recurrent harshness suggested a jay. He heard a cuckoo, and saw one too. Some lightly singing overtones were reminiscent of a hedgerow full of little warbling birds. There were no melancholy notes, either of the curlew or the gull. The whole effect was lively and glad. It was far more vivacious than one would have expected in an English ship, and more lyrical.

Yet these were the people who had built with such ponderous solemnity on the hillside of Hong Kong, who had charted the desperate seas, and conquered India. Perhaps, thought Juan, their sterner and more heroic qualities were developed only in a foreign climate. At home, perhaps, their characteristics were humorous and amiable. Once upon a time, before there was any suggestion that Britannia ruled the waves, England had been known as Merry England; and this leafy hedgerow chattering, which was English voices, was like a memory that would not be subdued of that ancient merriment. He drank his gin and tonic-water. Whatever the truth might be, he was delighted to be going home.

*Some other Penguin
books are described on the
remaining pages*

SWANN'S WAY

MARCEL PROUST

1244

Remembrance of Things Past is an enormous semi-auto-biographical novel which describes the progress of the narrator through childhood, social life, and love affairs, to consciousness of his literary vocation as he starts work on the novel itself. *Swann's Way* is the first volume in this work. The narrator's childhood is described with delicacy as he reveals his great attachment to his mother, the characters of his family and their neighbours, the diplomacy practised in the small town, the influence upon him of places and people – and especially of M. Swann. The story of Swann in the Bohemian world of Paris, in society, and in the provinces – each of which considers itself to be his exclusive world – and the account of Swann's love for Odette, her gradual incursion into his life, and the equally gradual dis-illusionment, is told beside the tale of the narrator's child-hood love for Swann's daughter, Gilberte. The way in which he plays on time and memory as if they were instruments, using and expanding themes, returning to them in different movements, gives the book a symphonic quality in which the beauty of his imagination is matched by the efficiency and imagery of his prose.

TENDER IS THE NIGHT

F. SCOTT FITZGERALD

906

Dick Diver, the central figure of a group of Americans on the continent between the wars, is a psychiatrist by training and married to a girl he first meets as a patient in a Zurich clinic. She is both beautiful and rich, but remains a mental invalid after they are married (her family regard Dick as a doctor who has been 'bought' to look after her). On the surface their life is full of glitter and without a blemish, and to Rosemary Hoyt, a young film star, the Divers seem the most charming and perfectly balanced couple imaginable. But, in looking after his wife, Dick gradually lets his work slip. Their relationship becomes more and more hollow, and his life without meaning. The apparent and real appearances of this relationship are reflected in the smart society in which the Divers live, which in this novel is shown to be both romantically attractive and undeniably corrupt. The Penguin edition is a reprint of the version which was considerably revised by the author on the eve of his death.

END OF THE LINE

STANLEY WADE BARON

1159

This is a novel that truly merits the epithet sensitive. The motives and feelings of the characters, in whose lives we cannot help being caught up, are honestly and compassionately portrayed. The struggle between Communism and the West is played out on one of its most fluctuating frontiers – present-day France.

The story tells of the barrenness in the life of Emily Halliday and her efforts to find something, anything, in the endless and desperate search of escapism. A fateful coincidence plays its part in the tense and inextricable entanglement of circumstance and feeling that brings disaster both to the young communist agitator, who is hunted by the police and the party which repudiates him, and the successful American diplomat, who comes to feel disillusioned about his career and the hypocrisy it entails. The families and friends of these bewildered people are also described with sympathy. And around all is the lively, uncertain atmosphere of Paris in the heat of midsummer.

DRINKERS OF DARKNESS

GERALD HANLEY

1258

Drinkers of Darkness is ostensibly an account of the cele-bration of Christmas among the isolated group of white people at Mambango in East Africa, which included only three women; the feast, an occasion for eating rather than worship, is to take place in a broiling climate, in heat and dust and dirt. A hard-pressed community is shown going ludicrously and half-blindly through the motions of tradi-tional festivity while around it the spirit of the old Africa is changing, new unrest stirring. To the Africans Christmas is meaningless, to the whites it means little enough.

Christmas at Mambango is a failure. It does not give the small pleasures that have been expected of it; it is marred by events, some of which are the consequence of the white man's predicament in Africa, and by others that have been many years in the making.

'The helplessness of even well-meaning white ignorance, the dark limits to the cleverness of trouble-making educated Africans are intelligently sketched.' – *Manchester Guardian*

NOT FOR SALE IN THE U.S.A.